# JACOB'S GOLD

I0647524

by Larry L. Maxwell

This book is dedicated
to my wife, Frankie,
for her love and support.

# Chapter 1

It was a time and a season of uncertainty in my home land of Germany, and life was hard. I was the oldest of three children. I had two younger sisters. They weren't twins, but my folks had named them Ilkey and Zilky. I remember that my father was well over six feet tall, and to me he looked like a giant of a person. But he was just about as kind and gentle as he was big, when it came to the family or helping someone. Yet there was a stubborn streak about him that came up often in our lives. My mother was as small and feisty as he was big. It didn't usually take long to work out the problems between those two. They saw to it that I always had to work, even as a little boy, but it was good to know how to work.

Our hard times began when my father went away to serve in the army. I can still remember the last time I saw him before he went into the military service for the Kaiser, never to return. He was handsome in his crisp military suit. With piercing blue eyes he seemed to search out my very soul. His last words to me were, "Son, I am leaving you in charge of the family. I leave you with a noble name, Jacob Waltz, but most of all, I leave you with my trust. " He held me close then and that is about the only time that I ever saw tears in my father's eyes. It seemed even then that he knew he would not be returning. I knew he didn't want to go away and leave the family, but he felt honor bound.

I was able to get a job with little pay working in a small shoe factory. The work was hard and the hours were long, but I didn't mind it. I had to do all that I could do to help the family. With the work I had, I was able to keep food coming into the home. The money that I made was for food and clothes. The rent on the little home wasn't very much, but it was hard to keep enough to stay there. I wanted to see that my mother and two sisters were taken care of first, so there

1

was little left over for me, but that was okay.

We didn't have money to send the girls to school, but my mother would teach them things out of the books that she could get. I had been able to go to school in my early years, before times changed. The school system required that we learn English, so I had spent some of my years of schooling doing that. Now my favorite book was one about America. I don't know where she borrowed the book, but I knew someday I wanted to go there.

Letters from my father never came, and we never heard what happened to him. I know he would have come home if he could have. Finally, after struggling through four difficult years without any word, I had to tell my mother and sisters that something had happened to our father. He was not coming home!

My mother grieved over that for several months. Without the hope of his return to cling to, she got work at one of the local bakery shops in the little town where we lived. This made life a little bit easier, with me bringing home good shoes for us all and now mother bringing home things to eat from the bakery.

In a few months, she met a young man who brought the supplies to the bakery. She told us that he was a good man, and it would be time for her to think of the family. He had asked her to marry him. It would be nice to see our mother happy again, and I could tell that this young man was bringing a welcome change to our mother. She had him over to our home to tell us of the upcoming marriage. I could not tell what would be the best. One of my sisters thought that Mother should not get married again, but I told her that we needed a man to help with the family.

After they were married, they seemed really happy. He took over the making of the money for the family, something that I had done since my father left, so things were very different for me. I was a man at twelve, and his coming along hadn't changed any of that. I would not move with them to his new home after they were married. I asked my mother if I could stay at the old home for a little bit longer and work in the shoe factory. They moved several miles away and so I stayed at the old home.

Thus, I found myself alone in the world at the age of thirteen. There was a certain excitement mixed in with all of the struggles, because I often breathed the magical word that I thought often, "America!" Anyone would tell you America was the place to go.

It didn't take much for me to live, and I soon began to save the money that I might need to get to America. I talked to others and they told me that you could own land there and get work and make a lot of money. Everything that they would say just kept building in my mind. If I could work only a few more months, then I would have some money to go and see about passage to America.

It was while I was planning this that the foreman of the factory said to me one day, "We are going to have to shut the factory down. The owners want to do this and there is nothing that I can do." When he saw my shocked expression he added, "I will lose my job, too."

I didn't have a lot of money saved, but since my family had what they needed I decided to go to the docks and find a ship going to America. I spent some of my money for food for the trip. I said my goodbyes to my family and then, with one small suitcase, I walked the many miles to the ocean and the shipping lines. What a trip that was to the docks.

It had been late one night after I got there when I learned of the boat that was going to America. The journey would take many days. I asked two of the crew, at separate times, to find out for sure where this ship was going. I didn't want to make the mistake of boarding the wrong boat. I waited

3

by the cargo loading area and after the cargo had all been put aboard, I pulled myself up one of the long anchor ropes tied to the dock. I had always been pretty strong, what with sewing shoes and working with my hands. I found I could pull myself right up to the side of the waiting boat.

I stowed myself in the cargo hold, still with an occasional horrible thought that I might not be headed for America. I didn't really like the idea of having to stowaway in the freight area to get there. But I reasoned that the ship was going anyway, and I didn't take up much room. I had selected one of the highest slings of freight after I had slipped on board. In the dim light, I wondered how long it would be before the ship would pull out of the harbor.

I must have dozed off for a while in the early morning because the noise from the men working topside had brought me from my sleep. I could hear the start up of the ship's big engines, and felt the slight movement now, as we must be pulling away from the dock. I was on my way. It seemed strange to be finally on my way to America.

I felt the desire to be out on the deck to watch us pull away from the harbor in Germany. I didn't want to risk the chance of being spotted and put back on the dock, so I decided to try and watch it in my mind's eye. I could hear the big engines turning and hear the bite of the big props into the deep water. I would be far down below the water line. It was a long way down here. Would the sides of the ship be able to keep the water out? I had never been on a boat of any size, but could only guess what it would be like.

It was as though a part of me was staying and a part of me was going away. To what? To where? What would it be like in America?

I could hear the water slipping along side of the boat, ever so slowly. It was going to take a long time to get anywhere at this rate. It seemed like hours before I could finally hear the power of the engines speeding our journey. They started picking up speed slowly, then moved up to what would probably be the normal speed. I wondered how big the props were that were pushing us along.

There was a feeling of excitement and just a little bit of fear as I wondered about what would be said when they finally found me out. I had very little money or food and they probably wouldn't throw me overboard. I also knew they wouldn't turn the boat around after we had gone out a couple of days.

I would need to slip out in the middle of the night and go topside for relief, but the stores of cheeses, dried fruit and bread would keep me several days if it had to. The small amount of water that I had brought aboard would probably be the first thing to run out. It was cool down here in the hold, so even that would probably last me four or five days.

The big ship kept going day and night. I had no idea how many days it would take to reach San Francisco, but each day was getting me that much closer. The routine that took me out on the deck in the middle of the night was working pretty well, and I even found a barrel of water to help with my water needs.

Eventually I decided that maybe all of the ship's crew didn't all know everyone, and maybe I could get into the mix without even being noticed. After all, I could hear some of the crew and they were speaking German, so some of my countrymen were working topside. This gave me some comfort. I decided the next day that I would try and work in with the rest of the crew. It would be good to be topside, out in the fresh air after four days down in the freight area.

I slipped out on deck in the middle of the work detail the next morning, grabbing a bucket and broom in my journey. I nodded to some of the crew who were busy with their many errands. Suddenly someone called me from what smelled like

5

the kitchen area. They needed my bucket and broom right away, so I hurried to the task of helping with the spilled pot of stew that had found its way onto the galley floor. The big cook was yelling something in Swedish to one of the helpers, who was trying to please him in every motion of his busy mop.

I didn't look up, but went about the big chore of helping clean up the mess. The other young man, who was about my same age, was ushered out of the room when the cleanup was done. His would be another job out on the main deck. It seemed he had lost his job with the chief cook, who now motioned for me to pitch in with pans and the cleaning chores, which I was glad to do. He motioned to me to put on one of the aprons hanging from the rack, and gave me a large bowl of potatoes to peel. He could speak some English, but preferred his native tongue. It seemed that I was to help the other two workers in the kitchen. I was anxious to be accepted, but I felt a little bad for the one that I had replaced. I could tell right away that you didn't get second chances when it came to the cook.

When the meal was ready and the hot cooked breads came out of the ovens, I followed the other two into the dining hall, where sat all of the crew that could be spared for the time. The good food was really tempting, but I dared not sample any of it until the other two helpers did.

It was easy to see who was the Captain. He sat at the head of the table, and motioned the two waiters over often to see to his needs. I had heard his sharp orders barked out at times to the crew. Yes, he was for sure in command, and was not one to get cross ways with. I kept my eyes down and stayed busy, not wanting him to notice me.

It was a busy time around the long eating bench, and one of my jobs was to keep the coffee cups filled. I could do that, as long as they didn't ask me to make it. I even came in behind the Captain and filled his cup, without his noticing me.

6

I felt much better when the meal was over and the men went back to their bunks. Some had to be on night watch, and they would be coming in later; but until then, it was our time to sit at the table and get our helpings. It was a nice change to be out among the gang and to feel that I was helping to earn my passage.

Things were working out better than I had expected. That night, I joined the others from the kitchen in a small area nearby for a night's rest. I had to move a little stuff off the one remaining bunk, but it was good to feel like I was fitting in.

I worked hard in the kitchen, and the head cook took special note of my efforts. He didn't say too much, but just moved his head up and down when he was satisfied with the work. When he had something special to do, he would leave me in charge of overseeing the other two. They were twice my age, but I jokingly told them that I needed more experience than they did. This seemed to smooth things over.

The days turned into weeks. We had stopped several times to take on cargo and other ship needs. Finally I could hold back no longer and I asked the man next to me, "How much longer do you think it will be?"

His answer offered little help. He just said, "I don't know. Ask the Captain."

I knew I would not want to ask him, although he spoke to me once in a while. Whenever I looked into his eyes, it was as if he was studying me out. My heart would just about stop, and I would turn away, fearing that he might see the redness that I could feel creeping up in my face. I know that he knew that I was German, as he had heard me talking to some of the crew at times.

It seemed the journey would never end. Then one evening, someone said that they thought we would arrive on the morrow. How excited I was at the thought of finally getting to America! I could hardly sleep that night. At first light, we were back in the kitchen, getting ready for the day. My excitement was soon drowned out when one of the cook's helpers came by me and said that Captain Olson wanted to see me in his quarters. I was so startled I even dropped the kettle that I had in my hand. Luckily it was empty, and I was quick to retrieve it and finish drying it.

What was I to do? We would be within sight of San Francisco any time soon, and the Captain had asked to see me!

My heart was in my throat when I knocked on the Captain's door. There was a silence. I wondered if they were trying to play some trick on me. Then the deep voice of the Captain came from the other side of the door, "Enter!" He had his back to me and was bent over some of the charts on a table. Now he turned to me and said, " Ah, yes, Jacob." I hadn't thought he even knew my name, but there it was. "Sit down."

I moved to a chair in front of his desk and he sat down across from me. I knew my face was flushed red right now, and I had nowhere to turn or run. What if he took me back to Germany and put me off the boat? I guess I deserved it, if that was what he wanted to do.

He sat patiently looking at me for the longest time. When he finally spoke to me, he said, "Jacob, I have been watching you for a long time. I know you are not one of the regular crew, for they have all been with me for several months."

I blurted out, "Sir, I am a stow away. I am sorry for that, but have tried to pay for my passage by my labors."

"Yes, I know, Jacob. I knew it the first time I saw you. Yet you are one of the hardest workers I have on the ship. Even that cranky old cook brags about you. How old are you, lad?"

"Fourteen," I said.

He rubbed his chin as if in deep thought. " So, what are your plans now?" he asked.

" I always wanted to go to America. I have little family, so I decided to leave Germany."

"Do you know anyone in America?" he asked.

"No, I know no one, but I am determined to make my way when I get there."

"Would you like me to help you find a good German family there? I have had some good experience with one Sepp Braun. He is from your country and, in earlier times, he worked for me a while. He will help you if you tell him I vouch for you. The last time I heard, he was running a fish market down by the waterfront on Market Street."

I could hardly believe my ears. I stood up, barely able to say, "Thank you, Captain Olson, thank you so much!"

He stood up, too. Pulling an envelope from his desk drawer, he extended it to me. "This is for you," he said putting the envelope in my hand, "and if you ever want to put back to sea with me, let me know." His voice was kind as he added, "You remind me of myself, so many years ago."

My head was spinning with excitement as I grasped his hand and looked into those kind gentle eyes. Yes, he would be one to put out to sea with, if you were going. But a shout from topside sent both of us scurrying to the deck.

Straight ahead of us was San Francisco! I could see the city rising out on the hills beyond the harbor. Many other boats were tied up to the large docks. I was about to set foot in America at last!

# Chapter 2

My first impression of San Francisco was that it looked like some kind of a temporary city, with buildings scattered around the hillside, mixed in with tents and a variety of dwelling places. It wasn't a city like the ones that I had known in Germany, but then it was a new country and would probably grow up into a big place someday.

Captain Olson had brought us in on the early morning tide, and we would be off the ship in the early morning hours. I said my farewells to those I had come to know. Soon I was racing down the gang plank with my meager belongings wrapped in a small tarp, heading in the general direction where the Captain had indicated I would find Market Street.

It seemed that the town was nearly deserted, and there were many unfinished buildings. I remember thinking to myself, "Where are all of the people?" Those that I did see had a stir of excitement about them, and most of them didn't have time to stop or speak. I couldn't imagine what was going on, but it was good to be here. It was good to be on the ground again, and yet there was a swaying motion still with me after the long trip.

"Here I am at last!" I thought. "Me, Jacob Waltz, in America!"

Before long the streets were starting to fill with horse drawn carriages and riders. Still it looked pretty deserted along the walkways bordering the streets. Here and there store owners were shaking things out and displaying them along the boardwalks. Some stopped to look at me, and nodded a good morning. Others didn't say anything or take notice.

I had to ask where Market Street was and was pointed east, paralleling the bay. It would be good to find the Braun family. It was not that I was worried, but it would be good to make a friend. The intense looks on the faces of some people I had passed on my way made me feel a little bit uneasy. I imagined that in the night it could get pretty bad.

As I approached the fish market, I wondered what the family would be like. I could see a jolly man with reddish hair, wearing a well-used apron and moving back and forth among the fish displays. He was talking animatedly to some of the people that had come to the market to make their purchases. The street was filled with small businesses, but it looked like the fish business was the busiest.

I stood to one side, not wanting to be in the way of things and waiting for a break to ask if this man was Mr. Braun. After he had wrapped the purchase of a fish for a little old gray-haired lady, he caught my eye, and gave me a nod. A few moments later, I asked in German if he was Mr. Braun. He yelled for someone to come forward and take his place and then motioned me around the back of the rows of seafood, extending his hand as he came around to greet me.

Mr Braun seemed glad to get to know me and asked several questions about the homeland. I told him that Captain Olson had told me to look him up and he would help me get started, at which he replied, "Yes, you will come and stay with us until you find your way."

I was introduced to the Braun family, which consisted of a father, mother and two little girls, who seemed to be ages six and eight. Unable to restrain my curiosity any longer, I asked Mr. Braun, "Where are all of the people? On the way across on the boat, some of the sailors told me that this was a busy place -- an exciting, growing town. But it looks pretty much deserted to me. Not many men around, especially."

He looked up and down the street and said, " It was. There were a lot of people here a month or two ago, but as you can see, something has happened to them. People around here call it the gold fever." He shook his head as he continued, "They have gone off and left everything, crops in the field,

11

animals to fend for themselves, buildings left unfinished. I'll tell you, Jacob, it has been a kind of craziness that has come over the people. They have run off into the hills to strike it rich and have forgotten everything else. Our business is still doing all right, but we don't have nearly the people that we used to have a couple of months ago."

He looked at me appraisingly. "You might have come at a real good time, if you have any money to buy anything with. Or, if you would work on shares for some of those that have left everything, I think that you might soon do well."

"I would be glad to help you get started with something," he continued. "Everyone is left short handed and paying pretty good wages. There is plenty of opportunity for someone like you." He pointed back toward the harbor. "In fact, there is no one to help with the loading and the unloading of the ship you just came in on. Since you know Captain Olson and the crew, you might check in with them, as I am sure he would like to be underway as soon as he can. They won't be able to get much cargo to take back with them, with most of the places closed up. But if he needs some things that I can help with, let me know."

I walked back down to the dock and the boat after I had stowed my things away. The sailors and the Captain were busy trying to unload some of the cargo, and find someone responsible to accept it and pay for it. There were two banks in town, but they didn't want to be responsible for some of those that had taken off into the mountains.

I pitched in with the loading and the unloading of the supplies. Captain Olson was glad to see me again. He told me that he was not prepared for this, and had heard a story about a big gold strike at Sutter's mill. He said that every time someone told the story, it seemed to get bigger and bigger. He told me that even some of his crew were getting the fever, and he needed to get unloaded and loaded quickly before they all took it in their minds to take off. I told him that I had talked to Mr. Braun and he had volunteered his help if needed.

The Captain said that many people had sent orders in for him to fill, and now they were not here to pick them up and pay for them. It was fortunate that some of the orders had to do with tents and digging things. Now the increased demand for such items would enable him to get much more than he planned on. They could double or triple their money on that kind of merchandise, if he could find the right ones to buy it. Otherwise, he would continue on with most of the cargo, and try and unload it further along the way.

He said, "I will tell you, Jacob, if there is anything that you might want that I have on board, I want you to have first choice."

I selected a sleeping bag, a few cooking utensils, and a shovel and pick. When he mentioned that he'd heard that rope was in short supply in town, I told him I would take a couple of coils of rope, too.

When I returned from carting my new equipment back to Mr. Braun's home, I had some good news to relay. "Captain, there may be a way to unload about all of your goods at a good price," I announced eagerly. "There is a merchant here in town that Mr. Braun knows, who is trying to outfit some wagons for Sacramento to open a store. If you could give him a good price on things and he would give you more than you usually get for your things, it might work out well for both of you."

A few hours later, I brought Mr. Braun's friend, Mr. Strauss, back to the ship to introduce him to the Captain. He said that he would take nearly everything that the boat had on it. It would be a good start for his new venture in Sacramento. It didn't take long for the deal to be struck and the cargo to be unloaded.

Captain Olson thanked me for helping to get the cargo moved and said that he would race back with a shipload of goods for the gold fields. He had just found out that flour was already thirty dollars a barrel, and many other things had gone wild with supply shortage.

"Are you sure you don't want to go back and help me bring a new cargo out as soon as we can, Jacob?" he asked. "There is a lot of money to be made in this right now. The ones who move first with the most will do well. We can get a head start and establish a trade route for the things they need. I will make it worth your time."

I thanked him again for the offer, but told him that I needed to stay and try to get my start now that I was here. Mr. Braun had told me that there was a lot of work and opportunity here for someone like me.

Captain Olson wouldn't let me pay for the things that I had received. He said that it was a trade for my helping him. He promised that he would be back with another boatload as soon as he could make the turn around.

The Captain had certainly been right about the Brauns. They put a bed in one of their small storage rooms in the house and it was nice to feel the comforts of family. They were a fine family and I knew they welcomed me.

I spent the next few days helping Mr. Braun with his work in the fish market. I tried to help out as much as they would let me, and there always seemed to be much cleaning up to do. As we worked, I asked him what he knew of the gold field. He frowned thoughtfully as he replied. "Well, some have come back to town with enough gold to buy anything that they wanted. Others have come back empty handed, but there was no talking to them. All of them have what we now call the gold fever." He shook his head at the thought. "For the most part, it seems that more are going without finding anything, than those that do. To me it seems to be hurting more people than it is helping."

Every day there was more and more talk about a new

gold strike, or how much some had dug out of the ground. Why, some even said that it was already on top of the ground and just had to be picked up. Whenever I could, I asked Mr. Braun about these stories. He could see that it had a lot of interest for someone like me.

Before long, I had seen for myself some of the gold that the miners had brought in to put in the bank. They would look at it and talk about how well they had done, and with just a little bit of effort, too. I soon found myself thinking about the gold fields, even dreaming about it at night. I guess I had the fever, too, or was getting it. It seemed to be in my thoughts all of the time. It was exciting to think about, and I just knew that I could find gold out there if anyone could.

Finally I talked again with my friend, Mr. Braun. He could see that the excitement in me was building each day. "What do you think, Mr. Braun? Is it possible for someone like me to do good out in the gold fields?"

"Anything is possible, Jacob. I guess if I was your age and this came along, I might be going right in there with you." He shook his head and smiled. He did not want to spoil my eagerness, but still felt that he had to give me a warning. "I only know that it is a thing of chance. Some have lost their lives there already. I understand there is no law or order. You need to know how dangerous it is, before you go running off into the hills."

I couldn't stand it any longer. I had to go into the fields and see for myself. This America was an exciting place to be.

Then one day Mr. Braun announced that his friend, Mr. Strauss, would be going to Sacramento in the next two days and he might let me go most of the way with him. I quickly ran to seal the bargain. Mr. Strauss too was of a good German family. He and his wife had a twelve-year old boy named Josef. They would indeed be leaving by wagon and team in the next two days, and I was welcome to go with them. I agreed to work with whatever he asked me to do along the way.

That night I began to pack up my belongings, thinking back to my departure from the ship and my leaving the Captain, Mr. Olson. I realized that I had never looked into the envelope that he had given me. Since I was too excited to sleep anyway, it would be a good time to do that while I was alone in my room tonight.

I had put the envelope in one of the inside pockets of my heavy coat. It had my name scribbled on the outside, "Jacob". I opened the paper to find that he had placed money wrapped up in the message, and I counted it out before I read the letter. I was excited! It was more than three months' normal pay at the shoe factory where I had worked in Germany.

The letter was scribbled out on the page. It read, "Hello lad, I am paying you for your hard work on the ship. Your passage is free." It went on, "You remind me so much of myself, Jacob, when I was about your age. I too worked my way around the ports of the world at a very early age. I never forgot to do my part and more if I got a chance. I too have been a stowaway when younger.

"Your great dream was to come to America. Mine was to explore the seas. I am only returning the favor of one great sea captain who took me in and helped me in my time of need. I have now advanced to the point of being the Captain, but I have never lost sight of those who helped me.

"May you set a straight course, young Jacob, and may the wind ever be at your back. Signed, Captain Olson."

I put the letter and the money away in a familiar place and thought of the great, gentle Captain Olson. What a good man.

Morning came early. The fog was just rising off the bay below when Mr. Braun called me to come and eat. It would be

16

hard to leave the Braun family, who had been so kind to me. I asked what I could do to pay for their help. Mr. Braun simply said, "There are many of our people scattered out now in the land. If you get a chance to help another, pass it on."

Though the Brauns wouldn't let me pay for anything, I asked if I might buy something for the two girls. I told the mother that I didn't know what dresses cost in America, but the two girls would be excited to get one, if I could afford to do that. It took some persuasion before Mrs. Braun accepted the money she said it would take to get the girls new dresses. She promised she would go that very day and make the purchase at one of the stores.

With the prospect of saying goodbye once again, my thoughts returned to Germany and my mother and sisters. I wondered if they were all doing well. The fellow that my mother married seemed to be a good and kind man, so I felt that they would be taken care of. Did they realize that I had actually been able to come to America? How I wished that I could let them know that I was doing all right. That afternoon, with Mr. Braun's help, I sent them a card from San Francisco. But I knew they would have a hard time trying to hunt me down with a letter once I headed out into the wilderness of the gold fields.

After dinner that night, Mrs. Braun brought the two presents out to the two girls and explained that they were gifts from me. Both of them cried with delight. It was not often that they had a new dress, and they were excited as they tore open the paper and then held the new dresses up to them. Mrs. Braun seemed to know their favorite colors. One was pink and the other yellow. They thanked me for the kind gift, and I thought of my friend, Captain Olson, again. It was some small way of showing my appreciation.

The next morning I joined the Strauss family for the journey to the gold fields. I insisted that they take the money that the Captain had given me to help pay my expenses. They didn't want to take anything, but I insisted, and they finally agreed to take half of the money I had offered them.

It would take several days with the horses and wagons to make the trip to Sacramento. Mr. Strauss had hired drivers and loaded four other wagons with merchandise to open his new store. The way to Sacramento was well traveled. The wagons creaked along under their heavy loads. In a few hours we were out of sight of San Francisco and the busy bay area.

My chance to help came when we stopped for the night. There was much to do for the animals and the feeding of the gang. I had learned some skills by working with the cook on the ship, and they came in handy now. I could tell how much food it would take to feed everyone, and Mr. Strauss let me do a lot of the cooking. I had even learned how to make good coffee, according to him.

Mrs. Strauss also helped with the cooking, and we made a good team. Of course I knew something about doing the dishes, but I had never seen anyone rub sand in the pots to loosen up any of the hard stuff and then rinse it out afterward. I thought about that little jewel, and decided that we didn't have much sand at sea.

I took my turn with the animals and found how to pasture from Mr. Strauss. I asked so many questions about the animals that he would sometimes just smile and shake his head. His son Josef was the best to ask most of the questions. He was always anxious to help me understand things that I did not know. I soon lost track of the days, as we seemed to do the same things about every day.

We met many travelers along the way who were going toward San Francisco. Most of them were anxious to stop and visit, but some came by without even a word. I asked any that I saw about the gold mining. Some were good to visit with, but most of them were coming from, not going to the gold fields, so

I guess that told you something. It hadn't been good for everyone.

They told some terrible stories about the robbing and killing going on in the area. Mr. Strauss asked me if I was sure that it was what I wanted to do. He said that he was sure that I could get a job in Sacramento if I wanted to go all of the way with them.

The bedroll that I had earned from Captain Olson, while staying with the Braun family, was feeling pretty good right about now, as we seemed to be getting into the higher country. I lost track of the days as we moved ever forward in the wagon column.

One evening after the chores had been done and the animals taken care of, Mr. Strauss said, "Tomorrow will be the jumping off place for you, if you are planning on going on into the fields." He said that I could follow one of the many trails that would lead into the gold fields. Then he asked if I had any way to take game or defend myself from robbers or people who might not be friendly.

I told him, "No, I will just have to be careful."

He said, "Jacob, do you have eight dollars that you can spare for a gun?"

I said I had the money, but I didn't know anything about shooting a gun. He proceeded to the back of the last wagon and came forth with a shotgun and a handful of shells.

"Here, take this. I will show you how it works." He carefully loaded shot into the gun and said, "Now point that thing at that rock over there. Hold on tight and squeeze the trigger."

There was a good jolt and I could see the cloud of dust as the shot found its mark around the rock. "Wow," I said, " I guess you don't have to know too much to be able to shoot this gun."

"Just seeing that you have one along will be enough to discourage most of the bad ones," he said.

The next morning I made a rope backpack to carry the food and things for my journey. As I said goodbye to the Strauss family, Mr. Strauss reminded me that I should be very careful and avoid people when I could. "They can be a mean lot," he said. And wished me well. I followed the trail that led off into the deep woods towards the gold fields.

## Chapter 3

I had only been gone away from the road a few miles when I heard riders coming up behind me. I made my way into a nearby thicket and watched quietly as they rode past. There were four of them, and they looked in no mood to talk. I was glad to have a gun along.

The trails were well marked from their much use. I camped well off the trails at night, where I could have a small fire. I watched the clear streams that I passed and wondered what it would be like to just reach down and pick up gold out of the water. With that thought, I reached down and swooped up a white rock that was a little different than the rest. I had heard that was the way of things sometimes.

The only gold that I had ever seen, and that not often, was fastened around someone's neck or to some fancy watch or other things like that. About all I knew was that it was yellow. Someone had once told me, "It makes your eyes light up and burn." "You will know it when you see it," others said. "It sometimes makes you go a little crazy with a fever."

I passed many on horseback coming and going each day. I would move to one side and, with a tight grip on the shotgun, let them pass. I knew I must be getting close now, as the trail was getting wider and more people were on the move. I kept to myself, even though I figured few would want what I had.

At last I could see smoke coming from the distant valley. I was excited to get it into view and found myself trotting forward. When I finally got to the place where I could see into the mining camp, I beheld an amazing sight. I could see dozens of men, in the water and along the banks, as far as I could see in either direction.

The town, such as it was, had only a few temporary-looking buildings. The surrounding hillside and valley were dotted with makeshift tents and camps. A few corrals had been built to keep the horses and stock, and some places had painted signs proclaiming their business hanging by the front doors. It was easy to see the place that was the busiest, the place to eat, and the place to gamble and get drinks.

Good roads hadn't made it into this area, and everything had to be brought in by small wagon, or pack train, or on horseback. I noticed a faint road of sorts coming in from down stream as I made my way to the place called "Millie's." The sign said "Fine Food!" A little further down Front Street was a store called Stewart's Mercantile. A few other businesses found footing there, but for the most part, the whole town seemed to be out looking for gold. Excitement was in the air.

I walked into Millie's and found that it wasn't too crowded at this time of day. "And there really is a Millie!" I thought as this large lady came up to me and asked, "What'll ya have?" I asked about the price of a meal and nearly bit my tongue when she told me the price.

I guess she could see the surprise on my face and said, "New, huh?"

I replied, "Yes, ma'am."

"Well, I always give the new ones their first meal," she said. With that she came back with a generous portion of thick, savory stew and hot bread. I told her she was very kind, but I always worked for what I got. She looked hard at me and said, "Okay. When you are through, follow me into the kitchen. There is always plenty to do."

The food was good and plenty. After I ate my fill, I picked up my pack and followed her into the kitchen. She motioned for me to lay my things over in the corner, and when I turned back around I looked at the largest pile of dishes and pans that I had ever seen.

A Chinese couple were working in the kitchen and everyone seemed to be in some kind of a race. I was not long in getting into the swing of things. Millie looked up with surprise and approval at my ability around the kitchen. She came over and said, "German, huh?"

I said, "Yes, but I speak pretty good English, too."

I would soon learn what the race in the kitchen was all about, as it wasn't long before the men came storming through the door for the evening meal. They were a mixed lot that came into the place that night. Some were surly and mean, some happy and talking, and others at all of the stages in between. It was as loud as it was noisy. Millie was quick to collect payment for their food. I guess times were good, because no one ever squabbled over the cost. More often than not, they would give her more than they owed. A few of the miners paid in gold, but most had paper money. All paid in large bills, and Millie didn't give back much change; but I soon noticed that some of the men would come in just to see her make change.

You see, she was very well built where women need to be and she wore this low dress that came down plenty in the front. When someone gave her a big bill, she would make change right there in that place and pass the change back to him. Everything was sold by the dollar, so there wasn't ever any of the other kind of change. That's why everyone called her "Hot Money Millie". It seemed a little bit crude, but she was really good to most people, and no one ever tried to take advantage of her.

We were all kept on the run with the service and cleaning up for others to come. I thought the evening would never stop, but finally Millie picked up a large spoon and whacked a big cattle bell mounted up high on the kitchen wall. I asked what that was for, and she told me it was the signal that they had five minutes left to finish and get out. Then the long evening of cleanup was to start.

"What time do they come back in the morning?" I

asked.

"About two hours before sun up," she said. "We have another crew that comes in and works all night. You can sleep in one of their bunks tonight."

It was good to feel tired after my work at the kitchen. I would just as soon have slept outside, but I had been warned that the people who frequented the gold mines were a dangerous bunch.

Morning came early and one of the Chinese had been sent to wake me up. Millie stood big and firm in her orders to us in the kitchen. She came over to where I was busy with the potato peeling and said, " Jacob, I see that you know your way around the kitchen. You also seem to know how to do the potatoes without much waste."

I told her that in Germany we had had to learn such things, as food was scarce all of the time. She shook her head knowingly and answered, "Food is hard to get up here in this country, too." She looked steadily at me and continued, "You seem to be willing to work, Jacob, and I could use someone with your talents in the place. Would you like to come to work for me? I can only pay you fifteen a day and keep."

Fifteen a day and keep? That was a small fortune where I came from. She said that I would need to work hard and be dependable. She couldn't stand the other kind, the lazy type.

I guess my face was a beet red when I managed to stammer out a "Yes! That would be good for me." I told her I needed to think about going mining sometime, but right now this would be great.

The next morning, I noticed someone about my age in the bunch who came in for breakfast. As I looked at him, and noticed him looking at me, we seemed to have some kind of silent understanding. He was taller than me and a little bit more slender. His brown weathered face told of his many days out in the reflection of the water. When he removed his hat, there was a white band on his forehead, where his hat had given him relief from the sun.

When he asked for some more coffee, I detected a distinctive German way of saying things. I asked him in German if he liked the coffee. At first he looked startled, but then a thin smile began to spread across his face. Then he got quickly up from the table and came around to me. He extended his hand and said, "Jacob, Jacob Weiser."

I answered his smile with mine and said, "Jacob, Jacob Waltz."

We wanted to talk, but Millie gave a sharp nod, and away I went, back into the kitchen in a hurry. I glanced at him a couple of times more before Millie rang the all clear out bell. After that, he was soon gone from sight. Throughout the day, I wondered about this Jacob Weiser. He appeared to be about my same age, and from what I had seen at the table, his father was not there with him.

Most of the miners wouldn't come back in to eat until just about dark. That meant I had a few hours to explore the town. I soon found myself at the south end of the camp in front of a large, boarded up building with few windows. It had a sign over the front that read 'Stewart's Mercantile", but everyone around just called it the trading post. It had about everything in it that anyone could want. They even brought in the fine dress things for the dance hall girls. It was a favorite place for the kids to hang out because Mr. Stewart was a friendly man who made everyone feel welcome.

When the evening rush for dinner was nearing its end, the saloon across the way with the dance hall girls and the rowdy bunch of miners would get things going. I would soon find out that gunshots were a normal sound in the evening, as the bunch became more rowdy and noisy. Fighting, too, was an ongoing thing, whether it was over some of the dance hall girls or quarrels with some of the claims.

During the next few days, I spent more of my afternoons at the trading post. I began to help Mr. Stewart with all of the odd jobs that he seemed to have. There were often wagons to unload at his place, with a variety of merchandise. He was always fair, but he was firm. Sometimes someone would come in and try to take advantage of his warm smile, but they would soon learn that he would not put up with any foolishness.

Not long after my arrival, he caught a drifter one day trying to make away with some of the foodstuff without paying for it. Mr. Stewart was surprisingly fast when he wanted to be and got between the man and the door. He made him unload all of his pockets. When he was through he asked, "Now, what do you think should be done about stealing?"

The poor old soul looked even more dejected and beaten when he asked him this. It was clear from the clothes that he had on that he was having a hard time getting by. After a few more questions without answers, the thief said, "I know I done wrong, but I haven't had anything to eat for three days."

Mr. Stewart looked the man in the eye and said, "I see that this must be so." With that he gave the man a towel and a bar of soap and ordered, "Go down to the river and get cleaned up. Then come back."

In a short while the man returned and looked refreshed from his bath.

"Now here is what I want you to do," Mr. Stewart began as he gave the man a large broom from behind the door. "I want you to sweep the store, both the front porch and the back. When you are done with that, I will give you enough money to go over to Millie's and have a good meal. You can sleep in the storage room a couple of nights and work here. Then I may be able to help you find a job."

I smiled as I went on with the unloading of the freight

wagon. "This Mr. Stewart is one good guy," I thought. He was always fair with me, and was one of only a few that I felt like trusting.

Over the next week, I managed to find out something about my new friend Jacob. He had been mining for this fellow by the name of Sanchez, a big ornery Mexican who walked around like he owned most of the town. I guess by some accounts he did. Some said that Sanchez had taken more gold claims than anyone in the area, and many of them he had taken at gunpoint. He had five or six heavily armed men with him most of the time. As if that wasn't enough, he himself wore two pistols strapped to his large waist. He was surly in the bars and dance halls and he was never very friendly to his workers.

I noticed that he would come into Millie's and everyone would give him room. If for some reason they didn't, he would have a couple of his men clear out one of the tables just for them. He didn't come to eat often, but everyone knew when he came in.

I asked Millie about him, and she said that he could be an ugly one, if you got in his way. On the other hand, he was usually generous when paying for his meals.

Clean up was always interesting after everyone left. It was my job to broom and scrub the place after everyone had gone. Millie's was one of very few places here that had been built with plank floors. This floor certainly was familiar with the broom, as it needed a thorough cleaning at least two times a day. Just about as often as the dishes, I thought. I wasn't long in noticing that sometimes a nugget or two had been dropped on the floor and got mixed in with leavings of the meal.

I was startled when I noticed my first gold nugget. It was kicked under one of the tables. I remembered the argument of the bunch sitting there, and the shoving and wrestling that took place afterward. Millie had stopped the fight by ringing the five-minute bell.

Some of the miners had just sat down to their meal and weren't too much interested in going without, so several took the two and threw them out the front door. With that the talking and eating started again with hardly any notice of those who had been tossed out. Millie later told me that it is a hard life here and you can see that everyone watches out for himself.

When I produced the large nugget that I had found on the floor, she took it from the palm of my hand and said, "Mine. House rules!" That settled any thought that I might have had about what to do with it. She said that she had been watching me to see if I was trustworthy or not, and the return of this chunk of gold convinced her even more.

I told her that I never would take anything that belonged to someone else. She said, " I know. That is why you are trusted with the cleanup."

It didn't take long to find out the price of things here in the mining camp. The sign in Millie's read, "Coffee, three dollars a cup. Bread, four dollars and fifty cents a loaf. Meal, seven dollars." I was glad for our agreement, for I could see that, even with my fifteen dollars a day, if I had to pay these prices I could barely afford to eat. I found out from others that a room at the boarding house was eight dollars a day. Mr. Stewart's place had boots for forty dollars. I sure wanted to get a pair, but right now, I made do with what I had.

Across the street at the saloon, a drink of whiskey was a pinch of gold. Who knows how much that was, as some got pretty generous with their pinch of gold. An ounce of gold was worth sixteen dollars. Most of the gold nuggets that were common here were about the size of watermelon seeds. Many larger ones were found, and so much guessing had to be done. The bar would just give a running credit until it decided that the miner needed to bring more gold in to pay for what he wanted. Usually the miner got the worst out of the bargains. Some would come in and spend all they had on the dance hall girls and drinking.

I asked Millie about that. "Some people run their business different," she said, shrugging her shoulders. "I never turn anyone away who really needs food, so in a way, they all help to pay for the ones who may not be able to pay sometimes. Some pay a little bit more than others. I try to be fair."

I worked at Millie's for about six weeks. She gave me a lot of leeway with things. She would often leave me in charge while she went on errands. During those times, I would work extra hard and careful, so everything would be on schedule when she returned. The work was hard, but I needed to get my start. This was one good way to get to know some of the miners and it was especially good for me, as it gave me a place to stay and eat. Still, I often reminded her that I wanted to go gold mining some time.

One day when things were quieter than usual, I had a chance to visit a bit with Jacob Weiser. I told him that I really wanted to get out in the gold fields and see if I could earn more. He replied that he was making much more than me, but he hadn't saved too much. He liked to go to the bar and the dance hall with the others in the crew. It seemed that they took his money pretty fast there. He said nobody seemed to mind too much, because he could go out the next day and get it all back again.

I thought about what he had said and determined that I wouldn't let that happen to me. I would save mine for some better purpose. But that didn't mean I wouldn't go and have a beer with him sometimes. We learned to drink beer early in Germany. It was something that people made at home. From what I'd had here, it didn't taste much like I remembered.

I asked my friend Jacob to see if there might be a place out in the fields that I could work. He said that he would ask Sanchez that very next day. When he came in for the next evening meal, I would be waiting for him.

Sure enough, I spotted Jacob Weiser quickly even though he came in with the big rush of men. Everyone quickly found their way around one of the four long tables. They would normally eat whatever was the choice of the day. If they wanted anything special, like a steak and the fixings, that would take longer. Most of the men just had whatever we had prepared. It tasted good after putting in a hard day in the gold mines. The portions were generous, and usually everyone was satisfied.

When the first rush was over, Jacob came over to me and said he had spoken to Sanchez. He had a job for me, and I could start the next day.

I didn't know what to think. How could I start the next day? What could I tell Millie? She had been so good to me and had helped me so much. I didn't want her to have problems with replacing me. I knew I couldn't just up and leave her without some kind of notice. I told Jacob thanks for looking into the job for me, but I needed some time to let Millie get someone to take my place.

A look of concern spread across Jacob's face. "I told Sanchez that you are a good worker, like me, and he said to have you come on to work. When he says something, you had better not turn him down or make him mad. I have seen him just shoot people for no good reason." He swallowed hard and continued, "You will just have to quit tonight and be ready to go to work in the morning, or I'm afraid he might not like it too much."

"Tell Mr. Sanchez that I thank him for the job offer, but I need a little time to help Millie find someone to take my place. He would want me to do the same thing if I was working for him."

Jacob drew in his breath sharply. "I'll tell him, but he

probably isn't going to like it."

When the dinner hour was over and the cleanup was done, I found Millie and asked if I might sit down and talk with her. She was in her room with the money and gold from the night's business, and was getting ready to put it away in her large safe. The door to the safe was open, and I couldn't help looking inside. I had never seen so much money and gold as she had!

"Millie, don't you worry about someone coming in and robbing you?" I asked.

"Heck, no!" she said. "They all know they would nearly starve to death if something happened to me! I am necessary to all of the miners and if anything should happen to me, they would all come to my rescue."

She told me that she sure did appreciate my good work, and took out one hundred dollars from the safe and extended it to me. That made what I had to say next even harder.

"I can't take that from you," I protested. "I told you that I had come into the country to dig for gold, and now I have a job offer from Mr. Sanchez to come and work for him. This is what I wanted to talk to you about. Do you think you can find someone to take my place?"

She looked at me across the small table where she had spread the money out. "Jacob, you are a rare one!" she sighed. "Is there anything that I can do to change your mind?"

"No." I shook my head. "But I will not leave you in a bind. I told them to tell Mr. Sanchez that I needed a little time to help you get someone else."

"Yes!" she said, "you are different! I knew or felt it the first time I met you. I believe I could go off and leave the whole place to you and it would all be here when I got back."

"Yes ma'am, you could do that all right. I sure wouldn't

take anything from you." I could tell that she believed what I said. "But, Miss Millie, on the other hand, I would fight for what is mine. I am not afraid to stand up for what I think is right."

She didn't seem to be surprised about what I said, and a light was in her eyes and a quick smile was on her face. "Well, I want you to take this money, no matter what," she said as she put the hundred dollars into my hand. "You are a good young man, and I want you to do what you think is the best for you. I just hope you didn't make Sanchez mad by not coming when he wanted you. He isn't used to not having his way with people around here."

The bed felt extra good that night. I was tired but excited that I might soon be able to work in the gold fields. At first it seemed that I would never get to sleep. The next thing that I remember was someone coming in to tell me it was time to get up.

# Chapter 4

We took over from the night crew and finished the breakfast preparations. Our supplies had come in, and we had plenty of eggs and sugar-cured ham, along with jams to go on the biscuits. As always, we had to prepare huge kettles of gravy and hot cereals as well. This crew of miners could eat a lot more than a ship's crew. Here were some hungry men, but we always managed to have plenty. We had scarcely finished with our cooking before the morning rush was upon us.

After breakfast, Jacob came by to tell me that Mr. Sanchez was not happy with me for turning him down on the job offer. "You might think about leaving town," he warned. "He is in one of his bad moods."

This made me a little bit mad. Here I was, trying to do the right thing with everyone, and Mr. Sanchez wanted everything his way and right now. The more I thought about it, the angrier I became. Well, there was no way that I was going anywhere, and maybe I wouldn't work for him anyway. Although I kept busy all day and time moved quickly, by the time the dinner rush began I was more that a little bit mad. I was good and mad at his reply.

As the men began to enter the large room, I noticed that my friend Jacob didn't come in with the rest of the bunch. I decided that he might have had something else to do for a while. The room filled rapidly with the usual buzz of conversation and eating. When the front door next opened, Mr. Sanchez and his men came storming into the room.

Some of the men opened a table for them and moved away with plates in hand. Sanchez and his men sat down at the empty table. In a loud voice he ordered, "Steaks all around," motioning to his crew. Millie came to their table with the coffee.

"I want this Jacob Waltz to wait on us!" he said.

Millie knew she was treading on dangerous ground, but bravely told him that Jacob was busy in the kitchen.

"I want Jacob!" he said in a loud voice. The room fell silent. Everyone stopped what they were doing, some with their forks in midair. Even all of the cooks stopped dead still as Millie came into the kitchen, with a look of fear in her eyes that I had never seen before.

She came over to me and thrust a handful of money into my hand. "Get out, Jacob! Now! By the back door."

What was she trying to tell me? Could this guy really intend to just shoot me for the fun of it? Now I was really mad, and I am sure the blood rushed to my face.

"I am not going anywhere," I told her, yanking off my apron and heading into the dining hall straight for Sanchez.

Sanchez watched me as I walked quickly up to his table. He could see that I didn't have a gun or anything to defend myself with. Two of his hired guns moved their chairs back away and to the side of him, so they could square off with me and defend their boss if need be.

"I am Jacob Waltz," I declared. "What do you want?"

"Do you know who I am?" he asked in a surly tone.

"Yes," I replied. "I have been told you are Mr. Sanchez."

He stood up and said, "I don't want anyone looking down at me."

I said, "Find me a place to sit and I will sit down and talk with you." This seemed to take him by surprise, but a moment later he motioned for the one nearest to me to give me his seat.

I sat down not knowing what to expect. He looked me over carefully and we looked into each other's eyes for what seemed to be a long time. I knew that he could shoot me or have me shot, and no one would do anything about it.

It was then that I noticed an ever so small movement in

back of his table, behind the big curtain that was there for closing off part of the room. If it was what I thought, there was someone behind the curtain with a rifle trained on the Sanchez table. I tried not to look too closely, but decided that someone was there ready to fire if necessary.

The silence was finally broken when Sanchez spoke. "I like you, kid. You have got some stuff. Now, how about those steaks?"

"Coming right up," I said, and I got up and headed for the kitchen.

"You have to be one of the luckiest guys around," said Millie. "I have never seen anyone sit there eye to eye with Sanchez and get away with it!" She breathed a sigh of relief and added, "Yes, I guess you have some stuff, all right! But don't let it get you into trouble."

It wasn't long before someone on the night shift crew said that they might know of someone who could come from Sacramento to help with the kitchen. Millie told me that she expected to get some more help in about a week, when the supply wagon returned. Sure enough, the next week brought a young couple from Sacramento. They seemed willing and eager to work. Millie said that she felt that it would take the two of them to do what I had been doing, but they seemed to fit in. I was free to go into the gold fields with her blessing.

"If you ever need anything, Jacob, I will be here," she said. I thanked her for her kindness to me and for all of the help she had been in my getting a start.

"I have something for you, Jacob. I don't know why I have saved it all of these weeks, but I want you to have that first gold nugget you found in cleaning up the floor." She pressed it into my hand with a smile. "Maybe you will get more to go with it."

I picked up my things and, with a nod, went out the door. My friend Jacob Weiser greeted me with a wave of his hand. Mr. Sanchez had let him have part of the day off to come and bring me back to their ranch near the diggings. I noticed as we passed through town that all of the miners called him "Dutch." He said all of the foreigners were called Dutch, except for the Mexicans and Chinese. Because there were two of us now, those that spoke to me called me Jacob, and him Dutch. It no doubt would have been the other way around if I had been first in the gold fields.

The only good thing to say about Sanchez was that he had a job and I needed it. The work was hard, but rewarding, as we were able to shovel ore into the sluice boxes and watch the water do its magic as it moved through the ripples and landings in the box. I soon learned to keep away from others and work hard. He liked that last part. Dutch and I could each do the work of any two men that he had. I guess he paid as much for help as about anyone else around there, and I guess that being mean-tempered kind of went along with having a claim. With five or six of his gun buddies always around, he didn't have much back talk.

Most of the help that Sanchez hired were Mexicans, and Spanish was spoken all of the time. At first the only one that I could talk to was Jacob, when he was around. We soon learned that, to get along with the Mexicans, we had better not speak German. We wanted to fit in with the least amount of trouble. I began to learn the language quickly, at least enough to talk with the crew.

I was able to tell, most of the time, what the Mexicans were saying. At times, I knew they were joking about me, this young kid who had come to join the crew. Someone would say something and the rest would laugh and look at me. I didn't mind that too much, until I asked the other Jacob, or Dutch, what some of the words meant.

He told me what they meant and asked which one had told me that. I repeated the words and took down one of the

Mexicans who had said that to me. Leaping across the dredge with fist cocked, I caught him on the chin and knocked him into the river. He went completely under and came up holding up his hands, saying. "No more, no more!"

The others just watched and wondered if they might be next. After the fight was over, I told Dutch to tell them that we wouldn't need to do this often, if they wouldn't call me those names. That seemed to put a smile on all of their faces, and some of the older ones laughed out loud and came forth to slap me on the back. It was then that I noticed Sanchez nearby, watching the whole thing. He too had a smile on his face, as he motioned for us all to get back to work.

One of my jobs each day was to take the horses down to the stream and water them, then throw them some hay and a little grain. Both the hay and grain were scarce and had to be hauled all of the way from Sacramento. It was very expensive, and I was told not to feed the horses much, since they weren't being worked hard. I liked to be around the animals, even if it did take some of the long hours of the day to tend them.

Eventually I told Mr. Sanchez that I could divert the stream up a little ways and dig a small ditch to bring running water into the edge of the pasture. This would save the need of taking the horses out to water. With his approval, we soon had made a ditch bringing the water out of the stream and right through the lower edge of the pasture. I made a larger pool in one place, where the water could gather up some and give the animals plenty of room to drink.

Mr. Sanchez liked the idea, and came out to look at it. It had taken us two days to finish the ditch, but the water was already moving clear and cold going through the end of the corral. He looked at it with an approving shake of his head and said, "Now Jacob, if you can get hay to grow in the pasture, we won't have much to do with the horses."

It was not in his nature to show appreciation to anyone

for anything, and I knew he would turn quickly on anyone that made him mad. I did ask him if it would be all right if Dutch and I bunked together, and he said that would be okay with him.

We were finally able to spend more time together, even though some of the others were in the bunk house with us a lot of the time. I learned that Dutch had done about the same as me. He too had found a hideout on a ship coming to America. Although in the old country he had lived only about one hundred twenty miles from where I lived, he didn't know any of my people and I didn't know any of his family.

Dutch never talked about things too much, and was a little bit of a loner, like me. It was good to converse with someone in my native tongue, but only if we were alone. We had to be careful to speak and try to fit in with English or Spanish. Dutch was good to help me with the things that I did not know how to say. Before long I felt pretty good about being able to speak and understand the new language of the Mexicans.

Our pay from Sanchez would make us about sixteen dollars to one hundred dollars a day. We could often make much more at times. It just depended on how much the find was each shift. It cost about half of the wage just to eat someplace. A bath in the big tub was three dollars and fifty cents, so we never did that. Bathing in the river was a lot better anyway. Each time we made a purchase, we had to act like it was about the last cent that we had. It was good to act poor around there.

One day a horse trader came into town with about twenty horses for sale. If we were ever going to get out and find any claim of our own, or if we ever had a need to move on, we would need some good horses. We decided that we needed to do something, even if it would take a large part of our savings. Even then, we were taken aback when the man said that we would have to pay two hundred and twenty dollars each for the fine horses that we were looking at. We wouldn't even have a saddle for that price. That would cost another forty-five dollars each.

This was getting to be a big decision for us. The trader encouraged us to try them out by riding them around the corral. We didn't know anything about horses, but the trader assured us that these horses were some of the best around. "If you ever wanted to sell one of them, or both, you would probably get more for them than you paid," he declared. "In fact, if you don't like the deal, next time I come around I may even buy them back from you."

We had just about decided to buy the two horses when Sanchez came up to the corral and saw the two of us on horseback. We told Sanchez what the trader had told us.

He said, "Get down off those horses and walk them over to me." He looked them over carefully. We didn't know what he was looking for. A horse was a horse to us. Of course we wanted it to have some spirit, like us, and then a good color would be nice, too.

Looking around at the trader's stock, Sanchez said, "Those two horses over there, the sorrel and the black one, bring them here."

We could only sit and watch as he looked them over from one end to the other. Sanchez motioned the horse trader over. Pointing to us, he told the man, "These two work for me. They must have good horses. How much are these?"

The horse trader seemed a little bit less sure than he had earlier. "Oh! I could let those two go for one-sixty-five each, without the saddle."

"You are going to let them go for fifty dollars each with the saddle, and that is all there is to talk about." Two of Sanchez's armed men came to stand at his side to insure that his orders were carried out.

The horse trader sized up the situation and said,

"Done."

I know that Sanchez wasn't overly generous, but he didn't want to lose us. It was business to him. We were the best two workers in his crew, and we would make him that much money in a hurry. Even so, we could hardly believe our luck that he had come to our aid and picked out good horses for us. Sanchez even let us keep our horses with his and they were taken care of with the rest.

As the weeks rolled along we realized that Sanchez knew his horses. I kept the sorrel for myself. He was gentle and dependable and we built a special friendship. It felt good to have him under me, and I was soon calling him Jake. Dutch took the large black horse. Since I was the one doing the naming of horses, I just called him Nighthawk. Dutch seemed to like the name, too.

One day I heard someone at Millie's announce that the gold mining would soon be slowing down for the season. I had noticed the weather cooling off some the past few weeks. The thick growth of wild flowers that were on both sides of the stream had already lost many of their leaves. I had felt the bite in the air in the early mornings and noticed that my hands couldn't stay warm if I got them wet. Early in the mornings, I could even see traces of some ice forming along the waterway. Before long deep snows were showing up in the high mountains, and the watershed of the Sacramento and the San Joaquin Rivers had dropped to about half the flow.

Our production had been down and Sanchez let us know that our pay would be down, too. He put many of his men on wood detail to chop wood for the months ahead. No one had spent a winter here, but the trappers that had come by now and then had warned us that it would get pretty bad. Many of the miners would have to tough it out through the winter, as they had to keep sight of their claims. Others decided that the digging and the getting were too hard and they would move out of the area.

Even though I had worked only a few weeks mining, I had managed to save most of the money I had made. There was no bank in the camp, but Millie had let me store my savings with her in her vault. We had heard many stories about people being killed as they tried to make their way back to San Francisco or Sacramento with their gold. It seems that there were those who lay in wait to take all a man had and often his life, too. I would soon have to decide what I would do this winter. If nothing else came up, I would just have to take my chances, too, and get out of here.

# Chapter 5

Before the rain and snow started falling and the ground got too hard to dig, we were still finding our share of gold. Some said it should be even better next season. I guess that is the way of the miner, always better tomorrow.

When the time came that I had to break the ice for the horses to drink several days in a row, and the little ditch seemed all but stopped, I talked over our prospects for the coming winter with Dutch. He said that the dance hall and the saloon would be mostly closed until spring. Millie would be boarding up her place next week, and Stewart's was also closing down for the season. Those that were going to leave would go in a large group so that they could get past the bandits easier.

I had more time now that the mining had stopped and the sluice boxes were stored for the winter. I thought I should talk to Mr. Sanchez and see what he was going to do. He told me that some of his men would stay with the things here and he would be going back and forth in the winter. He had purchased a ranch in the low lands and his horses would need good attention. He asked me if I would like to have a job taking his horses down to the low lands where there was good pasture for them. I knew that horses were at an all time high price, and had to be watched and cared for.

"What about my friend Dutch?" I asked. "Would there be work for him?"

"No, I only would have need for one of you, and I have been watching the way you take care of my horses. You are the one to do this." I could tell that he had already thought this through. "Some of my men will go with you and show you the way. You will leave with a large bunch of them in a couple of days."

I told Mr. Sanchez that I would need to go to Sacramento and, sometime in the winter, I would like to have a week off to go to San Francisco, but that is all of the time I would need for the winter. He nodded his head at that, saying," Yes, but just make sure that my horses are taken care of."

I told Dutch what Sanchez had said to me, and he sat without comment for some time. Finally he said that he thought he would go to Sacramento and spend the winter, but that he would be one of the first ones back in the spring. I knew that he hadn't saved much of his money, but he said that he would get work in the city, and that he had enough to see him through the winter. I wondered if I should offer to help him by giving him a loan until next year, but thought better of the idea. Maybe he needed to learn to stay away from the saloons and those that would soon separate him from his money. Besides, he had a proud streak running through him.

I went by to see Millie and found her involved with making the place as secure as she could. The young couple that had taken my place was still there and I had seen them often the past few weeks. Millie asked me what I wanted done with my money and gold, as she brought it forth out of the safe. "It's all here," she said.

"I know," I told her, "I never worried about it."

What I had was a lot of money to me, and I would sure hate to lose it. She had carefully kept track of my earnings and had been careful to keep mine separate from hers. Mine was a small amount compared to hers, but it was good that she let me keep it in her safe. She had told me that she knew she could trust me and somehow I knew that I could trust her. It's not to say that someone couldn't come in and rob us both, but that was a chance we both had to take.

Before we knew it, the time to leave arrived. I found out that the ranch was only about a day and half ride from Sacramento. Dutch went with us most of the way from the gold mines. When the trails parted, he went on his way, and we went to the ranch.

The ranch consisted of a main house and three bunk houses, a barn and corrals. The field around the corral was fenced off, and so there weren't many places the horses could get away. There was fine grazing here, and I knew that the horses should do well. I had a couple of helpers who stayed at the ranch, so they would be the ones to watch after the horses when I needed to be gone for a few days.

We had about sixty horses to take care of, and there seemed to be plenty of grain and hay stored in the barn. I thought, with plenty of gold, you could afford about anything. However, I knew that this many horses would be a temptation for Indians and thieves to come raiding. So I put one of the Mexicans in the barn every night to sound the alarm if anyone tried to get in and take some of the stock. We also had two dogs on the place to help patrol things.

I couldn't help but wonder what would happen if someone made off with any horses. Mr. Sanchez would probably take all of my one hundred dollars a month, and more if he really got mad. I wondered why I ever decided to take this job in the first place.

In the first month, I only saw Mr. Sanchez a couple of times. He was in a bad mood. I found out that the news was out on the gold mining, and people were already coming in from all over the place. Some had even been up to his diggings and tried to set some claim markers. He had them shot, but still others kept coming, even in the winter.

I heard that San Francisco was bulging at the seams with new arrivals every day. Everyone wanted to get in on the easy pickings of the gold.

I thought, if they are coming in during the winter already, what will the spring and summer be like? It was true, what Mr. Braun had said; there was a fever about the gold and the mining that just seemed to take good people and turn them into bad ones.

I managed to get to Sacramento the second month. It was a relief to finally be able to deposit my earnings from the gold fields in a real bank where I didn't have to worry about someone taking it from me. After my visit to the bank, I couldn't seem to find Dutch. There were so many new people in town, anyone could soon get lost in the crowd. I wondered where he could have gone. I began to worry that something had happened to him.

I remembered telling him about the Strauss family. Maybe he had gone by there and they would know where he was. Before that, though, I thought I would just check in with the local marshal's office and ask if they just might have seen him.

I told them that he was German and about the same age as me. "The miners all called him "Dutch" up on the digs, but his name is Jacob Weiser," I told the marshal. He replied then that he knew exactly where Dutch was. He was in their jail next door.

"Why is he in jail?" I asked.

"For breaking up the saloon at Sal's place," the Marshall said. "He got a little too much to drink and decided to take it out on the locals. It took five of them to bring him down, but he won't cause any trouble for some time now."

"Can I see him?" I asked. "We worked together this past season in the gold fields."

"Yes," he said, "follow me."

I followed the marshal through the corridors and passed several jail cells before we came to one at the end of the room. It was not very light in here, since each cell had only one small barred window to the outside. I peered through the bars and could just make out someone hunkered up in the corner. The marshal said, "Visitor for you, Weiser."

It was a moment before the hulk in the dark even started to stir, as if figuring out if it was worthwhile. When he finally did come out where it was a little lighter, I could hardly recognize him. His clothes were pretty well torn off him and he had been healing from some of the beating of the saloon fighting. When he came close enough to see that it was me, he finally came to the front of the cell.

"Jacob!" he said. "It's good to get a look at you again. How have you been doing?"

"Some better than you! What have you been into that has put you in jail?"

"Well, I wasn't in town but a couple of days when I found myself down at Sal's place and having a few drinks. You know how it is. I just can't seem to keep away from these places somehow." He hung his head and frowned before he went on. "Well, you know I thought I was pretty good at gambling, and in most cases, I can hold my own. Here in this town, though, have come some of the toughest gamblers that I have ever seen. I guess it's the gold that has brought them in. I guess I was no match for them, and before long we were in the thick of things, when I caught them cheating."

He raised his voice defiantly as he related the tale. "There were three of them. They were all together and they played as though they didn't know each other. It was like three on one. I held my own for a while, but they soon began to pull things. That's when the fighting started."

Dutch's hands clenched into fists as he continued his story. "The main man started to grab for one of those little hidden pistols. Just as I saw this, I reached across and let him have it square on the chin, breaking his nose and knocking the gun out of his hand. You see how it was don't you, Jacob?" He paused for a time, thinking about the moment. "If I ever get out of here, I don't ever want to gamble again. It seems like these gamblers are getting worse all of the time, and these guys are from the East coast. They play pretty rough."

Dutch started to pace back and forth as he continued

his tale. "Of course, when the marshal came in, things were in a mess. And of course, the three gamblers said that I started the whole thing. Of course it was three against one, just like I was telling you." He stopped pacing and grabbed onto the bars of his cell. "They told me I would have to stay in jail till I rotted or could find some way to pay for the damages."

"How much damage did you do?" I asked him.

"Well, it was a lot more than what money I had left. They said it was five hundred and forty dollars."

I had never seen Dutch look so bad. He was always neat and liked to look nice. These few weeks in jail had changed that. He hadn't shaved for several weeks, and it looked like he hadn't slept very well either. He was thin and dirty and probably didn't have a friend in the world except me, and it was by accident that I happened by.

He spoke in German now, saying, "I guess I should have never come here."

"How much of the five hundred and forty dollars did you have?" I asked.

"Not much, with them all three trying to take it away from me," he said. "The marshal said I had one hundred and seventy two dollars left, which he took and put against my bill." His voice was full of despair. "I don't know what to do. I sure have learned my lesson with these kind of places."

"Do you want me to talk with the marshal and see if I can get you out? I have enough money to do that."

A look of hope came into his face, but then the look of despair quickly returned. "I can't ask you to do that. I have no way to pay you back," he said.

"I know you are good for it in the spring, if you tell me you will pay me when you get back to work. But, you need to promise not to let yourself get into any more problems around here."

"If I tell you this, I am sure going to do it if you can help me."

I talked with the marshal and found him to be a fair man. He said that he would probably let him out in the spring anyway, but if I were willing to pay the balance of the charges, he would release him now. I went to the bank and brought the money back that he required.

As Dutch walked out, a free man at last, I asked if he had ever been in jail before. "No!" he replied. "And I sure don't want to ever go there again!"

I had been thinking about the name the miners had given him of Dutch, so I asked him what he would like me to call him. "Just call me 'Dutch'," he said. "I am getting used to the name."

I needed to get back to the ranch and see if everything was still good there, but first I needed to stop by and see my friends, the Strauss family. Everyone seemed to know where their store was and Dutch and I were soon there. It was great to see them again.

After introductions had been made, I asked Mr. Strauss if he knew of any work that Dutch might do. He said that he needed someone to make the haul trips back and forth to San Francisco. It didn't pay anything like what he had made in the gold fields, but it was a job, and they would give him a couple of sets of new clothes until his first pay day.

When I left there, Dutch looked like a changed man, in his new outfit and with a purpose once again. He thanked me for all of my help, and extended his hand as I made ready to leave. "I don't really know what to say," he said. "I have never had anyone help me like that. I am good for it, though."

" I know," I said, and rode down the well-used dirt road that led back to the ranch.

I had been gone four days and I wondered if things were okay at the ranch. The helpers that I had left seemed

48

pretty dependable, but I didn't know much else about them. I know they feared Sanchez, and would try to make things look good when he came by for a short stay, or when some of his men came down to relay fresh horses for those who stayed up in the gold claims.

From the number of people that I saw in Sacramento who were here in the area to try their luck at gold mining, I imagined that some would do nearly anything for horses. Even the marshal asked if I knew of any horses for sale. He said they were putting on more riders and the drain on their horses was showing up. I told him that I didn't think that we had any for sale, but if I heard of any, I would try and get word to him.

As I left early the next morning, my thoughts at first were on my friend Dutch. But by the next day, my fear of new troubles had taken hold. When I came within sight of the ranch in the early afternoon, I knew instantly that something was wrong. I couldn't see any signs of the horses or of the two men I had left to watch them. The dogs hadn't come to greet me. All was quiet -- too quiet.

I eased the rifle out of the scabbard and pulled my horse to a stop. I waited in a thicket and watched for a few minutes. There was no sign of life in the meadow down below. I decided to hide my horse in the thicket and approach the house and the barn from the rear.

I worked my way past the familiar landmarks with rifle at the ready and an extra box of shells in my back pocket. I waited and listened but the only sounds that came were from some of the squirrels and birds moving about. After a few minutes I had made my way up to the back of the house and looked in one of the windows. The place seemed deserted. I also checked the barn and found it to be empty, too. Then I found the two dogs down by the corrals; both had been shot. I was convinced that no one was here.

Even in my worst moments, I had not imagined that the

whole herd of horses would be gone. Now, all of the bridles and saddles were gone as well, along with most of the ropes. Whoever it was that came in seemed to have known exactly what to do. The ground was torn up with many horse tracks and riders as they made off with the herd. There was no sign of any struggle or shooting in the barn or in the house. From all appearances, it seemed that the two who had been left to watch the horses had been in on the stealing of the herd.

I quickly retrieved my horse and followed the tracks for about three miles. They seemed to be headed straight for Mexico. I went around putting the gates back up, though it seemed a useless gesture now. What would Sanchez do about this? He would be in some kind of ugly mood over the loss of most of his horses, and I supposed he would blame me. It was his helpers that had been in on this, not me, but I knew that he would blame anyone that he could. That's the way of things, I thought. Those that steal and rob others sometimes have it done to them.

I thought of those that Sanchez had run off their claims and then taken over for himself. He was fierce when it came to things he owned, or things that he wanted. I even wondered how he had gotten this ranch. Maybe he took it like he had other things so many times before. Maybe he had it coming, I thought.

I didn't know where to find Sanchez or any of his other men. So I decided that I would rub down my horse good, give it plenty of grain and hay, and be off to Sacramento early the next morning. I would leave a note in the ranch house about what had happened in case anyone came while I was away. A lot of the food had also been taken, but I found enough to make the return trip. I knew that there was no way for me to get the horses back by myself, and I didn't even know if the marshal would come and help with trying to get them back.

I rode all of the long day, walking some of the time to

spare my horse, and well into the night before I could make out the town of Sacramento in the distance. A few lights were around the town, but it was well before dawn. There wasn't a place on me that didn't seem sore or tired. I wanted to hobble my horse and get a good night's rest. Maybe even a couple of hours' sleep would be good, but I must move on. The chances of catching up to the horse thieves were getting worse by the hour. They would have a good start on anyone by now.

The one place that would still be open was the marshal's office. It never closes the doors. When I finally rode up to the jail, it was just beginning to turn light in the east. The town was asleep and quiet at this time of morning. I didn't see anyone on the streets and only a few signs of life, as some of the lamps were being lighted in a few of the places for the early risers. The sleepy eyed deputy, who was on the job, came to his feet as I tied my horse to the hitching rail.

I soon told him what had happened while I was away from the ranch.  He told me the marshal was away for two or three more days and that they wouldn't be able to help me anyway. It would take a large posse to go after so many. It was just something that they couldn't do. They had their hands full with things close to home. He said that they had other reports of thieves taking stock and burning buildings, but they were not even able to go and check on things like that. It was as I thought. No help from them, but I needed to try anyway.

I took my faithful horse down to the livery stable to be taken care of. I told the man there that I wanted an extra ration of everything for him, and a good rub down. I asked him if I could pay him something for me to have an hour or so rest on his pile of hay. He said that would be fine, and there was no charge for that.

I was awakened by the loud sharp noise of the blacksmith banging on his anvil. It was full light now, and I turned and pulled myself closer to the edge of the hay. I could see that people were making use of the street in the early morning. I had no idea how long I had slept. I knew it wasn't long enough, but it would have to do.

I pulled my boots on and found the horse trough to wash my face in. The cold water was just the thing to shock a guy right back into reality. I made my way over to the nearest boarding house that offered food and beds. It was just getting busy when I came in and I ordered a good breakfast. Not as good as Millie's, I thought, but the second cup of coffee seemed to put the right touch on the balance of the hot biscuits and jam. I felt a lot better right about now. I wasn't even as tired as when I first got up.

I was still sitting there after I had pretty well finished eating, when two of Sanchez's men came down the stairway from the rooms above. I didn't remember the names of both of them, but the one in the front was called Pablo. I stood up so they could see me and motioned them over to my table. I asked them if they knew where Mr. Sanchez could be and Pablo motioned with his head, upstairs.

"I must see him right away," I told him. "It is very important."

He said that his boss would be in no mood to be bothered this early. I told him that he needed to wake him up, that something had happened at the ranch. With that he turned and went back up the stairway. In a short while he came down the stairs far enough for me to see him, and motioned for me to follow him.

We entered the room of Mr. Sanchez, who was sitting on the edge of the bed with his pants pulled on. A nearly empty bottle of whiskey sat on the table next to the bed, and the room had the foul smell of things of the night. I told him what had happened when I returned to the ranch, after being gone four days.

On hearing my story, he jumped to his feet and let out

a loud string of bad words. He wasn't looking at me yet, so I thought he was saving the worst for me. He told Pablo to go and round up all of the men and have them ready to ride in an hour. Turning back to me, he asked, "Are you sure that it wasn't Indians?"

"No, I looked everything over pretty well, and it appeared that they were bandits, apparently some that the helpers knew." I described the scene back at the ranch. Then I told him about how I had returned to town to see if the marshal might come and help, only to find that he was out of town and his deputy said they were not able to give any help.

Mr. Sanchez asked what else I could tell him, and I said that I had followed the trail about three miles from the ranch and they were going south by east, in the direction of Mexico.

I don't know what the bandits were like who had taken the horses, but it was soon apparent that a bad looking bunch would be heading out after them. Sanchez had offered one hundred dollars to any who were tough and ready to go with them. He would pay half now, and the other half when they came back. They bought or borrowed all of the horses and pack animals they could find. Sanchez had even given the asking price for most of the extra horses that he needed. I guess he was too close to the marshal's office for anything else. It took about two hours before provisions and animals and men could be ready. It was a mean looking bunch that pulled away from town that morning.

When we arrived at the ranch, Sanchez told me to wait there. He dropped off four of the horses, telling me that he expected to have some horses back at the ranch soon since it was about time to rotate the stock of the ones from the gold fields. Some of them would need to be exchanged for those he left with me. He had also brought provisions to be left at the ranch.

Sanchez had even recruited an Indian scout who knew

the area into Mexico, and the area between. This scout had gone on ahead of the rest of the bunch, as they watered their horses and looked at the signs around the area. A short rest had been called for the horses to get some rest and feed, as well as the fourteen men who had come to go after the outlaws.

As they mounted and went out of sight down around the turn of the pasture, I thought, "Boy, I sure wouldn't want them coming after me!" It looked like most of them were thieves or bandits. They were a hard bunch.

It was pretty quiet at the ranch now, with only four horses and four packhorses to take care of. Four days passed by since the bad bunch had left to go after the thieves before the horses to be pastured came down from the gold fields. Two riders brought them in. I told them what had happened and that we only had four horses to replace the six that they had brought.

They said that there were still people trying to file over the claims in the fields and several shootings had happened. I told them that the people were thick in Sacramento already and that they could expect things to get really bad when the weather warmed enough for gold mining to get going again. They only stayed one day, and took the four horses that were in the pasture. When I suggested that they could also take one of the pack animals along to help carry supplies back to the camp, they decided that they could probably use some more supplies from Sacramento. They would go by there and spend a couple of days before returning to the gold mines.

A week went by and there was still no sign of Mr. Sanchez and his bunch. I began to wonder if they would ever have a chance to catch up to them. The Indian scout had told them that they had three days' start on them. With that much time, they could be a long ways ahead. I considered the possibility that a band of Indians had taken them all out, but

54

figured there wasn't too much chance of that, with the risk of a few horses and the loss of many in a battle.

While I waited, I had plenty of time to think about my trip to Sacramento. Before Sanchez had ridden out, he told me that I wouldn't have a chance to go to San Francisco this winter, as I would need to stay and watch after the ranch. I had guessed as much. I thought he would be really angry with me, too, but he seemed to read what had happened. I wished that I had reminded Dutch to check with the Braun family when he went to San Francisco and see if I had a letter from my mother. It would be good to hear from her.

# Chapter 6

The days were getting a little bit warmer and the pasture was doing better. Even the night didn't seem to be getting so cold, though it was still cold enough to enjoy a good fire in the fireplace. I wondered just when spring would come and how long it would be before we would return back to the claims. I lost track of the days since the thieves had been gone, but it must have been about twelve days later when I finally saw some riders coming in from the south. Behind the two front riders came a large group of horses.

I went and opened the pasture gates as they got closer. I could recognize Mr. Sanchez in the bunch. The Indian guide was the first one into the pasture and he came right to the ranch house. His horse was a different one than the one he had left on. All of the men looked like they were just hanging on, and some of them had been bandaged up. I only counted ten who had come back. It did seem like we had a good number of horses in the pasture, but many of them were new.

Sanchez rode up to the hitching rack of the ranch house and I took his reins as he slid off his horse. The horses were all unsaddled and let out to pasture and I soon had some hot food for the bunch of them. Some said they were too tired to eat and made their way to the bunkhouses or to the barn for some rest. No one was in any mood for talking until after they had rested some and had some food inside of them. They looked like they hadn't had any rest for days, and from the look of their horses, they had come a long way this day.

I rubbed most of the horses down and gave them a generous helping of grain and hay. The Indian scout took some food and was then told to go and watch the back country. I wondered about that, but asked no questions.

The next morning, I was up early and had the coffee pot full as well as a big breakfast for everyone. The men were eager to eat as they rushed up to the table, but no one seemed to appreciate that I had gotten up early to get the food ready. On the other hand, they were kind of a thankless lot. If I thought they were surly before they left, they were even in a worse mood when the came back, especially two of them that had been shot. All they could say was it wasn't worth the hundred dollars to run all over the place and get shot up, too. Of course, they didn't talk like this when Sanchez was around them.

A hundred dollars was a lot of money, especially this time of year when there wasn't much work. With the migration of people into the towns waiting for the gold season to come, all of the available jobs had been taken. Some had brought their families with them; so that was even more pressure to keep money coming in.

Sanchez was up now and room was made for him to sit near the head of the table and near the food. I still didn't know what had happened, and would probably never hear anything from this bunch. As soon as they finished eating, they all caught up fresh horses for their return to Sacramento. Sanchez selected the horse he wanted and I caught it for him. He was a large black horse that I hadn't seen before. He was ornery and a little bit mean as he tried to bite me when I put the bridle on him. I thought, just like Sanchez! It was probably a good match.

Sanchez made sure his cinch was good and snug before he pulled himself into the saddle. He came over to where I was standing and said, "You will have to stay with the ranch from now on. No going anywhere until it is time to go back to the mines." I knew from his tone of voice that he meant it.

He went on, "It took four men and eight horses we lost in getting them back. Now some may come along and try to claim some of these horses after we are gone." His eyes narrowed as he surveyed the corral full of horses. "We did pick up all we could find along the way, but don't let them have any of these horses. I will try and send you some help from town as soon as I get there. In the mean time, you will have to stay alert all of the time." As he turned to go, he added one more chilling comment. " I have seen to it that your helpers from before will not be back, ever."

About eight days after they had left, I could hear the creaking of a wagon and hear the sound of horses neighing as they caught wind of our herd. The wagon was loaded down with grain and other things that we would need. The two helpers were Spanish and were brothers who lived in Sacramento. They told me that they lived in Sacramento with other relatives, and when they took the job, they were told that if anything happened to Sanchez's horses, their relatives would have to pay.

"Do you think he would shoot any of our family if we let something happen to his horses?" they asked.

"You can be sure of it. That's why he hired you from a large family."

I continued to watch the trail that the herd had come in on in case some might follow and want their horses back. I didn't have to worry about my family being shot, but what would I do if some came after theirs and wanted to take them by force? Sanchez wasn't paying me enough to risk my life for his horses.

The days and weeks went by quickly and there definitely was a warming of things. Spring was here. Buds were showing up on some of the willows. Some of the mares were having their young, and it was good to see the new ones come along.

We didn't have any strangers come along and demand their horses, but we had lost one of them that had been wounded. I noticed that it was not doing very well and in a few days it had died. Another casualty, I thought. I wondered how many men and horses had been killed in the fighting, when Sanchez caught up with them?

The last relay of horses from the high country brought news that it was finally warming up there a little bit, too. From their best guess, it would probably be good to go in about three weeks. Word was passed on that Mr. Stewart was preparing to return. Also, Millie was anxious to get back. And, of course, the dance hall girls and the saloon keepers would be ready too. I know I was ready. It had been a long winter for me, but now that it was about over, it didn't seem that bad.

I hadn't seen or heard from Dutch since he went to work for Mr. Strauss in the freighting business. I hoped that he had kept himself out of trouble this winter.

Spring was already well along here on the ranch, by the time four of Sanchez's men came by with orders from the boss. It was still cool up in the high country, but everyone was anxious to get back and see about his or her claims. We would need to be some of the first ones in, as Sanchez had more that anyone else, when it came to claims. We only took about half of the horses, as feed was very scarce up in the camp and it would be a while before the wagon trail was passable. All of the hay had been used up, and most of the grain, too.

Stewart and others were waiting for the trail to open, but Sanchez wanted his people in place to protect his, and take some that he wanted. According to what I was told, there would be a relay set up until the roads could be traveled. I had been asked to help take part of the horses to a point about half way to the fields and exchange them for others that would be sent back to the ranch. Each week I would take eight horses to the point of return and bring back the same amount.

On my first trip, I could tell that it was still some time before the rays of the sun would get into the low lands of the river shed and warm it up much. It would be at least two more weeks before anyone could get a wagon through, even longer if we had a change in the weather. Sanchez had come out a couple of times to check on things at the ranch. I asked him if there was any way for me to get enough time off to go back to Sacramento. I really wanted to go to San Francisco, but it would take several days to do that. With the days warming up, I didn't want to be gone too long. Sanchez said that he would send some extra men out to the ranch to help. I was to tell them what needed to be done, and then go from there.

The two Mexican boys were good help, and had learned things well. In a couple of days after Sanchez left, four of his men came to stay at the ranch. He even sent a cook along and a wagonload of supplies. He said that he wanted to get all of his men out of town before long, and the ranch was a good place to keep them.

My sorrel horse had become my trusted companion through the long winter. I never let him be traded into the relay with the other stock. He was gentle and dependable, and it felt good to have him under me. I thought of what I had called him from the time that I first started using him. Now, with a gentle nudge of the spurs, I said, "Come on, Jake, let's move on into town." He seemed to sense that this would be a good easy trip this time, not like the two trips in a row we had made before.

It was nice not to have the demands of watching after everything at the ranch. The rolling hills and small streams that I crossed gave me thought once again of the water that washed the gold claims much further up stream. What would it be like this year? Would there be twice as many people as last year? Twice as much trouble and robbery?

"Well, Jake, we don't have to worry about that right now," I said, patting him on the neck.

The next day we could see Sacramento and I could almost hear the hum of people and smell the bustle and work of the town. I had nearly forgotten what it was like to be in a city. Jake and I stopped early that night. We were in no hurry and so we took our own good time. I had brought a feed of grain from the barn for Jake. After rubbing him down and putting the hobbles on him, I made camp by a small stream. It was quiet and pleasant here. It was so peaceful out under the big sky. I liked sleeping out under the stars, and I guess I would just as soon sleep outside as anywhere if I had my choice. I always slept with my gun close by and just felt better, knowing I would be able to defend myself if I had to.

There was one good thing about my winter on the ranch. I got plenty of practice in with the pistols and the rifle. I was a pretty good shot now. Though not real fast with the pistol, I was good for hitting the mark. The rifle was my best choice. As I drifted off to sleep there under the stars, I hoped that I would never need to use them.

It was early in the morning, about two hours before light I would guess, when something woke me up. The small fire had long been out, and there was a half moon showing overhead. Without wasting any time, I made my way down to Jake, who I could make out lying on the ground. I spoke to him in a quiet voice so he would know it was me. I grabbed his nostrils and patted him on the neck. He was soon on his feet, and I reached down and took the hobbles off him, talking softly in his ear all the time.

From where I was, I could tell that there were several riders and a large herd of horses moving. In just a moment, I had pulled Jake back into the soft deep shadows of the trees. I found the bridle and slipped it into his mouth. In the dim light of the early morning, I moved quickly, knowing I might be taking a chance of being found out.

I could hear the horses and the riders real close now. I talked quietly to Jake as I put the saddle into place and pulled the cinch up tight. If we needed to go in a hurry, we could do that. I would just go off and leave the camp stuff if I had to.

No one moved horses or cattle at this time of night unless they were stealing them. I thought of the ranch that was about ten miles away. I had stopped there a couple of times and talked with some of the cowhands. The owner was called Norris. From what I had seen, he had a good, well-kept spread. There were four cowboys, Mr. and Mrs. Norris, and two children, a boy and older sister on the ranch. They had invited me in for supper and I thought it would be good to do that and get to know them. I told them that I was watching the ranch for Sanchez, farther down in the low country.

I wondered if these horses might be from the Norris ranch. The sounds of the rustlers disappeared about as quickly as they had come and I thought I had better get my things together and go by the Norris place. It was just getting daylight when I could make out the smoke coming from the area of the Norris ranch. Something in me felt bad about what I might find there.

When I was close enough to see what was going on, it seemed that the ranch house was the only building left standing. It looked like it had recently been set on fire. All of the bunkhouses had been burned and the men inside were shot as they had come out. The corrals had been torn down, and all of the animals were gone except a milk cow and calf. The chickens had been scattered around the yard; not knowing what else to do, the rooster was sitting on top of one of the few remaining fence posts, nervously announcing the start of another day.

When those in the ranch house saw me coming across the meadow, they came out on the front porch with rifles in hand, both the mom and the dad. I was glad to see they had survived the night as I waved to them. The children were safe and told to keep back in the house.

Mr. Norris told me that a large group of rustlers had come in the night, setting fire to the bunkhouses. Those inside

62

didn't have any choice but to come out, and when they did, the rustlers shot them down. He said it was hard to see what was going on, but he managed to get one of them. They were able to keep them away from setting the house on fire.

"I guess they really wanted the horses, anyway," he said.

"What can I do to help you?" I asked. I told him of hearing the rustlers passing in the night and coming over to their place to see if they were okay.

"We had more horses than anyone else around. They were good stock. But what is worse is the losing of so many good men. Some of them have been with me from the start. I don't know what I am going to do; they were like family. When will we ever see law and order in this land?" he asked.

I could see the sadness in all of their faces as they thought of those who had been lost.

"Will you go by and see if the marshal can come and give us some help with our problems?"

I thought of the time recently when I had asked for some help from the marshal. Maybe, being closer to town, Mr. Norris would have more luck, and maybe he knew the marshal pretty well.

"Will you do one other thing for us, Jacob? Will you go by Sal's place and ask for Sal? Tell him we are afoot. He is my wife's cousin."

What memories that brought back to me, of having to bail Dutch out of jail for something that he broke up in Sal's place! I told him that I would, and needed to be on my way. The faster I made it to town, the better chance they would have to catch the rustlers.

It would normally be about a four-hour ride to town, but Jake responded to the hurry and we arrived there in about three hours, stopping only for a quick drink for him. I rode up to the marshal's office and found him inside. He recognized me right away and called me by name. I told him that I had just come from the Norris ranch and about what had happened there.

He shook his head in disbelief. "Not Tom Norris! He is one of the best liked people in these parts."

I could see that he had great concern for the Norris family. But shaking his head he said, "There just isn't anything that I can do. I've been trying to get more help, but right now, I only have two deputies. Even if we all went, we would be no match for the rustlers. I have no authority to call or pay for a posse. The town council has to approve that."

I left the marshal's and made my way over to Sal's place. I told the bartender that I needed to see him as quick as I could. He sent word for Sal, who came out of one of the back rooms. He wore fine clothes and had a business look about him. We sat at one of the tables and I told him what had happened at the Norris ranch.

He called one of the men over who was sitting near the window and said, "Randy, I want you to get all of the able-bodied men who can ride and shoot and have them meet here in front of the place in an hour. They will be on my payroll!"

He told me that horses were in short supply, but he had taken a small ranch on a gambling debt that week, and would take horses from there and send to his cousin, Mr. Norris.

I related what I'd heard in the middle of the night as the rustlers had passed, and made sure he knew the spot where I had been camped. He asked me to have breakfast and wait for a short while until he could get some of his men together. I wondered if he would be going with them.

The breakfast was good and I was on my second cup of coffee when the door opened to the saloon. In walked the

Indian scout called Shaunecey that had worked for Sanchez. I had always wondered about him. He never seemed to get tired. When he came back with the horses down on the ranch after the chase of the thieves, he seemed just as rested and alert as if he had just come in from a morning ride. I know one thing, he listened closely when I told him where I had been camped the early morning they went by with the horses.

He seemed to know exactly where that was and told Sal that the rustlers had made a sweeping turn from the Norris ranch. They seemed to be heading in the general direction of San Francisco. The horses would bring big money to those able to pay for a way to the gold mines.

I went out on the front porch to see this group get underway. It looked like Sal had managed to get six men, plus the Indian guide, to go in search of the rustlers. Their group was also made up of other ranchers and some of the local citizens. I thought, this is a much different bunch than I had seen go out with Sanchez.

Each was given instructions before they left. They might be gone up to four days or more. It was easy to see that Sal wouldn't be going along with them. He was the one doing all of the talking from the porch and he hadn't changed his clothes. I couldn't even see if he had a gun with him. From the looks of Mr. Sal, he probably hired his gun to get things done. When ready, they all raced out of town as if they were close to the rustlers already.

It was a good show, I thought, but that is probably all it is. They aren't likely to ever get close to the rustlers. They would wear out their horses in the first five miles out of town.

It was getting pretty warm by now and I thought I would go over to see the Strauss family. I might catch Dutch there. It would be good to see him again. With no real schedule, we might be able to make some plans for the spring digging.

65

When I arrived, the store was already getting busy. It seemed that you could sell almost anything you had to the busy town people. Mr. Strauss was not at the counter when I came in, and I asked if he was there. One of the clerks said that he would be there any minute if I would like to wait. I spent a little bit of time looking at the merchandise and was surprised at how much things had gone up in price. It didn't seem to matter to the customers. They were all looking through a new load of stuff that had just come in.

Mr. Strauss entered the store, but he was immediately surrounded by some of the customers who had come in to see if he was able to get their special orders from San Francisco. I waved a hello to him, and decided that he was just too busy to talk with right now. He finally made his way closer to me and said, "Jacob, come over to dinner tonight, about sundown."

I nodded a yes and went back outside. I asked one of the men if he knew where Mr. Strauss lived and he pointed to a house down on the right side of the street. "Sixth place down. The one with the flower bed in the front yard," he said.

I asked him if he knew Jacob Weiser, one of the freight haulers, and he told me that he had seen him last night at Sal's.

I thought, "Oh, no, not Sal's again!" I worked my way back over to Sal's to see if anyone knew where he might be. I was told that he worked and stayed down at the livery stables when he was in town. The stables would know where he might be this time of morning. It was good to know that he wasn't in jail. Maybe he had given up the nightlife.

The liveryman remembered me from the time before when I slept up on his haystack. He told me that Dutch was around back feeding the animals. Sure enough, there he was with pitchfork in hand and talking to the horses.

"Throw me a fork full," I said as I came up behind him.

He stopped what he was doing and came over and gave

me one of those big bear hugs. It sure was good to see him again and see him looking so good.

"How have you been doing these past days?" I asked him in German.

He answered that since getting out of jail, he was a changed man. It was hard to keep his promise to me of not getting in trouble, but he had done what he'd said he'd do. He said they had just returned yesterday with several wagons loaded with merchandise. Mr. Strauss had been really good to him, and when he was in town, he helped out around here for a place to stay and a little spending money.

"It don't take so much money with me staying out of the saloons."

He was about ready to go to breakfast, so I told him I would go with him. We made our way over to Sal's place and he ordered his breakfast I had another cup of coffee with him and we talked for about an hour. I would talk for a while and then it would be his turn.

When he was through with breakfast, he said, "I have a letter from home for you. I picked it up from Mr. Braun. He asked about you."

We went to the place he stayed and from a leather folder he brought forth a letter and extended it to me. I went over near the only small window in his room and looked at the date of it. It was about six months old. It would be good to hear from home. I carefully opened the letter and began to read it.

I didn't get very far when Dutch asked me what was wrong. I couldn't keep the tears back as I told him that my mother had passed away with a sickness. I couldn't go on for a few minutes until my eyes were clearer. It seemed that she became very ill. The doctors said that she died in the winter of sickness. My two sisters were being cared for, and I was not to worry about them.

My mother's last words were, "I wish my Jacob was here with me now."

I went outside to be alone and think about this great loss. First my father was gone and now my mother. Should I have stayed back, so I could be there for her when she needed me?

I had given some thought to the idea of going back and seeing her again. With a good year, I would have plenty of money to go, and then there was of course my friend Mr. Olson who would give me a way if I needed it.

I handed Dutch the letter on the way out, so he too would know my feelings. I imagined him sitting in there wondering what to say, or what to do. There was sadness now that I had never known. It was different from my father passing away, and yet it was the same, only more of it. I was a man now, and needed to act like one. I couldn't let anyone else see the sadness that this had caused.

I walked over to my horse and began to rub his neck. Jake always liked that and nudged me with his head as if he didn't get quite enough.

"They are about all gone now. Jake," I said as I rubbed his head between his ears. I know he didn't know what I was talking about, but it somehow felt better to tell someone. I bent over in the horse trough and washed away all signs of anything from the eyes.

The blacksmith came over to the other end and put a red-hot iron in the water. "I will have it good and warm pretty soon," he said as the sizzle of another piece went in the water. He had a smile on his face, and I couldn't help but smile back. I went back to Dutch's place and asked if he was through work for the day.

He came out and said, "I am through any time you want me to be."

"Let's go look around town today," I said.

He came out, gave me back the letter, and put his arm briefly on my shoulder. Nothing else needed to be said as we walked side by side along the stores, and on out past the houses.

Then we found a good shade spot and some fresh young grass to sit on and talk. I found out that we both had no one else. He had lost both of his parents and he was never planning on going back. We talked for several hours in our native tongue. It was good to talk of so many things.

"What are we going to do in the fields this year?" I said. "It sure would be good to find some place to mine for the two of us."

It was sundown before I knew it, and I told him that Mr. Strauss had invited me to dinner. "I told him I would come, but if you aren't going. too, I will go and tell them that I won't be able to make it tonight."

"You go on, it will do you good," he said to me. "If you are going to be around tomorrow, we could have some more time to talk."

I washed up and made my way to the Strauss home. I had noticed the flowers in our walk and Dutch had pointed out their house to me. They were anxious to talk with me and I was eager to hear of the many things that they would say. The meal was very good and I told them, "You just can't beat good German cooking."

After the meal I thanked them for all of the good food and told them I might be in town for a couple of days. I would at least drop by the store before I left town.

I went out into the night. It was good to feel the cool evening breeze as I caught my horse and left the lights.

*After Jacob had left, Dutch sat quietly on the horse trough in the evening light. He wished he could do something or* say something to his friend Jacob that would make it better. He could remember how he felt about losing someone.

His hand went down to the handle of the fine hunting knife that hung at his right side. That always seemed to bring his thoughts back to his native land. His memories were as clear as if it had only been yesterday that he lived in Germany.

Chapter 7

*Dutch's Tale*

It was a gray fall morning that found young Dutch on the "do not enter" side of the Black Forest. The dark shadow of the huge mountain was hardly discernible, but its ominous image only stirred the imagination and his desire to go past the keep out signs. It was as though the mountain and the signs challenged him, dared him. Sometimes it was just too much to resist. After all, he reasoned, he was going because of family need.

He remembered wondering the first time he had crossed over into the "keep out" side, what the sign said from the other direction. The sign said nothing on the back. It didn't seem fair, he thought. It was, as everyone in the town of Dirchwitz knew, off limits except to those up in the Johann Von Schtreicher Castle. The Black Forest belonged to them.

Jacob had left early and was familiar with the best place to cross the river that was the boundary. He had gone over into the restricted forest once in a while to hunt for deer, but only in case of great need for fresh meat.

It was always a wonder why the deer and other animals liked that side of the river, more than the town side. He knew the demands of wood burning stoves and fireplaces had taken the big trees farther back into the hills. He had gone along many times to help with wood harvest. Winter times were not kind to those who didn't prepare. Some families could hardly manage to keep warm in the long and bitter winter winds.

No one ever thought of starting a fire without planning on cooking at the same time it was heating the home. That would be called waste, and waste was not something they could do. He remembered helping in the gardens that everyone seemed to depend on for food. It was during a weeding time that he accidentally pulled up a turnip that was only half grown.

71

His father told him that was all right, but be more careful.

He was allowed to peel and eat the turnip right there in the garden. How sweet and juicy it was. It was like no other turnip he had ever tasted, so he asked his father why they didn't pull the turnips when they were about that size. His father looked up at him from the hoe he was holding and taught him a good lesson.

"Young son," he said, "we have only a small garden. We need to get everything out of it that we can each year. To pick the turnip, or any other vegetable before it quits growing, is wasteful."

Dutch thought about the last of the big turnips that they harvested each year before the freeze. They were woody and sharp tasting. Nothing like the one he had accidentally pulled. He knew his father was telling him right.

He thought about the rifle he carried with the one shell still in his pocket. The rifle belonged to his uncle Otto. It had been given him from the factory supervisor, after three years of good service. His uncle Otto had been sick for a while and not able to work. Even with his long and faithful service at the factory, when he became ill there was no paycheck.

Dutch's own pay was half of what grown men were given. Grown men were called 'number one worker' and the younger boys were 'number two.' They were allowed to work in some of the unskilled areas at half pay.

Even the knife that hung on his right side brought memories. It took two months of evenings working at the foundry to earn enough for the fine steel blade. Times were hard. He had carefully fitted the steel blade into the handle of a stag horn. That was off the horn of the first deer he had ever taken from the Black Forest. It took four trips for him to carry the big deer out. He would never shoot one that big again; there was too much risk of getting caught.

It had taken many evenings to fit and secure the two

72

pieces together, to make the hunting knife just right. As he thought of this, his hand went down along his right side to the familiar handle of the knife. No one could have known he had gone over to the side of the forbidden.

Some of the town folks told of those who had gone over there hunting and two of them had been caught, stripped to the waist and tied all night to the tall elm trees. They were told that it would be much more severe punishment next time. All the villagers got the message to keep out.

Dutch had gone over to the other side of the river once in a while for the deer that seemed more plentiful there. He could never seem to figure out why most of the animals knew that side was the best. It may have been a better place for them to stay away from people.

Any time he had been over in the area of the Black Forest, he was ever on guard. He always went very quietly from the town before it was light and never returned until it was dark. He didn't much like the idea of going over there too often, but it was a time of necessity then.

His Uncle Otto had been sick for a while and unable to work in the factory. There was very little to eat in the home, and good venison would bring a feast to them right now. However, he knew he risked getting caught by those on horseback who occasionally roamed the forest for the Baron in search of poachers. He had occasionally seen them from the town.

With this in mind he left the cover of the alders and elms that grew down in the low lands and headed straight into the Black Forest of pines and spruce. He would need to stay in the areas where the brush and trees were thick, but the real thing that he always needed was a quick escape if he saw horsemen, or heard anyone coming.

It had been a long time since he had been out in the forest and he would need just the right place and time to shoot one of the deer. It wasn't long before seven deer moved out of the thicket into a clearing. One was huge, with the biggest set of horns he had ever seen. It would be too large for him to pack out in two trips, but the blood raced through his veins as he saw the big fellow turn and look back at him.

He whispered in a low voice, "Go on, big fellow, this isn't your time."

Some of the others would do, but it was too open here. If he dropped one here, he could be seen from several places. No, this was not the place or the time. He would need to be close enough for a one shot kill, so that any that heard the shot from the rifle wouldn't know exactly where the sound came from. The thick forest of the big trees would muffle the sound, so it shouldn't carry too far. Dutch stayed in the thicket of trees for a period of time so the deer would graze out of sight and not remember his position.

His thoughts turned back to his parents who had lived a couple of days' travel up stream. He was ten years old at the time of the tragic plague. Some said it came from a new family that had come to town. Others thought it might have come from some birds not usually found around the area that suddenly appeared around the town.

Whatever it was that brought it in, it took the lives of almost all the people in town. Even now, after two years, it was almost too terrible to remember. Most people had no one to help them, but he had tried to help any that he could. He carried fresh water from the river and changed damp cool cloths to the heads of many. Then his mother and father fell ill and took all of his attention. At times he had to blot out others' discouraging and terrible cries for help. The young children were the worst to ignore. His family was one of the last ones to survive, but finally his father passed away. There was no one else but his sick mother at the gravesite he had dug. He carried her to the side of the grave and watched her sadly looking down into the pit that held his father. She gave a slight nod of her head but no words were spoken as he filled the grave. He wanted to fall down along side the grave and let out all of the tears and feelings he had at that moment, but he knew he had work to do so he must be strong.

When he finished, he put a small board up for the headstone and, without looking back, picked up his frail mother and proceeded to their humble home. His mother passed away three days later.

Before her passing, she motioned him a little closer and whispered to him a message.

"Jacob, my son," she said, "No mother could ever have had a finer son." It took her a while to get enough breath and then she started in again. "There is a small package wrapped on the upper shelf above the grain bottles. It is for you. We had hoped to save it until later, but now you must go to the river and use the soap we have made for washing clothes."

It was still another time before she could continue. He tried to get her to stop talking. He took the cold rags from the river water and tried to calm her down.

"Jacob," she said, "go to the river and wash yourself everywhere. Even your shoes, scrub with this soap. Don't pick up your old clothes again, but change into the new ones that don't have the sickness around them. Carry your shoes until they dry and go to Uncle Otto's home. Don't come back into this town when you are cleaned and be sure to go upstream to wash. There is so much I would like to tell you. Take some of the grain in one of the full bottles that hasn't been opened. If you are sick by the time you get to your uncle's, don't go into town. For some reason you are the only one spared for..." her voice trailed off and she was gone.

Dutch thought of how alone he felt. After he buried his mother along side his father, he did exactly what she had told him to do. The new bar of the yellowish green soap felt

75

like it was going to take the hide right off him; but if mother told him to go and wash everywhere, that is just what he would do, more than once.

His skin was a bright red from all of the scrubbing and it stung like it might never stop. With new clothes on and carrying his well-scrubbed shoes, he set off for Uncle Otto's place.

It took about two days to follow the road to town, but he had seen the horrible effects of the plague and decided to stay out in the hills a couple of extra days. He emptied the contents of the bottle into his pockets, scrubbed his hands one last time and skirted the town, not looking back.


It was about an hour before he moved carefully out of the thicket, stopping often to listen and watch. There was a wall of brambles a short way down the hill he could run for if he needed to escape anyone. His plan was always the same: if he spotted someone and they saw him, he would race for the nearest thicket and hopefully out run the guards of the forest. He thought of how hard it would be to throw the rifle away. Hopefully. he could throw it into a hiding spot, but he would do what he had to do to survive.

He was probably about two miles inside the forest now. It looked like a good place for some deer to be getting up from their beds. It would be full sunup in just a few minutes. Suddenly he saw three deer, just getting up from the night's rest. It was just the right place, too, with a large fallen tree just on the backside of a half grown buck.

He had never killed any other kind of deer and thought about that as he smoothly raised the rifle up for the fatal shot. It sounded unusually loud this morning and he worried that it might call attention down his way.

The young buck fell instantly and the other two bounded out of sight. Jacob pulled back into the heavy part of the thicket and waited and listened. Only the stirring of the soft morning breeze in the trees could be felt or heard, but an uneasiness seemed to come upon him.

He stood rigid and quiet, straining his hearing. There was something that just didn't seem right, but he didn't know exactly what it was. Was someone watching, maybe looking right at the thicket he was in? Could the wind have carried the sound farther than he supposed? There seemed to be something, but try as he might, he couldn't identify what it was that was making him feel this way. He would give it another few minutes.

He felt well hidden and allowed his thoughts to return to when he first arrived at his Uncle Otto and Aunt Elkie's home.

They had made him feel welcome and told him that their home was his home. The couple also had a six-year-old son, Lars, and a seven-year-old daughter, Gretta.      He later learned there was no longer a village where he used to live. The military had gone in, killed and burned all of the animals that were left, and covered everything over with piles of dirt. It was the only way to stop the plague.

He moved out of the thicket again and tried to hear or see any movement or sound. It wasn't until he had cleaned out the deer and had it ready to pack out that he heard a sound that stopped him still. He paused, then moved in behind the fallen tree. He looked down hill to the nearest thicket where he might need to run for cover, but he could not hear anyone or any horse movement.

He stayed real quiet, afraid to even breathe for fear he might miss something. There it was again; this faint sound, almost lost in the forest. He must get a little closer and move back around this thicket without being seen.

He left the rifle with the deer and, moving around to his right in a circular motion, proceeded up the steep, dark, rounded mountain, stopping often to look and listen. He walked quietly up the hill, trying to hear any sound that would bring a warning.

"There," he said quietly to himself. The noise came again almost straight on around the hill from where he stood. He could feel his heart racing in his chest.

The large thick trees offered good cover for him, but not as good as some of the thickets he could see down the hill. He looked back at the place where his gun and the deer lay and watched for a minute. It would be almost impossible for anyone to find that place except by accident. He marked the spot in his mind and after a few moments he decide to move forward.

The sun was up now and, in about an hour, would be around to his side of the mountain. Whatever it was, it didn't seem so much of a threat to him now. He could almost see where the sound was coming from. It sounded like the moaning of a child. There were no places where anyone could hide a horse, so he hurried across the small opening to the thicket that held the mystery.

It was a shock for him to see a young girl, who looked to be about six or seven years old, lying there in the thicket. It was obvious she was not one of the girls from town. He slipped off his light jacket and, brushing the dark brown curly hair from her face, he placed his well-worn coat over her. She never moved much, only cried out a little bit.

He tried to tell her that he would help her and make her better, but she didn't seem to hear anything he said. Her legs as well as her hands were swollen and had been bleeding. Even with all of her bruises, there was little doubt after looking at her torn clothes that she was royalty. Every part of her clothing spoke of this and his worn coat looked out of place, trying to make her warm.

It appeared that her right wrist was broken, and he could but only imagine the pain this little one was in. It looked like she had spent the cold damp night out in the forest. She was very cold and he knew he must get to help quickly.

He carefully gathered her up in his arms, trying at the same time to keep her as warm as he could. He opened his shirt up and pulled it back a little as he started to climb to the top of the mountain, hoping to warm her up even more. He wouldn't need any help keeping warm, as he moved quickly up through the forest. He came to one of the many small clear cold mountain streams. After cleaning his hands and knife of the deer cleaning, he cupped a little bit of water and asked her to drink a little. She was unable to respond so Jacob wiped the water across her lips a few times and a little went into her mouth.

He moved as quickly as he could. His legs and arms were strong and stout from working in the materials for the factory. Since the Kaiser had taken many of the men to be in his service, some of the younger people like him were allowed to work in parts of the plant. They must be able to do a man's work, or lose their jobs. Jacob was always early to work, worked as hard as any man, and was now thankful that this hard work had made him hard and strong. His job was to push the large handcart with its heavy frame and steel wheels into the storage area. He would often push three hundred pounds a load into the warehouse. It was more than any of the other boys who worked there could do. His hands were rough and calloused from the work.

This little girl would only be a quarter of the load of the deer far back down the mountain, he thought. It looked like he would be near the top in about another hour and he pushed on ever harder when he looked down at this little girl and realized that her life depended on him. She was a pretty little girl, even with her dirty face and fine torn clothing. He supposed that when she was well, the olive brown skin might be set off with dark brown eyes.

He came to a small channel of water. Although he didn't want to lose any time, he thought it best to stop for a quick drink and see if she would let him give her some water. Since he was nearing the top of the mountain, this might be the last water he would find for a while.

She wouldn't let him give her much water, but he coaxed a few drops into her mouth and he could tell she now had a fever. Pulling a rag from his back pocket, he washed the signs of blood away from the cloth from the deer cleaning and placed it on the girl's forehead. He thought for a moment that he heard her say thank you, but then there was no other sound.

His body and legs were feeling the added pressure she was putting on him now, and he needed to stop once in a while and take a quick breather. How could a little girl start to get so heavy all of a sudden? He remembered that he felt that way at times after a long run. He could run for hours, but when he had little more to give, he would feel suddenly tired every place. Then he would stop and rest.

The crown of the hill was in sight now and he would soon be up to the top. When he got to where he could see, he recognized the castle in the distance. He had followed the wagon road up through the pass about a year ago, where he could see the castle and some of the many buildings, corrals and fields belonging to the Baron Johann Von Schtreicher.

The stops were more frequent now as Jacob finally came to the crest of the hill. His clothes were dripping with sweat, and fatigue had its claim on his young strong body. He finally decided that he could go no farther. He leaned up against one of the last pine trees. From here, with the castle sighted in the distance, out across the huge meadow, he felt so close and yet so far.

Cattle were grazing in the big meadow below, but there was no sign of anyone. It was while he paused there that he thought he heard horses off to his right. As he listened, he could hear the men calling, "Erica! Erica!" This must be Erica here in my arms, he thought.

He was too tired to yell, but he had always been good for a loud whistle. He sent one out now in the direction of the riders. He heard the yelling as he gave his last whistle. He slid to his knees as the riders approached and found Erica in his arms. All consciousness left him as he felt himself falling forward.

His hearing and vision were slow to come back. All of the fine surroundings where he lay were like a dream. A servant approached the nice soft bed that he was lying on, and his first thought was how dirty his clothes would be in all of this finery.

"Are you all right?" came the quiet voice next to him. He sat up quickly as he remembered the things of the day. It seemed it had been a week since he left town for his hunt. He wondered how the little girl named Erica was, and asked about her.

"She will be just fine," came the response. "Thanks to you. The Baron would like to see you just as soon as you feel well enough to be up and around."

Someone had brought food and a towel and a dish to wash in. He ate a few bites and had a drink, then followed the servant into a more royal chamber.

So this was how the rich people live, he thought. He was wondering what to say when the Baron would surely ask him what he was doing in his forest. I might just as well tell him the truth, he thought. His mother said that was always the best.

A huge door opened and an escort brought him before a man sitting in a huge leather chair with a polished dark wooden back and armrest. He had never seen such fine furnishings. The man sat with his back to him looking out on the meadow through large rounded windows, draped with scarlet silk curtains. Large metal bars and framework were in place across the opening, with big thick shutters that could close off the light completely.

He knew it was the Baron himself who turned his chair around to look straight at Jacob. He was not a large man, but with dark hair and piercing dark eyes, he gave you the idea that he could look right into your heart. He was dressed in the finest clothes and stood up stroking his tailored mustache.

"So you are the one they found bringing my Erica back."

Jacob gave a faint nod.

"What is your name?"

"JacobWeiser," Jacob replied. He was afraid of the next question.

"What were you doing in my forest?" the Baron wanted to know.

"I am from the town," Jacob said. He chose his words carefully. "My uncle, who works in the factory, has not been able to work for some time. Things are not good and we have little to eat. I was hoping to find some fresh meat and help get back his strength."

The Baron stood up and came closer to Jacob. He looked into his eyes and there was silence for some time, as he studied out young Jacob.

"So did you kill a deer in my forest?" he asked.

With all that Jacob had gone through to bring the Baron's daughter back, Jacob became a little angry.

He spoke out, almost defiantly, "Yes, sir, a small one."

"And this is where you found my Erica?"

"Yes, it is the general area."

The piercing hard look of the Baron finally began to change. "My men tell me that you nearly gave your life, to save my daughter's life," he said. He turned back to the large open window, deep in thought.

The thought raced back into Jacob's mind of the two men the Baron hanged for hunting in his forest. Finally, after a long silence, the Baron turned back to Jacob. His face seemed softer now.

He asked, "What can I do for you?"

"Nothing," Jacob stammered. "I just want to go home."

"I will do something for you, and only you. I will give you my permission to hunt in my forest any time, if you promise not to waste anything, when you need food for your family. You are always welcome here in the castle any time, to stay as long as you like. I will send two escorts with you to pick up the deer and take it to your uncle's house, so that the townspeople will know that I have made this allowance for you. Thank you, young Jacob, and thank you for being honest."

With that he went to a large collection of military pieces on the wall and selected a beautiful hunting knife.

"This is for you," he said, as he slipped it back into the dark leather scabbard. Looking at the silver falcon head at the top of the handle he said, "The falcon, one of the greatest hunters, I give to you, another good hunter. Peace be with you, young JacobWeiser."

Jacob stood motionless for a while, not understanding the full impact of what the Baron had said. He had been raised with the idea that you never accepted a gift without trying to give something back. Often times there wouldn't be any gift to give, but one could always offer some service. Looking about at the magnificent beauty of things, he thought that surely the Baron could not need anything.

Jacob felt out of place standing there looking at the Baron and wondering what to do. He reached down at his right side and felt the handle of his hunting knife. Drawing it out of its sheath, he extended it to the Baron with both hands. He could still see blood markings in the grooves of the handle and wished he had cleaned it better. The Baron looked at the extended knife in the palms of Jacob's hands.

"I made this myself," Jacob offered.

It seemed a long time before anyone moved or spoke. The Baron looked at the knife, then back to Jacob, then back to the knife.

Jacob said, "I give you the best I have."

"I know," the Baron responded, taking the knife and sheath from Jacob. He held it for a moment, then turned and replaced it on the wall where the silver handled falcon knife had been. It looked out of place with all of the other great things hanging there, Jacob thought.

"I will hang your knife there as a reminder of what you have done for me and Erica. Since her mother's passing, she is all that I have." He continued, "I noticed the fine bone stag handle on the knife. Should I ask if it came from my forest?"

"No!" Jacob said. "Don't ask!" He saw a faint smile at the corners of the Baron's mouth as he turned and left the room.

## Chapter 8

Here I was, Jacob Waltz, out away from the town to camp under the stars. As I had hoped, it was quiet and peaceful as I looked up at a half moon. I was soon asleep.

I had taken time to visit with Dutch a little bit more in the two days that I stayed around Sacramento. I found that the Strauss store was less busy, too, now that folks had come in and picked up their orders from the last freight arrival. We found out that Dutch and I could become citizens of the United States, so we both signed to do that. I don't know about my friend, but it was special for me to make that pledge. Mr. Strauss had sponsored us. He was well known around there, so it made it easier.

Another thing I did was stop by the bank. I had about half of my money sent to my two sisters to help with their needs. I was able to send a note with it and told them that they could probably reach me at the Strauss store in case they needed to get word to me.

The big posse that had gone out after the Norris horses were already home. It was as I had thought. They returned without any of the horses. I felt bad for the Norris bunch, but knew they would get started again.

When I returned from Sacramento, the ranch was just about as I had left it. It had a few more men now, but the regular cook had come to take care of the meals. Some of the men were grumbling about no place to go and nothing to do. Sanchez's men couldn't seem to understand why they had to wait here at the ranch instead of in Sacramento. Some went for short rides, but all remembered that the boss had told them to wait here. Many were drinking a lot, so there was much trouble between them. In a short while they were out of anything to drink, and then they really did get ornery.

A few days went by before Sanchez finally came to the

ranch. Everyone was glad to hear him say that it was time to load some wagons and head for the gold fields. He sent about half of the men on ahead to the camp. Most of the horses went with this group. The only horses that did not go with the herd were the three with colts. He left the two Mexicans with the ranch. The rest of us would be going back to Sacramento first, and then on to the mines. Our job was to load the wagons for the first trip into the high country.

Many people were already scattered out along the way, each expecting to strike it rich at the very next creek. I had never seen so many people out looking for that yellow stuff. Some were walking; some had dogs along to help carry small packs of belongings. A few had horses or mules, and they were trying to get ahead of everyone else.

The stories that had been told that winter in the city had everyone frantic to get on the move. Mr. Strauss had told me that the people back East had finally decided that this was for real and now the big migration was on for Californy. He said that he could hardly keep supplies in his store.

"It is a crazy time!" he said. "Be careful, Jacob."

It was evident that Sanchez had plenty of money to buy supplies for his camp. The wagons were soon loaded with all of the things that would be needed for the start up. I found out that my friend, Dutch, was on a trip to San Francisco. He would be disappointed that he was not around when we headed out, but I was sure he would follow us very soon.

On the road up to the diggings, we passed several other outfits. I felt pretty bad for some of them because it looked like this was their last hope. Even those who seemed to be the poorest of the lot had their eyes light up at the word gold. I guess Mr. Braun was right; it was a fever. You had to be there to really get a feeling of it.

I was filled with excitement myself, even though I had already spent most of the season last year on the riverbanks looking for the stuff. It seemed that I had lost track of time, but was told that it was now 1849. I wondered what the year would bring.

It took a few days to get our loaded wagons through into the mining camp. From the condition of the roads, it looked like few wagons had made it ahead of us. It was good to finally round the curve of the river and look up into the valley at what was left of the old campsites and what was left of the buildings. It was as if winter had frozen everything in place, as it looked just like when I left.

A few tents were already set up, and the air was full of smoke from the many fires. It sifted out through the dense forest like low lying clouds. Here and there, some of the miners were milling around looking into the river and wondering what they would find this year. The first green signs of wild flowers were just beginning to show up along the banks. The next few days would bring in more people and the saloon and boarding house would open. It was good to be back in the fields once again.

Millie came in five days after we did and I went down to see her. She said, "Hello, Jacob, are you looking for a job?"

I already had a job to look after the horses, but I went down and helped her get things into the building. It looked like it had come through the winter pretty good.

Sanchez had one of his men post a sign down river from the gold fields. It read, "Keep out, or be shot!" I heard that they had already run off two miners near their claims. They were lucky they hadn't been doing any digging, or else they would have been shot. Each day, Sanchez would have some of the Mexicans test the banks of the river and see if they could dig yet.

Dutch had come up now and we went to our regular bunkhouse. He told me that he had done well with his side job over the winter and had put all but one hundred dollars that he owed me in the bank in town.

Mr. Strauss, while in San Francisco the last trip, found something that he thought we might like and need. He had sent each of us one of the new Allen's revolvers and a Bowie knife.

"It's the latest thing," Dutch said. "Mr. Strauss said that we could pay him the next time we get into town."

I strapped both the pistol and Bowie knife on. It felt good to have the very latest things to help us defend ourselves. "This Jim Bowie, whoever he is, sure knew how to make a knife! Here is a knife that will do about anything," I said, as I turned it over in my hand and examined it for balance.

Mr. Strauss had also sent plenty of shells to go with the pistols. We soon found out how good they were. The next day, we had several offers to buy the pistols, but we refused. I thought, "This is a big step up from the shotgun I had when I came here the first time!"

Mr. Sanchez came by often to check on the horses. He seemed to be in a better mood now, but I knew that could change in a minute. I told him I would like to talk to him for a minute about the dredges and sluice boxes.

"I think I have a way for you to get more gold out of the sluice boxes," I said. "Are you interested in hearing what I have to say?" I told him that not enough thought was given as to how the sluice boxes were placed. It didn't give the gold time to settle if the water went too fast, or if it went too slow. I had checked some of the tailings last year and found that a lot was lost because the boxes weren't level and didn't do the job right.

This caught Sanchez's full attention. "How would you go about getting more of the gold that went over the ripples, and what do you want out of this? If you can get more gold than we got last year, I will give you a good raise and put you in charge of all of the dredges."

I told him I wanted Dutch for my assistant. I also asked that the horses that belonged to me and Dutch would be kept with the others. A raise would be fine, too, once I proved that my ideas would work. He agreed to that.

In a few days we were ready to give my idea the test. It was trial and error at first, but soon the panning of the tailings gave a little sign of gold. The rockers were something else, but the same thing would apply to them. They would have to be at just the right angle when they poured off the remains. Mr. Sanchez told me not to tell anyone else. It would be my job to set all of the boxes, and no one else was to touch them after I had set them. With twelve of them to do, I made a continual round each day checking on them. My idea would soon bring forth results, and Mr. Sanchez became real friendly to anything I wanted to do.

The gold fields were in full swing now and it was like the old days. Dutch and I were glad to be working together. We found that it was good to have someone that you could trust and help watch after your things. We decided that we would be partners. It meant a lot just to have someone who would help you, someone you could trust. Everyone had to be watching his back side all of the time in that bad bunch.

We spent another season in the fields working for Sanchez, but it became evident that the gold mining in that area was slowing down. Most of the stream banks had been dug away and a lot of the miners had already left in search of new claims that were popping up in other areas.

One day someone reported that a twenty-three pound nugget had been found in one of the new strikes. Half of the miners were gone the next morning, each with the dream of finding one just like that or bigger. Many rushed to the new find on the south fork of the American River. The wild flowers were everywhere along the Trucee River, and so were the prospectors and miners.

Mr. Sanchez, true to his style, reduced our wages each week as even the leveling of the boxes failed to keep up production. Dutch and I talked often of what we should do. We had more free time, but for Dutch, that was more time to get into trouble. In the saloon, we often fought with some of those who had lost their hopes and fortune. Every one who remained was in an ugly mood most of the time. It was much different than it had been earlier. You couldn't always go out the next day and replace the gold you lost at the bar or in the card games.

We had done well in the work and I had saved much of my money, but Dutch still liked to go the dance halls and mix in with the card playing at times. I told Dutch that he better watch himself or he would be like some of those that had been reduced to stealing and begging. This seemed to take his attention, and he told me that he would stay out of those places.

Mr. Sanchez was a wealthy man by now and spent months at a time in San Francisco, which was turning into a large town. I told Dutch one day that I was getting tired of doing the same things over and over, just to make him more money. We had seen how he treated those who might come in by chance near one of his claims. He was just a mean guy who wanted it all for himself.

We heard that there wasn't a place anywhere that hadn't been dug up. Even Sutter's pasture was full of holes and hopeful miners. I was getting tired of so many people and so many problems that the gold fever brought.

"Maybe we ought to move on," I told Dutch one day. "We could go somewhere else and find a new life, or see some new places. We might even try one of the new strikes we've heard about."

If we left, we'd have to be careful. Reports were that many starved to death in their search for gold. There were those that would shoot you in a hurry for your claim, if they thought you were alone, and nobody would even take notice. There was very little or no law there, so only the strong ones survived. And, you didn't ever let anyone know how well you were doing. There were always the bars and dance halls that soon separated a man from his diggings.

We went down there once in a while to have a few drinks, but we were careful not to let the liqueur get the best of us. It was a way of letting off steam after a hard few days of working on the claims. With the mix of people there, every night was filled with noise and gunplay.

Once in a while we would get out in the hills and ride away from the gold camps. We enjoyed this time because it was always good to escape from the mad bunch down in the fields and return to our German talk. And it was good to give our horses a work out. They seemed to like to be away from the rest, too.

Dutch had laughed when I told him I'd named my sorrel Jake. He said I might as well be the one to give his large black horse a name, too. So I just called him Nighthawk. Dutch seemed to like the name, too.

One day, we found ourselves riding up near the edge of one of the mountains. The forest was very thick and it looked like it had never been traveled. A small stream was making its way down from the hills above and through the thick brush. We were having a pleasant time as we went farther up into the hills away from all of the noise and people in the valley down by the river.

We were just wading our horses up the small stream a short ways, when Dutch muttered something in German and fell off his horse into the water. At first, I thought that he had been shot. I pulled my horse up to a stop and yanked out my pistol. I couldn't imagine what he was doing. The water was about three feet deep here, enough to get him wet. Then he came out of the water, holding a large gold nugget as big as his thumb over his head and all but shouting to the world.

We quickly tied our horses up and looked back where we had come from. We wondered if anyone had heard his yell. We hardly went anywhere without our gold pans, and they came in handy now. In a short time, we had found several nuggets. We soon had several times as much as we would make in a good season working down below. We were both excited and laughed like two school kids at the find we had made. I sampled the nuggets and, sure enough, they were the real things.

We quickly made some markers around the bank of the small stream and staked out a claim. It wouldn't do any good if the likes of Sanchez found out about it, or anyone else who might be out in the hills. We could hardly believe our luck. We had finally found a great strike.

By nightfall I had explored the stream down below the find, where it went into the brush. There didn't seem to be any trace of gold at that point. And it went several yards before it popped out again. I checked the sand at the bottom of the creek and could see no signs of the gold anywhere below. Dutch checked upstream and soon found that the stream disappeared into another thicket of brush for several yards there, too. There was no sign of gold up there either. We panned the sand in several places, but there was little trace of any gold.

It looked like we might not be mining here too long, as the find was in a pretty small area. We knew that we would not be able to leave the area until we had taken all of the gold out that we could find. One of us must stay with the claim and the other would need to go for a few days' food and supplies. One of us would need to leave in the dark of night. We decided that I would go and Dutch would stay to keep watch for anyone that might come this way.

It was nearly dark when I found a way to circle around some of the dense thicket and come out onto the river below.

As I passed some of Sanchez's claims, I wondered if I would see anyone I knew. Would the excitement still show on my face? However, most of the men had gone to eat and to the saloon by the time I came to the Sanchez place.

I fed Jake a helping of grain and filled a saddlebag full to take along. It was pretty quiet here at this time of night. I went to the supply room in the main house near the kitchen. Luckily no one was there, so I fixed a bag of food to take along. By the time I put our sleeping bags across Jake's neck, it was black outside.

It was good to be away from the camp without being seen. Jake made his way up the west side of the river along the road and we were soon lost into the night. I waited upstream until what I thought was about an hour before daylight. I crossed the river and waited on the other side in the darker shadows of the trees until there was light enough to go into the woods.

Dutch and I both knew we must be careful not to let anyone know of our find. We already had much more gold gathered up than we would make working for Sanchez in a dozen seasons. As we buried the nuggets that we had found in a good place away from the stream, we decided that we had better make plans to leave.

One of the muleskinners that delivered freight up to the camp had told us that Mexico was a good place to go for gold miners. He had given us an old map. We had talked about going into Mexico ever since, and now determined that's what we would do. We knew we would need to have a lot of supplies to take with us. We decided that I would go back and collect our wages from Sanchez, and tell him that we would be going over to one of the other gold strikes. Dutch helped me make a list of the supplies we would need. I was soon on my way in the late afternoon, planning on getting to the lower river area just about dark. It was about a two-hour ride to get back to the main river.

One of the foremen for Sanchez paid us for the time we had coming. I told him we had been over looking at some of the other claims and we might be interested in going over to Placerville, if the mining slowed down much more. He said that Sanchez had talked about that, too. I stayed the night and went early the next morning to Stewart's, to make our purchases.

Stewart's trading post had grown over the past two seasons, and he had pack mules for sale, as well as a few horses. It wasn't long before I had selected four mules and packs. I gave Mr. Stewart the long list of things that we thought we would need. I told him we were preparing to go over to one of the other sites before too long, if things didn't pick up here soon. I hated to tell him something like that, because I knew I could trust him, but Dutch and I had agreed not to tell anyone about our strike. Besides, many of those who were left loitering around the camp would listen for any sign that someone might have any gold that they could get their hands on.

I told Mr. Stewart that I would be by about dark and pick up the animals and things. He said that he would have everything ready. With time on my hands I went over to Millie's to have a nice breakfast. I thought about the little bit of food that Dutch would have to eat while I was away; we had decided that we didn't dare build any kind of fire. It would be a cold breakfast for him. I wished there was some way for me to take some of this good cooking to him.

Millie was happy to see me. I told her that I might be going to Sacramento later on in the day and would need to take my money out of her vault. She asked me to go along with her into one of the back rooms where she had her safe. I noticed that it was locked and closed. I asked her about that.

"It's getting so you can't leave anything to chance

around here, Jacob. Times are getting bad and people are getting desperate."

I wanted to tell her most of all that I would be leaving in the morning and might never see her again.

She said that this would be her last year here in this place. She felt that by fall all of the miners would be gone and only the diggings around the water would be left. I thought of this as I stood outside of Millie's looking up the river. It wasn't nearly as nice as when I had first seen it last year. Some of the crazy miners had even dug up some of the street in their search. There were holes everywhere in all of the banks and even near the streets and buildings. It would never ever look the same as it did last year when the meadows along the river were pretty and full of wild flowers.

The clear cool mountain stream coming from the direction of Lake Tahoe may never be the same either. Many had diverted parts of the river to take the water closer to their diggings.

"I guess I have been a part of this," I thought, as I looked at the wasted area. I didn't feel too good about that. I hoped that, with floods and time, most of it would get back to where it started and all of the diggings close to the river would be covered over or washed away.

I went down to Stewart's to see how things were coming along. He didn't have nearly the business that he had going last year. I asked how long he was going to stay, and he said that he had already canceled the next freight shipment. When I asked him if he would take a message to the banker in Sacramento for me, he said that he would. I knew that I could trust him to do what he said; he was a different type than most of those in the gold fields.

With pencil and paper, I asked the banker to send all of the funds that I had in the bank to my two sisters in Germany. Mr. Stewart looked at the message and said that he would for sure do that. I told him that I thought I had enough money to pay for all of the things that we would be getting.

"Where are you going, Mr. Stewart?" I asked.

"This gold mining thing can pass as quick as it comes," he said. "I have done well here, though, and I think I will just go back to Sacramento. Maybe I'll get into the same kind of business there. It sure has been good to get to know you and your partner."

He showed me a pair of high top boots that he had in the store. "Now here is a pair that will stay with you, Jacob, if you are of a mind."

I thought that Dutch and I should both have a pair, so I added that to my list. I wondered if Mr. Stewart knew that today might be the last time that he would see me.

I went by the bunkhouse at Sanchez's again, wondering how I could gather up the rest of mine and Dutch's gear. I shouldn't have worried about it, though. Several other men were about the same business. The gold mining had slowed down for all of Sanchez's men. It was easy to join in conversations about looking in other places for a chance to get started again.

"We might need to talk with Mr. Sanchez when he comes back from Sacramento," I told the foreman. He told me that he expected Sanchez back tomorrow and would tell him I wanted to talk with him.

It was nearly dark when I went back to Stewart's for the pack animals and supplies. He met me around back of the building. Gas lanterns were being lit, and a few of the men were going to their favorite places: Millie's and the saloon. I paid for the things that he had put together for me that day. I knew we would have everything that we would need, and I didn't need to check the list with him.

He handed me the lead rope to the four pack animals and said, "Watch your back, young Jacob, and thanks for the business." As I looked into his kind eyes and face, I saw that he knew we would be making our getaway.

It was nice to have the pack animals as I skirted the lights and the nightlife around the few places that were doing business. I had to be watchful for any miners who might see me leave. I could see yellow lights shining through some of the tents, and some men were sitting around an open fire close by. They never spoke and neither did I, but they were very intent on the train of pack animals that I had in tow. I knew what was going through their minds as I made my way on up the river and turned away from the crossing that I would normally have taken to go where Dutch was waiting and watching.

I traveled upstream for about another five miles until it became too dark to see any more. I slipped off my horse and loosened the cinch and tied the animals to one of the limbs of brush. The mules never gave up a chance to get a mouth full and soon began to graze on the feed at their feet.

I had kept my rifle out across my saddle ever since I had left Stewart's, and still held it at the ready. There wasn't anything different with that than most who traveled through here. A man had to be ready for anything, and being ready often made the difference of saving his life.

"Watch your backside," Mr. Stewart had said. I guess he meant the front and the sides as well. Yes! He knew we were making our move to clear out of the gold fields, but I knew he would not tell anyone.

It would still be a couple of hours before the stars would give off enough light to be able to pick my way back across the river and return down the other side to the place that I had tried to remember and mark for going back into our find. I would be leaving a much bigger trail for anyone to follow than I had before, but if we were away the next day, it would not matter. If I could find the tree in the dark that had been struck by lightning, I should be able to get through the thick brush and back to our claim.

It was about midnight and the stars were dancing overhead when I finally came to the place where I should turn in and get closer to the mountains. Jake seemed to know where to go and led the others into the thick brush. Before long, I recognized that we were going in the right direction. Jake would take us on in from here. We traveled for about an hour, frequently stopping and listening, but could not hear anyone following.

In another hour I heard the sharp call, "Who is it?"

"It's me," I whispered loud enough that Dutch might hear. I had brought some food along that didn't need cooking and he ate it as I unsaddled the horse and the pack mules, putting the hobbles on them.

"I sure wish we could have a fire and cook a cup of coffee," he said, as we talked in low voices. He told me that he had pretty well cleaned out all of the gold that he could find, but there was still pretty good stuff down on the bed rock.

I told him about the day in the mining camp and that we would need to get going early the next morning. We tried to get as much rest as we could. Every night sound woke us up, but right when it was time to leave, we were sleeping pretty well.

It was then that Dutch told me that he just couldn't leave without going back one more time to the mining camp below. I tried to talk him out of this. I hadn't liked the looks of those that had watched me pass by with the pack train. But I could see that it was just no use.

He left just before daylight on his big black horse. I guess I might have done the same as him, if I had known that I would never see this place again, or some of the people. I would feel bad, too, about leaving.

I divided the gold with him that we had found. He had been good to stay away from the gambling and the fighting lately. I guess my talking to him about being a beggar had something to do with that. He put all of his gold in his saddlebags and headed down below.

I worked the stream for a while in the morning and looked after the animals. It would be good to have Dutch get back here and be off early in the morning. There was no good place where I could go back and watch the back trail. The brush was just too thick and you could only see a short ways. My best chance of knowing if someone was come was listening. The little stream was doing quite a bit of talking as it hurried on down to the thicket below, so I would have to move further up on the hill to get away from the rhythm of the water. I did this several times through the day.

I kept busy adding to our gathering of gold. I did find one place that had several small nuggets, and I thought we could probably find more gold if we stayed and worked everything in more detail. I decided to take down our markers and prepare to get out of there in the early morning. I staked out the mules and stored the packs under some of the brush nearby. We would need to saddle up and get all of the things ready in the dark of the early morning.

I placed everything in my mind, so I would know just where it was, and went through step by step in my mind the loading of the animals. I planned to load my gold on one of the packhorses and keep some on Jake. I believed in dividing things up. It seemed safer that way. We had enough gold to last us a long time; we could buy a ranch or about anything else we wanted to do. I smiled at that thought. We wouldn't need to depend on anyone else for the things that we wanted or needed.

I kept listening for any sign along the back trail as the sun went down. I figured Dutch should be along in the next two or three hours. I tried to get as much rest as I could and had rationed out a little bit of the grain for Jake. Then night came and still there was no sign of Dutch. He should have been here by now, but it was better to be careful and take a little bit more time than take a chance.

Then, morning was coming. The mules were packed and everything was ready to go. We should have already been gone an hour or so, but still no Dutch. I didn't want to unpack the horses and mules to go see what had happened to him. But after all, we were partners, and a guy just doesn't go off and leave his partner. There just didn't seem to be much else that I could do, and we sure wouldn't be slipping out in the night.

I hid my stuff again, unpacked the mules and staked them out to feed, caught up my horse and headed for town. I didn't want to leave, but there wasn't anything else that I could do. The ride down to the dance hall would take over two hours, and by that time the sun would be up. I followed the stream down to the fork, where it met with the larger stream. From there on I was on a pretty good trail.

As I approached the two steps leading into the saloon, I noticed that it was a lot quieter now than in the early hours of the night. I hoped that something hadn't happened to my good friend, but knew that anything could have gone wrong. It was quiet inside and the bartender was wiping off the bar, as if by habit.

"Have you seen my partner, Dutch? He came down here last night, and I haven't seen him since."

"He was here most of the night, drinking and gambling. Why, I never saw so much gold from one guy. I guess it was the card game that cleaned him out," the bartender said. "And to make matters worse, him and that half-breed, Indian Joe, got to fighting over Belle."

Now, Indian Joe was a mean cuss, but so was Dutch, when he got a little too much to drink. And Dutch was tall, young and strong. He didn't like to start a fight, but then sometimes he seemed to enjoy a good scrap. I usually tried to stay out of the fights, but when more than one jumped on my partner, I would jump right in, too. Sometimes we would do well, and sometimes we would get our fannies kicked. More often than not, it seemed that we usually came out on top of the heap.

"They went crashing around the room, with knives in hand," the bartender continued. "Then they went right out through this hole here, which once was a window. Since you are his partner, how about getting some money to pay for this stuff?"

"Why don't you just get it from Indian Joe?" I asked.

"Can't, your partner just did him in."

One of the locals told me that Dutch had gone down to the river, so I made my way in that direction. I found him lying on the riverbank, and I could see that he didn't get away from Indian Joe without a struggle. His thigh was bright red from blood and he had wrapped his shirt around the wound after he washed it out. I had never seen my partner look so bad.

"Dutch," I said, "what in the world happened to you? We were supposed to be gone by now."

He then told me of the night's events, and about Indian Joe forcing himself on Belle. "And what's worse, I have lost all of my money and gold. That slick card dealer got me to drink too much, and the next thing I know, I was fighting and the whole place turned into a free-for-all. Indian Joe decided to take his bad fortune out on me, and the fight was on."

"Come on, you aren't in good shape. How bad is it? Can you ride? We need to get away from here before the news gets out through the hills. Indian Joe may have some bad friends."

"I can't go, I just can't go! I have no money left."

"Partners are still partners, and I have been saving mine. We had better hurry back to our claim before we have company."

Jacob Weiser was a stubborn, proud German and wouldn't let me give him any help getting on his horse. It was

101

evident that it took all the strength and determination he could muster to mount his horse.

We rode upstream and then circled back to the claim, trying to throw off any spying eyes. Our claim was just as I had left it. The spare pack mules were still feeding, and we soon had them ready to go. The sun was full up by now, and the best that we could do, to slip out of sight, was to climb back up the small stream, keeping to the low land and away from searching eyes. Before we went too far up stream, we would need to circle back and cross over some of the lower ridges so that we would be out of sight of the old diggings.

We stopped often to listen and rest. Thunderheads were already moving in from the west, and if I guessed about right, we would be in the thick of it by noon. It was one of the best things that could have happened to us. The wind and the rain came with a fury. Lightning was crashing all around us, but we only held cover for a short while, as we needed to put some miles between the gold field and us.

I never asked Dutch what started the fight, or why he lost all that he had. I decided that if he wanted to tell me he would, and if not, then that is the way it should be. He didn't talk much about some things. I did tell him my fear that, when they saw how much gold he had back there in the saloon, it would be pretty easy to figure out that I had that much and maybe more with me. No one ever carried that much gold unless they were trying to leave.

We didn't have friends along the diggings, and kept from ever getting to know the next miner. It was better that way. Nearly everyone only used their first name. But we had been seen around together often, especially during the slow times lately. Someone was bound to remember the pack train, put two and two together, and come after us.

We would need to head towards Mexico and move as fast as we could. It would take a lot of money to get started again in Mexico, unless we got lucky in a hurry.

# Chapter 9

We rode hard for five days, without stopping much except to give the animals a little breather for a few hours and some quick grazing. Finally I was convinced that we were no longer being chased from behind, so we could go more slowly. That would be much easier on Dutch, who was looking kind of worn down from our forced ride. When we found a meadow with a flowing stream, I figured it was time to unload and give everything a rest before continuing our journey southeast, toward Mexico.

This was the first time that we had stopped to cook and bed down since we had left the Rio Colorado. Poor Dutch was feeling pretty bad. I could see the strain on his face from the effort of our flight. His tousled sandy hair seemed to show how bad he felt. He was always one to want to keep looking good, but right now, it didn't seem to matter much. He seemed to be getting worse instead of better.

I washed the thigh wound and put some salve on it. The only sound Dutch made was a quick breath as I pulled off the old blood-soaked bandage. It was a vicious wound, left from the knife fight. I wish there had been time for the healing to start before we had to move on. But Dutch was young and strong. With a little rest and some good food, he would soon feel better.

We could go more slowly now that our fears of being followed were over. Still, we were ever watchful as we moved along at a steady pace. When we came upon an occasional ranch, one of us would always stay back with the pack animals while the other rode in to find out where we were. Sometimes we were able to buy a few more supplies. Occasionally we would pass a larger town with a store and a bank. We discussed the idea of trying to get the gold exchanged into Mexican or American currency. It would be easier to carry, and maybe easier to hide. At least it would take the crazy look out of people's eyes when they saw gold.

It took us several days to reach the Mexican border. We saw very few people now, but we were alerted by one rancher that the Indians had been doing a lot of raiding. We needed to keep our eyes open. We had come to the demanding dry part of the desert, and it had been two days since we had left the last water.

According to the map that the old muleskinner had given us, a few more days of travel would find us deep in Sonora, Mexico. We would use the landmarks on the map to figure out our route. We were heading for Sonoyta, and then on to Arizipe.

Dutch was fairing some better now, and even had that old sparkle back in his eye. One night we sat down around the glowing remains of our campfire. After we had put away a lot of coffee and food, Dutch said to me, "Why didn't you just go on and leave me there? No one would blame you if you did."

I thought of what he said for a few minutes. He looked at me, waiting for some kind of answer. Finally I said, "It never came to mind to do that. You would have done the same for me."

"But sharing all of the gold that you have left, just to take me along, no one has ever done anything like this for me before."

"Dutch, we are a long way from home. We have nobody else, let us remember that. Real partners are not only when things are going good, but for the bad times, too."

Tears came to his eyes as he caught the meaning, and he choked some when he tried to talk. He extended his prized knife, the one he had brought from the homeland, and offered it to me across the fire.

"Here take this! It's the only thing that I really have left to give. I want you to have it."

"I can't do that, Dutch,! I can't take that from you!"

"You must! This is the way it should be, and I have another that I can get by with."

I could see that there was no talking this hardheaded German out of this, so I told him that I would treasure it always. He didn't say more, but only nodded his head as if to say, "Yes, this is good."

I turned the fine knife over in my hands as light from the glowing embers brought out the beautiful workmanship of the tool. The handle was inlaid with stag horn from the Black Forest of the motherland. The knife and shaft were joined together with the finest of silver, capped with the royal German crest of the falcon. I knew how much he prized the knife, so it was even more special. He never mentioned how he had come by this knife, and I never asked, but I had seen him holding it and looking at it at times in deep thought.

We saw even fewer people once we crossed into Mexico. The land felt more barren and much hotter. We needed to fill our canteens more often now. We didn't know how long it might be before we were able to get fresh water. Perhaps that was why, when we came unexpectedly upon a little meadow with a small running stream, I told Dutch that we should rest up a while. It seemed a perfect place at the base of the mountain range. Large boulders laced the upper hillside and extended all of the way up the steep incline.

It would be good to get Dutch fully healed up before we went much further. His wound was starting to do better now, and it looked like it had no infection in it. It was still hard for him to walk, but a few days here would be good for the body and the spirit. Dutch became more talkative now, and since we hadn't been pushing too hard, things were better.

The idea we'd discussed earlier about changing our gold into Mexican money seemed even better now. We hadn't thought how hard it would be to bring gold into a country and try to get along. I decided that I would split up our finances again and give Dutch another half. I insisted that I wanted to do it this way, and I thought it would make him feel better, too.

He didn't want me to do that, but I insisted. I told him that I was getting tired of doing all of the talking and the cooking, so he had better get on with doing his share of those things around here again. I divided up the gold I had brought. I told him that it would be up to him to keep hold of his diggings this time. Besides, I might be the one that would be in trouble next time.

We sat and visited by the campfire each evening. The nights had taken on quite a chill and it made the blankets feel real friendly. We talked about our time back in California, and how by chance we had come to be partners. We talked about our trip from California, and how the Spanish we had learned while working for Sanchez would come in pretty handy here in Mexico.

When we started off again four days later, we continued going south. I noticed that we were coming across more ranches and a few farms that had been settled in the low lands of the watersheds. We had decided that we would stay pretty clear of any towns of large size, but we still needed to find one with a bank in it to change our gold to paper money. It wasn't too long before we found one of the small towns that had a good-sized bank.

We sat on one of the ridges overlooking the town below. Dutch didn't say much, and that was a sign that he again wasn't feeling very good. Maybe we would be able to find a doctor to look at him when we got to the town. We decided to hide most of the things that would give our wealth away. We only kept our pistols. We had even hidden our knives. We would just tell anyone who asked that we were passing through. We wouldn't let people know we had been anywhere near the gold mines. We knew that we would need to show the gold to the banker, but decided that it was a chance we must take.

Luck was with us as we turned our horses and mules down the narrow street that went into the little Mexican town. Some nodded and some just watched, but everyone knew when a stranger was in town. Dutch hid the old bloodstains away from sight with the slicker thrown over his saddle horn. We were careful for him to get off between the horses to be less noticeable from prying eyes.

The sign on the front of the building where we had stopped translated to 'Teresa's Fine Food.' We would just have to give it a try. We made our way inside to one of the tables. Only a few people were inside, and we sat so we could watch our horses and pack animals. We had watered them at one of the troughs before we got all of the way into town.

A large lady came over to take our order and motioned to the hand scribbled sign on the wall describing what was to eat that day. We both ordered a hot meal of the day, with plenty of coffee.

We didn't want to talk to too many people, but the man sitting across the small dining room asked, using English, "New in town?"

We looked quickly at each other as I answered, "Just passing through. If we can't find any work on some of the ranches," I said.

He replied, "You might find some work at a couple of the ranches out east of here. It seems everybody and their dog has gone to the gold fields in California. You fellows planning on going there?" he asked.

"No," I said, not wanting to talk about that. "But I have heard that some have found gold in a few places."

"You should stay here a while and you will see all kinds of people on their way there. They tell all kinds of crazy stories."

"Probably just stories, is all they are. We are going to spend our time thinking about ranching." I said.

Looking at Dutch, I motioned toward him with my hand and asked, "Is there a doctor here about? My partner here hasn't been feeling too good lately. Maybe it was something he ate."

"Sure, go see Doc Swenson. He does the horses and people."

I nodded thanks to him and we soon finished our meal without any more talking.

The doctor was not in when we got to his place, but the young boy who was cleaning up said that he would go fetch him. He was over at the saloon. We waited a few minutes before the Doctor came in.

"What's the problem, fellers?" he asked.

I told him that my friend had been in a fight in San Francisco a few days ago. Dutch dropped his pants and the doctor had him lie down on the table. He didn't mind yanking the bandage off Dutch, who let out a smothered word in German. It was good he didn't say what he was thinking, as the doctor began to pry open the wound and swab it out to look inside more.

"You have lost a lot of blood the past few days," he said. He was soon through with cleaning it. He then poured something into it and said, "This might hurt a little bit."

I could see the look on Dutch's face as he gritted his teeth.

"It has been too long for stitching it up," the doctor said. "It would be better if you could take it easy and leave it open so it could heal on the inside. The stuff I put on should make it start feeling better in three or four days. Come on back then and I might be able to stitch it up some, if it looks like it is healing inside. What did the other feller look like?" he

asked.

"He didn't look so good," Dutch said.

With clean bandages and a hand full of the salve and bandages to take with us, I asked him how much.

"Three dollars," he said, as he wiped down the table where the fresh bleeding had started again. I paid what he asked, and nothing more was said.

We went out onto the front porch and Dutch found a bench to sit on for a while. "I will never let you talk me into going and seeing him again," he vowed. "It's a wonder the horses don't die, too, as rough as he is." I felt bad for him, and told him that I thought he would feel better tomorrow.

We needed to go to the bank next and see if they would cash us out. It would be good to be out of town by sundown. I hoped no one here would follow and try to take our things away from us. Dutch's next comment told me he felt the same uneasiness.

"Did you see how everyone watches us? It is like they can see right through our stuff and see the gold we are carrying. There are a few over there looking our way; they seem to be no good."

"Did you see the one dressed in full buckskins? He looks like some of those we have seen up in the diggings."

"Do you think we could stop off and have just one drink at the saloon before we go to the bank? I think it would make me feel a lot better," Dutch said.

I told him to go ahead and I would go down to the bank and talk with the owner. It might be better if they didn't even know there were two of us until we got our money.

"Now don't be going and getting into any trouble. That is sure something we don't need right now," I said.

With a wave of his hand he turned and walked inside the saloon.

It was early afternoon when I went into the bank. I waited back for a few minutes and let the townspeople who were talking to the banker finish before I moved toward him. I took off my hat and held it in my hand as he motioned me through the half-sized door that separated him from me.

"Ellsworth Kennard," he said. "What can do I for you?"

He was well dressed and had a slight moustache, which was turning gray to match the small amount of hair above his ears. I thought about the small round glasses that he had on and wondered if all bankers looked about the same. His soft, smooth hands told of the easy life he had as a banker.

"I am Jacob, and I wanted to exchange some of the gold that I brought with me for paper money," I said.

He looked thoughtfully at me for a minute and I think he was wondering how someone as young as me could have much gold. I began wondering if he would even exchange it down here. Maybe they didn't deal in gold this far away from the gold fields.

"Where did you get the gold?" he asked.

"From some of the streams up near Sacramento," I said.

He sat there in thought without saying anything. I became a little bit uncomfortable about the silence, when in walked another customer and he called him by name. The banker said, "Wait a minute, Charlie."

I finally blurted out, "Do you take gold or not? If you don't, just say so!"

"Of course we take gold. It's sixteen dollars an ounce. Bring it on in and we'll weigh it up."

I told him I would be back in a short while and went out the front door just as a couple of more people came through it. I found Dutch leaning against the bar, and it was evident that by this time he had something to ease his pain. I had a beer with him and told him that we needed to get going.

The doctor was sitting in one of the corner tables and pointed me out to some that were with him, probably telling them of patching up my partner and that we had come to town together. I thought, news travels fast in a small town. "Travel fast -- that's what we need to do," I told Dutch as we made our way out into the sunlight. I could tell he was feeling no pain as we walked across to the front of the bank.

"Get hold of yourself," I told him. "We are not out of trouble yet. I don't exactly trust this banker, but I don't know what else we can do. We should be well into Mexico tomorrow if things go all right."

I thought we should talk over our situation before we went to the bank. The place where we had eaten was just a few doors up, so it seemed a good idea to sit down at a table there and get some strong black coffee into my partner before we went any farther. We moved the horses back up the street and tied them in front of the boarding house. It was still pretty empty, and the fellow who had talked to us earlier was not there.

I ordered two coffees and made sure that Dutch drank them both. He argued and fussed with each swallow, but I could see the effect on him.

"That's terrible stuff," he said. "I think it is going to make me sick."

I asked the waitress what time the bank closed and she told me it would close in about half an hour. When we went back outside, I could talk to Dutch better than when he first came out of the saloon. I could tell he was coming around when he began to complain.

"First that horse doctor, Swenson, with those beady little eyes and thick glasses! And now pouring that coffee down me with no sugar!"

"Can you understand when I tell you that we have to be

on our toes and ready for anything?" I warned.

"Yes, tell on, partner. I am full awake now, and my side is starting to hurt again," he groaned. "Do you know that Swenson came up to the bar and asked if I was going to buy him a drink?" he asked in disgust.

I just shook my head and said, "Listen! We have to decide what to do. Shall we take part of the gold into the bank, or all of it? Before dark, the whole town will know how much gold we have or how much money we have. We have a real good chance that some of these no goods around here will come to try and take it away from us."

"You make the call," Dutch said. "You have always been the one to do that in the past."

"Let's go for it, then," I said. We both took our shares into the bank in our own saddlebags.

"Are you ready?" I asked the banker. He turned and called the clerk out from behind his cage to weigh us in. As we started getting our pouches of gold out one by one and placing them by the scales, I could see the shine in the banker's eyes.

"I want to put down the weight of each pouch as we go," I said. There was greed here, I thought. I could almost feel him thinking about how he could get it away from us. He had the fever all right, but he wasn't willing to work for it. He would just as soon get his gold the easy way. Take it away from those who had it, one way or another, I thought. Even the clerk could hardly keep a smooth voice as he tallied up the amount that we had. When it was all done, the banker turned to the clerk and said, "Horace, get them their money."

I told him that we would take part of it in Mexican money.

"Would you boys like to open an account with most of the funds?" he asked.

"Maybe later," I said as we carefully placed the large

amount of money in our saddlebags and left the bank. We stopped by the general store and picked up a few necessary supplies. We didn't want to add too much to the packs, as we might need to move out pretty fast before morning. Then we walked our horses and the mules over to the livery stable and asked that they each get a good portion of grain and hay for the night. We paid for their board in advance, and asked the caretaker if he could recommend a room for the two of us for the night.

"Only a couple of places in town," he said. "Kind of depends if the noise bothers you." He mentioned a couple places we could stay.

"What time do you close down?" I asked. "And what time do you open in the morning if we decide to get going a little bit early?"

"The boy, Dan, stays here all night, but I will be calling it a day in about two hours. If you want to leave by sun up, just wake Dan up. He will let you have your animals."

Dutch had let me do all of the talking as he had spent some of his time around behind the barn. It sounded like he was sick. Finally he came back and splashed some cold water on his face.

"Just right," he said.

"What's just right?" I asked.

"Me," he said. "I knew you was going to ask me how I was, and I thought I would tell you first and save you the trouble of asking."

I smiled at this a little, but I knew he was not smiling as we put our saddlebags over our shoulders and made our way to the boarding house. I paid for our room and we both went in. It wasn't much, just two single beds in the room with one small window overlooking the street below. We could see the saloon just a couple of buildings south of us across the way.

"Pull your boots off and wash up, just like we were going to stay the night," I told him in a whisper. "The whole town will soon know that we have all of this money and that we exchanged the gold. Keep your gun ready all of the time and get a little bit of rest. Do you feel like eating anything?" I asked.

"No, I don't think I will ever want to eat again," he said.

I left my saddlebags with Dutch and went down to the lobby. The food smelled good coming from the eating room, so I went in and sat close to the door. A few people were eating and a lot of talking was going on. It kind of reminded me of Millie's when it got real busy there, but this bunch of people didn't look like the bearded, grizzly-looking lot that would come in from the gold mines. Most were cowboys; a few of them were Mexicans. We were pretty close to the California border, I thought as I looked at the mixture of people.

A young Mexican girl came over and took my order and then returned into the kitchen. She brought the coffee and it smelled good. I thought of the coffee that I had to nearly pour down poor Dutch. I thought of him now and hoped that he was getting some rest. He put the chair under the doorknob like I told him after I had gone out into the hall. It should keep anyone from slipping up on him in case he was asleep.

From where I was sitting, I could see the stairway up to the rooms. If anything looked out of place, I could move quickly up from the table. I was glad that we had not decided to stay over the saloon.

It was dark now, and if anyone were thinking of giving us much problem, they would probably come in the early morning hours, when they figured we would be asleep. Maybe I was just getting jumpy, but I had a bad feeling about some of the men I had seen that day. I didn't like the way the banker acted, either. Whoever had a first name Ellsworth? What kind of a name is that?

I finished the meal, and stepped out onto the front porch and stood along side of the door. I was in the shadows more here and could listen and watch across the street. I could even hear some of the conversation from inside. I heard about two guys coming into town with a lot of gold. I guess they didn't know I spoke Spanish and could understand everything they said. The word was out, just as I thought it would be. By now, the town also knew that Dutch was hurt and all about that, too. The doctor had said he wouldn't be able to do much for three or four days, but he didn't know that stubborn German like I did. One thing was sure; he couldn't jump out the window like I could. It would be too much for him.

I wondered how we might get out of the room without everyone knowing about it. I moved along the outside of the building, past one of the windows in the dining room and on around the corner to where our room was. I could see the light from our window and some of the others. If we could get out that way, it looked like we might be able to slip around behind the boarding house and make our way to the livery stable without being seen.

What I needed to find, without getting away too far, was a rope. I soon found one on a saddled horse across the street. I didn't know to whom it belonged, so I took it and left five dollars wedged under the saddle where the rope used to be. I hoped that the owner would see the money and be able to buy half a dozen ropes or more with the money.

In the deeper shadows, I pulled up my shirt and wound the rope around my body, then pulled my shirt back down. This was how Dutch would have to get out of the window and onto the street in the dark. It was already full dark, and I felt uneasy with Dutch up in the room alone. I had been gone only a few minutes when I entered the lobby and made my way up the stairs.

I knocked and in German told him I was alone. I could

116

hear him getting out of the bed to open the door. I watched the hall to see if anyone else heard me speak to him. I slipped inside and we secured the chair back under the knob. I asked him if he was able to get any rest.

He whispered to me, "No, too much to think about."

I nodded my head in agreement and whispered to him that word was already out about us and about our gold. I had heard it on my way in to eat. We would need to go soon. I showed him the rope that I had brought and told him he would have to use it to reach the ground. I looked out the window and wished that we were already on our way from here. The most important thing we must do now was get out of here without causing any noise.

In a couple of minutes, we had pulled one of the loose ends of the rope around the legs of the bed and pulled against it to see if it would hold us. With both ends of the rope ready to push out the window, we were about ready. We carried the bed and pushed it against the wall. It seemed like it would hold our weight. It was time for us to go.

I took a look outside to see if I could see anyone in the shadows. I watched for a few minutes and then gave Dutch a sign to blow out the light. Then we waited for any movement below. We must have waited for about five minutes, when finally the waiting was rewarded with seeing someone come out of the deep shadows. He looked up at our room and headed down the street for the saloon.

"Hurry," I told Dutch. "He's gone to report in."

I slipped out the window first, then waited with my pistol in hand as Dutch tied the bags on and let them out the window without a sound. He slid out over the windowsill and was soon at my side with pistol in hand. With a little jerk, I was able to pull the rope from around the leg of the bed and rolled it up as it came out of the window. We moved quickly around the building, sticking to the shadows.

I was glad that it was too early for the moon to be up. It was increasing in size and getting nearly full. In a short time we came up to the livery stable from the east side, away from the lights. I called out for Dan, and a light began to show back in the barn.

"I will give you twenty dollars to help catch up our mules and horses and help get them ready to go. We are in a hurry!" I said. "And don't light any more lanterns!"

Well, that was more than Dan made in a month. He was full awake now. Moving quickly in the dark of the night, he soon came with all of the animals tied together. I wondered how he was able to find them so fast in the night. He said that he just left them in the feed area where he had given them grain. We fastened our belongings onto the mules in the dark by feel and whisper.

"Now Dan, you won't tell anyone we are gone, will you? I have another five dollars you can make if you will take this rope to that big gray horse tied up just past the saloon and tie it back on that saddle. You will find the five dollars wedged under the saddle blanket where the rope goes."

He shook his head as I handed him the rope, and we were off into the night and away from the little town. We had seen the road earlier that led off to the south and soon had the animals stretched and moving away from there. It would be possible that they had someone watching the road, and so just in case we tried to leave without them catching up to us.

We could make out the wagon trail, but were unable to see very far ahead. When the moon came out, if we didn't meet up with any bad luck, we should be able to move even faster. I turned to look back at where the town was, but could not make out anything or hear anyone coming behind us.

*In the saloon, Stoney came in to report to Wedlo. "They have gone to bed and tuned out the light," he said.*

Wedlo turned to the others who were sitting around the table with him.

"We will wait a couple of hours and let them get to sleep. After all, they are just kids. I told Ellsworth that we would have his money all back by morning. Remember, there is twenty dollars in it for each of you. Try not to do any shooting, unless you have to. I don't want the law coming down here and looking into anything."

When the time came to rush in on the two sleeping upstairs, Wedlo checked with the lookout he'd stationed at the bottom of the stairs.

"They are still up there in their room," he said. "They haven't come down the stairs, and the night clerk has been long gone."

This felt too easy, Wedlo thought as he dispatched four men up the stairs to take care of things and bring the saddlebags back to him in the lobby. Two more were left by the front door to keep anyone from coming in or out. There wasn't much chance of that in this early hour of the morning.

He had known Ellsworth since he had come to the area about three years ago, and had done a few jobs for him when he needed someone roughed up or run off their ranch. Ellsworth was from California, and tried to work both sides of the border for his gain.

What really kept Wedlo going, though, was that good-looking daughter of Ellsworth's. Ellsworth was starting to show some interest in Wedlo, and this just might be the thing that would get him in real thick with the banker. He often thought about this young and pretty Nancy that the banker had for a daughter. He had danced with her once at the last dance. She seemed to have a lot of friends, but if he could do this one big thing for Ellsworth, it would look pretty good for him. She was probably the prettiest girl in town. It sure wouldn't hurt to be married to the banker's daughter, he *thought.*

He could just imagine taking the money back into the bank in the morning and turning it all back in. Of course Ellsworth had paid him well for the things he would do, and three hundred dollars to "handle it" would be good pay for a few minute's work. He would be sure to check the saddlebags himself and take anything else that he might want from them. They might even have more gold in there that the boys didn't show Ellsworth.

Wedlo's thoughts were interrupted by the crash of broken wood. He could hear the men entering the room of the two young boys. He listened for shots, but heard none. There was cursing as the men came back down the stairs and said, "They are gone!"

This brought Wedlo to his feet. Not only would he not have the money to give the banker the next morning, but all of his plans for the banker's daughter were gone, too.

"Twenty dollars!" he shouted out. "Twenty more dollars each to get them and return the bags to me for Mr. Ellsworth. Shoot them on sight." He would negotiate the extra charge with Ellsworth when he returned with the money.

"Be ready to ride at first light, when we can find out which way they went."

To the seven that were in the group with Wedlo, twenty dollars was a good month's pay around here. And now the stakes were at forty. They would find the two boys.

# Chapter 10

The moon was showing some light in the east and we could make out the road now. I looked over at Dutch and wondered how he was holding up. We put our horses into a good pace to cover as many miles as we could before we might be followed. I didn't think they could do anything but wait for light to get a general direction of where we were going. But one thing was for sure: they would be coming after us and our money.

We stopped to give our horses a quick drink at two of the small water crossings. It would be important to spare them as much as we could and yet cover as much ground as we could, too. The horses felt fresh from the good feed and short rest they had at the stable. The mules had been packed with an equal amount of weight and seemed to gallop along with ease as they came along in tow. They are probably the only ones that can keep this pace up all day, I thought.

I could just make out a low range of mountains ahead of us. The road made a sharp bend and went up toward a pass that I could see on the horizon. That would mean no water for a while, I thought, and no time to look at the map. It would be nice to get to the top of the pass and look at the meadow that we had just crossed. We would be able to see a long way back toward the town from there. The wagon road went along the side of the hill for a ways before it went into the pass.

When we reached the pass, I turned but could not see anyone or anything following us. But that didn't mean anything. Those who would be after us would be able to travel just a little bit faster than we did. I figured that we should have about a three hours or maybe more start on them. The only problem was, they knew the land and trails and we didn't. I thought of this as we pushed on toward the top.

It was getting steeper here now and more winding as

we neared the top of the gap. In a few minutes we reached the gap and pulled the animals off the road to give them a breather. We loosened the cinch on the horses, but left the pack mules tied to a bush. They immediately started grazing as if nothing was wrong.

I could tell that Dutch wasn't moving too good and wished that we could wait somewhere for him to get better. He didn't say anything.

In no time at all, we resumed our ride, following the trail as it started down the other side. We moved quickly through the open area below. This wouldn't be a good place to get caught, so we hurried across the two-mile flat and into the foothills and brush on the opposite side.

We hadn't come to any water since the trail started climbing, and I had a suspicion that it might still be a while before we came to water again. I could see a pretty good mountain range to the east and thought it was about ten miles away. We should be able to get there in about half a day, if the road stayed this good all of the way.

The days had been getting warmer the farther south we had traveled, but the nights stayed cool. We kept looking back at every chance we had, but it was harder to see very far now. We kept up a good pace until we reached the rim of a drop off into a canyon. I pulled up and walked over to look below. There was a good stream of dirty-looking water down in the canyon, but so were about a dozen Indians.

The way they were traveling, they could be up to the road in just a few minutes. I motioned for Dutch to turn back into the brush along side of the ridge and move farther down stream away from them. They didn't look like they were too friendly as they and about ten horses moved up stream.

I wondered if they would keep following the water or turn and come our way. We couldn't take the chance of letting them see us. It had been good luck that we held the horses back and walked to where I could see over the other side, before riding on down to the little river below. They would have seen us for sure.

We tried to brush out our tracks where we moved off the road. We knew we were using valuable time, but maybe the ones who might be after us would move on down into the river below. Who would stop this close to water and not decide to go down the ridge anyway?

As we moved away from the bank a little bit, it was much easier going because the brush was not so thick. We made good time for the next hour, but the animals smelled the water below and needed to have some of it.

We were just making our way down through the brush and into the river area when we heard gunshots ring out from the area where we had left the road. We stopped to listen; the gunfire went on for some time.

"I guess we know where the bunch is that was following us," I said.

After looking up stream and down, we decided to move on out into the water and give the animals a drink. We followed the stream on down for about three miles. The high sandstone walls were closing in all of the time. I finally found the place I was looking for: the place where we must leave the river. We got out on the rocky bank and followed it along the river for a short ways until we headed up one of the little canyons that led into it.

I looked at Dutch and he didn't seem to have any color in his normally tanned face. We had to find a place soon where we could rest the animals and Dutch for a while.

The canyon was narrow and full of brush, but we were able to pick our way along for about a mile from the river. It became more rocky and hard now and I thought I noticed the sand was taking on some color as we got nearer the top. It might even be getting a little damp. Upon rounding one of the corners, I looked up ahead and thought, "Yes! Oh yes! Let there be water in that thicket of green reeds that are in the canyon ahead."

I was excited to find that the draw widened out a little bit. I could see clear water in some of the pools of the bedrock. There would be enough feed for the horses and mules for a couple of days. It looked like we would be away from prying eyes down in our little canyon.

"This is where we can camp for a little while," I told Dutch, as I took the saddle off my horse and carried it up on the bank.

In a short while we had all of the packs off, and the mules and horses hobbled. They made for the reed patch where the grass was tall and green. It wouldn't take long for them to clean that out, and then they would have to move back on the banks to the dried grass.

With rifle in hand, I told Dutch that I thought we were near the top of the ridge and I would go and look over the other side. We would need to keep our eyes open for Indians now, too. From the top of the ridge, I could see smoke coming from far down in the valley. That is probably where the Indians got their horses, I thought.

As I sat thinking about that, I thought back to the Norris ranch and how they had been wiped out. America and Mexico were good countries, but it was sure hard for people sometimes.

Since we no longer were threatened by any who had followed us from town, we could stop here for a while. The rest would do us good, and maybe Dutch could get some strength and feel better. It would also give those Indians another day to get farther away. I gathered some small oak brush that was good and dry from up near the top of the ridge. We would chance making a fire tonight after dark. It would be good to have a hot meal and something hot to drink.

I walked back to the horses to tell Dutch to keep watch below, but he was fast sleep with his rifle over his lap. The afternoon sun on the grassy hillside was just too much for him. I was glad to see him getting some good rest and decided that I would just stay up and watch for a while.

I had brought the map along, but things just didn't seem to be the way the map was drawn. We might have passed some of the landmarks in the night without seeing them. For now we just needed to keep going toward the morning sun each day.

It was nearly dark when I made my way back to where Dutch was lying. He woke up a little as I broke some of the branches and arranged them for a fire. I thought a good stew might be just what he needed to make him feel better. In no time I had found what I needed. Using some of the fresh stuff that we bought in town, I soon had our dinner cooking and smelling delicious. I made six biscuits and placed them in a frying pan.

"It won't be long now," I said, as Dutch moved closer to the small fire. The oak burned hot. I raked some of the coals out of the fire and put them to one side. Then I set the pan with the biscuits on the coals. I raked more coals together and put them on the cupped lid. It was only a short time before we were sitting around eating. We had bought some honey and finished the biscuits up with the sweet stuff.

It was good to see Dutch feeling like eating again. "I thought you told me you would never want to eat again," I said.

He looked up long enough to pitch a small stick at me.


*Wedlo and his bunch were ready at first light. When someone found the mule tracks, they knew which way to go. It wasn't long before there was enough light for them to see the trail plainly before them as they urged their horses on.*

*"We should catch up to them before we get to the*

125

river," he told his men. "And when we do, just shoot them! We'll take the animals and all that is on them."

When they got to the high rise of the first mountain, he said, "We are getting close, boys. We should catch up to them by the time we get to the river, or just beyond."

With that they rode quickly down the other side and soon closed the gap across the flats to the edge of the river. Their horses were getting winded, but they could have a good drink after they got the money back.

The Indians, always looking for any sign of trouble, had gotten out on the bank of the river and sent one of their own up on the ridge to look ahead. He came racing back saying that a bunch of riders were coming fast from the direction he was pointing.

The scout told the leader how many were coming. The leader didn't want to lose the horses they had taken, so they decided to stay and fight. They turned the horses in against the brush on the west side of the river and spread out, waiting for those who were coming.

Wedlo led the race down toward the river bottom. He was looking up the other side, expecting to see the pack animals and boys any minute, when shots suddenly rang out. The two riders next to him were shot off their horses. He was shot in the arm as he stopped and wheeled his big gray horse back the way they had come.

The Indians shot one more rider from his horse as they retreated back up the ridge. Several of Wedlo's men had exchanged fire with the Indians, but they came off badly. The Indians did not follow their group.

It was a sad looking bunch that made it back to town just before sundown that day: three men missing, Wedlo shot in the left arm, and no money for the banker.

The story would get bigger and bigger every time one of the survivors told it. Of course they had killed several of the Indians, but there were still about fifty or so left. They for sure had gotten the boys and all of their stuff. No one would have had any chance against that many Indians.

The banker called Wedlo in to see him, and Wedlo could see the anger in his face.

"I gave you one simple little assignment: to go and get my money back. And look at you! I never would have let them have all of that money if I had thought there was any way that I would not get it back," he said.

Wedlo thought he had better not ask for any extra money for the losses they had, but did ask if the banker would give him the money for the men.

"For what?" Ellsworth demanded. "If I was you, I would get out of town and take that shiftless bunch with you. Eight men against two boys and one of them bad hurt . . . ! Some help you are. If word ever gets out around here what really happened, you will be the laughing stock of the West. I had better not hear my name mentioned in the conversation."

The third day after we had left the little town, we continued to make our way east. We had circled around and got back on the road again, but before long it seemed to turn in the wrong direction. We were about to leave the road when we noticed a couple of wagons coming our way. We thought they didn't seem any threat to us and they might be able to point the way that we needed to go. We decided to move on down the trail toward them.

When we got closer we could see that there were two wagons and two riders along with four extra horses following behind. We waited by the side of the trail as they pulled closer to us. We each had our rifles lying across our saddles in case they were not friendly.

We saw that they were Mexicans and soon got to use our Spanish. It seems they had gone for supplies and were returning to the area we just came from. They knew of Ellsworth, the banker, and spoke his name with disgust.

I told them we were on our way to Sonoyta and asked if they could point the way. I showed them the map and pointed out what it said. After some talking between the two, the older one seemed to know where we wanted to go and pointed to a distant mountain. He told us if we would stay to the left of the mountain, we would find the things on our map.

I asked him about water on the way and he took a stick and drew a map on the ground. He explained that we would be going into some dry lands with little water if we went straight for the distant mountain range. If we would take a different trail, which he sketched in the sand, for two days, we would find more water. Then we could get closer to the mountains, too.

I asked him if he would take a note to Ellsworth for me. It was a joke, I told him, and he seemed anxious to do that. So I found a scrap of paper and wrote: 'Ellsworth Kennard, Thanks for all of the money. Your two young friends.' I folded the paper and, knowing that neither one could read what was written, did not worry about sealing it. The older one put the note in his shirt pocket. He said that he would give it to the banker as soon as they got to town.

Several days passed without us seeing anyone or anyone seeing us. Many stories, maybe some of them true, had come out of Mexico. They told how banditos had taken all from the gold miners, including their lives. Very few ever came back to tell of these experiences, so we were ever on our guard. We didn't want too many to know that we were even passing through the country. We got used to having only a small guarded campfire that couldn't be seen from any distance. We never stopped for long, and it was beginning to show on Dutch again.

Our map seemed to be better now. We used it to find a

water source. The ground was pretty firm, but a recent rain had left some deep depressions filled with water. Deer and many other animals of the high desert had visited the water hole in the little grassy meadow. It was hard to decide just what else had been there. We wondered if Indians, or bandits, or even the Mexican patrols might have passed this way. We could find no signs that horses had been to the water hole the past few days. Because it was one of the few water holes for miles around, we decided to take our chances and stop. We could see a short way down stream, and the mountain to our backs seemed to offer good cover in case we were forced to move quickly.

Heavy clouds rolled in, and the wind started to blow from the south. There was an uneasiness that we both felt, but neither of us talked about it.

Our coffee was nearly gone and our food was getting down to the point that we need to think about getting more pretty soon. We thought about chancing a shot at a young buck that came down for his evening drink in the fading daylight, but decided we dared not fire any shots. Two does were already in the water hole alleviating their thirst, but they soon departed. They didn't even seem to be bothered too much by our horses hobbled in the upper part of the little grassy meadow. We watched the fine young buck come in. He wasn't too eager to get his taste and now stood looking straight at us. We didn't move from our hiding place, a little above the meadow.

We had put all of our camp stuff behind the bushes, so that they wouldn't get any bounce from the sun and bring unwelcome eyes our way. We knew that anyone who came within view of the meadow would see our horses and pack animals hobbled in the grass. But the animals needed the feed and rest as much as we did.

I was still watching the way the deer had gone when I noticed something or someone coming into the lower end of the meadow. Dutch had been lying down on one of the saddle blankets and using the saddle for a pillow. He was asleep now. I pushed at him and he sat straight up with rifle in hand.

A group of eight or ten riders would soon be upon us. If they were bandits or Indians, we would be no match for them here where we were. We ran up the hill into the cover of some large boulders, just as the shells started to break and bounce around us.

All of the bandits were shooting at us every time we tried to see how many of them there were. They had moved much closer now; they were shooting from where we had been resting a few moments earlier. Their leader was yelling out orders to those in his group.

I motioned Dutch to get up higher in the rocks so they couldn't get around behind us. We used the large boulders as a shield and kept moving ever higher. Each time we showed ourselves, the fire from the bandits below increased. Once a bullet came so close to my head it broke off a fragment of the rock and the splinter cut a gash across my right cheek.

There was a narrow opening between two of the rocks that I was behind and I could see them unhobbling our horses and pack animals. I recognized that they had loaded all of our camp gear on the pack animals. They had about everything that they wanted now, except us.

We decided to get a little farther apart, hoping that maybe we would get a chance to get some of them. Dutch got a good shot away, and one of the bandits went down. I was able to get one in stride when he tried to get to a better vantage place. The loss of the two bandits seemed to change their idea of coming up after us. We increased our shooting at them now. The leader of the bunch motioned to leave and they started out of the meadow with all that we had.

Suddenly Dutch got out from behind his hiding place. In the loudest German that he could shout, he called them some names that I wouldn't want to mention. Upon hearing this, the leader held up his hand and stopped the others from leaving. It was about then that I wondered if Dutch had done the right thing. Maybe they would come back and finish us off.

The big bandit turned to face us on his horse. Even from that distance, we could hear him say in broken German, "I leave you something." With that they cut loose the last pack mule and rode off. The last we saw as the robbers went out of the meadow around the bend were my sorrel, Jake, and Dutch's black horse, Nighthawk. Gone were our best friends.

We could hardly believe our ears to hear German spoken in this place. We waited for a few minutes and watched and listened. Maybe it was a trap. Finally, we had to take a chance. They had left Chancey the mule, who was as hard headed as they got. If we didn't go after him soon, he might just decide to run off after the others.

We spread out and made our way back down to the meadow. I noticed that Dutch wasn't walking very well. The familiar bright red place was again showing on his thigh. He hobbled along and we soon were able to get close to Chancey.

From everything that we could see, it looked like the banditos had gone; but we couldn't be sure. One of us had to make a move into the clearing and one had to stay back at the ready. I decided that I should be the one to go forward; and I did with gun in hand.

Chancey didn't even seem to know or care that we had just been through a gunfight. He began to eagerly nibble at the grass. I gathered up the rope that was trailing on the ground and motioned to Dutch that they must be gone. I went far enough down around the turn that I could see the heavy running tracks of the animals as they made their getaway. When I returned with Chancey, we decided the safest place for us would be back up against the mountain amid the large rocks.

Dutch could hardly walk now. I looked at him and he was pale, as if all of the blood had drained out of his face. He picked up a dead stick to keep himself from falling. When we had run up into the rocks to take cover behind the huge boulders, I had seen him fall and heard his muffled cry. Having to move so quickly, plus the fall he'd taken, must have opened up the wound again. I took the pack blanket off the mule and the saddle and tried to make him as comfortable as I could.

He said. "I am sorry, Jacob. If it hadn't of been for me, you would be in Sonoyta by now. I have just held you back again."

"I don't want to hear such talk!" I replied. I refused to let him take the blame. "We might have run into this bunch out in the open and lost our lives. We are still alive, and we will get out of this some way. Besides, calling that leader all of those names in German was what got us Chancey and a little bit of food."

There was a quiet time as we thought of our chances now. Would the thieves return? Or would some other party, hearing all of the shooting, be guided our way? We talked it out and finally decided that they would probably not come back. They already had nearly everything, including all of our money.

I said, "Dutch, we are right back where we started from, maybe a little bit more in trouble. We are in an unfriendly country, where we are fair game to anyone that wants to come our way. You are hurt and cannot walk very far. They did leave us a mule, but it could have been any of the other animals. This Chancey is about as bad and ornery as they get. We still have a couple of pans and a small amount of food, along with one canteen for water. It could be worse, much worse. We still have matches, a little flour, salt, and a few pieces of jerky that we bought from that last Mexican family we found. There's even one slicker tied on the backpack."

# Chapter 11

The sky was turning an ugly, dark color and the wind had continued to blow. I spread the slicker out to create a makeshift tarp for Dutch. Then I took the canteen and Chancey down for a drink. I didn't take long to water the mule and myself. I would take Dutch a drink. Tonight I wouldn't leave Chancey hobbled in the pasture, but would tie him securely at our camp. We couldn't stand the risk of losing him, since he might be our only chance to get out of here alive.

I no sooner got back to Dutch than the clouds burst open. Poor Dutch was stretched out on the ground and there wasn't room for his legs to keep out of the rain. I sat close to him and tried to shelter him from the storm. Even in all of the rain, we were bone tired and drifted off to sleep once in a while. Dutch groaned with pain throughout the night, and I didn't know what else I could do to make him feel easier.

I thought the night would never end. Even Chancey hung his head and was still. Gradually the rain let up, and in the east the gray dawn started to appear. I welcomed the warm morning sun, hoping that it would quickly thaw us all out. The meadow glistened in the early morning. It would usually have been a beautiful day, except for our circumstances.

I had noticed a small cave up on the hillside not too far away and decided that maybe there might be some dry brush or sticks that I could use to start a fire. It was as I had hoped it would be. There was a small amount of brush and weeds at the mouth of the cave. I even found some dry sticks inside that had been carried there by some critter over a period of time. The pack rat mound would help to warm us this morning and maybe get Dutch to feeling and doing better. We hadn't had a chance to talk. When he felt up to it, we would need to decide what we should do.

It wasn't long before I had built a small fire near

Dutch. I gathered some of the other sticks and placed them around the small fire so they might dry out some. We would need a fire for some time today, and I would gather more wood for the night. As the wood from the cave burned, I kept stacking more close by and adding whatever finally got dry enough to burn. It left quite a trail of smoke going up, but it didn't worry me now. In the daytime it wouldn't be seen too far, and the smoke was going up in the rocks and breaking up.

I felt chilled clear to the bone, but the warmth of the fire brought back hope and a little bit of comfort. I watched Dutch as his pants started to steam from the rain of the night. The exertion of the gunfight yesterday had torn his leg wound back open. The bloodstains had soaked through his pants once again, but he appeared to have stopped bleeding. He had been real quiet, and I knew that sleep and food were the two things he needed the most. Dutch wouldn't be moving very far or very fast for a while.

As I considered our prospects, my worst fear was that we would meet up with more bandits, Mexican patrols, or Indian raiding parties. Some said that the patrols were just as bad as the bandits. And the Indians were in a bad mood all of the time and would take on nearly anyone or anything. One thing was for sure: we were in a heap of trouble. I didn't want to tell Dutch what I was thinking. I thought it best not to worry him too much about just how bad our situation was.

The fire was really beginning to put out some heat, and in a few minutes the sun would be high enough to be shining right down on us. Somehow daylight made everything seem better. I didn't know how, but some way or other we would get out of this.

When the sun had been up for nearly two hours, I walked down around the end of the meadow. I could see no sign of intruders. When I returned, my partner was making his first stirring.

"Hello, Dutch, how are you fairing?"

"Oh. partner, am I ever feeling poorly!"

I could see that his words spelled out a truth. He could hardly roll over to give his back a rest. I propped him up and gave him a cool drink of water.

He said, "After all of that rain, you wouldn't think that we would ever need another drink."

I felt I needed to look at his wound. It was actually two wounds. Indian Joe's knife had entered the fleshy part of the thigh, hitting the bone and glancing off into a small exit in the back. We had tried to keep it clean and get the smaller wound to heal over. It had been doing real well up until now.

"Here! Let me have a look at that and see where we are now with things. As soon as we get this taken care of again, I will get you something to eat. We are lucky that they left us some food." I hoped he wouldn't ask about the scant food supply that we had left.

I peeled the blood soaked bandage off his thigh. He let out a sharp smothered cry at the pain it caused him. I tried to be as careful and easy as I could be, but I could tell the pain was there by the way he tightened up his lower lip and set his strong chin. It was not quite as bad as I had thought, but the wound had opened again, and now we had no salve or ointment to make it better.

I thought that the warm sun and open air would do it good for a while. I went down to the spring to gather some fresh water to boil the bandages in. If only I could figure out a way to keep the edges of the wound from getting too stiff and drying around the cut. Oil would let me take the next dressing off without removing the scab. But we didn't have any grease, or any oils.

I must find an animal soon that would provide some fat that I could use. I decided that the very next deer that came into the meadow would need to be taken. With all of the rain, though, it might be several days before the deer found a need to return to the watering hole. For now at least, they would be able to find water in many places.

I was watching out across the meadow when something took my eye. There was a slight movement in some of the green brush on the other side. By instinct I grabbed my rifle and put it to my shoulder. Nothing seemed to be moving as I watched the spot that had caught my notice. Whatever it was couldn't have been very big, and there wasn't enough cover to keep it hidden for long.

I kept watching the spot and waiting. What could it be? Suddenly, there it was! A porcupine waddled out of the undergrowth. Excitement filled me as I thought of using this creature. In no time I made my way across the clearing. With club in hand, I soon had him where I needed him. I cleaned the animal and thought of the fresh meat, something we had not had for days. It was a big rascal, and I thought that there might be another farther down around the stream. For now, though, we had food without a shot and hardly any sound.

I soon dispatched the hide and took the meat across the meadow to where Dutch lay. In a short while I had meat cooking in one of our two small pans. With some of the remaining flour, some fresh fat, and salt, I put on four biscuits. We would both feel a lot better with the food we were able to have. Maybe our luck would be in for a change.

Dutch seemed to relish the food when it was done. I had him drink plenty of water, too. That would help flush out his system and keep things going. Someone told me that water was good for more than just the thirst.

After we had eaten and I had put on the rest of the porcupine to cook so it wouldn't go to waste, I said, " Partner, we need to do some serious thinking of what it is we can do. The chance of someone coming back into this water hole are pretty good, and we sure won't be in any shape to run or fight for a long time."

He just nodded and sat thinking about what I had said. By now the hot food was bringing the color back into his face. As I looked at him across the campfire, it struck me that, even with his muscular build, he was still just a boy. He had told me earlier that he was just about the same age as me when he got to California. So, even though we were both young and strong and had worked in the gold diggings for about two years, neither of us needed to shave yet.

For some reason, it seemed that boys just had to grow up sooner in this part of the world. We certainly felt that we were now young men. What we had decided early in the fields was to keep our mouths shut, work hard and save our money. We had no one to turn to if we didn't have a job or money. We had seen others that had given up; or worse, they had become beggars in and around the gold fields. They were at the mercy of anyone that wished to take advantage of them. This was not going to happen to us. We had come too far, and there was no going back now.

Right now we had to face up to some tough problems. As I wondered what we were going to do, I decided I might as well tell Dutch how it was. He would really want to know.

"Dutch," I said, "we have to decide what we should do now. We have no horses and very little food. Our money is gone. Even dividing it up didn't help too much. The six gold nuggets that we each kept are gone, as well as all of the money that we had. We should have been able to live for years in Mexico on a part of what we had. But now that's in the past."

He just nodded agreement, so I continued, "I know you can't walk very much yet, and need time to heal. It appears that time is one of the things that we don't have. We have that crow bait ornery mule, which as you know was the worst animal that we had. Now why couldn't they have cut out any of the other horses or mules? We can't go back to California. Even if we dared go back, we would never be able to get over those mountain passes before the deep snows. Besides, we would need to be well and ready for a trip like that."

I went on and on, listing all the things that could happen and the things that we should think about. Dutch just sat there the whole time that I was talking, listening to me tell of how bad our situation was. He just sat there playing with a stick in the fire, deep in thought, without any answers.

When I finally ran out of steam, he looked up at me and said, "Let's see what we do have instead of the other way around.

"We are still alive, we have just had a good filling meal, we still have our rifles and a box and one half shot each left. We still have our pistols with good firepower there. We still have one mule, a canteen, matches, salt, a little flour, some jerky. And, if we wasn't doing this, we might be out getting into some fool trouble."

That brought out a laugh that I just couldn't hold back. Then he was laughing and poking the stick at me across the fire. We laughed until our sides hurt and tears came into our eyes. There we were, just like old times, I thought.

I made my way down to the meadow, shaking my head at what my partner had said. It brought a smile to my face again every time I thought of his words. I dragged a big stump out into the meadow and tied the mule to it. Old Chancey would need to get all of the water and feed that he could stand, because we'd be getting out of the valley soon.

I spent the rest of the afternoon gathering wood to keep the fire going through the night. By the time I finished all this and hauled more water back to camp, the sun was setting. We would need to stay the night right where we were.

As I climbed back up the hill and reached Dutch, he was sitting up. "Here, pull off my right boot and give my foot a rest, will you?"

I gave it a good smooth pull, so that it wouldn't hurt his thigh, and it finally slipped off. I noticed that a waxed flat pocket came out with it.

He said, "Open it up." To my surprise, I saw that he had stowed several dollar bills inside his boot. What he said next surprised me even more. "My six gold nuggets are down in the package of flour in the mule's pack."

I went to look and, sure enough, when I got the flour off them, they sparkled and shined more than any I had ever seen.

"Dutch, how did you ever think to do something like that?"

"Oh, I learned that little trick from a partner of mine. Don't ever let yourself get flat broke."

He took the nuggets that had come out of the flour and divided them into two piles. Then he divided up the money from his boot. "Take yer pick," he said. It wasn't a large amount of money, but it would be a way to get through and maybe start again. We both felt good.

I pulled the saddle blanket up over him and built up the fire. All I could say was, "Thanks, partner."

Morning took its time getting there. I knew that the dew would be heavy and that it would bring a chill in the air. We couldn't afford for Dutch to get sick right now. I tended a small fire throughout the night, drifting off to sleep once in a while. Once a coyote's mournful howl brought me full awake. I listened for any other sounds in the night, but heard only the wind in the trees.

I thought about the coyote. It hunts all night and sleeps through the day. That would be how we would need to do our moving around. We must be slow and careful. Any bad judgment or decision would bring our downfall. I watched the morning come and added a small amount of wood to the fire.

Somehow I just felt better than yesterday. Maybe it was the old spirit of my partner, or finding that we still had some money to help us get along in this strange land. Whatever it was, I just felt better about things.

Dutch hardly moved at all through the night. Would he be better this morning? I wouldn't be long in finding out. I looked across at the meadow and spotted Chancey right away. That was a relief. I knew that I was taking some chance with him down in the meadow with his drag, but he was lying right there beside it in the tall grass.

It was then that I decided that the only thing we could do was get Dutch on the back of Chancey. I would lead him along the route that we would choose. With our map now gone, along with most everything else, I tried to remember what I could about the territory. My best guess was that we had about four long days' ride to Sonoyta. We would decide our next move after we got there. We might never arrive at our destination, I thought. One thing for sure, if we were to have any chance at all of getting as far as Sonoyta, I would need to find out if Chancey took to carrying someone rather than something.

I remembered the first time that we had tried to get him to carry a pack. It was a terrible sight. He bolted and bucked and fell all of the way down, but the pack wouldn't come off. He then switched strategy real fast and made for the nearest oak tree. There was a rattling and snapping of the belly straps when he pulled the pack off. There wasn't much left of the pack, either. We never could fix the darned thing and finally had to get another one.

The next time, though, we were ready. We had tied a strong rope around his neck and to that same oak tree. We made sure that he was headed the other way when he made his run. We tried to stop him, but there was just no way. When he finally came to the end of the anchored rope, he was going full speed. The rope tightened around his neck and jerked him flat on his back. He did a somersault backwards and ended with his legs straight in the air.

Dutch said that I had broken the durned fool's neck, but in a little while he got to his feet, breathing heavily. I was able to walk right up to him. When I slipped the rope off and on his neck, he never moved a muscle. From that time on, whenever a rope was pulled around his neck he would come to a stop. He didn't seem to be too much bother after that, no more than the other horses and mules. He was about one of the biggest mules that I had ever seen.

Now Dutch was up and walking around. He went into the brush for his morning need. It was good to see him up. I warmed up the remains of the porcupine and even stirred up a little gravy to pour over the fixings. We could have stood to have a few more things to make a meal with, but it filled us up. As we ate, I told Dutch that we needed to try and slip out of here. I had a feeling that we didn't have much time, and to stay much longer was really pressing our luck. He started packing our meager belongings while I went down to get on the mule and ride him back up to the fire.

As I approached, I could see that the darned mule was up getting his fix, too. I knew I had to be the first one to ride him and kind of get him used to things before Dutch got on. Chancey would hardly notice the extra load, for we didn't have too much left to take. But it wouldn't pay for him to get too rough on Dutch.

I had carried the blanket and packsaddle down with me. Luckily the bandits hadn't taken the gear we'd purchased back in California. The lead halter on the mule was solid and stout, and the lead rope of twenty feet or so was also new and solid. I went right up to him and patted him on the neck. He seemed interested to see me and I let him smell the saddle as I scratched his long ears and nose. He kind of liked that, and I placed the saddle blanket on his back.

I had learned that the trick with animals is not to get them too excited. I could see that Chancey wasn't too excited, because he started to feed again with the blanket on his back. He was at the limit of the rope tied to the hardwood stump, but there was still plenty of food here.

I looked back up the bank at Dutch, who was watching all of this. He had his rifle slung in his arms and kept glancing off down the trail and in every direction. He was ready to move on.

I talked to Chancey and told him that we would be doing something different today. He would like it, and besides my friend Dutch couldn't walk very good. I told him that the next time we stopped the water may be even sweeter, and the grass higher. He could roll all around in it that way.

I put the saddle on his back in one motion. He stopped eating. I reached under and cinched the cinch strap and tightened it on his full belly, talking all the while and patting him anywhere I could reach. I then caught the other strap and buckled it. He seemed to stand frozen. I was about to untie the log drag and get on in the normal way, but something told me I had better not.

Now that was silly. Chancey knew who I was, and he would come around pretty quick. It made me more than a little bit nervous when he laid his ears back along his head. Now what's the matter with this hardheaded mule? I patted him a few more times and he seemed to relax some.

This wasn't going to be so bad. I tested my weight on him by hanging onto the saddle. He moved a little bit sideways and his ears came back again, but pretty soon I talked him into standing still.

Dutch was really watching all of this intently. I bet he would have let a whole raiding party slip up on us right about then. We didn't have a lot of time to mess around, so I decided to pull myself up on Chancey's back. Okay! That's more like it. I could see Dutch still watching all of this, and I gave him the thumbs up. He responded with a quick raise of his rifle over his head.

I guess this was the signal that mule was waiting for. It seemed that he jumped ten feet high with his back bent. He made three jumps sideways, two without me, and down I came flat on my back. Even the grass was no comfort to land in from that distance. It knocked all of the wind out of me. And Chancey was trying to run away with the stump.

I got slowly to my feet, and things seemed to be spinning round. Dutch might have been busting loose inside but he didn't dare let me see him smile. Now this sure enough made me mad! I soon caught up to Chancey when the log caught up in some brush.

"Now, Chancey, this is the way it is going to be," I gasped through clenched teeth. I pulled myself back on, with him trying to get out from under me.

This time it was four jumps and then open air; or was it three? I kind of landed on my knees this time. As soon as I could get back up, I got on again. I didn't know which of us would have the strongest will. What Chancey didn't know was that we had no other choice.

This time, I was able to hold on through all the bucking. It was kind of nice not to hit the ground again. When he finally stopped, I reached over to pat his neck. I shouldn't have done that. He threw me right over his head.

I didn't know if I could get back up again. That sure did hurt. It was while I lay there that something came to mind. I got up and went over and undid the rope from around the log. He had it all twisted and tangled up. When I had the rope loose, I fashioned a loop and went over and put it around his neck. He stood deathly still. I climbed on his back and loosened the rope on his neck so he could hardly feel it. He knew it was there, so as I nudged him with the halter in one hand and the rope in the other, he went right to Dutch without any problem.

I slid off his side and handed Dutch the rope around his neck. "Now if he starts to act up any, just tighten the rope around his neck and he will stop."

With Dutch on his back and me leading him on, we left the valley the way the deer had come into water. I hadn't seen the other side of the ridge, but I reasoned that if the deer could hide there, then it might be cover for one fine mule and us.

It was about as I expected, except the trail turned sharply up the ridge, staying in the thick scrub brush. It had been used often by deer, and now it would have man and mule tracks for anyone that might want to follow.

We kept up a steady pace. Chancey had no trouble matching my quick strides. It would have been nice to just get out on the valley floor and go as quickly as we could from place to place, but without horses we couldn't move fast enough across the open areas. Staying concealed was our best chance, maybe our only chance.

The sun was now up, and warm enough that the shade brought welcome rest. Dutch seemed to be doing fine. We hurried along as quickly as we could, wanting to put some distance between us and the pasture and water. I could see the valley opening up now; a high range of mountains backed it.

We walked all day without much stopping. I only paused when we came to some small clearing, just long enough to watch for anyone that might be coming. At one place, we spooked a large buck that went crashing down the mountainside until he found a new place to hide. Sometimes the trail would take us down and then turn back up into some steep sharp climbs, but Chancey was up to it all.

The sun had passed to the other side of the mountain and we were in the shade most of the time. I estimated that we had about three hours of daylight left. Our rest stops had been few as we tried to hurry all that we could, but the next time the game trail took us near the summit we stopped to get a drink. I passed the canteen to Dutch. While he was getting a drink, I slipped out two pieces of jerky from the slicker. We would need to find some water by nightfall if we could.

It was then that we noticed something in the far distance. It looked more like a dust-devil than anything else, but there was not a breath of wind anywhere. We concealed ourselves and waited to see what was coming up the valley floor.

There wasn't much for Chancey to eat, but he seemed to find some pickings under the trees and small brush. It was a poor exchange for the tall sweet grass that he had for his own the past few days. I told Dutch that he would have to pull the rope tight when the dust cloud got closer. We had our rifles out and ready just in case we were found out.

"Do you think it's Indians, Mexican cavalry, or bandits?" Dutch asked.

"I don't know what to think, but whoever it is won't be friendly."

In just a few minutes, we could make out some riders ahead of the main group. Before much longer, it was easy for us to see two scouts on their Indian ponies. They were ahead of a large raiding party of fifty or so braves, led by an Indian chief in full war paint, with his large feathered bonnet trailing behind. He was a fierce looking warrior, sitting proudly on top of a fine Appaloosa horse. This was an Apache raiding party, going back across the border. Some poor rancher had lost several of his horses, and maybe they wiped out the whole family. They seemed to be taking their time, maybe daring anyone to follow them.

When they were about even with us, the leader signaled for the main body to come to a stop. For a moment, we thought we had been discovered as he looked our way. We pulled way back into the brush and tightened the rope on Chancey's neck. We gripped our rifles as we looked at each other.

Not believing that they could see us, I peeked out through the small clearing under the thick brush. Then we heard rifle shots and the shouting of several of the Indians as the chief directed them toward the mountain. Our hearts nearly stopped. What was going to happen next?

I took another quick peek and looked back behind us to see what cover we might have for an attack. It didn't look good. The thickets would hold a hundred Apaches, and they could be down on us before we'd ever see them. My heart was racing now. We would be little match for them here.

Suddenly there was much shouting and cheering as the Indians retreated from the base of the mountain. The big buck that we had seen earlier hadn't been so fortunate as we were for the moment. The Indians soon had the animal on one of the horses that they had stolen and were on their way. No doubt that would be food for them that night.

As soon as we were sure that they were out of sight, we continued on our way. The trail was starting to go down a little bit now, and it was easier going. We didn't say anything, but only wanted to put as much distance between the Indians and us as we could. It was starting to get dark now, and we needed to find a place soon where we could spend the night.

The trail eventually led down into one of the largest little draws that we had seen, and we decided we would be safe there, at least for the night. When we finally reached the sandy bottom of the small canyon, Dutch got off the mule. He could hardly walk the first few steps that he tried, but his muscles loosened up as he continued.

Chancey seemed ready to get on with eating as he started nibbling on some of the small scrub oak brush. There was even an occasional clump of dried-out grass in the bottom of the creek. It would be here that we would tie him up. I went on up the dry streambed to see if the rain had left water holes.

I found the granite floor of the creek was showing up more. Just as I had hoped, one of the large rocks had a depression in it where a good supply of water had collected. I would need to bring Chancey up here in the morning to get him some water. I filled the canteen and went back to where Dutch was sitting quietly on the bank.

"Boy! That was close, wasn't it?"

"Yep! I don't want to get it any closer than that!" he said. "What if they go into that water hole and see all of the signs we left?"

"I don't know," I said. "I do know they know where that water hole is, and all of the rest of the drinking places around here. I wish that I could be just a little bit Apache and find all of the places to drink."

Chancey was already chomping away at the dry tall grass and everything else that he could reach within the twenty feet of rope. A mule was much better than a horse for finding something to eat. I checked the halter and the rope to see that all was still good and strong. I thought that maybe letting him drag that hardwood stump around might have weakened something, but the halter still held him fast.

The next thing we needed to do while we still had a little bit of light was check Dutch's wound. Dutch said he thought that he should walk more tomorrow and give his body a little bit of a workout, but when I pulled the bandage back to look underneath, I heard him take a sharp breath. I could see it was still bleeding a little bit; but at least it looked like it was starting to mend.

We would need to have a cold camp tonight. I brought out the last of the porcupine that we had cooked and we sat quietly eating our portions. We didn't take long to eat what we had, and it didn't fill us up like the first meal we had from it. We broke open the bones and sucked out the marrow. I made sure that Dutch got a little bit more than I did; he needed it more than me. Things were probably going to get even worse for food, and without a fire, we couldn't fix any biscuits or anything else. Maybe it was just as well; we would probably need that little bit of food later on.

We were both very tired. Dutch was soon fast asleep, and I knew he wasn't doing as well as he let on. I knew he didn't want to worry me. I seemed to hurt all over, more than any one place, from my riding and trouble with Chancey earlier that morning. I lay there wondering how many more days it would take to get to Sonoyta.. We had planned on going on to Arizipe but, without a map, we might miss both of them.

It seemed to take a while for me to go to sleep, but finally the body gave up over the mind and I dreamed about being back on our gold mine claim. It was so nice there, and we could get fresh game higher up in the hills when we needed it. Then I dreamed it had started to snow, like it does there in the high country. I couldn't get a fire started. Dutch was there and he couldn't get one going, either. We were both freezing from the chill of the night.

I was awakened and came to my feet when I heard Dutch cry out in his dreams. I was freezing cold, and I rubbed at my arms and legs trying to get the blood flowing. I could tell that Dutch was shivering and I pulled the slicker tight over him and lay down at his side. This made it some warmer for the both of us. I wondered how it could get so hot in the day and so cold in the night.

When I woke up a bit later, Dutch was shivering violently but also seemed to have a fever. There was no choice now; I must find something to build a fire and get him warm. I remembered seeing some sticks just a little ways down the wash. By the light of a half moon, I could see enough to travel

148

that short distance. I soon found what I was looking for, and also gathered some of the dry grass to kindle the fire.

I drew one of the matches from my hard leather container. We had both found out long ago to never go into the hills without some matches. I soon had the dry grass smoldering under the few sticks of wood that I'd found, and the blaze leaped quickly up the wood pieces. It should be hard for anyone to see a fire at this time of the morning. They would be more apt to smell it than see it. Even that didn't seem to matter too much right now. Getting warm was the most important thing that we needed do.

I built the fire as close to Dutch as I dared. He was moving around now and moaning some with his turning. I couldn't tell if he was full awake, but I rubbed his legs and back until the fire started giving off some good heat. I could see a few more chunks of wood now that the fire was burning higher and set out to fetch them closer.

I wished I had some good food to heat up and put into him. Instead, I poured some water into one of the pans we had and broke up some of the jerky into small chips. I noticed that we only had four pieces of jerky left; we sure needed to get more food soon. I added a little bit of salt and stirred some flour into the mix. How I wished that we might have some hot coffee, or maybe tea would be the best for him right now.

Someone had pointed out to me a bush that could be used to make tea. I didn't remember seeing any of those bushes around here, though. They probably only grew out on the plains. They called it Mormon tea. Some of that would sure be good right now. Heck, nearly anything would taste good about right now. I sure hoped this stuff that I was stirring together would be edible.

First light was showing up over the tall mountain range to the east. I reckoned we would have enough light to see a little bit in the next thirty minutes. I kept the fire burning and the stew cooking. I even borrowed some of the fat that I had along for tending to Dutch and put that in the pot, too. When it looked done, I set it aside to cool a bit.

I made my way back upstream above Chancey, and he hardly even moved. I wanted to get some fresh water for Dutch when he woke up.

When I got back, Dutch was sitting up by the fire with the slicker and saddle blanket pulled tight against him. His head was bowed toward the flame and I could imagine that he could hardly get enough of the heat to make him warm. He looked up when I got close.

"I just went up and got some fresh water. It would be good if you could drink the whole canteen full." I handed him the canteen. He opened up the slicker just enough to drink his fill. By this time the stew was just right, and we each drank from the pan.

It was good to feel it warm my insides. With all of the added things that I had thrown in, it was actually pretty good. Dutch didn't seem too hungry, but I told him he must eat and get some food into his body. He continued to drink slowly from the pan. He knew what I had said was right, so he drank more than he really wanted.

I left the pan sitting close to the fire so it wouldn't get too cold before we had finished it. If Dutch were getting warmed up now, it might be better not to put any more wood on the fire. But sometimes there is nothing that will take the place of a good fire, and this seemed to be one of those times. So I reached over and put on the last of the sticks I'd gathered.

Dutch had stopped his shivering now. With the warm food inside of him, he seemed to feel a little bit better.

"Better clean her up! It's going to be another long day," I said. Any other time, we could both have eaten more. But, without saying anything, we knew that the food and the water were both going to be scarce for a while.

I told Dutch that I was going up to the hole in the rock with Chancey and get him a good drink. I decided to stay with him for a few minutes and let him graze on some of the dry grass in the streambed. Sometimes when he ate a little bit, he would drink again. I had a feeling that he would need to have all of the water he could stand, because we might not find another rainwater well like this again. There sure wasn't going to be any water in the valley we now had to cross, and maybe not on the other side either. Maybe it didn't even rain over there. I didn't want to think of all of the problems that might happen. I had enough on my hands worrying about Dutch.

It wasn't too long before Chancey had cleaned out all of the quick grass bites around the water hole. Then he was back getting another drink as if he had read my mind. I walked him back to where Dutch was. The last of the coals was just about out, and it was getting lighter by the minute. I was really sore this morning from tangling with Chancey, but I tried not to let Dutch see me walking gingerly along. I could tell in the early light that he was feeling much worse than I was.

"How are you doing this morning?" I asked.

"Oh, about like yesterday, I guess."

I looked at him and could imagine that he felt pretty tough. But what choices did we have?

"Do you want to move on, or spend another day here?"

"I guess we can keep going if you're ready. We will never get to where we are going if we don't," he replied.

I knew he had to muster up about all of the strength and spirit that he had to make it look good to me. If we stayed another day, we would be taking a chance that the Indians would come along our trail by evening, maybe sooner. They would be able to travel a lot faster than we did, and even the worst tracker in the bunch could follow our trail. On the other hand, if we stayed another day, we would have water for the

151

time being, and maybe Dutch could get to feeling better. After considering everything for a while, I finally decided what we should do.

"Dutch, what I think is this. We best lay low here until evening. If we get lucky and the Indians don't come on us, then we can light out at night and try to make it to the other side of the valley while it is dark. If we try crossing in the daylight, once we are out in the open we could be seen for miles from either end of the valley. We must do this at night." I hoped my words would convince him that I didn't see we had much choice.

"What do you think our chances are of the raiding party coming back on our trail?" he asked.

"Well partner, we just have to hope for some luck," I said.

It was settled then. I made sure that Dutch drank every last bit of the stew. I told him to get as much rest as he could possibly get. Then I went to tie Chancey up to some new feeding ground. After that, I went looking for a point back along the trail where I could see if any of the Indians would be coming our way. If they did, I would get back to where Dutch was as fast as I could, and we would make our stand.

We had both had a lot of practice with the pistol and the rifle. We learned early on to save our ammunition and try to hit whatever we shot at. Sometimes Dutch would surprise me with some of the shots he was able to make, and sometimes I would get the best of him. I guess we were about equal with that.

By the time the sun finally peeked over the tall mountain range, I had found a good spot where I could see for some distance in several directions. It felt nice to have the early morning warmth today. It made me forget how hot it had been yesterday, and how thirsty we'd been. I had left the canteen with Dutch so he would have plenty of water. I thought that I could go without for the day since I wasn't moving around much. It would probably be my stomach that would complain first about going without.

I hadn't liked either of our choices very much, but as I looked out over the big valley floor I knew I had been right. We would certainly have been seen if we were trying to cross right now. As far as I could see, the valley floor looked pretty smooth. I couldn't let that fool me, though. I was sure there were some gullies out there, and maybe even a few deep canyons that couldn't be seen from here. Shoot! There might be a thousand Indians, bandits and Mexican soldiers between us and the other side, I thought.

I turned my head to watch our back trail, where the Indians had surely camped near the water hole we'd left yesterday. I thought about the fix we still might be in if they decided to follow our tracks. Whatever came, we would just have to do our best. If our luck held out through the day, we would race to the other side tonight under cover of darkness.

# Chapter 12

The sounds of the morning were beginning. I saw a squirrel or pack rat dart across the trail on the far end. The mansanita were thick in that area and I guess the rodent found plenty to do and to eat. I made myself about as comfortable as I could get behind the nearest thicket, where I was still able to see out through a small hole down the back trail.

I continued my vigil but could see nothing else moving. The sun was warming everything up, and I guessed that it must be somewhere around ten o'clock. Dutch would probably be finding some shade about now.

As I sat watching and waiting, I wondered whether we would find any gold here in Mexico. Some experienced miners had told us that most of the gold here was found in veins, along with the sand. Instead of getting gold out of the river and its banks with gold pans or sluice boxes, we would need to explore the sand a little bit, looking for ore-rich veins. This would be something new for us, but we would learn fast enough. One thing for sure; we knew what gold looked like! I touched the three nuggets hidden inside my belt in a small cloth wrap.

I waited about three more hours with no sign of pursuit. Boy, that ornery mule Chancey had sure put a hurting on me! I just couldn't find any place that was comfortable for too long, but I dared not move very far. I had to stay where I could see the trail down below.

It was getting on toward evening now, and I thought that this was about the time that the Indians would show up, if they were coming. It startled me when I saw a bird fly out of the thicket down the trail. Something had caused it to move, because it flew away instead of just flitting across to another bush. I tightened the grip on my rifle and wondered if my cramped legs would carry me quickly and silently to warn my partner. I watched and I waited. My mouth was dry and I thought about how much I'd like to have a big drink of water. I probably couldn't even muster up any spit. I pulled off one of the oak leaves and chewed on that for a while. It seemed to help.

I did not take my eyes off the spot that the bird had left. Something had made it fly, but I could hear no sound. Then suddenly in the trail stood two deer, a mother and a small one. At first I thought it was about the best thing that I could have hoped for. But then I wondered if the deer could have been spooked by Indians coming up the trail. Why else would they be up and moving around at this time of day? It was too early for them to be feeding, but how could I know for sure?

The deer left the trail now and vanished into the thick brush. I waited, thinking with every breath that the Indians would be coming behind the deer. I listened with my head cocked that way, but could hear nothing. In fact, the only sound was the pounding of my heart.

An hour went by this way. Even though the sun had gone to the other side of the ridge, I found myself wringing wet with sweat. I brushed it away with the back of my hand, never taking my eyes off the trail. I could probably get at least two or three if I had to make a stand here, but they would soon vanish into the brush and then we would be found out.

Another hour came and went, and nothing showed up. I had kept my eyes keen on the trail and didn't allow my thoughts to go for very long. Each minute that I waited there without them coming improved our chances. I finally decided that they must not be coming, and it was time for me to slide back along the trail and get things ready before it got too dark.

I turned and started my retreat back to camp, feeling pretty good about this, when I saw something moving out on the big mesa. Whatever it was, it stirred up the dust and seemed to be moving quickly. From this high up on the hillside,

155

I would be able to make it out soon. Then I must get back down and warn Dutch to put the rope tight on Chancey's neck again.

I waited until I was sure what was coming our way. It turned out to be a large Mexican patrol of about forty cavalry and horse packs, probably hot in pursuit of the Indian raiding party. Two front scouts were about one fourth of a mile in the lead. It was easy for them to follow the raiding party's tracks. With the open space, they didn't need to worry about ambush. The sun glistened from their sabers, and even from this distance I could see that they had come to fight.

I moved quickly now, wanting to get back to Dutch before they came even with our camp. He was standing up with his gun in hand when he heard me coming. I told him of the large patrol who appeared to be after the Indians. Maybe this was why they decided not to come after us when they found our tracks at the water hole.

I told him that we would need to get as ready as we could for a night crossing of the valley floor. He said that he was ready, so I moved Chancey back up to the pool of water. I drained the canteen, then filled it up and took it back to Dutch. Some food would have tasted good about now, but neither of us mentioned anything about it. We had only four pieces of jerky left now, and we would just have to go the night without any more. I told Dutch to drink all that he could hold. It would be a long ways to the next water hole.

As I came back from filling the canteen once more, I wished that we could take some more of that good water with us. My eyes fell on the rain slicker that Dutch had been sleeping in, and I wondered if the thing would hold any water. It kept the rain out; maybe it could be used to keep water in. It was worth a try, so I went back up to the water hole one last time to try it out. I knew Dutch would miss having it during the night, but maybe with us moving and the warmth of Chancey he would be all right.

I pushed the slicker into the pool and, holding the sleeves and the tail, pulled it back up to see if the water would stay in or seep out. I tied the arms together and pulled the tail and neck together, making a carrying sling of sorts. It seemed to hold the water cache, and I even had a pretty good handle to hold on to. This might be real handy before we found our next water.

Dutch was ready to go when I returned with the two or three gallons of water I had trapped in the rain slicker. We loaded up quickly and started down the trail. It would be dark soon and we needed to hurry. If we didn't make it down to the valley floor by the time it was dark, we might never be able to get through the many thickets that covered the hillside.

We stayed on the trail as long as it kept getting closer to the bottom. We didn't have to worry about the party of Mexicans; they would be long past us before we finally got out in the open. When the trail turned parallel to the hill and stopped going down, we decided to take the next draw that led down. At times it was so choked up with brush that we would have to go around it some, but we soon found ourselves out on the flat valley floor. We got there just in time, for within a few minutes it was too dark to see.

During the long hours of keeping watch, I had plotted our course across the valley. With any luck, I hoped to wind up just below the tallest peak by the time morning came. We would be feeling our way along until the half moon came up, so it would be slow going at first. I hoped that we would not fall into some big hole or encounter other dangers that we could not see. I heard that horses and mules have a pretty good sense of things, and I had fashioned a handhold in Chancey's lead rope.

After the rugged hillside, the valley floor seemed smooth and easy walking. Now I worried that we might get turned around out in the open and not go in exactly the right direction. It wouldn't take much to miss the mark in the night. I wished that I had studied the map out better before it was stolen. The moon would be up in about four hours, and then I could get a fix on the mountains for sure. Until then, we would go with the best guess, keep up the pace in the general direction, and hope that we would come to Sonoyta sooner or later. Just the thought that the darkness would keep us safe from prying eyes as we crossed this flat made me feel better.

After the long day of keeping watch, it felt good to get out on the flat and leg it off. The pullover boots I'd bought at Stewart's trading post had been put to the test the past few days. I was glad that he talked me into getting them. "They are made to stay with a man," he'd said, "and if you keep them greased up, you could wade right through a foot of water and never get your feet wet." When we bought them, I never thought that I'd be walking half way across Mexico. Now, at the rate we were going, if wouldn't be many miles before I worked all of the soreness out of me.

I knew that Dutch was half asleep in the saddle and that he was just awake enough to hang on. There was no reason to talk even if we felt like it. Sound would travel for miles in this kind of place. Nothing seemed to travel farther than talk, except rifle fire.

I changed hands many times, never letting go of Chancey's lead rope. I knew if I fell down, I would probably lose all of the water that I was carrying. I wondered how such a little bit of water could be so heavy. But then, I thought, it must not be leaking much to still be this heavy.

The stars were full out now, and that helped us pick our way along. It seemed like we had been on the move for hours, but it had probably been no more than three or four. A brightness along the eastern horizon signaled that the moon would be up in less than an hour. As I studied its location, I realized that we must have drifted down the valley a ways. I quickly made a correction in our travel. We sure didn't need to do any extra walking tonight! I wondered if we might be getting close to half way. When the moon came out, I would be able to judge our position. We could also pick up the pace some when we had the advantage of more light.

In the dark we never knew when it was that we crossed over the raiding party's tracks or those of the cavalry who followed. This valley had been a busy place today, but we were content to pass by unnoticed and let them have at each other.

The only sounds in the desert came from Chancey's steady plodding. I wondered what we could ever have done without him. That struck me as funny, since I usually wondered what we were going to do with him. Somehow he seemed to sense our problems now, and no one would ever guess that he had been so ornery a couple of days ago. He had taken to carrying Dutch with ease. It was good that he was so big and strong, for there would be little rest tonight.

The night air had a chill to it, but it seemed refreshing because of the effort of walking and carrying the water cache. Before long my thirst grew strong enough to convince me that maybe we should just stop for a quick break to get a drink. We wouldn't be able to have much, but it would sure help us. When I whispered as much to Dutch, he answered in a quiet voice, "Let's have a short drink of water."

He pulled the canteen down and we had a quick drink. I wanted to give Chancey a drink, too, but decided against untying the coat. I poured a small bit of water into the palm of my hand and rubbed his mouth with it. He licked my hand for more, but there wouldn't be any more for now.

When the moon finally came up over the mountains, I could see we had been drifting to the south of where we wanted to go. I felt bad, because we had lost some precious time going a little bit the wrong way. But at least it looked like we might be about half of the way to the far mountain range.

This was a good thing, since half of the night was now gone. We could go faster now that the valley was bathed in the moonlight.

I planned that we would not stop again until we reached the other side of the large valley floor. Hour after hour went by, and the moon eventually disappeared over the hills and out of sight. It was full dark again, and I supposed it would be about three hours before daylight. I knew we must be getting closer to our destination, but everything ahead of us was swallowed up in the darkness. I had to trust the course corrections I'd made in the moonlight and hope that the early dawn would bring the welcome sight of the mountains at our feet.

It was hard to tell how long we had traveled since the moon had gone down. Whenever I found myself wanting to rest for a few minutes, I checked with Chancey. He was not breathing too hard, just plugging right along. So we continued our steady march without any more stopping. From somewhere in the vicinity of the mountains I could hear a coyote call. Then came the answering cries from others that seemed to be near by. They were our fellow travelers through the long night.

We were still going along good when Chancey suddenly yanked back on the reins. I had just finished changing hands with the water pouch, and he almost jerked it out of my hands. Chancey had come to a dead stop. I couldn't see anything or hear anything, but this brought Dutch full awake.

He whispered, "What is it? What is going on with this darned mule?"

I could only guess from what the mule was doing. I found a small stick on the ground and gave it a throw forward. It seemed to take a long while before I could hear it hit down below. This sent a chill up my back. Chancey had just saved us from walking right over the edge of a steep canyon cliff! We moved back a few steps and Dutch got down off the mule. We

160

would have to wait for some light before we could even think about going on.

I told Dutch that I had considered the possibility of running across something like this the day before. There was no way that we could have seen this from the other side. We had no idea how deep it was or how far across. We would just have to wait it out until daylight. Hopefully we would be able to get out of sight early so we might be away from prying eyes.

"It makes sense to me, Dutch, that we are close to the mountain range. This kind of a cliff ought to be close to the hills."

I threw another chunk of wood forward trying to get some idea what it was like ahead of us. It only confirmed that we weren't going any further in the dark, and that Chancey had probably saved our lives. I helped Dutch find a level place where we could stretch out for some rest. Then I pulled the saddle off the mule. He deserved all of the rest that he could get, too. How I would have liked to reward him with an armload of that soft green grass from the meadow! He wasn't worrying about food too much, though. He just rolled around on the ground for a few minutes and then lay still.

We all dozed fitfully, waiting for the first rays of light to show up in the east. As dawn approached, we began to trace the outline of the canyon rim. It was pretty good sized and we could just make out the far bank. As details of the canyon gradually came in sight, we tried to measure the depth in the early light. We saw that we had nearly gone straight over a drop off of at least seventy feet, and we still couldn't see the bottom. We wouldn't have been able to survive such a fall without serious damage.

We looked for a way that we could cross the canyon from this particular place. It was important that we get out of sight as quickly as possible. Chancey was back up on his feet, and I soon had him saddled. I just couldn't help stopping long enough to pat that mule on the neck, and he put his big head and mouth under my arm for more.

"You don't think that he has had a change of heart?" I said. I vowed I would never say and think hard things about him again. Even about the old aches that he had given me, which had returned since our rest.

We started walking along the canyon rim to find a place where we could get down into the bottom. The thick brush kept us choosing our path carefully. It took several minutes before we found a place which looked like it went all the way down. It was steep, but would keep us out of sight.

We had some tough going in the brush that grew along the sides of the canyon. It had not rained in this part of the country for a while from the look of the trees and brush. It had been some time since they had a drink. At some time or other, though, a flood had raged high up against the canyon walls and had left the telltale signs of driftwood a good ways higher than where we were riding right now.

It was good and light by the time we reached the bottom of the wash. We could see the tracks of coyotes and other small game who tried to survive in this dry land, but there were no cattle or horse tracks in the floor of the canyon. I felt a lot safer now than I had for the past day or so. We could not be seen from above now, so we had made it safely across the big valley. The only danger now would come from someone coming up the canyon, or someone who just happened to look over from the other side.

I thought my arms were going to come off as I kept switching hands back and forth to carry the water. I would have bet that Chancey could drink all of that up and look for more. Since we didn't need to hurry quite so fast, I took time to scan the walls of the canyon for any indication that we were close to a water hole. We hadn't gone far before I noticed that the cliffs seemed to be getting a little bit lower. This was good

162

and bad all at the same time: Good that we didn't see anything coming our way that would give us cause to hide or fight; bad that we hadn't come upon any natural spring where horses or cattle would come across the canyon.

I could see several places now where we might be able to get out on the other side of the canyon. The next time we came to a small patch of shade, I helped Dutch down so he could sit on the broken limb of an oak tree. Chancey immediately began nibbling at the leaves trying to find just a small nice bite. Handing Dutch the water, I scrambled up one of the openings to see what was there.

I peeked over the top carefully so that it would be hard for anyone or anything to see me. The mountains were close by, as I had expected, but ahead of us was some pretty rough terrain. I could see more dips and arroyos like the one we were in, outlined with a thick growth of scrub oak. There were even some larger oak trees above the rim of the canyon that we were in. It would have been a great find, if only they had been in their nut season. There was a little grass up on the bank, so I gathered some and took back a handful for Chancey. He seemed to smile at me as he eagerly took it from my hand.

I gave Dutch a report on what I'd seen. He wasn't any more eager than I was to hike up and down through any more of these sharp canyons, especially if we were going to travel only by late evening and early morning. We sure couldn't take a chance on Chancey pulling us back again in the dark of the night. I said that I thought we needed to work our way south anyway. That made it easy to decide that we should do our traveling farther away from the mountains. We determined that we would go on down the canyon we were in for another two or three miles.

After about an hour we were ready to set up camp and get some rest. Whispering, we planned to stop just around the next bend of the canyon so that we would have the advantage of seeing what was down beyond. We hadn't quite made it that far when we noticed something had crossed the canyon floor up ahead. We immediately took cover and waited and listened. Dutch had the rope tight around Chancey's neck. I signaled him to wait while I went on ahead to see what it was that had torn up the floor of the canyon in its crossing.

I inched my way down along the east side of the canyon wall, stopping every so often to listen and look. The tracks seemed to have gone into the canyon and right on through. When I squatted down for a better look, I could see the prints of several horseshoes, plainly visible in the hard dirt. I noticed something else, too. They were traveling with maybe two or three mules.

It must have been bandits. It looked like it had been a couple of days since they had crossed. That would have been about right. They were probably the bunch that had jumped us back at the water hole.

I hurried back to tell Dutch what I had found. This seemed to make him mad all over again, and he started using some of his pet German names for them. I reminded him they could have left us with nothing, so maybe we shouldn't forget that. We talked of how nice it would be right about now to have our pack animals and our two horses back once again.

After considering everything for a few minutes, I said, "I think they may be headed for a town or a ranch to sell our stuff! If they are, they know where the water holes are. So, if we follow their tracks, we might do the right thing."

Dutch couldn't remember the map any more than I could, since we had mainly picked out the landmarks that marked the next water hole. He seemed satisfied that this might be our best chance. We both knew we wouldn't last too long out here without water. I looked at the water bag that I had been carrying and it still looked like it had most of the water in it.

We went ahead with our plan to stop beyond the turn in the canyon. We had a clear view to the south a few hundred yards before it turned again and was out of sight. And we were out of sight of the place the bandits had crossed, in case others came the same way. This would make a good place to stop and rest.

"I think that I should stir up some of those fixings that we had yesterday. This canyon should hide the smoke pretty well. If we use some of the real dry stuff, there will hardly be any smoke at all. Besides, there are just some things we have to do."

I wasn't long in stirring up the food we would be having. I used two of the last four pieces of jerky, and we emptied the canteen into the kettle to give it the necessary juice. Dutch was to stir it a little and not let it get too hot while I climbed higher up on the banks of the canyon to pull up some of the tall dry grass. I would gather as much of it as I could for Chancey, since he would not be able to find much by himself near our camp. I was really beginning to like that mule, and I could see that the bandits had done us a real favor when they left him for us.

As I was pulling up some grass, thinking about how nice it would be if we had something more to put in the pot, a rabbit unexpectedly appeared not twenty feet away. I took a throw at him, but missed him by a mile. He even let me have another throw before he ran away. Though I normally was pretty good with throwing rocks, I guess I was trying too hard.

When I got back to our camp, Dutch was sitting by the fire and tending the pot. He hadn't talked too much lately, and we hadn't looked at his thigh either for a while. I could see some dampness in the area of his wound. Maybe he was hurting a little bit more than he let on.

He tried to cheer me up as I came with the armload of grass and put it at Chancey's feet. The mule seemed real anxious to get it down. I knew he had to be about as thirsty as we were. I patted his neck and went back to where Dutch was sitting.

The stew was hot and he passed it over to me. I ate some and passed it back to him. We kept that up until it was gone. Each time I tried to take a little less without him knowing it. I didn't want to say anything to him, but I had been worried ever since the night he'd had the fever and chills, one right behind the other. Then he'd had to drink a lot of water to try and cool off. If that happened again, it would be hard on our meager supply of water.

Dutch helped me untie the water pouch. I dipped the canteen into the water and filled it. I said we should put some water in the kettle and give Chancey a small drink, too. He could smell the water and put his head right into the half filled pot. He wasn't long in getting all of the water out. I could hear his long tongue licking the kettle. I knew it wasn't much, but we had to make do.

The sun was hot and nearly overhead now. We tried to keep in the shade as much as we could. It wouldn't do to get too hot and thirsty. I could tell by looking at my partner that the loss of blood and the strain of traveling for the past few days had taken their toll on him. He didn't have good color and he was still too quiet. I was afraid that the dust, or worse, had gotten to the wound. It was time to get the wrapping off.

I told Dutch, "Here! Let me have a looksee at your leg."

He dropped his pants so that I could get to the bandage. I lifted the edges in hopes that the porcupine fat had worked well enough that the scab wouldn't come off, too. It seemed to come off most of the way, but the seeping part held fast to the bandage. A few traces of new red blood had shown up again. I wondered if we would ever get time for the thing to heal.

Warning Dutch to grit his teeth, I gave it a good jerk

166

and exposed the wound. Sure enough, it looked like it was infected. I wished we had some medicine to put on it to make him better. I could see that I needed to clean him up some. Carefully, I poured some of our precious water into the other pot we had so I could wash the wound. When I had done the best that I could, I told him to leave his pants pulled down so that the air and the sun might help.

I washed out the bandage in the pan and hung it on a nearby scrub oak to dry. In the desert air, it would be good and dry before we needed to put it on again. I made sure the water pouch was tucked away in the shade, so it wouldn't accidentally spill. The morning fixings felt good and we had another drink from the canteen. Then I told Dutch I would take the first watch and would wake him before too long for his turn.

The sun was full out now, and the warm air, the warm meal, and the long hours of walking through the valley were taking their toll. I had to keep moving around some to keep from falling asleep. To pass the time, I wondered about the tracks that we had seen. Were they really our horses and mules? It might be; but then it might also have been just a couple of fur traders or prospectors like us. Using mules to pack with was fairly common, even here in Mexico. And there was no way to know just how many were in the party. The one sure thing was, whoever it was knew exactly where they were going and didn't mess around much in getting there.

I wondered how many times they had ridden out in the open. Riders on horseback could travel fast, even across places like this. They could travel during daylight and keep their sights on the place they were heading for. I wished we could do that. I needed to get Dutch to a doctor so he could get help soon. That was the most important thing I could do right now. Our plan to leave just about sundown and follow the trail of those that had passed seemed like the next best thing.

We took turns resting and watching through the long afternoon. I don't remember going to sleep there under that big oak tree. Dutch gave me a push and it brought me full awake. I think that I could have slept for a week. It was already cooling off and the sun had just about disappeared. It was time to move on.

Chancey was up looking for something to eat, and I wished I had gotten up sooner so I could fetch him another handful of grass or two. I noticed that Dutch was able to pull himself on the mule after we wrapped the bandage and put some of the fat on the wound again. That fat was beginning to smell pretty bad, but we would just have to get along.

We made our way back up to where the horses had crossed the canyon. We climbed up the other side, and I stopped just as we reached the top to look back out across the valley floor. I could see no movement. Chancey spotted a few clumps of tall dry grass and just had to have some. We thought that he did, too, and gave him a couple of minutes before we were on our way.

The trail that the horses left was easy to follow and we made good time. The farther we went, the more concealed we were from the big valley. It would take some accident for anyone to see us now from behind. What we needed to worry more about now were the things in front.

I reckoned that we traveled about two hours before we had to find a place to stop and unload before it got too dark to see anything. We decided we would rest until the moon came out, then travel on as far as we could before it dropped behind the mountain peaks. We took a drink just before we started out again, and filled the canteen. The water pouch was a lot lighter now. We didn't give Chancey any more and felt a little bit bad about that, but Chancey might be able to get a few nibbles in the morning, and the dew would be good for him.

Knowing that the moonlight wouldn't last very long, I

tried to pick up the pace to get as much distance as I could. The ground was harder here and had many little sharp washes to cross. It was much slower going than out on the big flat. We knew we had been right not to try to travel it in the darkness.

We finally stopped with just a speck of the moon still visible in the west. Dutch slipped off the mule and began to take the saddle and gear off and tie him up. It looked like a good place for a few hours rest and Chancey was even able to find a few nibbles where we had tied him.

Even with walking in the cool night, we found ourselves thirsty, and of course still hungry. We decided to eat the last two pieces of jerky that we had left. I gave Dutch the largest one, but there was very little difference in the two. We dared not have any fire tonight. I hoped that Dutch would be warm enough with just the small saddle blanket. There was no time to look at his wound or do anything for it. We were both soon asleep and so was Chancey. Only the lonesome call of the coyote came across the silence of the night.

I woke up every hour or so. I could hear Dutch in deep troubled sleep and wondered if he was warm enough. I ached from the distance that we had covered in the past few days. I guessed that most of it was from carrying the water. I rubbed at my shoulders and arms. Yep! They hurt, sure enough. I thought about the precious water. I was certain we had used over half of it. We had to find water today.

I didn't know how long I had been sleeping, but as the first light appeared I dared not go to sleep again. We didn't want to miss the early morning going. I wanted to check Dutch's wound, but it would have to wait until our next rest stop. Whenever that might be, I knew it must be where there was water.

We soon had ourselves ready to travel, and Chancey was ready, too. I noticed that he didn't even need the rope to be tight around his neck for Dutch to get on and off. We started down the trail, straining to see our way. We had to go slowly at first, but when it got a little lighter, we speeded up. By sun up, we were coming into some rolling hills. There were lots of ups and downs, but it wasn't too steep.

We were moving along at a good pace when suddenly something caught my eye on the next ridge. I immediately gave a warning sign and pulled Dutch and the mule into the nearest thicket. I motioned for Dutch to stay hidden while I scouted ahead for a closer look. What I saw was something that I never expected.

Over on the other side of the ridge was a mean-looking Texas longhorn bull. I could hardly believe it out here in the middle of nowhere. I watched, but he was the only one that I could see. I made my way back to Dutch and told him the news.

"We must be close to water!" I told him. "Maybe it will be within the next four or five miles. Maybe we will come to a ranch house or some other type of settlement!"

"I don't know," Dutch said. "I have heard of those animals going for days just living off the dew. They are a tough bunch."

Well, if worse came to worst, we could take our chances and shoot the big fellow. So we continued to make our way on down the trail. The big critter saw us coming. When he was convinced what we were, he turned and ran through the bushes like a deer. Boy, would he be hard to round up! We searched for more signs of cattle or riders, but his tracks were about the only ones we could see. We still felt hopeful, anyway. He had to come from somewhere.

# Chapter 13

I was walking ahead, keeping a lookout for danger, when I suddenly recognized the distinctive sound of a rattlesnake. Almost at the same instant, Chancey gave an awful sound. He yanked the rope right out of my hand, pulling me down along with the water pouch. I looked up to see Dutch flying downhill through the air. The snake must have struck at Chancey, or worse, bit him.

I ran towards Dutch, giving a wide berth to the snake, which was moving away from all of the commotion. My poor partner had landed right on a pile of rocks on the side of his wound. I heard him let out a big groan. He couldn't get up, but only rolled with the pain. Chancey had run off a few yards and was looking back at us.

I finally reached Dutch and asked, "How bad is it?"

He answered through clenched teeth, "It ain't so." He tried to sit up now on the pile of rocks. "Just let me sit here a while and go see about the mule."

Now this could be a challenge all of its own. If the rattler had hit Chancey, he would be in no mood to let me get close to him. As I looked back up the trail, I could see the last of the water running out of the pouch. That meant that our canteen of water was the only water we had left, and it was still tied on the pack. I faced a real dilemma. If he started to run away, would I would have to shoot him to get the water?

I had my rifle in my hands. I didn't want to scare him any by pointing the rifle. Maybe I could talk my way up to him. I sure didn't want to shoot him; I just couldn't stand the thought! He had saved our lives more than once already. Besides, I kind of liked the hardhead. But how could we survive without that water? If he decided to run, would I let him go?

I moved slowly toward Chancey as he stood looking warily at me. The halter rope was down by his feet. I looked

171

for something to coax him with, but there was no grass around. I would just have to act like I had something for him to eat. I was talking to him all of the way, trying to get him to calm down, telling him that everything was all right. He backed up a few steps at my approach, and I wondered what he was going to do. I guess he wondered what he was going to do, too.

That big rattler had sure done his damage with us. He had let me walk right by him without a rattle. Then when Chancey came along he set to rattling and scared the mule nearly to death. I still didn't know whether the snake had also struck him.

Chancey was still backing up, but I could tell that I was gaining on him slowly. The lead rope was stretched out toward me. Was I fast enough to run and jump on it? I stood still for a minute and offered out my closed hand to him. How could he know that there wasn't something good to eat in it? I moved ever closer, close enough to nearly grab the rope.

It was then that I saw something in Chancey that I hadn't seen since our workout down in the meadow. He laid both ears back along his neck. I knew what that meant, so I made my jump for the rope. I was able to get hold of it just as he turned to run. Suddenly he was dragging and bucking and pulling me through the brush. I tried to get to my feet, but finally thought it best to just hold on. When he stopped at last, I wrapped the rope around my waist and snubbed him down.

"Now why did you go and do a fool thing like that?"

I retied the loop and slid the rope back over his neck. I rubbed him and talked to him. We went back to where Dutch was still sitting and watching all of this. I tied Chancey securely to some brush. I went to look for the rattlesnake, but he had crawled in a hole or something. I picked up the water pouch and climbed down to my partner with it. I untied it and we both licked at the last wetness where the water had been.

"Do you think that Chancey got struck by the snake?" I

asked.

"I don't know," he replied. "I was as much surprised as the mule, and then I was flying through the air. You were right about one thing, that mule sure can buck."

It hurt too much for him to laugh or even smile. But he wanted to say something. I could now see that he had skinned up one wrist and elbow from the landing, too.

"Do you think you can stand up?"

"Give me a hand and I'll give 'er a try," he said. It was with some effort and a little bit of wincing that he was able to stand on his feet.

"I don't think anything is broke," he said, "but it sure is tender about everywhere." He hobbled back to the mule and just stood hanging onto the saddle. "What do you think we should do now?" he asked. "Do you think we should press on, or rest for a spell?"

I looked at him and the mule. Our chances were not too good right now. I wondered if Dutch could even stand riding. We couldn't stay here for long. Our water would soon be gone, and we wouldn't be any closer to help.

"If you can stand it, I think we had better move on. We might find some water that way."

Dutch wasn't able to get aboard the mule by himself. I knew how stubborn he usually was, and when he let me help him up without an argument, I saw that the last few weeks had really taken a toll on him. The loss of blood and the wear and tear of our journey had taken all of the fight out of him. He didn't look like the young scrapper that I had known around the gold fields. He was having a hard time just hanging onto the saddle yoke. As for Chancey, if the rattlesnake bit him, he didn't seem to show any signs of it.

We traveled more slowly now. When we had gone about three miles, I noticed more cow tracks crossing the trail. The tracks crossed over those of the riders we'd been following and were probably made yesterday. I kept a sharp lookout to see if I could spot any of the critters, but the brush was pretty thick and we didn't get many open looks. I could see a high dark mountain range, though, several miles to our east. Dry grass was getting more plentiful and the land seemed to be changing from the desert that we had crossed. We even saw some deer tracks. That meant there had to be water close by somewhere.

Gradually it looked like the country was opening up some ahead. I knew Dutch must need a drink of water pretty bad by now, so I stopped and extended the canteen to him. He was kind of groggy. As I watched him, he seemed to be a little out of his head. He was able to drink some of the water. That seemed to wake him up some, but he had the look of fever. I was afraid that the infection had spread and things were worse. Definitely things were worse.

I poured a small amount of water into my hand and let Chancey lick it up. I didn't drink any myself, although I sure wanted to. The sun was bearing down now and we needed to find some shade to wait it out for a while.

We found a good thicket where the oaks were a little bit taller and would give us more cover. It wasn't long before Dutch was sleeping fitfully and shivering there in the shade. I took the saddle blanket, still warm from the ride, and carefully covered him. Then I stretched the slicker over the top. That seemed to warm him up enough that he stopped shaking.

Chancey was checking the browse by testing the length of the lead rope. There seemed to be a little more grass here and it looked like it had rained more often. I tried chewing on some leaves, but they didn't taste too good. I lay down, too, and was soon asleep beside my partner. In my dreams, I walked beside one of the clear mountain streams that we had crossed in our travels through California. If only I could bend down and get a drink . . .

We must have slept for three or four hours, judging by the position of the sun when I awoke. My body felt rested, but I was intensely thirsty. I was still half dreaming about that mountain stream when I heard a distant sound that had a familiar ring. A horse or horses must be coming our way! I woke Dutch up and slipped over to tighten the rope on Chancey's neck. Whoever it was would be passing close by, moving in the same direction we had been traveling. Had someone been tracking us? I could see that Dutch was trying to come awake. He had his rifle on his lap, but he wouldn't be too much help if we got into a gunfight.

When we had left the trail to find a place to rest, we had backtracked a bit to climb high enough to get the shade that we had wanted. This was probably a good thing, because we would be behind anyone who saw our tracks leaving the main trail. We had moved off into the brush enough that it would be difficult for anyone to see us. Now a rider was passing the very place we had left the trail. I could hear the creak of his saddle as the rider slowed and then stopped to listen.

I listened and looked, but no one came into view at the place where we could see the trail. It seemed like hours, but was only a few minutes before I could hear movement again. It sounded like only one horse, but maybe it would be a lead scout with a big bunch close behind. I had my rifle ready when the horse and rider came into view. I could see that it was a vaquero, or Mexican cowboy. He had his gun out, too. I could shoot him easy from where I was, but he didn't look like a gun fighter.

In Spanish, I asked him to stop. At the sound of my voice, he whirled around to face me. When I asked him if he was a cowboy, he said he was. I then walked down toward him and lowered my gun. I asked him if there was a ranch house where we could get some help for my friend.

The cowboy must have thought the German accent of my meager Spanish was amusing, because he smiled frequently as we tried to understand one another. He said the ranch he came from was big and had many vaqueros there. It was about six hours ride away. He told us that he was out checking the range for strays when he came across all of the tracks. He was worried that someone was after their cattle, so he was following the trail to see what was happening.

He offered to ride with us and show us the way to get to the ranch. The thought of getting some help was so good that we packed up Chancey and were soon speeding along. The Mexican didn't have to wait on us! We followed him down the trail for a ways until it split in several directions. He waved us onto the right trail, then turned off and headed south. We drank the last of the water out of the canteen and hurried along.

The ranch came into view about an hour before sundown. It was a beautiful sight! Up against the tallest of the south mountains, the large ranch house and buildings were cupped into the side of the mountain like a large bowl held in a giant's hand. Big red rocks outlined the sky, and the thick juniper and pine trees had been cut away to make room for the house. The large green meadow leading up to the buildings was filled with corrals and cattle, and many horses were grazing in the valley. A large clear stream of water meandered down the slope and out of sight to the south. Near the water, the grass was even higher and greener than in the rest of the meadow.

"See there, Chancey, I told you it might be this way." He seemed to pick up his pace at the smell of the water and all of that good pasture.

When we came to the first place that Chancey could drink, he took a long time to get his fill. Then he kind of shook himself as if to shake the long ride off him. He immediately had to have some of that tall green grass, and would have gone for a second helping if we hadn't pushed him along toward the main buildings.

I could see that this was no small outfit. The house was large and spacious. Out front were some hitching rails where many horses could be tied up. There seemed to be three large barns. In one of them, someone was working the anvil, hammering and fixing shoes for the horses. Several stopped what they were doing to watch our approach. I guessed we looked quite a sight, all except Chancey, who strutted right up to the hitching post with Dutch.

A slight-built Mexican in his middle years came out to greet us. He was clean-shaven except for a small mustache, and his clothes were of good quality. One could see that either he was the boss or the owner or both. He graciously welcomed us to his ranch and told us that his name was Luis Ortega. When he shook my hand, I could feel the firm grip of much hard work. He was obviously not one to sit by and let others do the work. I liked that about him right away.

I introduced Dutch and myself and asked Señor Ortega if he would help us. Upon seeing Dutch's weakened condition, he quickly gave some orders to those in the house to come and help with him. When I told him that we had a little money and could pay for his help, he held up his hand in protest and said, "No, no, señor!" He said that he would make room for us in one of the near bunkhouses, and the men he had summoned carefully helped Dutch dismount and head that way. I followed along and stored our gear in the bunkhouse. Then I let Chancey out in the pasture with the other animals.

There was a spring right by the corner of the house that had been rocked up for some distance before it flowed on down to the larger stream. I thought that I had better not dirty up the fresh spring water, so I went further downstream to wash the trail off me as best I could. When I returned and sat down wearily on the front porch, Mr. Ortega had food brought to me there and sent some more in to Dutch in the bunkhouse. I was reminded of the beggar who came to Stewart's who hadn't eaten for three days. He must have been just about as hungry as we were right now.

I couldn't help but feel amazed to have entered this nice, lush valley. It wasn't too many miles ride back west when I had wondered if we would ever find any water. I told Mr. Ortega that it was the most beautiful ranch and valley that I had ever seen. He seemed pleased with my comments, but insisted that I call him Luis. He told me that the ranch had been in his family for many years. He had grown up here and learned ranching from his father. He introduced us to his wife, Elisa, and his children. His oldest son, Lollo, was about our age. They all made us feel welcome in every way, and we were grateful for their hospitality.

Luis told me we were welcome to stay as long as we needed to rest from our ordeal. He said that the medicines he had should start to make Dutch feel better soon. If they didn't, he would send for the doctor in Moctezuma, which was about a day and a half ride each way. It was then that I realized that we had passed our two first stops altogether. We were miles and miles from where we had planned to go. When I mentioned this to Luis, he confirmed to me that we had gone too far north and passed them on our way here.

As I ate, I told Luis about the bandits who had taken everything from us. I told him of Dutch yelling some bad things in German, and how the leader had stopped, cut Chancey out, and said, "I leave you something." This caught my host's attention, and he asked me to describe the leader. I told him he was a big man with cartridge belts wrapped over each shoulder. He wore a large black hat and had a heavy beard and black mustache.

"Boracho," he said, nodding his head. "I know him from your description. Some say that his mother was German and he came from down near the gulf. He and his bunch have come in and stolen cattle from us before. They roam the hills at will and the patrols are not able to do anything about it. They are a bad bunch, and you are lucky to be alive! But, I am afraid that your horses and mules are forever gone."

Sleeping in the bunkhouse was a luxury after the places we were used to camping for the night. Knowing we were safe put my mind at rest, and I guess my body's need for rest just took over. I slept deeply without any dreams to trouble me. If Dutch made sounds during the night, I didn't hear him. It was good to have a full night's sleep.

Morning came early on the ranch, and I could hear the wrangling of horses as the cowboys got ready for their riding chores. Dutch was still sleeping soundly, so he must have rested well, too. I hoped that he was going to feel better this morning.

I had asked Mr. Ortega if I could help with anything while Dutch was recuperating. He had said that I could go along with Pedro, the cowboy who had shown us the way to the ranch. He was riding back up to try to find that stray bull and drive him down closer to the rest of the cattle. Pedro caught one of the good ranch horses for me, and I helped with the saddle and gear. We took our rifles with us, along with some extra water out of the cool clear spring by the house.

I thought this was about the best water that I had ever had, and there was plenty of it. As a matter of fact, the whole meadow seemed to have a plentiful water supply going underground through it, because it was nice and green with grass. It was easy to see why Mr. Ortega's parents had chosen this spot to settle in. It seemed an ideal place for a ranch.

Pedro indicated that it was time to eat before we went on our way, and we joined the others in a big serving and eating room next to the main house. There was more food there than I had dreamed of. It was real cowboy cooking, with fresh meat and biscuits and all of the trimmings. I knew that I ate more than I should have, to be going riding right away, but I just couldn't seem to get enough. We even packed a small amount of food to take with us because Pedro said it might be late before we could get that big bull moving in the right direction.

Breakfast was soon over and the dozen or so hands that were there for the meal began to file out of the cookhouse. We started on our way just as the light was starting to appear in the east. I followed Pedro back through the hills, thinking that even this land looked better with rest and good food. We certainly made better time going than we had coming.

It felt good to be riding and not walking all of the time. I was pretty good at walking, but my feet were sore from the days past. Ortega had given me some salve to rub on them and they seemed to feel better now. The horse Pedro had picked out for me was sure-footed. I could tell he was used to being ridden through the brush. He was probably trained to cut cattle, too, as most ranch horses were. Riding him would give me some good experience.

After we got into the high country, Pedro warned me to keep my eyes open. We would need to be alert, for we might come upon anything at any time. He said that the Apaches sometimes raided their herd, too, and they wouldn't be likely to give them back without a fight.

A few hours later, I recognized a familiar trail, a little bit to the west of where I first saw Pedro. He stopped and listened more now, and watched for any movement. We continued to backtrack to the place where I had last seen the large bull. Finally I was able to point out the ridge where I first spotted the stray.

It didn't take too long to find the tracks of the bull, and Pedro set out following them through the brush. When he got to an area that was choked thick with brush, he motioned me around the outside of the thicket. He whispered that the steer was probably half wild from being out on the range and would spook easily. He would wait right here to see if the bull came out the way he'd gone in.

I took a westerly direction around the place. In a little while I was on the backside of the huge draw. I couldn't see very far into the brush and continued to circle it. I was pretty well convinced that the big fellow was still in there, or I would have seen his tracks coming out the other side.

I decided to climb a little bit higher up on the side of the canyon wall so I could see down into the brush. My horse responded and moved sharply up the slope. It was here that I really understood how sure-footed my horse was. I could take him almost anywhere. When the trail leveled off some, I would be able to look straight down into the thicket.

It was a good place to see from, and I spotted the bull pretty well out in the middle of the brush pile. He had heard our approach and was looking straight at me. There was a clearing right in the middle, but it would nearly tear me off the horse to try and get down to him. The leather chaps that they had given me that morning would sure come in handy in this brush.

While I was sitting there on the horse trying to decide how I could best scare the critter out toward Pedro, my eye caught sight of something else. I slipped off my horse so I could pull him around into the next thicket of brush. I had no way to let Pedro know that there was someone coming unless I could get where I could see him. I left my horse tied and worked my way up higher. I could see Pedro just about where I had left him. Whoever was coming would be going close by him.

I waved my arms until he finally saw me up on the side of the hill. Sensing that something was wrong, he gave a quick wave, then got off his horse and led it up into the thicker bushes. He knew that I wouldn't be up there without my horse if I didn't need to be.

I untied my horse and moved back the way that I had come. All I could see was some dust and movement coming our way, but I could not stay up high enough to see what it was and still be close enough to Pedro to be of any help. We would just have to let the bull stay where he was for the time being and worry about helping each other. I planned to get down close to the trail so I could see who was coming. Then, if need be, I could give some fire power to help Pedro out.

In a few minutes, I could make out the sounds of cattle coming our way. Rustlers more than likely, I thought. I wished that we had time to go get some help, but they would be long gone before we could get down to the ranch and back.

I picked a place where I would be concealed and still have a good look at the trail. I could hear the cattle moving closer now. I could see two openings in the trail, one to the east and one just ahead of me. I would get a good look at them before they got even with us. They would be coming between Pedro and me in the next five minutes.

As I sat motionless on the horse, I wondered if he would react to me shooting off him if I needed to. I had never shot anyone before, but I had learned to protect what was mine. In this case, it was Ortega's. I was sure they would shoot to get me, so I had better make the first one or two shots count. My hand was gripping the rifle, and I was glad I had a good number of shells to go with it. It would be nice if I didn't have to use very many.

Just as I anticipated, within minutes a rider came into view. His rifle was cradled in his arms, and he was scouting out the trail ahead of him. He was Mexican, and had his hat pulled down so he could see out from under in the morning sun. He was mean looking, and I thought he would shoot me in an instant if he saw me. He was followed by two more riders. Behind them came about twenty-five head of cattle. I guessed that there might be three or four more riders bringing up the drag; I could hear them as they pushed the cattle quickly up the trail.

It was then that I heard a shot ring out. It was followed by another, and then another. I saw one of the rustlers fall from his horse and the horse began to run away. When the lead bandit got even with me, I fired one shot at him. He flew off the saddle from the force of the bullet. The last bandit who had been riding in front moved into the brush and started firing at Pedro. The cows began to scatter. The remaining thieves decided to take cover until they could decide how many of us were shooting at them. They had lost two of their three front scouts; and maybe Pedro had even hit the third.

I stayed where I was. They didn't know for sure where I was as I had only taken one shot. They did know that they would be between our guns if they continued on this way.

I had dismounted now and tied my horse to the brush. I didn't hear any more shooting and wondered if they might have gotten Pedro. I waited for several minutes, not daring to show myself. I couldn't tell if they had given up, or if they were slipping around in the brush trying to get up on us. I took a drink from the canteen and patted the horse's neck to keep him calm.

I waited and watched for nearly an hour. Nothing moved that I could see or hear. I finally decided to slip back across the trail and see if I could find Pedro. I whistled and waited. Finally he whistled back from about the same area that I had last seen him.

I walked back, got my horse and mounted up. I moved cautiously around the Mexican that I had shot. I could see his horse grazing a ways down the trail. Pedro came out into the clearing and held up two fingers. When I got close enough to talk to him, he said he had hit two.

I told him I'd got one, too. He went to check the one

that I shot. He said he didn't know any of them. We loaded them on the one horse that was left behind. Then we rounded up the cattle and headed them straight for the ranch house. All the way there we kept a sharp lookout, not wanting to run into an ambush ourselves.

It was getting dark before we came out onto the meadow. Pedro knew the way, and as soon as the cattle were there we turned our horses straight for the corral. A large barking dog signaled our arrival, and several men came out to meet us. When we got close enough to them, Pedro yelled out something in rapid Spanish. They came forward to take the packhorse and the three who were tied over the saddle. Pedro was still telling them what happened when Luis came out of the main ranch house. He had someone bring a lantern. Another held up the heads of the rustlers in its light.

"Not anyone I have ever seen before." He instructed four men to take them down the meadow a ways and bury them. "Scatter any extra dirt and move the grass back on top of the graves," he said, as they went off into the night. "Don't leave any marker."

I thought about what he said. It would seem that Luis Ortega was pretty well able to take care of anything that came his way. His men followed his orders with no questions. I wondered how many times they had done this before. I had noticed a small cemetery up on the hill on the south side of the house. It was neat and well kept. Later I learned that it was mostly for family, but that some of the old timers had been remembered there, too. It was only for those with honor.

I went over to our bunkhouse to see what kind of a day Dutch had. He was dressed and sitting on the side of the bed when I came in. He said he was feeling a lot better. They had washed all of his clothes and changed the bandage twice that day.

I could tell he was feeling a lot better and I asked,

"Who took the clothes off you and washed them? I know it is the women that have been taking care of you, so which one pulled them off when you was feeling so bad?"

It was the first time that I had seen the old smile on him for a long time.

"You know that big one? Why, she yanked them right off me without even blinking an eye! She is big enough that you don't want to talk back to her."

I smiled and had to agree with that. I told him of the cattle thieves we had come across that day. We still didn't get the bull pushed back toward the ranch, but I had seen him.

A few days later I happened to tell Luis about the Indian raiding party and the Mexican patrol that seemed to be after them. He had me describe exactly where I had been and then asked several questions about the direction in which I had seen the smoke. He had not heard of any raids, but said it sounded like they may have raided the Vargas Ranch.

He was very concerned. Apparently the Ortega and Vargas families were good friends. Luis told me that they often got together for some fun activities each year. They would sometimes combine their two herds for the long cattle drive to market. He said that he even went down to help out once when Vargas was thrown from a horse and couldn't ride for a while. Luis had taken some of his hands and gone down to help with the roundup. Now he decided to send Pedro and me over to their place to see what had happened. He told me he wished that I had told him sooner.

The next morning we left early with a packhorse and two extra mounts. We would need to make as much haste as we could to check on the neighbors. It would take about a day and a half to reach the ranch. We might meet some outriders from the Vargas Ranch before that.

# Chapter 14

We rode south through the big meadow and then turned west a little bit. The hills were more rolling and the brush not quite so thick as up in the higher country. The grazing seemed to be pretty good, a sign that they had rain pretty often down in this part of the land. We kept up a steady pace most of the day before we changed mounts.

Our instructions from Luis were to help the Vargas family if they needed it. If they needed more help than we could give, we were to send word back to him. Pedro didn't say too much as we rode along, just that he knew Vargas wouldn't give up any of his horses or cattle without a fight. He only hoped the thieves hadn't taken lives.

With fresh horses under us and with the packhorse loaded light, we pushed on until dark. Pedro found us a good camp with a small flowing stream. After putting the hobbles on the horses, we gave them a chance to eat a small amount of grain that we had brought. I wondered where they got grain for the animals and asked Pedro. He said they brought it from Moctezuma, down on the Sonora River, when the wagons made a trip.

Next we set about cooking some food for ourselves. The coffee pot was the first thing to go on and we had brought plenty of food for the few days that we would be gone. We even brought some handmade tortillas from the ranch.

Morning came early and we were anxious to check on the Vargas ranch. We still hadn't seen any sign of other riders, but it looked like it might have rained the past few days and probably washed out any tracks. We even started to see a few cattle, but we still couldn't see any riders. Pedro felt that something must really be wrong. He pointed out a distant hill to me and said that we should be able to see the Vargas ranch when we got over that ridge. It looked about an hour away.

When we rode over the top of the hill and looked out at the valley below, we weren't ready for the sight below. It looked like all of the buildings had been burned to the ground except for the ranch house. There were no horses in the corral or in the pasture. We could only see dead animals around the field and yard, and many died close to the house. We put our mounts into a gallop toward the standing ranch house.

Someone saw us coming and came out into the yard to watch us. He yelled back into the house. Three or four more came out now with rifles in their hands. When they recognized Pedro, they became more relaxed. One vaquero related everything that happened.

The attack had come just a little after sundown and just before dark. The Indians had been waiting there, hidden in the trees and brush, until most of the vaqueros had gone to the bunkhouses. The main party had waited until a few scouts set fire to the buildings. Then they attacked before the men knew they were here.

The Vargas family had been fortunate to all survive the attack. Mr. Vargas was shot in the leg. Fortunately the bullet hadn't hit any bone, but the wound would be tender for some time. His wife and daughter, as well as the women who worked in the main house and their children, were safe.

They had lost eight men in their battle with the Indians; many of them lost their lives in the bunkhouses before any warning shots were sounded. When the battle started and the outbuildings were set on fire, some of the hands retreated back into the main house to protect it. Only six of his hands had survived, and one of them had been shot in the arm. The entire attack only lasted a few minutes.

When the Indians ran off all of the horses in the corral, they then made their escape. About ten Indians had been killed in the attack, but a few of their comrades returned and took their bodies away in the night.

One vaquero who had been out on the range before the fight occurred was sent to the mission to get word to the Mexican patrol. They came quickly but didn't take time to bury any of the dead for fear that they wouldn't be able to catch up with the raiding party. They only paused to doctor the ones who had been hurt. Then they were on their way. When I told them that my partner Dutch and I had seen the Indians and the patrol going up the big valley, with just a few hours between, they were glad to hear it.

We gave the two extra horses that we had brought along to two of the ranch hands so that they could go out and round up some more horses. With this help they were able to find nine and bring them back into the corral. Then Pedro and I helped drag the dead animals away from the ranch. The men who had been killed in the fight had already been buried. The evidence was the fresh mounds that we could see.

We slept outside that night with the other hands. It was good to be out watching the moon come up. It was full now, and seemed to bring a peace on this burned and damaged ranch. Yes ,they were lucky to have anything left at all, even their lives, I thought just before sleep came.

They posted guards throughout the night and I was to take my turn, which came kind of early. I got up and went to the front porch to watch and wait. Many thoughts were going through my mind. I used to think that California was a tough and wild place, but a man might get into more trouble in one day here than in a month there.

I wondered how Dutch was doing. If he were here and could see that oldest Vargas girl who Pedro had said was sixteen, he would sure get all prettied up. She was a good looker with that long black hair and friendly smile. Yep! That would make Dutch get to feeling better right away. He liked the ladies anyway, and one like this, well, who knows?

Both her mother and father were handsome people,

too. They reminded me a lot of the Ortega family. Maybe Lollo Ortega had his eye on this Catrina Vargas. Wouldn't blame him any if he did.

I was surprised that the Vargas ranch was so similar to the Ortega ranch. It too had a large valley and stream, and the ranch house seemed nestled in the hand of the mountain range for protection from the winds and thieves. In fact, both looked as though their owners had carved out a mountain to put their ranch houses in. The way they backed up against the mountains made for good defense. We wouldn't need to worry about any large group coming in from that direction. The trees had been cleared from behind the house, leaving only the shale of the exposed mountain in the back. Someone could walk over the high ridges, but would have trouble getting close to the house without being seen or heard.

My watch lasted until daylight. I was supposed to see that everyone was awake and ready to get going, but before long I knew that I wouldn't need to wake up anyone. As I walked around, I could hear them up moving around. I had seen a light in the main ranch house about an hour earlier. Someone was up cooking and getting things ready. I could already smell the coffee and the bacon frying. I was hungry.

Before the raid, the cowhands always went to eat at the cook shack. Since it had been burned down with the other outbuildings, the ranch house and the outside were being used. Mr. Vargas assigned the morning chores from his chair in the living room. He sat with his injured leg propped up on a low stool that was placed in front of the fireplace. The happy sound of the crackling fire filled the room. Its warmth was just as welcoming after the chill of the night before. I asked Mr. Vargas what I could do to help out.

I tried to pay attention but was distracted. His daughter, Catrina, was helping with the breakfast and she seemed even more beautiful than I had thought yesterday. I tried to rub the hair back from my fresh-washed face. She looked at me and smiled.

"More coffee, Yacob?" she asked. Her smile made me forget what she was asking. I muttered my thanks back to her and she went on around the table with the large coffee pot.

It sure looked to me like she had given me an extra big smile and stayed a little bit longer filling my cup. I had not dared to look up at her soft eyes as she leaned against my elbow. Now I could see her looking back at me across the table.

Flustered, I returned to my food. Like most of the rest of the hands, I ate a healthy breakfast. I had learned that out here a person could never know when he might have to go a long way without food or water. Most of the group had left the table now, and it was time to be up and on my way. It was good to get outside now and away with my thoughts.

Maybe Catrina was trying to be friendly. Yes, that was probably it. I would never do anything to hurt my relationship with Mr. Ortega, after all his kindness. I knew he was a good friend to the Vargas family, so I had better be careful to keep my thoughts to myself.

Mr. Vargas had said that if Pedro and I could stay three or four days, we could help him check on his herd. The cattle thieves or the Indians might have run off some of his stock. We had told him that we had been instructed to help wherever we could, so the next three days were filled with trips to check out the range. I was given a different partner about every day, and sent off in a different direction. I enjoyed the chance to ride the ranch and see new country.

I was on watch at the main house porch before daylight another day when I heard the screen door open behind me.

"Coffee, Yacob?" came the soft voice. It was Catrina.

I had tried not to watch her too much when I ate in the house, but I couldn't keep my eyes off her. This seemed to make her smile at me more. I know I must have turned a bright

190

red many times. It reminded me of the time that my partner had seen the gold nuggets in the stream and dived into the water to come up with one. He got so excited that his face turned beet red. I hoped the others weren't noticing any of this red face stuff on me, but I caught Mr. Vargas looking at me with a small smile once.

I turned to face the beautiful girl. There she was. It was just the two of us. She knew I would be on watch on the front porch and we would be alone. She asked if I wanted a cup of coffee.

My heart was racing when I finally answered, "Yes."

"Can we sit in the swing and talk a few minutes?" she asked. "You can still keep watch from there."

She sat down and I sat close to her. It wasn't because I wanted to, but because she didn't leave me too much room to sit.

"Tell me about yourself, Yacob," she asked.

I didn't know just where to start. I only wanted to tell of the things that were good, so she could see the best of me.

I told her about Dutch, who was wounded and resting over at the Ortega ranch. Both of us were the same age, sixteen. I told her how we had become partners in the gold mining in California and had done real well until the bandits robbed us of all that we had. Then we escaped across a big valley at night to finally find Pedro, who took us to the Ortega ranch.

"And what about your mom and dad?"

"Well, my father died in the war in Germany. He was a soldier. Life was hard for my mother and little sisters. I worked at what jobs I could find, but we often had to go without food at times."

She was silent as I told her this. I could not get her to understand how far away Germany was, but she had seen the ocean three different times. I explained to her that Germany was a long, long way across the water. It was many, many days by boat. I had hidden aboard one of the boats coming to America. Many German people had come from there and some had helped me to get to California.

My partner, Dutch, was about the only family that I had. And he was my very best friend. We came to Mexico to search for gold. Some traders had told us this was probably a good place for gold miners to come. I told her that we had made a lot of money and we could have bought a nice ranch here in Mexico or some other place, but now it was all gone.

She sat in silence for a few minutes. I wondered if I had said what she wanted to hear. I hoped that I hadn't told her anything to make her not like me. It was getting light now and she came quickly to her feet without a word. I stood up with her close and she kissed me on the cheek and was gone.


*It was going to be a great day, Catrina thought as she waited for the men to come in for breakfast. She didn't get to see many young men her age, not any that she had any interest in. And now here was a handsome foreigner.*

*She knew she couldn't quite pronounce his name correctly, even after being sent to the mission school to learn English. She hoped he didn't mind. She wondered what this shy Yacob would be thinking right about now.*

*He was a handsome young man, with that curly yellow hair and deeply tanned face. He was something to look at with all of those curls and deep blue eyes. He was well built, about six foot tall, and ever so bashful. She could tell that he was used to hard work, and now he had told her that he was used to taking care of himself, too.*

*She knew she would be expected to find someone on her own before too long, and she might just as well see about this Yacob. It all seemed kind of sudden, but in this land there*

*was not a lot of time to sit around and think of what you should
have done, or whom you should have pursued.*

*To think how bold she had become! She had never done
something like this before, but she just couldn't seem to keep
away from the kiss. How surprised he was when she did that!
She hoped that it would not make him run away. She had
sensed that, when she got too close, he wanted to do just that.*

*He would be coming in soon, and she would see if he
would look at her more.*


As the hired hands seated themselves at the large
breakfast table, I held back a little. I wanted to be in the
middle of the group, so I would not be sitting on an end. But as
everyone settled onto the benches, I found myself at the end
once again.

Food was brought in to the table and the men started
their usual conversation. In the background were the sounds of
the forks on the metal pans and the metal coffee cups hitting
the table. It was really noisy in here, I thought. But, since I
wanted to see Catrina again, and didn't want to be too obvious
about it, all of this commotion might be good.

Suddenly she came sailing through the door right
toward me, carrying a large plate of food to be passed around.
She seemed to float, more than walk. It was like a sound heard
out in the mountains, a peaceful sound that I couldn't quite
identify. As I watched her move on around the table, I
wondered if her feet were really touching the ground. She
quickly moved from one to the other, calling them all by name.

She moved over against me and set the food down. She
was as close as she had been that morning when she moved
forward and gave me a kiss. I could feel the redness coming
into my face, and wished that I hadn't come in for breakfast.
It felt like everyone was looking in my direction, even though I
knew they were all mostly busy with eating.

Then Catrina's father glanced down toward the two of us for a moment. I quickly picked up my knife and fork and began to eat.

Breakfast was over quickly, and then I slipped outside in the fresh new morning dawn. I tried to think of other things. Heck! I couldn't let this be happening to me! Now, my partner, Dutch, well, he was another story. He would have been courting the young lady at every chance. But when she was close to me, I had a hard time thinking straight. I had to get back in control of things, but there was something telling me to spend more time with her. I wondered what she did when she was not helping with the cooking. I knew there was always much to do around the ranch each day, but she must do something else once in a while.

The next day as we were checking over our assigned section of the range, we found four more horses that had been injured and needed some doctoring. This caused us to return to the ranch much earlier than usual. We had just finished putting the horses into the corral, and I was about to pull the saddle off my horse, when I noticed someone far out in the south pasture. I could tell even from such a distance that it was Catrina.

I decided not to take the saddle off, but tightened the cinch back up and rode toward her. I wondered what excuse I would make to come over and see her. Maybe I could tell her that it was still pretty dangerous around here. There could be some of those Apaches lying around out there. Or, I could just tell her that I was worried about her and came out to see if she was all right. That would probably be the best thing to say, even if it wasn't exactly true.

She stopped and waited when she recognized me coming toward her. In a few minutes, with my horse loping along, I soon closed the distance to where she was.

"Yacob," she said, "you are home early."

I didn't want to seem too forward and decided to stick with my plan of telling her that she should be careful out here. The ranch house was still in view at the upper end of the long meadow, and I really couldn't see any place that anyone could hide, but I wanted to make her think that is why I came out to see her.

She seemed to fill out her riding outfit in all of the right places, and I became a little bit embarrassed with that thought, too. It was not like I had never been with the dance hall women, but this was different. I had never seen anyone so beautiful. I wondered why some of the young Mexicans hadn't ridden a hundred miles or so and courted her. A hundred miles wouldn't be much, if she gave them one of those smiles like she was giving me right now.

"Have you ever been on down the stream where it comes into that mountain? My father said that as more streams come into it, it gets deep down there. There are many fish farther down. Will you take me there, Yacob?"

"I don't know. It could be really dangerous, and we might not have time to get there and back home before dark."

"Please, Yacob, take me there."

She was right by my side. As I looked down into those soft eyes and warm smile, what could I say?

The sun would be up for about four more hours. If we kept a steady pace, we should be down to the mountain that she had pointed to and headed back home before dark. It would be close. I was wondering if I should have promised her that I would take her that far. After all, it hadn't been that many days since the Indian attack.

I had never had the assignment to come down the valley in this direction, so it would be new to me, too. The valley seemed to be narrowing down some, and we saw some cattle from time to time. I guess the vaqueros had tried to get them closer to the ranch since the attack, but with the shortage of cowhands, there were many strays. I made note of this and planned on reporting it when we returned.

We were about halfway to the mountain now, and the brush and trees were growing more thickly here. Big juniper trees mixed with pine came almost down to the meadow, with a few large oak trees popping in occasionally on the west side. But the east side of the valley was mostly tall grass. Higher up on the bank the oak thickets seemed to act like a border. From the large trees that extended up the mountain, I could see that we were going to be there pretty soon. We crossed little streams that gave strength to the larger main stream.

Catrina was something to see in her riding outfit. Her long black hair flowed out from under a small black hat. The silver band around it seemed to set off the turquoise necklace that she wore. Her skin was fair and soft, and she moved as one with her horse. Every time I looked at her, she would be looking at me. This made me feel a little bit awkward.

Catrina would talk once in a while, but just being with her was all that I could think of. No wonder she made it hard to talk when she was close to me. I kind of forgot what it was that I wanted to say. I had never had trouble like that before. I sometimes stumbled in my Spanish to her, so she tried to help by mixing in her mission school English.

As we got closer to our destination, the brush around the stream seem to get thicker. The water was channeled up more, heading for the mountain. We had to move a little higher up on the hill to make it easier going.

After a bit I told her we had better not talk much as sound carries out here in the open. We didn't want to invite anyone else. I had to whisper that in her ear.

She whispered back, "Okay, Yacob," as she pressed my hand.

From higher up on the ridge, we could look down at the fast moving stream as it gathered speed in its rush down the mountain. The water was crystal clear until the rush over the rocky face of the mountain created white rapids which fell into the large pool below. It was a beautiful place. No wonder she wanted to go see it.

The climb down to the pool was easier than I had expected. We got off our horses, tying them under one of the large pine trees, and walked over to look into the water. I picked up a small oak leaf and pitched it out into the dark pool. A large rainbow fish came up and took it from the surface. Catrina just laughed and clapped her hands at what she had seen. There sure were a lot of fish here. We sat down in the grass on the bank above the pool, and she moved in at my left side.

"Yacob, when will you have to leave?" she asked.

"I don't know, but if we don't get some word back to Mr. Ortega soon, he will come or send more men to see where we are."

"He will come," she said. "He will come if you don't let him know soon. That is the kind of neighbor he is. We help each other often. Out here you have to help each other."

I told her that was the way it should be. I told her my partner was like that, and I was like that.

That was the first time that I had thought much about Dutch for the past three or four days. Maybe it was a good thing to leave your partner home once in a while. Besides, I didn't like the thought that he might be the one here with her now instead of me.

Her hand felt soft and smooth in mine now and she was close as she said, "Yacob, I hope you don't think bad of me for stealing a kiss the other night. I want you to know that I am a nice girl, but I just couldn't seem to help it."

I didn't know what to say. She was so close and warm, and we were alone. I probably did the worst thing that anyone could do when I blurted out, "I don't know much about girls. I guess I don't know much about these feelings that I have had."

I felt my face flush again. This brought an even bigger smile from her.

"That's what I like about you, Yacob. I can tell you have a tender heart. I have had other young men come by and see me from time to time. Some of them work in the mission. There are other ranches about four days' ride from here, where they have many men. Some of them are young. They usually come to our gathering each year when we all try to get together. We spend the whole day at one of the ranches with music, food and dancing. Do you like to dance, Yacob?"

I told her that I never had much chance to learn to dance. The barroom women were more interested in other things.

"Will you dance with me, Yacob? Will you dance with me here? I will show you."

I stood up with her as we moved back away from the edge of the pool and she whispered a sweet song in my ear. I was clumsy at first while I watched her small boots move with the sound. It was then that I remembered she had been humming the same sweet sounds as she moved around the breakfast table.

It made my heart race to have her so close and feel her near me. I don't know how long we danced, but then we stopped and kissed. I had never felt anything like that before. She put her head on my shoulder and whispered in my ear.

"Yacob, I have never found anyone before like you," she breathed as she squeezed me tight.

I ran my fingers through her long black hair. I guessed this must be what Heaven was like. At least it felt like what the preacher who came through the camps had described. I didn't want this moment to end.

It was while we were there holding each other close

that I saw movement that brought me quickly back to reality. I put my hand over Catrina's mouth and pulled her to the ground. I pointed up stream.

A band of about twelve Indians was just coming out of the brush to the west and heading down to the stream.

We moved quietly back into the brush where our horses were tied and caught the nostrils of each of them so they wouldn't give us away. I slipped the rifle out of the scabbard and thought how foolish I had been to be this far away from the ranch with Catrina..

I peeked out from behind the thicket that we were in to see if they had seen us. It looked like they hadn't, as they began to water their horses. And we could hear them about one half mile up stream.

I wondered what they were going to do. What we were going to do? It would be dark in a couple of hours. From the look of things, they planned to spend the night right there. I watched as they posted a scout back along the way that they had come. He was soon out of sight. I guess with the clearing and the stream to the east, they felt pretty good that no one would slip up on them from that direction.

I looked at Catrina and she looked back at me. She didn't have that warm smile that she had earlier, but she still held my arm close. It was good that she had brought a rifle along, too. She assured me that she knew how to use it if necessary.

The hill that we were on sloped back to the east. I saw some possibility of going that way to get around the raiding party, especially since they had not posted a sentry across the stream. I told Catrina to stay close to me and we would see if we could walk our horses around them. I told her that if we ever got into sight of the long valley back home, and they started after us, to ride for the ranch without looking back.

I could see the concern in her eyes, and wondered at

the thoughts that might be going through her head. Had her father ever told her to not be taken alive by the Apache? I didn't like to think of the stories that I had heard of what they did to women captives.

I told her to do exactly what I said: move very quietly and be ready for anything.

The brush seemed to afford us enough cover to get off the mountain and into the lower places. The sun had set and it was going to get dark early. I hoped that we would have time enough to get around their camp before it got too dark. I never was one to find a way in the dark without a few falls.

We had moved around by now, and it appeared that we were about even with them. If we could get on past them about one half mile, I would feel better about being able to get out of here. I knew we could never outrun them all of the way to the ranch down the long meadow unless we got a good start on them.

We tried to move quickly forward and stay out of sight, but we had to backtrack often. I wondered if Catrina was getting tired of walking. Maybe she wished that she had never seen this "Yacob." I looked back at her and she gave me a little nod, as if to say that everything was fine.

My mind was racing as I tried to see our way out of this. If we could climb just a little bit higher, we should be able to see the valley soon. I could make it out now. It would be dark soon; maybe we should wait at the edge of the meadow until it got dark enough to ride. I could see the meadow now, just a few feet ahead of us. We should wait in the trees along the bank for it to get dark. I must not let anything happen to her.

# Chapter 15

*Vargas had seen the sun going down and began to question the ranch hands about whether they had seen Catrina. He found out Jacob was missing, too. The vaquero who had helped Jacob bring in the injured horses said that he had seen Jacob ride down the pasture to meet up with Catrina.*

*"They were still riding away from the ranch house when I last saw them," he said, pointing down the pasture.*

*Mr. Vargas was getting sterner as he ordered about half of the hands to saddle up their horses and the other half to stay and guard the ranch. Though dinner had been set out on the long tables outside, and everyone was ready to eat, only those who were to remain behind would take time to eat now. The riders took some lanterns out of the house in case they needed them. Each man wondered what they might find. Catrina was special to all of them.*

*No one had heard any rifle shots, and that was good; but maybe they had been jumped and didn't have time to get their rifles out. All kinds of things were going through Vargas's mind as he set the pace by putting his horse into a gallop down toward the setting sun.*

It was time to move quietly out onto the pasture. Catrina was still close by my side, but I had to forget all about the feelings that I'd had earlier. There was only one thing to focus on now.

We walked the horses out onto the meadow. It was good to feel the grass under my feet. I wondered how I would ever explain what had happened to Mr. Vargas. And even worse, what would Luis Ortega think of me?

"I think we should walk the horses for a few more minutes before we mount up. And then," I told her, "we must go slowly. One of the horses could step in a hole or something in the dark and could fall."

Finally the darkness was complete. I could not see Catrina, but felt her by my side as I whispered the direction to mount up. Once we were astride, we could just let the horses find their way home. Surely the Indians couldn't see us, if we couldn't see each other. It would be a long way back in the dark, but the darkness was welcome.


*It wasn't long before the riders from the Vargas ranch came to the last place that the two had been seen. The tracks were plain in the soft meadow as the two headed on down toward the mountain in the south. Most of the riders had been down to where the stream boxed up against the mountain. As they started for the place, Señor Vargas remembered how Catrina had asked him if she could go there sometime. He had told her that it was just too far for her to go. Things weren't much different in those days. A man had to keep his stock close to the ranch and in sight. And he didn't want his daughter's rides to take her out of sight of the ranch. She needed to watch where she was going all of the time.*

*He remembered how she had been when she was little. She wanted to go riding every chance she had. She loved the outdoors and the ranch. When she was four he had given her a young colt. It was hers to keep and take care of. He remembered how an Indian raiding party had caught some of the horses out on the pasture and made away with them. One of the horses was her very own Chico. It broke her heart when they were unable to recapture the horses, although they did get some of the Indians. The rest escaped with the herd. Catrina had learned early in life that sometimes her father couldn't make everything better. She cried through the night.*

*Señor Vargas was secretly proud that Catrina had learned to ride as well as any of the hands. She was equally*

*good with the rifle. Why, last year, she had won the shooting
contest over at Ortega's ranch. She beat all of the men with
the rifle. Some of the old timers just shook their heads and
laughed.*

*Yes, if she had a chance with her rifle, she sure would
make them think twice about shooting. And, he reminded
himself, she was tough inside, though the soft look of her
fooled many. At the same time, she was also soft and sweet
inside and would make someone a fine wife one day. There
wasn't much she couldn't do, from cooking to taking care of
the injured.*

*He had noticed that she had taken a fancy to this
young, good-looking Jacob fellow. He was so shy; she might
never get very far with him. But he had a feeling that Jacob
would be able to handle most problems. He had watched him
work the past few days, and had heard the stories of what he
had been through before that. Yes, honor would he have when
it came to his Catrina. He had always been a pretty good judge
of people. He felt that this Jacob had some good qualities;
honor was one of them.*

*With those thoughts and the darkness coming down he
put his horse again into a gallop and so did the rest of his men.
He must find her soon, or no telling what would happen.*


Catrina and I kept our horses at a steady walk back to
the ranch. It was hard to tell just how far or how fast we were
going, but the horses just kept on with the reins loose. I would
have to see that they got an extra ration of grain tonight. That
was one of the things I had noticed that hadn't been all burned
up.

I wondered what Victor Vargas would be thinking right
now. I was sure that he would have gone out and searched in
the last evening light, but by now would have had to turn
around.

It was just at that moment that I heard two rifle shots in the distance. I dared not answer them. I reached out to touch Catrina's hand and whispered, "We cannot answer."

Victor Vargas had gone with his group as far as the light would let them go. The horses were thick with sweat from the quick ride down the meadow. They would need to turn back soon. If for some reason the two had met up with cattle rustlers or Indians, they would already have been caught by now. As for his men, lighting the lanterns would make them easy targets for anyone who might be out there.

He told his men to turn around and get back home. It was pitch black, and they could not help anyone now. Before he turned, he fired two shots from his rifle up into the dark of the night.

What would his Maria say when he returned home without finding the two? What could he say, except that they would be out before first light with most of the men to continue their search.

It took them over two hours to get back to the ranch.

Back at the main house, the men had built up the fire high in the yard in front of the house so it could be seen from far off. Under Pedro's direction, they built two more fires farther away and spread out some, so that they might be seen more easily. The fires gave out their light in dancing shadows. Whenever the men added more juniper to fuel the fires, they sent off a shower of sparks.

Pedro went inside the house to check on the women, and found them all gathered in the living room. Maria Vargas sat closest to the fireplace, rocking slowly back and forth with her head buried in her hands.

He said in his soft-spoken way, "They will be all right. I

have ridden with this Jacob, and though he is young, he is able to take care of himself. He was the first to spot the bandits on our ranch the other day. She couldn't have had a better one to be with. He will see to your Catrina."

Maria looked up at him and thanked him for those encouraging words. Victor had said that Catrina seemed to like Jacob. And she had noticed how excited her daughter was when she expected him to come in. She would go to the mirror and see if her hair was combed, or check her apron to see how she was looking in it. She was a joy to have in their family and seemed to make up for not having a boy on the ranch.

She remembered how sick she had been when Catrina came along. Victor had to go for the doctor in Sonora to help her. He rode through a day and night and half the next day without stopping. After only a short rest, he returned with the doctor, hardly stopping on the way back. He had borrowed fresh horses at the Ortega ranch both ways in the ride.

When the doctor arrived, he had looked at her and told Victor that his wife was very sick. He didn't know if he could save the baby and her, too. When Victor was told that, she could barely hear his answer. He said, "Save my Maria!"

The doctor had worked throughout the night. By the morning, Catrina was born and Maria was still hanging on to life. It took two days before she seemed to get better, and Victor never was far away. The doctor told them they wouldn't be able to have any more children. They named Catrina after her grandmother.

The distant sound of gunfire brought her back to the present. Two shots were fired. She knew that meant one of two things: either they had found the lost ones, or they were returning and had hoped that those lost might be able to answer and let them know they were all right. Just two shots . . . and then there was only silence.

Maria thought about the other women who lived on

their ranch. Two of them had small children that brought much joy into the home. The wives of three permanent ranch hands had been helping in the main ranch house when the Indian attack occurred. Now they stayed in the guest rooms at the back of the main house. She was glad that they had built the extra rooms. They were such good help and friends. They were there to comfort her now.

Victor and the men had rounded the last curve into the large meadow and could see the fires in the distance. It was slow going, but the lights up ahead made things easier and they moved steadily forward. They could make out someone putting wood on the fire, and before long they were able to call out into the night. Those around the fires could hear their approach before they could see the riders. Faces peered out into the darkness, anxious to see if they had brought Catrina and Jacob back with them.

Maria was told of the group's return. She came out to wait on the porch. When Victor rode up to the house, she could see by the look on his face that he had not found them. She put her hand up to her mouth as though to catch her breath at the news.

Victor dismounted quickly and stepped up the three porch steps, his strong arms holding his Maria. Everyone was talking all at the same time, but his voice carried over the crowd. He ordered the other women to see about their husbands and to bring the men who had come in from the search to the house to eat. Saying that he was not hungry, he went with Maria to their private rooms so they could be alone, and that others might not see the tears in his eyes.

I stopped to listen now and then to see if I could hear anyone calling out into the night. I felt that we were getting close to the place where the two shots had come from earlier, but I couldn't be sure. We would have to wait until we could see the lights of the ranch before we could send two shots to let them know we were coming.

In another fifteen minutes or so, we were able to see three fires in the distance. I touched Catrina to let her know that we were safe now. I whispered, "I will fire two shots into the air and they will be able to hear them."

She pressed my arm, and I felt that she was smiling at me once again. I forgot to ask her if her dad had a mean temper over such things as this. I guess it was better that I didn't know.

I had carried the rifle cradled in my arms all of the way and so was prepared to fire two spaced shots into the air.

*Pedro was one of the first to understand what the rifle shots meant. He ran from fire to fire yelling, "They are coming! They are coming!" Those in the house had not heard the shots because of all the commotion of eating and conversing. Pedro raced to the house to spread the news. Everyone came out on the front porch, including Victor with Maria close behind.*

*Victor yelled for the men to put more wood on the fire. He sent one of the hands to saddle his horse in a hurry. Grabbing a lantern from the house, he got on his horse and rode as quickly as he dared down the meadow once again. It mattered little to him that he might be a good target to any one that would want to take a shot at him. His only thought was for the safe return of his precious daughter.*

*Those waiting on the porch watched the lantern. It seemed to float off down the meadow as if by itself, searching through the night. At a point about half way to the big bend, the lantern stopped. Then it was lifted high in the all-well signal.*

Catrina and I could see the light coming towards us through the night. I whispered, "It looks like one of the riders has come down to find us and help us get back."

"That will be my father coming for us. He would not send anyone," Catrina replied.

I thought of her words and the way she had said them. I knew that the rider moving quickly our way would be Victor Vargas.

In a short time he closed the distance enough that we could call out to him and let him know that we were all right. He held the lantern over his head so that he could see for himself. He rode directly up to Catrina. Getting down, he pulled her into his arms. It was good to see him holding her close with one arm and waving the lantern in the other. He turned back toward the camp and gave the safe signal.

As Vargas helped Catrina back onto her horse, he simply asked me if I was okay, to which I answered, "Yes." Catrina rode at her father's side in the light from the lantern. I hung back a bit, wondering what else Catrina's father would say to me. I wondered what I would say to me, if I were him. In this land, having someone gone for a few extra hours in the dark normally spelled tragedy. It was a demanding country, and often didn't give anyone an extra chance.

As we rode along, Catrina explained to her father what had happened. She said that she was sorry she had gone so far away. Her father reached over and patted her hand as she finished telling him of the past few hours.

It would be good to get back to the ranch house. I was hungry, but more tired than anything else. Tomorrow would be another day.

*At the Ortega ranch, the injured Dutch was soon up moving around. During the past couple of days he had even felt good enough to lead two of the men back up to where the big* range bull was last seen. It took a couple of days for them to find the critter and drive him back down into the meadow.

Dutch watched Chancey out in the pasture, lying in the tall grass and getting his fill of resting and eating. He could walk right up to the mule now and put a halter on with ease. He had asked Mr. Ortega if he could just feed him a little grain, since he had saved their lives. Mr. Ortega had smiled at the friendship that he felt toward the long-eared mule, and said that he could do whatever he wanted.

Each day he walked down to the meadow with a handful of the delicious grain for the mule. And each day Chancey would put his long nose and mouth under his arm after he had eaten the grain. He liked to have his ears rubbed, and Dutch was glad to do it. He talked to Chancey about Jacob, and wondered if he was all right.

"I think he should have taken you along, so he would be able to come back. Some of these other range horses would be no match for someone like you, if Jacob really got in a tight place."

Luis Ortega was a strong-willed and proud man. He had to fight often to keep the things he had on the ranch. Sometimes he even had to fight the military forces that would come in to take it away from him when the rulers of the country changed. Right now though, he was friendly with the patrols and would offer them the comforts of the ranch whenever they passed by.

Once Dutch had asked him what they would say if they saw Jacob and him there. After all, Mexico had recently been at war with the United States, and they were obviously not Mexicans. Ortega assured Dutch that they would not be bothered; he would simply tell them that these gringos were working for him.

If they were ever caught out alone, though, that would

be another story. The soldiers would probably take them to their headquarters, and they might be thrown in some of their jails. They would be treated as bandits or thieves, and that was something they would never want to have happen. If it came to that, if would be worth a try to tell them about working for Ortega, or maybe Vargas. At least right now they were all friendly.

Dutch had looked around at the fortified ranch and asked if Ortega had much trouble with bandits. He said, "Yes. And the last few years we have had trouble with the Indians, too."

There was an Indian headdress mounted over the main entrance to the ranch house and Dutch had asked him what the three Indian feathers in the leather headband meant.

"Well, about seven years ago, the country had some deep and heavy snows, not like the small ones we have now. It was the coldest winter that we have ever had. In fact, it was so bitter cold that the ice had to be broken off the spring so the animals could get water.

"We brought in a large storage of wood, so we could keep warm. Our horses had to be in the corrals most of the time, and often we had to heat the barn to keep them warm.

"We had put up our cutting of the hay into our barns and stacked the feed in the corrals like we do now, but there was little range for the animals. We would sometimes ride our horses out to check on the stock that we could not get into the corrals. Somehow, some of the range cattle were able to find enough food to survive.

"It finally looked like we had made it through the worst of the winter, and the grass was starting to come up just a little. Most of the snow was gone, and we could put the animals out for a while. Then we had some visitors across the meadow.

"I could tell that they were Indians, dressed in all that they owned to keep warm. They came straight for the house with their hands held up in peace. One of my men had been a scout for a while and had picked up some of the Apache words. I had him come to me and translate what they wanted.

"An elderly chief slid quietly to the ground. He said that he was chief of his tribe and his name was Black Eagle, pointing to the three eagle feathers trailing down his back. I could see the deep creases in his worn and tired face, representing the many years of his life. Only the sharp dark eyes, piercing in their glance, revealed the great chief he had been. Deep down inside a strong spirit still dwelt, for even in his age, he stood tall and proud as he began to talk.

"His braves stayed back on their ponies. They had not come to raid, but to see if they could get food. As we sat squatting on the ground around a small fire, he told us of the deep snows that came upon his people eight days' ride from here. The snows had been so deep that they could not hunt food, and many of the little ones had died, as well as some of the older ones. It was not easy for him to ask for or take help from anyone; only the suffering of the tribe brought him forth.

"Using my translator, I told him that I was Luis Ortega. I had food brought from the house and gave it to the chief. He began to roll it into a skin as if to take it back with him. I told him that we would give them more food to take with them, but to eat this. He went and offered it to his braves first, and then they all began to eat the tortillas and jerky.

"I asked him what we could do to help, and he pointed to the cattle in the pasture and held up four fingers. I told a couple of the hands to round up about fifteen of the best cattle, the ones that looked like they would make the trip, and cut them out from the rest of the bunch.

"I asked some of the others to round up six horses, without saddles, and to lead them out. I also had them bring two pack mules with packs ready so that we could load them up with food.

"The old chief could hardly believe what was happening when I told him they would be his. And then I sent to the house for a piece of paper to write on. I wrote, "If anyone stops this party with my animals and cows, they are a gift I have given to take to the starving people of this tribe. This is Black Eagle and I am Luis Ortega.'

"I told the chief that, if anyone stopped him, he was to show them the message. He seemed to understand as he stood up. He offered me the only thing of value that he had. It was that headpiece over the front door. The Indians watched as I directed it to be hung right there over the top of the door."

"Did you ever see them again?" Dutch asked.

"Yes, the next spring he came again and stopped across the meadow with his hand raised in peace. He only had four braves with him this time, as they led our six horses back toward the ranch, with one mule following.

"I greeted him . He came up to me and held up his thumb. With one quick stroke of his knife, he drew it quickly across the thumb and waited for me to do the same.

"I accepted the great offer to be his blood brother. This is the scar that it left on my thumb. Black Eagle returned to his braves and they went back the way that they came. I never saw him again, but for several years, the Indians were never a threat to our herd. I'm sure that by now Black Eagle has gone, so perhaps some of the braves from his tribe may come on raiding parties again."


Dutch appreciated Mr. Ortega telling the story of Black Eagle. It told him a lot about Mr. Ortega, who had been just as kind to Jacob and him. He had refused Dutch's offer to pay for some of the medicine and help that they received. Even if they still had all of their money and could easily pay him for the many things that he had done, Ortega would probably have

212

still refused it. Dutch could hardly imagine anyone not liking the man.

Ortega had begun to wonder what was happening at the Vargas Ranch. The two men he had sent, Jacob and Pedro, should be coming back soon with some news. Finally he declared that if no word came from the Vargas ranch in the next two days, he would need to send someone else to check. This time it would be himself.

Dutch was glad to be able to ride and help out around the Ortega ranch, but he couldn't help wondering what had happened to his partner and Pedro. They should have been back by now. He wondered what he would ever do if something had happened to Jacob. He was about the only family that Dutch had. Dutch hoped that Mr. Ortega would let him go when they sent someone else to check on the Vargas ranch and see about Jacob.

The next evening, Mr. Ortega said that he would be going to the Vargas ranch to check things out. He wanted Dutch and a few others to join him, and Dutch was glad to be included. They wouldn't follow the old wagon trail to the ranch, but would go across the meadows, a steeper way. They made preparations to leave before daylight. Ortega gave instructions for the rest of his men to stay close by the ranch house in his absence.

A crisp cool morning welcomed the group when they pulled away from the ranch house before dawn. The coyotes were howling in the distance. In the early morning light, Dutch could see several deer out among the cattle, feeding in the meadow and getting their drinks from one of the many little streams that emptied into the main channel. A few of the stock were up grazing, but most of them were still bedded down. The deer were wary as they approached, and moved back toward the tree-covered mountain.

No one paid much attention to the deer as they rode past. It wasn't at all unusual to see several deer in the large valley early in the morning. One of the cowboys told him that they only took what they could use, and only when it was cool enough to keep. Dutch hungrily thought of the fresh fried steaks that they had been having for meals. Venison sure was good with those biscuits or tortillas! That jerky the ranch made was probably venison, too. It was the best he'd ever had.

He could see that it didn't make a lot of sense for a rancher to kill one of the cows for food. They would be saved for the market. Besides, a guy would have to go someplace far to get something better than that good venison. He should know.

The large heard of deer were well up in the trees now. Dutch had noticed that all of the game seemed to go to the mountain. With all of the water coming from there, and the feed so good, maybe it was the place to be. Especially considering what the land was like a few miles to the west.

They continued south and a little bit west. With fresh animals, the miles seemed to go by quickly. Mr. Ortega had no doubt gone this way many times before. They had brought three pack mules, including Chancey. The beasts were loaded with much more food than his group would eat in the next few days. They soon left the big meadow and climbed west over the hills. It wasn't an easy ride, and a wagon could never go this way; but no doubt it was the shortest way there.

The sun wasn't nearly as hot as it had been a few days before, and the nights were pretty cool, too. It would be just right for real good sleeping, and now for riding. When sundown approached, Dutch could tell that Mr. Ortega knew just where they would spend the night, as he motioned them over the next ridge.

When they reached the spot, Dutch saw a small catchment of water in the little valley. It looked like others had used the spot often. Dutch could barely make out an old wagon road that headed in the direction of the Vargas ranch. It hadn't been used often, but this must have been one of the necessary stops. Mr. Ortega said that they would be at the Vargas ranch before noon the next day.

When he found they would need to post a watch for the night, Dutch volunteered to take the first shift. Ortega said that would be fine. He promised that as soon as they had a fire built and someone finished eating, he would send them up so Dutch could come and eat.

"It was nice that he trusted me to do this," Dutch thought. It was nice to have the assignment to keep a keen eye out. If the watch failed at his job, many lives could be lost. It was also nice to be up here alone. It gave him some good time to think. He chose the spot to watch from, a place where he could see down into the group and for a ways onto the other ridge. The coming change of the season was showing up in some of the trees. A few leaves were starting to turn a little bit golden. The trees here were pretty good size for the little water they had. Near the water below was a grassy little meadow, but the large oak and juniper were thicker up on the ridges. Not too far away there was even a half-grown pine mixed in.

"What was the pine doing there?" Dutch wondered. It looked out of place down here in the low country. Maybe it was a little bit like Jacob and him. Maybe they were a little bit out of place here, too.

It was getting dark now and Dutch pulled his slicker a little tighter around him. The cool wind started to pierce every place that wasn't covered. He found an old stump and leaned up against it, hoping that nothing would try to sneak up on him in the dark.

It wasn't long before one of the cowboys came up to relieve him. He headed back down to the small campfire burning in the flat below. Dutch bet that many fires had been there over the years, and it looked like they had all used the same spot to build on. The walk did him good and the exercise helped to warm him up. He could smell the hot coffee from a long way off.

When he finished eating, he returned back up the hill to replace the watch. He whistled lowly when he got close to the spot, and the other man answered back. He could hear the coyotes calling from somewhere nearby, and others answering in the distance. He remembered the time that Jacob had said that they would need to be like the coyotes and only travel at night and rest in the daytime. He had sure been right about continuing to travel. Dutch had really been sick a few times when they had to move. If Jacob had left the decisions up to him, they would still be out there somewhere, left to the scavengers.

Yes, Jacob was a good man. Dutch hoped that nothing had happened to him. He couldn't do without his partner.

This watch lasted three hours. Then relief was supposed to come and replace him. "I will be ready for some rest," Dutch said to himself.

# Chapter 16

I couldn't seem to get to sleep once Catrina and I had made it home safely. The night was dark and silent, and my thoughts went back over all the events of my life. Had I told Catrina everything? My life in Germany, my trip to America, the gold fields, the desert? Was there anything else that Catrina would like to hear? I wondered about this for hours as I lay in my bunk before sleep finally took over.

Early the next morning, Vargas said they needed to get some word back to Ortega. They needed to let them know I was all right. It had been six days since Pedro and I had come to check on them. The decision was that a rider would leave the following day. Vargas felt that he could not send more than one rider back, as they were so shorthanded already. He chose Pedro to return. And then he asked me if I could stay for a while longer. I could think of nothing better to do than this. Luckily, he hadn't been too angry with me about the night before, and even said that I had made a good choice to try and get out around the Indians.

When I walked into the dining hall, I saw that Catrina was up early as usual helping with the food. And she had on that warm smile again. I didn't want anyone watching the two of us make eyes at each other, so I set about eating a good breakfast.

I got into a conversation with Pedro, who told me that he would be leaving early the next morning. I asked him to tell Dutch that I was fine and would look forward to seeing him soon.

The next day Pedro left before early light. He wanted to ride right on through the night and make it to the Ortega ranch in a long day and part of the night. He took an extra horse and rations for the fast ride. He knew that they would be getting anxious back at the Ortega ranch. He should make the water hole where he and I stopped on our way here at about the time that it was getting good and light. He would need to be careful in his approach there, since others might be using the familiar pasture and water. He tied on some extra water in case he had to go around that place.

I had drawn a map on the ground for Mr. Vargas, showing him where I had seen some of his cows on our trip to the mountain. He was familiar with the place and assigned me to take two of the hands and try to retrieve some of the strays if we could. It meant riding toward where the Apaches had camped for the night. Mr. Vargas said that we would really need to keep our eyes peeled and watch out for them. He thought that if we stayed in the valley, it would be unlikely that twelve of them would come out in the open against the three of us.

It seemed different going down the valley without the conversation and the excitement of Catrina with me. I couldn't get her off my mind. I'd have bet my partner wouldn't have stumbled around his words as much as I had. He had more of a way with women. What would I do if he met her and started to like her a lot, too? What would she do?

I could see the bend in the meadow now that would take us out of sight of the ranch house. We should find the strays in the next two or three miles, unless the Indians had run them off. When we finally got around the turn, we were relieved to see several cattle feeding in the meadow about two miles away. It would be good to get them and any others that we could find without going into the brush. Our only job then would be to head them toward home. We wouldn't need to take them all of the way to the ranch, but just get them closer so they would be easier to roundup later.

During roundup time, I thought, it would probably take thirty or so cowboys to round up the range and get the cattle to market. Normally that would be happening in the next two or three months, but I had heard talk that, with so few men left, they would have to postpone the trip.

　　　　Luis Ortega was up early the next morning. Dutch had been in his bedroll only three hours. It seemed that he had just gone to sleep when he smelled the coffee cooking and heard stirring around the camp. Someone had already gone into the meadow to fetch the hobbled horses and lead them up to the camp. Though Dutch's injury was still a little tender, and a nasty scar was forming, he found that the more he moved, the easier it got. He was also anxious to find out about Jacob, so he was one of the first ones ready to ride.

　　　　They had barely climbed out of the pasture area and out onto the high ground when Mr. Ortega held up his hand and said, "Rider coming."

　　　　Dutch looked in the direction that he was pointing and could see a lone rider with two horses coming their way. Whoever it was saw their group about the same time that they saw him and came to a sudden stop. He appeared to be waiting for them to get closer before he decided what to do.

　　　　Luis had a keen eye and said, "I think that is someone from the Vargas Ranch." It wasn't long before he recognized Pedro and motioned with a wave of his hat. Pedro answered with the same wave and they rode quickly towards each other. As soon as they were within earshot, Ortega started asking Pedro what had happened at the Vargas ranch.

　　　　Pedro answered all of the questions as briefly as he could. He was not used to doing a lot of talking, and thought that Ortega would rather hear it from his friend Victor Vargas anyway. He turned around to join them on the return to the ranch, which was about three hours away.

　　　　When Luis Ortega came upon the ridge overlooking the valley of his friend Victor, he stopped and looked at what the raiding party had done. He shook his head without saying anything, and then proceeded on to the ranch house.

Some of the men out in the yard had spotted them as soon as they came over the top of the ridge. They had been real careful to watch out for anyone that would come their way. Victor had told them he needed every man that he had left. Defense of the ranch house was number one priority.

After they rode in, Dutch quickly learned that Jacob was out on the range. He was introduced to the Vargas family and the other Mexican families that were staying in the ranch house with them. When he first saw Catrina, he could hardly believe there was someone so beautiful. Little wonder that his partner, Jacob, was willing to stay behind while Pedro rode back alone to report. He would have to ask Jacob about her. He knew how quiet Jacob was around women, though. He had probably never even gotten in much of a conversation with her.

Dutch remembered how quiet his friend became around women. He hadn't gotten him to take much interest in the dancehall girls, not even when they'd had a few drinks. Some of the miners said he was bashful; others said that he was a loner when it came to the women. Dutch guessed that it was something that his mother taught him while he was young: to be respectful to females.

A meal was soon brought out for those that had just come. Catrina was ever the helpful one in the kitchen and around the long table. She could see Dutch's eyes on her and gave him a quick smile. She said, "Yacob told me about his partner. He said that you were the best friend that he ever had. That makes you a good friend of mine, too." Dutch was too surprised to reply.

Victor Vargas was happy to see his good friend Luis. As they ate, he explained in detail about the Indian attack. "I guess we were not on our toes, to let them get so close," he said. "I feel so bad for those that have been lost. I don't know if any of them have families, but I am trying to find out. I sent

*Reuben to the mission; he was the one shot in the arm. He has not come back with word of anything yet. I know a couple of the men came from Moctezuma. Maybe we can ask around there. They were good men, and had wages coming. What do you think I should do, Luis?"*

*"I don't know what you can do. I do know that if you just send a message that someone can pick up their stuff, no telling who would come by. If I lost that many men and didn't know how to find any of their families, I guess I would do just like you are doing. I would let the mission know that some men had been lost in a raid, without giving names.*

*He thought for a moment and then added, "When you get to the Sonora outpost, you can also let the patrol know, if you haven't already done that, of the men that have been lost. If they have any family, someone may contact you for their things. I don't know what else you can do. You know how they move around the country from ranch to ranch."*

*They continued visiting long after the meal ended. Luis directed the men he had brought to go out and see if they could help with any of the work.*

It was after sundown when I returned with the Vargas cowboys. We had been west, where the land was thick with scrub oak and buck brush. The range cattle seemed to like to get away from the rest and go into these thick places. In the course of the day, with the help of three other hands, I had been able to haze out about twenty-five head of stock. Some of them were plenty wild, and it would take a good rider to head them off in the chase. The brush tore away at our chaps.

I wondered if they had to go through this all of the time, so I asked the nearest one to me. He said that the range cattle had a liking for the meadow and the easy feed, but because they were more used to the range, they preferred the rough and ready places.

I considered what he had said as he raced off to head another steer that seemed set on going a different way. Maybe that is a little bit like people, I thought. They don't always take the soft and easy way. Sometimes there is a little bit of wildness in them, too, like Dutch and me.

Who in their right mind would be way off down here in Mexico, with their lives threatened so many times? We had certainly had enough money to move away from the gold fields and buy a place in California. We could have done well by staying there and picking up a good little ranch or something. In fact, we had talked about that at different times. Always, it came back to the same thing. That quiet life wouldn't be a lot of fun. It just wouldn't scratch an itch we both seemed to have. Besides, how could we ever know what was over on the other side of a choice if we didn't go and take a look?

When we finally got the cattle back onto the pasture and mixed them with some of the others, we headed for the ranch. One of the riders in front of me pointed out that company was at the ranch. Two more riders came down the mountain to join us. It was Luis Ortega and some of his boys for sure. Maybe Dutch would be with them. It would be good to see him again.

The house was full of people and a table had been set up outside where everyone could gather to eat. Lanterns were being lit so that all might be able to see around the large dining table. People were coming in and out of the ranch house, as I made my way through to find my partner.

A shiver went through me when I saw Dutch sitting in front of the fireplace talking to Catrina. As anxious as I was to see him, seeing him with Catrina held me back for a moment. But then Catrina saw me and gave me a warm smile. I moved toward them.

Dutch got up from the chair and turned to meet me. In a few short quick steps we had closed the distance and caught

222

each other's arms. Our words tumbled out.

"How are you feeling? How is the leg?"

"Oh I have been up for days. I have been helping around the ranch the past three or four days. I guess if I would have had some of your porcupine stew earlier, it might have only taken one day to get better."

Here he was, the same old partner. "I see you have met Catrina."

"Oh yes! I have met all of the family. I would think that a guy could get himself in a lot of trouble around here," he said with a smile.

I don't know why that bothered me so much, but I decided to shrug it off. Maybe the best thing to say was nothing at all. I wondered what Catrina thought of Dutch. As he told me about what had happened while I had been gone, it seemed like weeks, not days. I didn't dare tell him that some days I hadn't even thought about him.

The women cleaned off the tables when everyone was finished. Some of the men gathered around a campfire that they had built. That would be where many would sleep tonight. Many of the cowhands knew each other and the conversation and the laughing carried well into the night.

My last thoughts were about Catrina. I wouldn't be able to see her alone tonight, with all of the extra work the visitors had made. But at least I didn't have to stand watch. The extra sleep would be good.

Morning came early on the Vargas ranch. Luis had told Vargas to use his men to help where they were most needed. Vargas decided to send riders into the high country where no one had been since the raid. I was assigned, along with Dutch, to go along into the hills and check on the stock. We would travel in a large group so we wouldn't be too apt to find anyone willing to take us on. A big raiding party might have chanced it, but there weren't enough horses left to tempt them into taking

223

such a risk.

We all ate in the main ranch house. It was good and warm in there from all the cooking going on for the past hour or so. I could see Victor and Luis over against the fireplace, leaning back with cups of coffee in their hands. They were evidently talking business. I usually said my hellos, but this morning I felt that I shouldn't interrupt them.

Catrina came through the kitchen door with her arms full of delicious food. Just as I started wondering if anything had changed between us, she smiled and gave me a little wink. Boy! I hoped no one else saw that! What would Dutch have thought if he had seen it? Luckily he was fixing his plate when she came in.

The horses were frisky and ready to go by the time we mounted up. The high country we were heading for was west of the main ranch and across the meadow. We traveled north by west, climbing gradually until the trail crested a high ridge. From here we began to fan out toward the high range of mountains. There were few clearings visible, and brush choked most of the land. It looked like a thousand Indians and cattle could hide in there and not even see each other.

As we spread out, we spent most of our time looking down at the ground as we picked our way along through the brush. I still couldn't imagine why any cow in its right mind would leave the meadow for this. It was true that there seemed to be some feed down under the brush, but it wasn't easy to get at. If they could survive out here, it didn't take a lot of food for them to be able to get along. Maybe they ate the brush right down to the ground. One cowboy had told me that these range cows would eat about anything that did not eat them.

Dutch was on the far outside with me. We found cattle over the very next ridge. We wanted to get around to the back side of them before we turned them toward the ranch. They would be easy pickings for rustlers out here.

The leader of our group said that there was a small water catchment called Dripping Springs about two miles away. We would have to look sharp when we approached it, because it was a good place for thieves to hang out. As we neared the place, we could hear cattle bawling close by. The foreman signaled for us to stop.

"Something's wrong," he said. "These cows don't bawl in the middle of the day without a reason." We waited for some time before he decided that he would ride ahead to where he could look into the little hidden valley and see if it was being used. He told the rest to wait until he came back but asked me to go with him. We rode toward the springs until we could hear the cattle just over the next ridge.

He gave the sign to dismount and pulled his rifle from its scabbard. He came over to me and whispered, "I think we have cattle rustlers here. Maybe they've stopped here to change the brand. If I'm right, they will have a lookout posted, so watch for one. We will go in together and try to get a look without being seen."

It took several minutes for us to creep through the brush to where we were able to see into the small meadow below. It was as he'd predicted. The thieves had built a makeshift fence below the springs. This kept the cattle from getting out at the base of the rocky formation, where the water was seeping out. The sides of the ravine were too steep for the cattle to climb out around it. The rustlers were able to keep several cattle boxed in there while they used the running iron to give them new brands. No telling what they were making the Victor Vargas, V/V brand into.

We counted about a dozen in the group, and there could be even more men on their way in with other cows. Our own crew numbered seven, which was about half their numbers. They were moving fast to get as much branding done as they could. There was room for several to be working at the same time. As I surveyed the busy scene, I noticed the man they'd posted to watch for them. He was on his horse high up the opposite bank in the thick brush. I pointed him out, and the foreman nodded back that he could see him.

We slipped carefully back from the crown of the ridge. The foreman whispered to me, "I don't think they know we are here. They must think that with our problems, we would not be able to cover this part of the range. But they seem to be in a big hurry anyway." He jerked his head in the direction of the lookout and continued, "Boracho! He was the one up on the ridge as look out."

The mention of that name brought back a flood of memories. He was the man who had taken all that Dutch and I had! What had he done with all of our money? That should have lasted even him a long time. Yet he was out here rustling cattle! And he now seemed to have about twice as many men as he did when he robbed us.

We made our way back to our horses, watching carefully to see that no one followed. When we reached the rest of the men, all but the lookout they'd posted were sitting down or leaning against the trees, taking advantage of the shade. Cowboys learned quickly to rest themselves and their horses every time they could. The cinches were all loosened and the hands sat silent and listening.

The foreman gave his report, drawing the layout with a stick in the dirt. All of Vargas's men had been to the springs and could see in their minds how they were closed in with the huge rock face to the north. The brush was thick there except for the small meadow and large pool of water from Dripping Springs. They listened intently as he told them of the rustlers and Boracho and then reminded them, "You know how we treat rustlers around here, with a bullet or a rope!"

The foreman suggested that the safest way to

approach was probably the way that we had just been. If we walked our horses down to the place where we had tied them before, we could spread out on the east side of the pasture without the thieves knowing we were there. We could pick our cover and maybe keep ourselves from getting shot. Then, at a given sign, we would open up on the rustlers below.

It went without saying: the rustlers were well-armed and always expecting trouble. It seemed a vicious law of the land, but when it came to rustlers, the ranchers took no prisoners. They couldn't just take them in and have a trial and put them in jail. The Mexican army didn't do business that way, either. Landowners were expected to keep what they had, any way they could.

I wondered why people turned to rustling and stealing. I guess they just didn't believe in working for things. Maybe to them, this rustler's life was an easy way to take what they wanted. They just had to be bad enough.

Dutch came along with me as we went up the backside of the pasture. He remembered as well as I did that this Boracho was the one that had taken all that we had, except Chancey. He whispered, "I wonder if they still have our two horses with them."

While we waited for the signal, I spotted my sorrel horse being used to haze the cattle back into the holding area. I wondered why I had not seen him sooner. The bandit riding my sorrel was going to be my target; of course, I wouldn't turn down a chance to get Boracho, too, if he came across my sights. I pointed out my horse to Dutch, and we started looking for his black one. Nighthawk was not in the group.

The branding suddenly stopped when our rifles spoke. The man with the branding iron fell forward. Others in the bunch ran to their horses as firing sounded from both sides. I shot the rider off my horse as he tried to make it up the other side of the little valley. Two more thieves went down before they could get up the other side. The cattle broke loose from the holding corral, and a couple of horses followed the cattle as they fled out to the south of the watering place. The only cow left was the one that had been tied down for the branding. It was trying to get up but kept falling over with its legs bound up.

Heavy fire began coming our way when the rustlers realized we were across the meadow from them. It was like the foreman had said; we kept low and tried to get as many of them as we could without getting shot in the exchange. The battle only lasted a few minutes before we heard them sneaking away through the brush. With the loss of all of the cattle that they had rounded up, four men dead and one other shot in the arm by Dutch, it would probably be some time before they would come back here and try this.

Dutch and I went after my horse, which had galloped off with the reins dragging. We found him a short while later. He seemed to know us and even whinnied a little bit as we approached. I climbed down from my mount and walked over to him. It felt good to rub his neck. He still had my saddle on him, and my slicker was still tied on behind. It was good to have him back again. I just wished that we had recovered the black, too.

When we were sure that the outlaws had gone, we set about rounding up the herd. The outlaws had been busy the past two or three days. The good part about it was that they had gathered about one hundred head of cattle into the area. This made our work of finding strays much easier.

The hard part, though, was still ahead. It would take many more riders than we had to get all these cattle through the rough places and back to the ranch. Someone would need to go back and get most of the boys to come help. The rest would have to concentrate on getting the herd back to the springs and guarding them there until help arrived. Then, when we finally got all of this bunch back into the corrals, they would all have to be looked over to see if the brand had been changed. Any that had been branded at Dripping Springs by the rustlers would have to be branded again when we got back.

I explained to the foreman that I had recovered one of the horses that Boracho had stolen from us earlier. He asked if I would be willing to take the extra horses and be the one to go back to the ranch to get some more riders. I told him I would do that. By leaving right then, I should be out onto the valley about dark. If I changed horses along the way, I could make good time.

I waved to Dutch and headed toward the ranch. I rode without stopping until about an hour before sundown, when I stopped to change mounts. I could see the mountain that backed up to the ranch. It looked like I could ride straight over to it in no time, but I remembered how we'd had to skirt so many thickets in our trip over here. It would still be awhile before I would make it onto the meadow.

It was good to have my own horse under me. I was sure glad to have him back. I reached over to pat his neck and give him encouragement. "Let's go, Jake," I whispered into his ear.

As I rode along, I thought back to the gunfight at the springs. Now I had time to wonder where Boracho had gone. Somehow he must have sensed danger and ridden away. I was sure that, once the shooting started, he was not on the ridge where we had seen him earlier. Even then, I had just had a glimpse of him. It wasn't until the foreman had said his name that I recognized him as the same bandit I'd encountered before. Obviously he was careful not to let anyone have a good look at him for long.

As it got darker, I had to slow down some. The horses behind were leading well and sensed that we were going home. They had enough slack on the rope to never need to be pulled along. I could probably have just untied them now, but they still had saddles on and might not go straight to the corral. I was relieved when I reached the level part of the meadow and didn't have to go through the pucker brush after dark.

The lights of the ranch house guided me a little bit to the south after I came onto the meadow floor. I rode straight to the main house and tied up to the hitching post. Some of the men came to ask where the others were. I told them briefly that they were bringing in some cattle the next morning and would need a lot of help.

Luis and Victor heard me ride up and came out on the front porch to meet me. They asked me inside, where I related all that had happened. I told Mr. Vargas that his foreman wanted him to send all of the men he could spare to help with getting the cows back. I told the story of our fight with the rustlers who were changing the brands on some of his cattle. When I mentioned that we had seen Boracho, both men instantly came to attention. They fired questions at me about how many men we had seen. I answered as best I could.

Luis said, "This Boracho has really increased his payroll and become more bold in his raiding. I wonder where he got all of the money to pay for his help."

It was then that I told them just how much money Dutch and I had when we got robbed. This took them by surprise.

"No wonder!" Luis exclaimed. "With that much money, he could hire rustlers by the dozen."

It made me feel bad that our money had gone to the bandits and now was the cause of so many more problems. They repeated the amount over again as if to ask if I were sure about it. I answered yes, and told them how we got our gold exchanged at a bank in Mexico near the border of California.

"You two had all of that money and came to Mexico to look for gold?" Luis asked.

I said, "Yes, that's about right. We hit it big in California."

Victor said, "Well, now we know where his money came from. There is going to be no stopping him now, unless we actively pursue him. The next time we see Boracho, whether he's stealing cattle or not, we have to just shoot him. That may be the only way that we will put a stop to this." He turned to me again and added, "I am glad that you got your horse back and saved some of the herd. We will ride at first light with most of the hands."

He turned to Luis. "My friend, we need to make some plans."

I was the only one at the dinner table that late at night, and I asked if they would just bring out a plate and not go to much trouble. I was happy when Catrina came into the room with it. She walked up by my side and said, "Yacob, I am glad you are here. Where is your partner?"

I told her a little bit of the events of the day and of the cattle thieves. She was happy that none of our men had been hurt in the shooting. She asked me whether I would rather eat out on the porch where it was a little bit cooler.

She moved my plate out to the porch and set up a table at one side of the door. It was almost the same spot where she had given her first kiss to me a few days before. She brought water from the house and coffee to drink. She was right; it was much nicer here than inside. She pulled up a chair and sat close to me as I ate the supper she had brought. She offered to go and get more if I would like, but I assured her that I was having a much better supper than those that had been left to watch the cattle.

I knew that I hadn't had too much time to clean up before I had the meal, and I felt a little bit uncomfortable with her being so close and me smelling from the travel of the day. She didn't seem to mind. She had something she wanted to ask me and so she started with, "Yacob, how long do you plan to stay?"

I hadn't thought too much about my future since I had been there. So much happened each day, there was little time for long-range plans. So I told her, "I don't know. I would think that we would stay for a while to kind of pay back Luis for the things he has done for us. We might help out with the cattle drive. I haven't talked to my partner at all about what we should do."

She seemed to like the idea that we would be around for some time if we stayed for the drive. She reached over in the dark of the night and squeezed my hand. The thought occurred to me that I might never leave if life could be so nice with Catrina. But there didn't seem to be much of a hurry to figure that out right now.

# Chapter 17

Victor rushed out the door after his meeting with Luis and began shouting orders to the men who were down by the campfire. He and Luis would ride out with most of them the next morning. This time I was appointed to stay behind with two other men. Our task would be to repair one of the large corrals to hold the bunch that would be driven in. We were to take what boards we could salvage from the buildings that had been burned and use them to patch up the fences.

I was up when the riders came to the breakfast table to eat. I stood back, knowing that I would take a turn after they had left. I helped them load up, and then they were off in a hurry for Dripping Springs. It still wasn't very light when I went back into the house. The other two workers were waiting at the table and had already poured their cups of coffee. It would be a hard day for the three of us, but we would get it done somehow.

Catrina came gliding through the door with fresh food in hand. She had on her warm smile for me when she looked my way. It was always good to see her. I wondered if she ever slept. I knew the women were always up an hour or more cooking before we ever came in to eat, and they were cleaning up long after we had gone outside.

I went out in the yard to size up the corrals that we needed to make ready. The only corral that was intact would need to be used for the horses. We absolutely had to finish the biggest one before the cattle got here. It would take all of us to get the gaps closed in this large corral. The Indians had pulled down much of the south wall when they made off with the horses, and many of the boards had been broken and crushed with the animals running over them.

We found the necessary tools and set about digging the posts into the ground again. It helped when we could find the same hole where the last post had come out. I sorted out all of the lumber that we could find for the rails and it looked like we'd have enough to do the job. As we carried the usable boards from the pile of rubble, we spaced them between the posts. In about four hours we had most of the main poles set and lumber arranged to go back on. We hadn't stopped since first light, and the cool chill in the air was welcome.

Catrina came down with tortillas, coffee, and water. We stopped long enough to eat and thank her, and then we turned to the task of rebuilding. Neither of the two Mexicans was as big as I was, but they kept right up with the work. I imagine Victor had assigned them to stay behind to fix the corral because they were both such good workers. He had given me the assignment to get it done and the men who could help me do it.

About mid-afternoon, Catrina called from the ranch house to come and eat. I was really starved with all of the work that we had been doing. I hadn't done so much shoveling since we were on the gold claims. It was good to use some of the old muscles.

She was humming a nice little song when she came around the table to serve us. I recognized it as the same music I'd heard the first time I met her. And, it was the same melody that she had whispered in my ear when she had tried to teach me how to dance. When I thought of this, I could feel red creeping up my face again. Why did this always have to happen to me? Why couldn't I be like all of the rest and not get too bothered when I thought of her, or any other woman?

The dance hall women would go out of their way to tease me just to see me blush. That is when I would usually leave. I had never forgotten what my mother once taught me about women. She said that there are all kinds of women, some good, some bad, and some kind of in the middle. When I met those who would cheat, or lie, or sell themselves for money, I

234

should stay away from those kind. She said I would know when the other kind came along because my heart would tell me. When that happened, I should be kind and gentle, and they would treat me the same way.

"Life is a lesson of doings and feelings," she would say. "Let those good doings go first, and then the good feelings will follow."

"Well, Mom, I am at that point of learning those good feelings," I thought.

Too soon it was time to get back to our assignment. The work on the corral was going well, and I could see that the Mexicans had done a lot of this before. I wondered if things were going as well on the cattle drive. It was getting close to sundown when we put the final top rise on the corral and added a string of barbed wire. That would do the job nicely. In fact, it was probably better now than it had been before the Indians destroyed most of it.

Just as we finished the corral and were putting our tools away, one of the Mexicans gave a yell. He pointed out across the meadow, where we could just see the first of the herd come out of the brush. We saddled up our horses and rode out to meet and help them. With so many hands, the herd was moved right into the large holding corral.

Victor Vargas rode up and inspected the new fence. "Good job," he said with a sweep of his large hat. "Muy hombre."

After dinner I waited around the house in hopes that I might get to see Catrina. She was always on the go, but at times I would see her smile as she looked at me.

The next day would be Sunday. I had noticed that it was the only day of the week that things changed much in that area. It was a time for all of the ranch hands to do whatever they wanted, except for the few chores that had to be done. The food was put on the table about ten o'clock in the morning

235

and covered up. Anyone that wanted something to eat would help himself or herself. Sometimes somebody would ask for some extra time off to go somewhere. Some of the men had girlfriends or liked the cantina crowd. Victor usually let them go by pairs, so it wouldn't leave the ranch too shorthanded.

I wouldn't have to wonder long about what would happen this Sunday, because Victor came outside and announced that we would need to start the cattle inspection early. If any of the riders wanted to take the day off, they needed to let him know now. No one stepped forward. He went on to say that we should get done early if we all pitched in with the work.

Morning came with the usual smell of coffee and breakfast. Dutch and I both went into the house at about the same time. I thought that we would have a little time to talk about our future plans. Talking confirmed my thoughts; he wanted to help Luis out for a while. He said that he had offered Luis money for the medicine that he received, but Luis refused. The only way that Dutch could think to repay him was to help him a few days. I told him that this was about the way I saw it, too.

After breakfast we went outside in the early light and caught up the horses for those that would be roping cattle. Victor asked us if we had ever done any branding or roping. We told him not much roping and never any branding, but we would be willing to learn.

He gave us the job of putting the cows through the chute and checking to see if the work had to be done again. It was something to see the ranch hands all working together this way. One vaquero would lay a loop around the neck of the steer we needed to brand, while another would come in, catch the back legs, and pull the animal down. Others had their jobs as well, keeping the iron hot and the fire going. We had enough room to have three sets of different workers. Men were going everywhere and the properly branded cattle were ushered out into the pasture.

After about two hours of this, a new pair would take over the roping and heeling. The horses needed changing often, but whoever came with the rope was as able as the last to do the work. Dutch and I had tried roping a few times, but it wasn't as easy as they made it appear. Occasionally we managed to throw the loop around a log or post, but we never had much luck with a moving target. We definitely weren't any match for these cowboys.

With everyone working, we were done before noon. I was glad to be done early, because I wanted to go upstream with some of that homemade soap and get a real good bath. Maybe I'd even wash out my clothes at the same time. I had noticed that Dutch had some different clothes on. He said that Luis had given them to him. He said they weren't much, but it gave him a change. Then he surprised me by saying he'd accepted two sets of clothing and had brought one of them for me.

We were soon riding upstream away from the house and out of sight to where we could get cleaned up. We left our horses tied to the tall grass and peeled right down to the hide. It was good to get into the water, even if it did about take our breaths away.

I saw the long scar that Dutch had on his thigh and asked if it hurt any more. He said it was doing real good. He said that Luis had sent a rider all of the way into Sonora near the outpost to get some medicine from the doctor. With that and all of the care that they gave him, it would be hard for a man not to get better soon.

Before many minutes went by, I told him that I'd had about all of the fun in this ice water that I could stand. If he would pass the soap over to me, I would get on with the getting on. This brought a laugh out of him, and he pitched the soap to me. It was hard to get a lather up, and that homemade soap just about took my hide off.

We both finished up about the same time and pulled our new borrowed clothes on. He said that the women at the Ortega ranch had just thrown his old ones away while he was asleep. I noticed that his clothes fit a little tight, but mine were about right. I told him that he shouldn't be so tall. We enjoyed the warmth of the sun as we sat on the bank and talked of things gone past.

"If you'd had a chance for a lucky shot back at the springs, do you think you would have shot your German friend?" I asked.

"Well, that Boracho will never be any friend to me. And, besides, if we had shot him, we could have found out if he still had some of our money left. I wonder how he sneaked out without anyone getting a shot at him. I sure would have liked to find my horse," he said.

"Maybe between the two of us, we could work out one of the rustler's horses. At least that would give us some way to get around. Course, I noticed that Chancey came up to the corral while we were working, and you rubbed his big ears for him. Maybe you don't need anything else."

He gave me a shove as if to push me back in the water, but when he could see that I had a tight grip on him, he let me loose. We both laughed at that. It was good to be alone again and see him feeling so good.

"Say," he said, "what do you know about this cute thing, Catrina?"

I didn't know exactly what to say, even though I'd known that before long he would be asking me about her. I decided I would meet the question head on. "I like her a lot," I told him. "And I think she likes me, too."

He turned around to me as if he couldn't believe what he had heard. "You what! You and Catrina? Have you ever even talked to her?"

I told him that I had, and that brought a slap on the back and a hearty "Way to go, partner!"

When we got back to the ranch, several of the men had gathered under the shade trees around the yard. It would be some time before we would have supper, and it was good just to talk and rest.

I looked around for Catrina. I hadn't seen her all day. Someone mentioned that Señora Vargas was not feeling well and needed extra attention. She was suffering from the stress of losing some of her close friends and worrying about all of the other losses besides. Catrina must be tending to her now.

Some of the men had set up a makeshift card table and had a card game going on. Others were talking about the events of the past few days. We overheard lots of talk about what Victor Vargas was going to do, and whether he would rebuild the ranch. Maybe he wouldn't need so many people at the ranch. Maybe some would be let go after the cattle drive. Everyone had their opinion and shared it freely. Dutch and I sat close to the rest of the bunch, but not too close to visit and put our two bits in.

"Do you think Mr. Vargas will rebuild the buildings?" I asked. "It will cost a lot of money to rebuild everything. The barns will need to be the first thing to get done. Winter will be here soon, and without a good barn or two, he would be hard pressed to bring all of the stock through the winter. If they have a bad one, like the one Luis told me about, even with a barn they would probably lose a lot of stock."

I wondered if Victor even had the money to rebuild, and where he would get the help to do it before winter. He definitely had a lot of things to think about, what with the herd needing to be gathered for market, and all of the buildings fixed, too. We sat in silence thinking about what would happen, and how all of the things would get done.

"You know," Dutch said, "staying outside right now isn't too bad, but when the rains come and it gets colder, he will need something and some place for the boys to stay and keep warm. The horses won't do well out in the open either, with no place to cool them down and dry them out. I wonder how long Luis can stay away from his ranch, too, with the cattle thieves in the area. You know, they might have figured out that Luis was here helping, and be making a raid on his cattle right now."

"I have thought of that, too," I said. "He must be some kind of a good friend to take such a chance."

Just then the card players got into a fight and before long, several were trying to break it up. It seemed that one of the cards had fallen off the makeshift table and when it came back up, it was different than when it went down. Every one soon agreed that it might not have been cheating, and the two antagonists shook hands and decided not to play any more cards right then.

I told Dutch that even the men were on edge now. Having to live outside and work extra hours was making their nerves thin.

"Maybe they all need to be thrown into the cold water," I said. "That would calm them down for a while."

A few got up and challenged others to a horseshoe game. Before long, they were all into the game, and the earlier squabble was forgotten.

Victor came out of the ranch house and walked toward where we were sitting. "Hi, boys," he said. His face was still lined with concern over all that had happened. He pointed down the pasture and said, "I guess we could use a couple more nice deer. Do you two think you could go down and bring in some fresh meat?"

I told him that we could do that, and we would have it back in plenty of time to skin and hang up, so the cool night could chill it out good. It was good to have something to do. We

240

caught up our horses and headed down the pasture just a little before sundown.

"Did you see the worried look on his face?" I asked. "He doesn't look like he has slept much lately."

"Yes, he looks tired," Dutch said. "I wish there was more that we could do."

"He is a proud man," I said. "And he doesn't want to ask anyone for extra help. He even seems to have trouble accepting help from Luis, now that he has little way of returning the favor. It's times like this when I wish we had our money back. I would loan him my part to get the things he needed -- if he would let me," I said.

Dutch nodded in agreement and we got on our horses to search for deer. He rode along deep in thought. When I asked him again about what we should do to help out, it was as if he didn't hear a word I said. In times past, his silence was because he wasn't sure, or just wanted to think about the choices. All I knew was that when Dutch didn't want to talk about things, I might as well let it ride.

We continued on down toward the pasture that went up against the hill. We always saw a lot of deer coming down to feed and water there. The trees were taller up on the hillside and it wasn't long before we were right up on a herd of about fifteen deer. We could see more getting up in the shadows of the trees on the hill.

Dutch looked at me and we both put our rifles up at the same time. I selected a nice four-point buck. They were fat this time of year and the meat had been really good and tender so far. I sited in on the young buck and gently squeezed the trigger. I felt the rifle recoil and he went down. Dutch had picked out a little larger one and dropped it neatly as the herd started to run. After the rest of the deer fled, we went to clean and carve our game. Before long, we had them dressed and across the shoulders of the horse in front of the saddle.

"They sure have lots to eat here," I said. "Just look how fat they are."

When we arrived at the ranch, we went around back to hang the meat. It was cool on this side of the house, out of the sun; and by morning, the meat would be chilled real well. I could see by what was left hanging that we did need the meat, as there was little left from the last one. While we were hanging the meat, I heard the back door open. Catrina stood there looking at what we had brought in.

"Well," she said, "Yacob and Dutch, now they have you bringing in the food." She looked tired, but smiled at the two of us and said, "Did you save the heart and liver?"

I told her we did and, if she would get a pan, I would get it for her before we skinned the deer. She soon came back with a large metal pan, and I put the parts into it. She looked up at me in a searching way. I wondered what she wanted to say to me, but Dutch was there with me.

She finally whispered to me, "Here, after supper."

We turned our horses in with the others in the corral. Dutch had been riding one that had belonged to one of the bandits. He said that it was a pretty good horse. But something in his eyes as he looked at my sorrel told me he was thinking about Nighthawk.

Right after we turned our horses loose, Dutch walked down the meadow toward the creek by himself. I guessed that he was still trying to figure something out. I was busy myself, wondering what it was Catrina wanted to talk with me about. It was always good to see her and be near her, but right now she seemed to have other things on her mind. I guess with her mother sick, she had a lot to think about.

I noticed that as soon as the sun went down, it turned pretty chilly, especially with that breeze blowing off the south pasture. Some of the cowhands had built fires around the yard near where the barn used to be. It would be cold tonight. All of our blankets would feel good, and the heat off the fire would be welcome, too.

As soon as it was dark, someone came to the front steps and called everyone in to supper. The crew moved in around the large table in the ranch house. I noticed Victor talking to Luis again by the fireplace. They were sipping their coffee and looking into the blazing fire. Luis took a poker and moved one of the logs into the flames. I could hear him say something about needing to leave soon and get back to his ranch. Then the conversations around the table got noisier and I couldn't hear any more.

The men were seated on long benches down each side of the plank table. Each of them had hung their pistols up on a rack at the front door before sitting down. I couldn't see Dutch anywhere around the table and asked some of the ones closest to me if they had seen him. One of them said that he had seen Dutch saddle up his horse just before dark. The woman who was pouring our coffee said that Dutch had borrowed an extra canteen and had picked up a small ration of food from the kitchen before he left. He hadn't said anything to any of them about his plans.

It was odd that Dutch would just be up and away without telling anyone. I looked around and guessed that if anyone knew anything, it would be Pedro. I would ask him as soon as supper was over.

Catrina didn't come into the dining hall. I supposed she was with her mother. There was a passage where the women could come and go from the kitchen without coming into the room where we were. Later I would go around to the back of the house and wait for her.

I finally saw Pedro get up to leave and caught him at the door. I pulled him over to the side and made room for the rest of the bunch to get out. I asked him if he knew anything about Dutch. He told me that Dutch had taken the horse that we had brought in from the bandits, the one he had been riding, and rounded up a small amount of food. Then he said that he was going after the bandit Boracho. He would be gone up to five days, and didn't want anyone to follow him.

I wondered what that hardheaded German was up to now. He probably thought that somehow he could find the bandits and get his horse back. I knew he had a bad temper when he got mad, and I hoped that wouldn't get him in trouble.

Thinking that I should tell Vargas and Luis about this, I went over toward where they were talking at the fireplace. I waited for a minute until one of them looked around and saw me there. They invited me over to sit with them and I pulled up another chair.

I told them about Dutch taking the spare horse and a small amount of food and going in search of the bandits that still had his horse. He had told Pedro that he could be gone up to five days. I told them that sometimes he would do things like this, but usually he was pretty levelheaded. It must have been me getting my horse back and not his that had got him so riled up. I related how he had hardly even talked to me when we went after the venison.

After listening to my story, Luis told me that he had decided he could only stay one more day right now. He would leave three of his men to help out and all of the extra horses that they had brought. He was going to ask Dutch to stay, too; but since he was gone, he could not plan on him. Victor interrupted to say how good it was for Luis to come and help out so much already. Both of them had agreed that Luis needed to get back and check on things at his own place. They told me not to say anything to the rest of the men. They would tell them tomorrow.

It was past supper by then and I hoped that Catrina hadn't been waiting on me. I hurried around the outside of the house to see if she was there. I waited by the back porch and wondered what she would say. It was only a few moments until I heard the screen door open. As I turned to look, I saw her standing there inside with the light at her back.

"Come in, Yacob," she whispered. "Come inside."

She pushed open the screen door for me and we moved back into the room. I had never seen the back part of the house. It appeared that there were about four large bedrooms, a small parlor, and I could see the kitchen beyond. She told me that if we stayed close here in the parlor, she could hear her mother if she called out for her. She motioned across the parlor to the room on the other side.

"It was good of you to come, Yacob," she said. "We have not had too much time to be together for a while."

"How long has your mother been sick?"

"Three days now," she said. "And she doesn't seem to get any better. Hold my hand, Yacob. I feel better when you do that."

I could feel and see her concern when she spoke of her mother. I held her hand and looked into her soft eyes. I wished that somehow I could make everything better for her.

"I am worried about my father, too. He doesn't get much rest with worrying about mother and all of the things on the ranch. I don't know what we would have done if Luis hadn't come over to help us." We sat in silence as I thought of what she had said.

"They are going to send for the doctor tomorrow, if she isn't better by morning," she revealed. She said that she had fixed her mother some good soup and coaxed her to eat some of it. If the fever was down by morning, they wouldn't need to send for the doctor.

I told her how Dutch had gone off on his own to try and find his horse. I didn't see how he would know where to even start looking for that bunch, and then he would have to see them first.

"Where do you think the bandits might be right now, Yacob?"

I thought about what she asked and finally said, "They would be more apt to be up on Luis's ranch trying to get some of his cattle, since it didn't work out too good for them here." I hoped I was wrong, but Dutch and I had talked about this some, and we both thought that they might go up there. If they did, with Luis and about half of his help gone, they would make it pretty hard on those that were left behind.

"Will you stay with us and help us out, Yacob? I don't know when my father can pay you."

" Yes, you can count on me."

Right then her mother called out for her and she said, "Yacob, thanks so much. I must go."

When I got back outside, I could see several of the men sitting around the four fires that were scattered through the yard. We had been lucky that it hadn't rained on us while we were camping under the stars like this. I picked up my saddle and found a place by one of the fires, pulling a blanket and the slicker over me.

It was always peaceful to breathe in the fresh air and look up at the stars that were just beginning to appear. I wondered how big those stars would be if I could get right up to them. I thought of seeing Catrina again and how nice it was to spend just a few moments with her. Did she really ever think that I wouldn't stay and help them?

The men were up early the next morning. Victor had spread the word around that those who would be going back with Luis would be leaving right after noon. They would need to get an early start for home so they could make it on the next day. I had been asked to stay and help if I wanted, and I liked that. I had planned to do just that. Catrina's mother had started to feel better that morning, so it seemed that they wouldn't need the doctor right away.

The experienced ranch hands decided to try and get some more of the stock closer into the valley, so each trip that day took us a different direction. I wasn't near the ranch when Luis and his men left for home, but I knew they had gone. I could picture them trying to make the water stop by night, and then on to the Ortega ranch tomorrow.

I wondered where Dutch was right then. He couldn't have gone very far the night he left. It bothered me some that he just decided to slip away. He probably didn't want to have to answer any questions. I hoped that he didn't get himself into a lot of trouble.

Each day saw many of the cattle moved back in towards the flats. Some of them no doubt moved back into the brush, as we didn't have any way of keeping them out of there. All we could do was hope that the good pasture would make them want to hang around. Finding the cows and learning that Catrina's mother was feeling much better meant that all seemed better at the ranch.

We still hadn't heard from Dutch, and it had now been four days since he had gone. I was beginning to worry more about him. Since I didn't know for sure which direction he had taken, I kept a watch every time that I could on both ends of the pasture. Often I wished he had let me go with him. It would have been much better. When the fifth day came and went with still no Dutch, I kept asking myself what could have happened to him.

# Chapter 18

When Dutch rode away from the Vargas ranch that night, he didn't plan on going too far before he stopped for the night. He would head up the pasture and in the general direction of the Ortega ranch. He thought that it just might be possible to run onto these rustlers without getting shot. If he saw them first, he might have a chance of waiting for a good time and getting this Boracho. The bandit would no doubt have many men with him, and it may not be possible to get at him, but he wanted to try any way.

It was after noon the next day before he came to the end of the pasture and had to choose a direction. He had not traveled through this part of the country before, and he waited until he had no other choice but to ride up one side or the other. He finally chose the right side, which would be closer to the Ortega ranch. He hadn't seen any horse tracks in the flat, but he knew rustlers would be too smart to get caught out in the open anyway.

The going was much slower now and he stopped at every place that allowed him to see for a ways and study out the area. He hadn't seen any cattle tracks for a while now, either. There was only a very small stream of water and he took his last drink before climbing up onto the brushy ridge. It would be getting on towards sundown soon. He would like to find a place where he could find shelter for the night but still see some of the area around.

He finally found the place that he was looking for. From where he was up on this ridge, he could see any one coming his way from two different directions. He had a cold supper and got his horse something to eat. He wished that he could have turned him loose down in the valley below for a good feed, but that wasn't possible. Instead he gathered up some of the dry grass and brought it to his horse.

Darkness came soon even up here on the ridge. As he drifted off to sleep, Dutch's thoughts were of his partner, Jacob. His friend would have insisted on coming along if he had shared his plans. But the Vargas family needed Jacob's good sense and resourcefulness to rebuild their ranch. Besides, it might get real bad when Dutch caught up with the rustlers, or they caught up with him.

The night passed without incident and the light came early up on the ridge. Dutch watched the open areas all morning, but all he saw pass by were three deer. When he was convinced he wasn't going to see anyone pass that way soon, he saddled his horse and continued his hunt. He rode a cross pattern from ridge to ridge, trying to find any sign of horses or cattle being moved through. It was no use; he couldn't find any trace of the outlaws.

About mid-afternoon, he thought that he would move more toward the Ortega ranch. He was able to find a small amount of water in one of the canyons where he saw a few deer moving about. He watched for a long time before he dared venture forward. He found only a few small puddles where moisture seemed to have seeped up from the ground. Only deer had watered there.

Working his way uphill, he could see the formation of a rocky bottom. The sand was wet here, and when he dug down about a foot with his hands, water filled up most of the hole. As soon as it cleared a little bit, he got a drink and then gave the horse a few drinks. He had to wait for a little while before the hole would fill up again. He would need to remember this place, and tried to fix some landmark to measure the spot.

It was close enough to dark that Dutch thought he would stay in the area for the night. He pulled back up the way that he had come and made a quick camp not far from the water hole. Just before dark, he saw several deer come down to water. One walked right by where he was and looked at him,

249

then walked on to the water hole. He had brought a few handfuls of grain for the horse and fed him a small ration. The horse ate everything and was looking for more. Dutch went to sleep that night wondering what the next day would bring.

It was late on the third day out that he finally came across a number of tracks going toward the Ortega ranch. He got down off his horse and studied the ground. They were pretty fresh, but some deer had been over them since they were made. Could this be some of those rustlers that he was looking for? It wasn't Indians, so maybe so.

He decided to follow along the trail and see if he could get closer to them. The tracks could be as new as three days. He could tell a lot more if he could see some horse droppings. He wished that he had picked up this trail early in the morning. As it was, it looked like he would only be able to follow it for about two more hours. From the direction of the tracks, he guessed they were heading into the Ortega ranch for sure.

He was up early on the fourth day and decided to give his horse a double handful of grain that morning. They hadn't been able to find any more water, so they continued on. It only made sense that the rustlers would have to find water, too. So if he kept on their trail, they would lead him to the next water hole. His horse was getting pretty worn out from climbing and going without good feed. Dutch got off and walked from time to time to ease this burden, especially up the steep places.

When he came across some horse dung, it told him that the trail was about two days old. The riders he was following could be nearly anywhere in that time, or they could just be over the next ridge. Dutch made camp off the trail that night. He could sure have used some of that good cooking from the Vargas ranch or the Ortega ranch.

The next day, he got another early start. His horse had little to eat or drink the day before and the same would most likely be true today. Somewhere, Dutch needed to refill his canteens today. As he poured a little water into his hand and gave the horse a taste, he also knew he would have to walk more today.

Dutch spent the next several hours following the trail on foot. His horse had picked up a stone bruise and hurt his right hind leg. He could walk on it pretty well, but he wouldn't last long with a rider on him. He would be fine in a while if he could get back down to the grass and pasture. Dutch got to thinking that it would be a long way to walk over to the Ortega ranch, which lay just under that mountain range visible to the east.

He was resting under the shade of an oak tree when he heard the sounds of cattle coming his way. His instincts told him it would be the rustlers. Quickly he looked around for a place to lie in wait. He knew immediately that he would have to leave the trail and climb higher on the ridge to get around behind the advancing herd. Any riders coming in front would be sure to see his tracks and suspect that something was wrong, and he wanted to be behind them before they did.

Knowing that he could make much faster time on horseback than on foot, he decided to mount up and put his horse's lame foot to the test. The animal limped a little bit, but seemed to be able to carry his weight up the hillside. He knew the herd would be sticking to the low land and would pass close by him. His mind raced from one plan to another as he searched for cover. Should he ride away as fast as he could, or should he pick a place and take his chances on getting some of them first?

He had brought some extra shells for his rifle. They would come in handy. Where could he retreat if it got too hot for him? He wouldn't be able to withstand their firepower for very long once they found out that he was alone. They could ride around him in time and trap him here. He would need to stay up high enough that he could make his escape off the back of the ridge. He knew that when they found his tracks, they would come looking for him no matter what he did. He might as well get as many as he could before they knew he was there. He slid the box of extra shells out of his pack and put them within easy reach.

Dutch reckoned there would be about two more hours before sundown. If he could hold out until then, maybe he could slip away in the dark. He had a few minutes before things broke loose, so he gave the horse another handful of the grain. He didn't want to harm that injured foot any more, but he might not have any choice except to ride away as fast as he could. He would have to take a chance if it came to that. He stroked the horse's neck to keep him calm and prevent any sound that might alert the riders that they were being watched.

The sound of the bawling herd was getting closer now, and he wished that his partner were here. He had selected a hiding place where he had a clear view through a gap in the trail below. If he were ready, he would have about twenty feet of opening to shoot through.

The lead riders were entering the gap now. They came along looking sharply from side to side, and the cattle followed behind. From the sound of things, they had a lot of cattle. More riders began to file through his line of vision.

Where was that Boracho? If he was among them, Dutch was going to get him. In the next few moments, the front riders would reach the place where he had left the trail. He didn't have much time left before his chance to surprise them was gone. He could shoot a couple of the riders and scatter the herd. He guessed that was what he would do; he might as well make all of this count for something.

Two more riders appeared at that very instant. Dutch saw his black horse, and Boracho was riding him! He had been ready to shoot and he did, but not before the sound of a warning shot from those ahead signaled they had found his tracks. He could see Boracho holding on to the saddlehorn, and then gunfire seemed to come up toward him from every direction. He couldn't see if Boracho slid off the horse or not, but he knew his bullet had hit its mark.

Dutch knew he had to get out of there, so he raced off the back side of the ridge, firing a couple of times in the general direction of the thieves. His horse responded well to the downhill travel. They were running though the brush and the small clearings as fast as he could go. Dutch's hope was that the rustlers might be more cautious, not knowing how many men were shooting at them. But they would soon figure that out.

He was just about out of rifle range when the first bullet came whizzing by. If he and his horse could make the next few jumps without getting hit, they might slip away altogether. But the firing from the ridge increased, and suddenly his horse went down. Dutch was thrown a few feet away and landed in some scrub oak that helped break the fall. He still had hold of his rifle and looked up the hill to see riders coming his way. He ran into the brush in the bottom of the little canyon and pulled himself into the thickest part of it. It would be too thick for them to ride horses in here. If he stayed still, they might think that he had gone on over the ridge on foot.

Before long his pursuers reached the place where his horse had fallen. Would they remember that it had belonged to one of their friends who had died at Dripping Springs? He held his breath and his gun close as they rode by just at the edge of the deep thicket where he was hiding. He heard them say, "Where did he go?"

Two rifle shots sounded up on the ridge he had come from. Someone shouted that they needed to get Boracho to the doctor. In a few minutes he could hear horses climbing the slope that he had come down. He waited for some time before he decided that they had really gone. But he would wait until dark before he slipped back up to his horse to see if they had left anything. He knew they had killed the horse.

Dutch knew he was a lucky man to have been able to get away from that bunch. He nearly tore his clothes off by the time he crawled out of the thicket, and his boots looked like they sure needed some more grease on them.

Warily he made his way back to where the horse lay. They had taken the canteens and everything else they could get. He guessed they didn't want the slicker. That would come in pretty handy tonight and in other nights that he might spend out here. They had tried to pull the saddlebags off, too, but one side was wedged underneath. They had just taken what they wanted from the other. Dutch knew that the one under the horse had some grain in it. If he could get it loose, it might make for pretty good eating before he could get to Ortega's ranch. With some pushing and pulling, he finally moved the horse over enough to pull the saddlebag out. In the morning, he would head straight for the Ortega ranch.


Luis Ortega made it back to his ranch before sundown the second day. It was always good to get back to his own place. Those he had left behind greeted him. Some of them met him down in the pasture and followed him home. With the shortage of help, they had not been able to ride the range too far. He said that he hoped the cattle were still okay. They would need to check things out in the morning.

During the evening hours, he told everyone of the past few days and answered any questions asked. Many of the hands had friends at the Vargas ranch, and sat quietly as he told them of those who had been lost. He asked if any of them knew of any family, but they were little help. Some had been around for years, but seldom would anyone talk of family.

Luis had told Victor that he would ride to Sonora and send some wagonloads of material back for rebuilding the Vargas spread. Victor had given him a note to take to the merchants there who were his friends. If they would send the lumber and other materials out, he would pay the drivers for their work. He had to ask the merchants to wait until after the cattle drive for the balance of payment. Luis planned to visit them personally and urge them to extend the credit to his friend.

Though Luis needed to get to Sonora as soon as he could, he first needed to get a feel for his own operation. He would take four or five days to see about the cattle on his own ranch. In the crisp, clear morning, he started out with some of his men, giving each an assignment before they rode away. The day passed without incident. They located a lot of the cattle, but this was only a beginning. It was getting dark when they finally got back to the ranch. Everyone reported in, and the horses were put away for the next morning.

It was well past supper and about time to turn in when the dog started barking. Several lanterns went out into the night and voices asked, "Who is there?"

Dutch yelled, "Hello, the house!" He was soon in a circle of light on the front porch, and what a sight he was! His clothes were in rags, and he was about worn out from his two nights in the open and his three days of walking. He had chewed on the horse feed to give himself some extra energy, but he couldn't eat too much of it as it only made him more thirsty. He had stopped only once that day, and that was to finally get a drink out of the stream in the meadow. The water had turned the trail dust into mud, which was now caked over his arms and chest.

In spite of this, Luis quickly drew him into a chair near the fireplace and sent for some food. Then he listened while

Dutch told the story of his run in with the cattle rustlers. He became agitated when he heard that they were driving so many head from his range, but he listened in silence while Dutch told how he had waited and watched until Boracho finally came into view.

"It was just plain bad luck that someone sounded a warning shot just as I was getting a good bead on Boracho," Dutch complained. "I know I had to have hit him. From what some of his men said, they were going to have to get him to a doctor."

"Can you take me and my men to the place where you last saw the cattle?" Luis asked.

"Sure! I can tell you about where it is, and you will know the best way to get there."

"I hope they didn't take time to round up the herd after their boss was shot. If they didn't, we may have time to go and get them back." Luis turned to the listening ranch hands. "We will need to leave early in the morning. Take a pack along. We may be gone more than one day. And be ready for trouble."

Dutch drew out a map as best he could, and Luis was familiar with the place. He said that nearly all of the cattle rustlers moved cattle through that general area. They had some area up near the big mountain where they had water. They would either hold the stock there until they had a buyer, or drive them on south across the big mesa.

Luis seemed to be in a hurry the next morning as he gave orders to the men. He had decided to leave only two hands at the ranch to keep watch. The dog should give them plenty of warning if anyone approached. As an extra precaution, he had them saddle and tie four extra horses around the yard before it was light. He said that should keep any one guessing.

The rest of the men were soon out on the flat, heading a little bit upstream from where Dutch had come in. They climbed rapidly up toward the mountain range that lay in the distance. Luis was in the lead, his ramrod musket close by his side.

Even though it had been cool in the night, the sun quickly warmed them up. In the daylight, Dutch had a chance to inspect the new used clothes that Luis had given him. They were a much better fit this time, though maybe a little too big around the middle. He could now also see the many scratches on his arms and face. He smiled as he thought of what Luis had said when he saw him last night in his ragged clothes.

"It looks like you have been sorting out wild cats," he'd said with a smile. He had quickly sent one of the men to the bunkhouse to find Dutch something to wear. Dutch remembered how embarrassed he had been to be hanging out every place when Luis's wife had walked into the room.

They were steadily moving up toward the mountain range. It had been some time since they could see the valley floor below. It would be hard to find anyone in all of this brushy country. It was well after noon before Luis stopped to rest the horses. They had brought food along and water, so they pulled the saddles off the horses while they had something to eat.

"The way I figure it," Luis said, "we should be cutting their trail in the next hour if we keep on this direction. And that should only be about an hour or so from where Dutch had his run in with them. We had better look sharp! We don't want them to get the drop on us."

It was from this point that Luis sent two wing riders out away from the rest of the group. He picked out a point to meet just in case they all got separated. Those two were soon out of sight. Luis led the rest of them in the direction that they had been going earlier. They continued forcing their way through all of the brush and little openings, only to find more of the same. It was hard riding, and they couldn't see very far ahead. Whenever they came out into the open and had a better chance to see, he would hold them up and study the area out before they passed through.

Once as they waited and watched, they heard the movement of something coming their way. Luis silenced the riders and they spread out and waited. Before long, they heard a faint whistle, and then an answer as one of Luis's men came into view. He had found the tracks of the herd just a little ways ahead. Luis waited for him to lead the way, and before long they were looking at a well-worn trail of many cows. Luis got down ad studied the cattle tracks; they looked really fresh. He posted riders up and down the trail to watch.

"Do you think this is about the place where you came across the rustlers?" he asked.

Dutch answered in a quiet voice, "Yes, it's close. But a little bit farther to the west."

While they were looking ahead down the trail, Luis's other wing lookout joined them. He said that he had come from down the trail about one half mile, and he hadn't seen anything but tracks.

"It looks like a lot of riders are heading toward Sonora, maybe all of them. You must be right, Dutch. You must have hit Boracho. Otherwise they wouldn't have left the cattle. He might have left some men to take the cattle on, but it looks like a lot of riders went the other way."

Luis decided to hurry forward and see if he could find any of the cattle. In about an hour they came to the place where Dutch had been hiding when the bandits came through. He showed where he had hidden and where he shot Boracho. There was a lot of blood on the ground for a few feet, but then horse tracks covered over any other sign.

"I would say that you hit him pretty good. It would be a shame if that mean cuss didn't make it to town," Luis said.

They proceeded on up the trail with caution. It wasn't long before they spotted the herd grazing off to the side of the trail. Luis said that they would need to get them rounded up and try to hold them for the night. It would be a long way back to any water hole, and he knew they had been pushed hard by the rustlers.

It was then that Dutch thought of the little pocket of water that he had found. He told Luis that it must not be more than a couple of miles to where they could probably get enough water for the herd before heading them back to the ranch.

Luis said that he had never known of any water around these parts, but that he had seen deer sometimes and wondered how they survived so far from water. It would mean going the opposite direction from the usual water hole, but Luis knew the cattle would suffer if they tried to drive them all of the way back to it.

He told Dutch to lead the way and had one of the outriders accompany them. When Dutch finally came even with the landmark that he had picked out to mark the spot, he led the way off the trail, knowing it should be less than a mile to the place. He went ahead of the cowboys and cattle to find the best way to the springs.

It was as he remembered it. He could even see the place where he had pooled the water earlier. Many deer had left tracks here, and the water was almost running now. They took their shovels off the packhorse and started digging a long ditch. In no time it was nearly full of water.

Luis rode back to the rest and pointed the way down to the small meadow and the water hole. When the cattle got close to the water, they didn't need any more help. They ran right into the pools, drinking and bringing down the banks the men had dug.

The vaqueros had to move them away and dig more ditches before they got all they wanted. Luis seemed happy to *know that there was a source of water here. He decided they should bed the cattle down right where they were and start back early in the morning. He ordered the men to have a cold camp and posted lookouts all night.*

*It was good that Dutch didn't draw any lookout assignment. After the exercise he'd had yesterday, he certainly needed the extra rest. Besides, Luis probably figured he deserved some reward for finding the water. He fell quickly asleep, thinking of his partner and Catrina.*

Our heavy and steady riding on the Vargas ranch was bringing some good results. Many of the cattle had been driven back to the pasture and seemed ready to stay there for a while. The big meadow was dotted with the herd.

When the five days had passed, I wanted to go out and try to find Dutch. I visited with Catrina about this and wondered if her father might be able to spare me, but they needed everyone to help with the cattle now. After seven days, I knew it had been way too long for Dutch not to return, and this worried me a lot. I thought I would ask Victor again about going to look for my partner.

The next morning right after breakfast I found Victor at the fireplace with his wife. It was good that she was feeling so much better now.

"Mr. Vargas," I said, "it has been eight or nine days since Dutch has been gone. I am real worried about him, and have been thinking about him. I need to go see if I can find him."

Victor turned to me and said, "Yes! This is something you need to do. Take whatever you need. I hope you find him well."

I told him that I would only be gone three days. If I didn't find him by then, I would be back. I caught Catrina's eye and nodded toward the front door. She gave me an okay nod and in a few minutes we were out on the front porch away from the rest. I told her that I was going after Dutch.

She came close, held me, and said, "Yes! I know you need to do this."

I didn't want to leave her, but she seemed to know how much I needed to go. She gave me a quick kiss on the cheek and said that she would get me some food to take along.

In a few minutes, I had my horse ready to go. It would be good to ride out on my own trusty horse, Jake. It felt like putting on my favorite hat. Catrina came out with a bag full of food and handed it up to me. The sky was getting lighter now as I looked down at her. She had her hand on my leg and was looking up. I wondered what I would say if she asked me not to go right now. But she didn't ask me that.

She smiled up at me and said, "Dutch wouldn't think you were much of a friend if you didn't come to help him."

I nodded a yes and rode out into the early light. I had been wondering for days about the place Dutch would be most likely to go. I thought he probably would have gone up the meadow and toward the distant range of mountains. There was good cover in most of the area I had seen there, and Mr. Vargas had said that the cattle rustlers often used that route.

It was good to be out doing something. I had been worried about Dutch every day, even the first two or three. Now that he had been gone more than twice that long, I really was beginning to get concerned. It was not like him to not show up, unless something had happened to him.

As I rode through the pasture I looked for any tracks that might be his, but there was no way of knowing. The crews had been working the area hard close to the ranch, and tracks went everywhere. The sun was up now and it looked like I would reach the other end of the pasture by about noon and then climb out on one of the banks. I could still see an occasional cow, but most of them had been driven back toward the ranch.

The water was only running in a small stream here. It was quite a contrast to the large streams of water that Catrina and I had seen several miles to the south. I had taken three canteens to fill in case water became difficult to find. I enjoyed riding along without having to go running through the brush after those half wild cattle. I wondered how they would ever get them to market. Maybe they were better when you kept them in a herd.

I had left the chaps that I normally wore behind and I looked down at the shoes on my feet. There were several deep slashes and cuts into them around the toes. None of the cuts had come all of the way through, but they looked real used and worn. I would really need to get them oiled up when I returned.

After a few hours, I found myself at the end of the meadow. The brush choked up the little canyon that led into it, so I needed to pick out a place to get out on the ridge. I couldn't see the distant mountain range now, but knew that I would be able to when I got out on top. I wondered if Dutch had come this way. He might have gone further west, and I might not be anywhere near where he came out of the pasture. At least I was out trying to help, anyway. And if I didn't have any luck, at least I would know that I had tried.

Just then I saw what looked like an easier way to climb out of the little canyon on the right. I started up that way, and within a few minutes I could see the tracks left by someone going up at the same place. The tracks were old, but I could see them plainly in the soft ground, leading up the hill.

"Yes!" I said out loud. This had to be where Dutch left the valley. I kept a sharp lookout as I rode along, but the tracks soon vanished as the ground become more rocky and firm. When I looked back along the trail that I had come up, I could see very few of my own tracks, either.

I sat looking in all directions for a bit, wondering what to do. I felt sure that this must be the way that Dutch had come. Why would any other lone rider have come up here like this? I already knew the answer. It could have been one of our riders from the ranch. They might have wanted to make a circle at the end of the pasture to look for cattle.

When I got up in the higher country, I found a better place to look out. The canyons and draws were brushy. I would need to be careful and go slowly. It wouldn't do for me to get caught alone out here.

I decided to pull the saddle off my horse and give him a good breather. I had been pushing him along pretty hard since we left the ranch. I opened the food that Catrina had sent along. She had rolled some of the tortillas with beans and they sure did taste good right now. She had also sent along a good helping of jerky and even some biscuits from the morning meal.

I thought of her as I started to eat. She was a dandy! And she would make someone a good wife to settle down with some day. I could see by her willingness to work that she was an 'up-and-at-em' kind of person. The past few days had been hard for her. She worried about her mother and her father, too. She had told me they had planned that this year's roundup would give them some additional money for improvements and a few luxuries around the ranch. Her father had looked forward to increasing the size of the herd and hiring more riders to work there. But their recent losses would keep that from happening.

Victor had told me one evening that he had sent Luis with a message to have lumber shipped to help rebuild his ranch. He had also ordered four large tents, and asked for more men who would be available to help with the construction. He was counting on having five or six men arrive along with the materials.

The regular hands would have little time to help, with the roundup coming. It was more important than ever that Vargas get his cattle to market. And he had to get a good price for them in order to be able to pay everyone off and have enough left for the cost of the new buildings. Things didn't look very promising for his prospects of having any extra funds this year.

I had seen that Victor had enough cash to be able to pay those that would take a couple of days off to go to the towns. I wondered just how much money he had. Losses like he had suffered could wipe out a lot of ranchers. Losing his horses and buildings would be hard, but the loss of his workers, many of whom were also friends, was the worst. It was difficult to get good men.

Nighttime found me well up into the rolling hills leading toward the mountain range. After taking care of the horse and giving him some of the grain that I had brought along, I selected a good place for the night. It wasn't long before I could hear the cry of the coyotes. That was the last thing I remembered before the early dawn came and I found myself awake.

Something hot would sure be welcome right now, and I could see that Catrina had sent some coffee and sugar along. I always liked to have sugar in my coffee, but some of the others just liked it straight. Unfortunately I knew I wouldn't be having any fires up here. I pulled the blanket and slicker back over me as I thought about getting up. It would be a few more minutes before it was daylight and I really needed to be able to see pretty well before I left my spot.

If Dutch was out here he would be getting up at about this same time of morning. I wondered if I would be able to find any trace of him. He could be anywhere; even worse, he might be dead by now. I would only have this one day to look before I would need to start back. I shifted and felt the small pains and stiffness that came from a steady day of riding out in search of the cattle. So far they had always gone away when I got to stirring around.

My horse was up and looking around for something to eat. I had spotted some dry grass a little ways away and went under the brush to pull it for him. I yanked my hand back when I saw movement at the base of the brush. I had nearly pulled a large rattlesnake out with the grass! It was cold and the snake moved slowly, so I was able to get clear of it without getting bitten.

Maybe something like that could have happened to Dutch; maybe he hadn't been so lucky. There were a lot of things out here in the hills that could bring death, and I was reminded of one just now.

The horse seemed glad to see me as I whispered to him and rubbed him. He was warm and felt good to my cold hands right now. I waited until sun up before deciding to ride on; it seemed to stay dark in the low places for a long while this morning.

I continued on toward the mountains that I could see in the distance. I would really need to start back before nightfall, if I could. In the meantime, I needed to keep a sharp eye out. We worked our way down through and around the brushy washes. There was no sign of anyone coming this way, and I knew there was only the merest chance that I would find any tracks out in this kind of terrain.

I rode and watched until about noon. I decided I needed to take a little rest and give my horse some more feed. I put some grain into my hand, and he licked every bit of it up. Then I let him stop and have a few mouthfuls of the dry grass. I decided to give him most of a canteen of water. I poured it out slowly to make sure my hat would hold it without leaking. That would have to last him until we got back down on the pasture tomorrow.

I still had one canteen left and took a quick drink from that. I knew from our last trip up here in this general area, when Dutch and I had first come into the country, that water was pretty scarce. Even when I reached the mountain ahead, I could still be quite a ways from any water supply.

I thought that if all went well, I might be able to make it to the area in about three hours. If I didn't find any trace of Dutch, then I would need to start back toward the ranch before dark. It was a little bit easier going now and the brush wasn't nearly so bad. There were a few clear spaces that I judged to be about three hundred yards wide. Instead of riding right through, I tried to go around the edges. I didn't want to be seen by unfriendly eyes.

In about two hours, I came upon something that brought me up short. Right in front of me was a well-worn trail. I got down and began to study it out. It looked like a large number of cattle had been going west. Horse tracks were everywhere. But then, only a little distance away, I could see signs of a lot of cattle being driven to the east. Many horses were going that way, too. From the looks of things, the cattle were being driven back toward the Ortega Ranch.

I looked in the direction of the Ortega ranch, and decided it would sure be a long and hard ride to make it there in one day. What did all of this mean? Ortega's men wouldn't have come this far if those cattle hadn't been rustled, and the cattle would never have been that far away from water unless there were pushed. I didn't think that any of the canyons that I could see would produce any water. One thing for sure, the cattle had to have been driven into this area, and someone was taking them back toward the Ortega ranch.

This find gave me a lot to think about. With so much activity going on, Dutch may have found some of the riders. If he hadn't run into the rustlers, maybe he would have joined the riders who were returning to the Ortega ranch. If he was still alive, he might be safe and helping to return the cattle. If not, then what?

As I turned to head toward the Vargas ranch, I

decided I would ride back a little bit to the west and see some new country. Maybe Dutch would be back at the ranch when I returned. The setting of the sun found me happy to be alive and anxious to reach the ranch. I really didn't know what to think about my friend Dutch now. The things I found caused about as many questions as answers.

As I rode into view of the ranch, I realized it had been a long three days and I was glad to get back. Some good warm food would be waiting. And of course seeing Catrina there would tend to take some of the tiredness out of me. Heck! I might not even be tired at all if I could be alone with her! Maybe Dutch would be there, too. This would sure be a relief, but deep down I didn't expect to see him.

It was still light enough to see when I got to the corral. After taking care of Jake and giving him a good rub down, I made my way to the ranch house. After washing up I went inside. A couple of the hands had nearly finished eating, so I found a place among them and joined in their talk.

I asked about the day's ride out, and was told that one of the cowboys had been thrown from his horse. He had been chasing one of the young steers when his horse stepped into a hole. It had broken the horse's leg, and he had to be shot and left out in the hills. I had seen the horses come up lame at times, but I had never seen one of them break a leg. Here was another loss for Victor. The cowhand was pretty dinged up, too, with a swollen arm and scrapes. He hadn't broken his arm, but it would be painful for a few days and he wouldn't be able to ride for a while. This riding and chasing wild cows was dangerous and tiring work.

After the crew had gone back outside, I told Victor that I had found evidence of a large movement of horses and cattle up in the high country. I told him I thought that I had found Dutch's trail at the north end of the meadow, just before the hills. He agreed that it was probably Dutch's, since he hadn't sent his men that far away yet. I did tell him that I had spotted about twenty or so head of cattle a long ways up the valley and described the last place that I had seen them. He thanked me for that and said he would send part of the riders up there in the morning. If I felt good enough to go, I could show them the cattle. I assured him that I would be ready to ride with the rest the next morning.

Tomorrow was Sunday. If we brought the cattle in early, we might have some time off. A rest would be welcome.

# Chapter 19

Luis Ortega was a man determined to keep what was his. He sent a rider ahead to scout for any danger, and pushed the cattle forward toward the ranch. They would not reach the familiar range in one day, but if his men could hold the herd together without water and keep them from running away during the next night, he would be able to get them home.

Dutch rode along with them, thinking of his partner over at the Vargas ranch. He wondered about asking Luis if he could cut out of here now and return to tell them that he was safe. He knew that Jacob would be worried sick about him and probably would be getting ready to come and see if he could find him. Before long, however, he could tell that it would take all of the help that they had to get the cattle safely back onto the range. He decided that maybe he should just not say anything.

By nightfall the cattle were milling around. They were more thirsty than tired. Luis had said that they could not drive them as hard as the rustlers had. The front riders had been pulled back to camp by now. Luis decided to post lookouts, but said that they could have a small fire to cook up some hot food. He designated one of the hands to stir up some food. In a short while, he called everybody to eat. The stew tasted especially good with the tortillas that they brought. Several said that this vaquero made the best stew in Mexico. Dutch thought they might be right, or else he was just extra hungry.

Luis had picked out a good-sized clearing surrounded by oak and juniper trees. When it was Dutch's turn to ride the circle around the cattle, he noticed that the juniper smelled good this time of the year. Some said the berries were good to eat, but he hadn't liked them much when he'd tried them.

Riding the circle around the cattle gave him time for some good thinking. He wondered if Jacob would still want to go to the Sonora River country. He seemed pretty stuck on this Catrina, though. And it was true that she seemed to like him a lot, too. She was something, all right.

He wondered if they would ever get back to their gold mining dreams. They hadn't even been able to think about such things as that. It was sure one busy place around here, and a guy could get himself killed real easy if he let his mind go to dreaming. It was a different kind of danger than in the gold fields, too. It wasn't easy to see coming, and there wasn't often a chance to get help.

The only thing Dutch knew for sure was that they had to stay and help out here for some time. Within a month both the Ortega and Vargas cowhands would round up the cattle to drive them to market. Not much could be done to help Victor restore his burned out buildings until after that. He didn't see how they could leave before the first snow to go anywhere else. And maybe Jacob wouldn't want to go then, either.

"If I had a gal like this Catrina, I guess I would take my time about moving on, too," mumbled Dutch. He still couldn't imagine his partner falling for someone. Jacob must have learned real fast out here.

He smiled as he remembered how the dance hall girls used to sit down on his partner's lap, wrap their arms around him, and give him a great big kiss on the neck. Then the crowd would laugh and tease him as he left the saloon.

The only one that wouldn't do that was Belle. She was different from the rest, more their age, or maybe just a little bit older. She was usually the one that would come and break it up, helping poor Jacob out of the pickle he was in. Dutch didn't like that kind of treatment much either, but there was nobody to fight. He couldn't hit the dance hall girls. On second thought, maybe he should have just swatted them one.

Of course this made him think of that card shark, Slippery Jim, who was always hanging around with some of the regular dance hall gals: Sadie, Big Hattie and Careless Ida. Yes they were a bunch. If he had slapped one, then they would all be in for a fight. That may have been better. Jacob could take care of himself, and sometimes Dutch, too, when they got to slugging it out. He was a little bit shorter than Dutch, but he was real strong and fast. Yes, he guessed that's what they should have done. Jacob didn't like to fight as much as he did, but when pressed, he was one to put your back up against.

Dutch could hear the next watch coming to relieve him now. He would need to hurry and get some sleep. A thought popped into his head. "You don't need to sleep too long, if you can just sleep fast." That was what Jacob said.

The cattle were up and moving at first light. Luis sent a rider forward to check the trail ahead. At first they would be moving right back down the trail that they had just come over, so they knew the going would be easy for now. But Luis would have them leave the trail before too long and head straight for the mountain that rose above his ranch.

The hands were hazing the herd forward in a steady walk. Occasionally a stray or two wanted to get out of the ranks and into the brush. No matter whether they wanted water, a bite to eat, or just to rest for a while, the vaqueros would push them back into the flow. Luis estimated they had about a hundred head of cattle, and he was glad that the rustlers hadn't changed the brands yet. They probably intended to do that when they reached the holding area up at the base of the big mountain range. Luis was upset that some of the cattle buyers would purchase the stock without worrying about the owner's brand.

After about three hours of travel, Luis decided it was time to head them toward the ranch. It was hard to get them off the trail. It took the short rope and a little yell to get them turned the right way. If they ever got close enough to smell water, then they would get down to that in a hurry.

It was harder going now, and Luis sent a few hands to scout ahead for the best way to take the bunch. They tried to keep them closer together, too, but often found themselves dashing after strays that bolted away from the rest. They were anxious to get back into familiar country where the going would be easier, but it wasn't until about three hours before sundown that they finally came within view of the valley.

From a long ways off, Dutch could see the grass and the shimmering water that found its way down through the pasture. It took another hour before the cattle became aware of it and started running for the meadow and the water. The riders tagged along behind to see if any strays were left, but the whole bunch rushed forward and down into the meadow. Luis may not have wanted them to run off any of their fat before market time, but nothing could keep them back now.

When the herd finally reached the pasture, Ortega ordered all the men to dismount and stretch their legs. He had them wait for nearly thirty minutes so the horses could feed and drink their fill before going on. Dutch had often wondered why Luis was always so interested in taking care of the horses. Now he understood that it was probably the difference between a good rancher and a bad one. Horses were most important out here at the edge of the wilderness. Just thinking of the long walk he'd had earlier when the rustlers shot his horse told him that.

Dutch still felt really bad about that. The horse had responded even in pain and had run full out down the ridge. If he hadn't given his all, Dutch wouldn't be here today thinking about it. That horse had saved his life.

He was glad now to get down and let the horses drink. They would push the cattle on into the pasture and leave them there where they could feed for awhile before the men would come back to bring them on in. It would be well past dark when

272

they arrived at the ranch.

The dog sounded their approach when they arrived at the ranch. There was always something good about getting home, even in the dark. Luis gave instructions to the returning riders and then went into the main house to see how things had gone at the ranch during their absence. The two men he'd left behind had been busy, keeping the extra saddle horses in sight and moving around the yard enough to make it look like others might be there, too.

It was that special time of the night when the call to supper was made. Some of the men were too tired to eat and just fell into their bunks. The rest went into the long cook shack and found a comfortable place at the table. The room was big enough for at least twice that many to eat at one time. At roundup, it would probably get pretty crowded inside, but room was always made for whoever came. Tomorrow would see the herd back near the ranch.


Dutch wondered what Jacob was doing right now. It would be good to let him know what had happened with Boracho and his band of thieves. Could he get permission to ride back to the Vargas ranch?

The next morning, before he had a chance to ask if Luis could spare him, the rancher invited him to ride along to Moctezuma to see about the lumber shipment. The small town of Moctezuma was down on the Rio Matape River in the state of Sonora, where many of the bandits liked to go and spend their time. If they found Boracho there, Dutch might be able to identify him and have the soldiers arrest him for rustling. It could be a chance to put him away for a while.

Dutch hesitated for a moment, not sure what to do. They really did need to get this ringleader out of the way. He knew that someone else would probably move in and continue the rustling, but having Boracho arrested might slow it down some. But if he went with Luis, how would he ever get word to Jacob? Dutch finally decided he should accompany Luis now and hope that someone from the Ortega ranch would get word to his partner soon.

They left early the next morning, taking along one of the wagons to haul back supplies for the ranch. It was slower going with the wagon and team, but the road was pretty smooth down along the edge of the pasture. The four horses stepped lively with the empty wagon, and the skinner sat back in the seat and talked to them. The wagon held enough supplies for the three days' round trip, and Dutch was excited at the thought of going to a new area and seeing new places. This was going to be an adventure.

Dutch wondered why there seemed to be more places for water on this side of the meadow than the other side. It must have something to do with the mountain range that was behind the Ortega ranch. He guessed the water flowed both ways from the range. The grass was thicker here, too; not as lush as out in the big pasture, but plenty for good grazing.

At dusk they stopped to camp by one of the small watering places. So far they hadn't seen anyone on the trip, even though Dutch had expected that the thieves might give them trouble on the road to town. The country had been pretty open most of the way. Without good cover for an ambush, any attackers could expect to lose men in a fight. The few horses and the empty wagon probably weren't worth the risk. It was still good to keep a sharp look out, though.

As they continued on the next morning, Luis pointed out a ranch in the distance. "Those are our closest neighbors," he explained. "They are good people, and we help each other. Often our cattle get mixed up, and we just take them on to market and sort them out. I let them do the sorting. "I want them to know that I trust them."

As they neared Moctezuma shortly after noon the next

day, they passed through fields of different kinds of crops. This was where Luis got the grain for his animals. A small detachment of military troops was stationed just outside the town. Dutch could see them moving around their courtyard. They had many horses in the large corrals.

Dutch was surprised that there weren't as many big buildings as he had expected to see. The town had a bank, mercantile store, several cantinas, a place to spend the night, livery stable and several houses along the two or three streets. There was also a church with a big bell. The more he looked around, though, the more small businesses he could see. As they rode along he spotted a blacksmith shop, tannery, leatherwork, and a couple of small stores besides the mercantile, which sold everything. It seemed like a quiet town, and Dutch mentioned as much to Luis.

"Wait until the sun goes down!" he smiled. "The military patrols will be back, the ranchers will come in, and it will get pretty noisy then."

Dutch could see the women of the night outside the cantinas, visiting with each other or those that would pass by in the street. Some of the Mexican wives would jerk their husbands away if they paid too much attention. Maybe they had reason.

Luis reminded Dutch to look for his black horse, since that might help them find Boracho. He also warned him to stay close by in case the Federalies came over to question them. Now Luis added a caution that he would need to stay out of trouble.

"Now why did he say something like that?" Dutch wondered. He didn't know Luis knew he sometimes got into a little bit of trouble.

The big sign over the mercantile read, 'Sonora Mercantile. Armando Marino, Owner.' The man in the mercantile was friendly as Luis introduced Dutch to him. What was more exciting, the owner pointed out his daughter, who was working with another woman folding and stacking clothing. She seemed to know Luis very well, and came over to them. Dutch hadn't thought it possible that there could be another one around the area who would be as nice to look at as Catrina. He smiled as Luis introduced her to him.

"This is my good friend, Rosa Marino."

She was tall and slender, and seemed to be just about his same age. She was very easy on the eyes. Like most of the women in Mexico, she had long black hair that hung nearly to her waist in the back. It was held in place by two small combs. She was warm and friendly as she smiled at him. Her skin was light in color, set off by two dark brown eyes and nice soft tanned skin. Yep! She was easy on the eyes.

Dutch visited with her for a moment, before she was called away by a customer. As she moved away, she said, "Luis, you must come and have dinner with us tonight."

Now this was something to come to town for, Dutch thought, as Luis answered, "Yes! We will be there."


Luis was soon busy getting the supplies ordered for the ranches. As he walked through the building with Señor Marino, checking off items from the list, he realized how lucky Victor was. All of the supplies that he would need were there in stock. Even three drivers were located who would freight the things over to the Vargas ranch.

While Luis was making the arrangements, Dutch noticed the loud noises coming from inside the bar across the street. "They must have a pretty good crowd in there already," he thought, as he counted eight horses tied to the hitching rail. His black horse wasn't among those that he could see from here. He wondered if Boracho was even in town. Maybe the bandit had made off for some other place, or maybe he wasn't hurt as bad as Dutch had thought.

276

Dutch told Luis he would go over to the livery stable and check the corral. By the time everything was ordered, he should be back to help get things loaded. He knew that they would need to be on their way the next morning.

Dutch could see several people coming and going around town. Some of them were about his age. Some of the girls were pretty good looking, too, but not as pretty as Rosa. He went over to the man in charge of the livery stable and asked how business was. He asked if there were any horses for sale, just to get the conversation going.

The man took Dutch around back to the large holding corral which had several horses in it. It was there that Dutch recognized his black horse. The blood seemed to boil in him as he leaned over the corral for a better look. The brand had been altered, but he could still make out the old tracings of the brand it used to have when he first got it.

He asked whom the horses belonged to, and the owner said that most of them belonged to the same group of riders. He didn't want to call them any names. It wouldn't be good for business.

Dutch asked him if the black horse was for sale. He said no, but pointed out five or six others that he would sell. So Dutch asked him who owned the black horse. He said that it had been led in without a rider. He didn't really know who it belonged to, just that it wasn't for sale. All he had been told was that it would need to be looked after for a few days.

Dutch quickly returned to the mercantile. Drawing Luis aside, he gave him the news that Boracho was still here in town somewhere.

"He will likely be staying there," Luis said, pointing out the place over the two-story saloon, which had rooms for rent. "My friend Armando has invited us to stay at his place for the night. The hotel would be the only other place to stay." He looked cautiously up and down the street, then asked, "Do you think you would be recognized by any of the cattle thieves?"

"I got good looks at the ones who passed me before Boracho rode up," Dutch replied, "but none of them got a very good look at me."

"Let's hope not," Luis said. He walked back to Señor Marino to finish ordering the things for Vargas and for himself. When he was done, he passed Dutch on the way to the door. "I think I will go over to the military headquarters and see if they will come and arrest Boracho for cattle rustling. You stick around here and get the wagons loaded."

That would be something, if he could talk the garrison into coming down and taking care of these outlaws. That would be something Dutch would like to see. They just had the wagon loaded when Luis came back. They could tell by his face that he hadn't been able to get the soldiers involved in going after Boracho.

"No use," he said. "They said it wasn't their problem." Dutch wondered aloud whether the bandit had some friends among the soldiers. Luis said that some of the men weren't very loyal and would be hard to trust. In this land of changing rulers, he just tried to stay friendly with every one. Since the military was one of the largest buyers of his cattle, it wouldn't do to go getting mad at them.

Luis suggested their next step. "I know the doctor who is in the town. Maybe we should check with him and see if he treated this outlaw."

The doctor was gone when they went into his office. Only a young man was there, cleaning up. Luis asked him if the doctor would be back soon, but the young man said he didn't know. When Luis asked him if the doctor had treated a large Mexican for a bullet wound lately, the young man stopped his cleaning. He struggled a moment, trying to think of what to say.

He finally said, "We were told not to say anything. I cannot tell you."

As they turned to leave the place, Luis told Dutch, "We might have learned more from the boy than the doctor would have told us. It looks like Boracho threatened them both."

"Well," Dutch told Luis as they walked along, "in the morning I'm planning on leaving with my horse."

Luis shook his head. "There is no way to prove it is your horse!" he said. "If you get caught stealing it from the stable, the owner would be within his rights to shoot you."

That didn't make Dutch feel too good, to hear this from his friend.

He fished a little bit of money out of its hiding place and asked Luis if he would like to go over to the cantina and have a drink. They might be able to find out more in there, especially if Boracho was staying above the saloon. Luis said that might be okay. He didn't have a drink very often, but the long ride into town made it sound good. They waved the driver over and invited him to go with them.

Walking through the double swinging doors into the saloon, they saw several men sitting around the large room, playing cards and talking. All of them came with plenty of firepower for anything that might come up. Dutch recognized one of the men sitting at a table over in the corner.

Looking for a place to sit down, Luis picked one of the tables across the room and a little bit away from the group that were nearer the bar. He recognized some of the men and nodded to them as he passed. In a few moments, one of them came over to their table and asked Luis if he were going to need some help pretty soon with the roundup.

Luis said he would need several riders this year, and Vargas would need several, too. He went on to tell about the men that Vargas had lost in the Indian raid and asked if any good men were ready now to go to work on the Vargas spread.

That man called over five of his friends from a nearby table and said he knew of four or five more that might be *interested in going now.*

*Luis talked to the men and selected three from those that came forward. He had hired them before. He asked about four or five more who had worked for him before, and sent word that he would like to talk with them, too, if they would come to town tonight. He said they would be staying with Armando and his family for the night.*

*Then Luis asked his friend about the man sitting over in the corner whom Dutch had recognized. Glancing cautiously over his shoulder, the man turned back and lowered his voice.*

*"I don't know him. He came in with a big bunch, and they seemed to about take over things here. There was some gunfire, and one of the local cowboys was killed. They had a big man with them who had been over to the doctor's office. It was all they could do to get him up the stairs here. He looked like he had been shot in the left shoulder. He was cussing and swearing all of the way up the stairs. I have not seen him come down any more, but I do see the doctor going up there every day. His men hang around here and cause lots of trouble. We do not mix with them."*

*Later that afternoon, they drove their loaded wagon down the street to the home of Armando Marino. As they came to the house Luis had pointed out, their driver said that he had decided not to come inside with them. He would feel better staying with the wagon and supplies. Dutch wondered about that, but said nothing.*

*When they pulled into the courtyard, Dutch noticed that the grounds were well kept, in contrast to those of some of the neighbors. The flowers seemed to reflect a woman's touch; probably Rosa or her mother were putting effort into the home. The yard had a white wooden fence around it.*

*Armando greeted them warmly and ushered them in. Rosa was not in sight. The home was large and spacious, and servants quickly took the guests to their assigned rooms and* saw to their comfort. The living room had a large fireplace with a cheerful fire burning in it. By the time Dutch had washed the trail dust off his hands and face, he found Luis already sitting down near the fireplace, chatting with Armando.

Again Dutch looked around for Rosa. Was she getting ready for supper? When would she come into the room and join them? What about her mother? A woman was arranging the dining table, but her looks and manner told Dutch she was probably a servant, not Rosa's mother.

There were many fine things from the mercantile in the home. A picture of some Mexican general hung over the fireplace. The candle holders looked like they were the finest silver. As he looked at the large formal dining table with its elegant glassware and place settings, Dutch felt as if he hadn't washed enough or dressed enough. If he had not wanted to see Rosa again, Dutch would have joined the wagon master outside and eaten in one of the cantinas. He stood awkwardly looking out through the fine, lace-covered window. Then someone made an announcement for the evening meal, and he turned back toward the table.

There she was, with her hair pulled up and lace flowing down past her face. She had on one of the prettiest dresses that he had ever seen; it only made her more beautiful. She noticed him coming to the table and gave him a warm smile. He chose a place across the table from her, as Armando took his seat at the head of the table with his pretty wife at his right side. As he was introduced to Señora Marino, Dutch could see where Rosa got her good looks. Armando wasn't exactly ugly, but he didn't have the posture and handsome look of either Rosa or her mother. All Dutch could do was nod politely.

Servants came in with the meal, the likes of which he'd never seen before. They carried in all of the fruits and grapes of the season. He wondered how long it took to transport them here. A large turkey had been roasted, and dressing was piled along side. The tastes seemed to melt in his mouth as he ate. Of course what really helped during the meal was Rosa sitting across from him. When she noticed him watching to see which piece of the silver to eat with, she gave a small smile.

Dutch wondered if this was the way they ate every day. The home no doubt was accustomed to entertaining guests. He ate so much that he was getting a little bit uncomfortable. Rosa had long since finished and sat with her cloth napkin covering her plate.

Dessert followed the big meal, and Dutch thought, "I can't eat another bit." But when hot apple pie was served, he just couldn't turn it down. Rosa had a small piece of pie and picked away at it as if she didn't want to hurt it. Dinner finished with wine for those who wanted some. Dutch did turn that down, as did Rosa.

Armando looked at Rosa and said, "Why don't you show Dutch some of our family treasures?"

They moved their chairs back from the table. Armando, his wife, and Luis moved over to the fireplace to enjoy the comforts of the home. Rosa took Dutch around the room and began to explain the history of the items displayed on the wall.

"That sword, hanging there in its sheath, belonged to Maximillian, a great cavalry officer."

Dutch pulled it out and examined it. It was a beautiful sword with silver and gold inlaid on the large handle. He had to use both of his hands on the grip. It was too slow and heavy, and certainly wouldn't be a practical weapon in a life and death situation.

They then moved on around the room to some of the family portraits. Armando had been in the military for a while and was shown mounted on a fine horse with lance and sword. He appeared in another picture with many other officers. Next came a large painting of the mother, Carmen. She was beautiful even then, and Dutch told Rosa that she surely did look like her mother.

At that moment Dutch felt even more out of place in his worn clothes and dusty shoes. He thought, I don't belong here! Rosa seemed to sense what he was thinking; taking him by the hand, she guided him on around the room, showing him one thing after another.

This was the first time that he could ever remember feeling awkward around a woman, and she was a fine woman. She finished the tour around the big room and asked if he wanted to go out on the porch, away from the grown-ups. She had the softest voice. And he did feel a lot more at ease outside than inside. It made things seem a little bit easier.

There were several places to sit on the long porch, and she selected two chairs away from the door. Light was coming through the window, and Dutch could see her sitting across from him.

"Tell me," she asked, "what brings you here?"

Dutch never had any trouble talking with women before now, but this was different.

"I work for Mr. Ortega," Dutch said. "We came to town for supplies."

"He is a good man," she said. "I hope he will stay a couple of days with us."

"We have to leave early in the morning," Dutch told her. "I was wondering, what do you do for fun around here? Do you ever go to the cantinas to dance, or anywhere else?"

"Oh, no!" she said. "My parents would never allow me to go into places like that. We have our dances here in the home, or sometimes a neighbor's home."

There was something in the way she said things that bothered Dutch, and he tried to figure out what is was.

"Do you have many young men call on you?" he asked.

"Not many," she said. "My father doesn't allow many

since I have come back from school. Some of the soldiers came by the store and wanted to take me out or come and see me, but my father makes all of the decisions when it comes to men."

Her voice trailed off as she said that, and Dutch felt the sadness in her voice. He had heard that some of those who had money and means were careful to keep their sons and daughters away from the common folk. Anyone could look at them at this moment and see that Dutch was one of those. But he figured out that his being here was because of Luis. He was a friend, and that made Dutch a friend.

Rosa said sometimes she enjoyed riding and sometimes her father would let her go by herself. Dutch told her it would be fun to go with her sometime. She looked at him and smiled and said, "Maybe some time."

They could hear the others up and walking about in the house and then her father called out to her. She stood up, saying, "I must go!" and went into the house.

Dutch felt a little bit uneasy about staying the night in the home. When Luis stepped out onto the porch, he mentioned that he would rather sleep out on the wagon, too. Luis turned to walk back in the house, but then came back where he could whisper, "Don't try and get your horse tonight. We can't afford trouble right now." Dutch wished he had his black horse to ride back to the ranch, but decided that Luis probably knew better.

Early the next morning the crew that Luis had hired all assembled back at the mercantile loading area. Marino's servants had brewed up a pot of coffee for the group. There were six new cowhands, four drivers, two men to help build the barns and bunkhouses, and Luis and Dutch. Luis told the men that they should make it to his place in a little over two days. That part of the road was used more often by other ranchers, so the going would be relatively easy. After that, it would take

284

about five or six days to make the trip to the Vargas ranch. The wagons would need to return once more for the balance of the needed materials.

The town was pretty well asleep when they left. Dutch's thoughts were all about Rosa. It was probably too much to think about, her and him. She was of the upper class and was guided by her father and family. No wonder she didn't have too many young men come by and see her. It would be hard to ever find her alone where he could talk to her again. But if he ever did get that chance, he would be sure to look a lot better. Maybe he would even buy himself a new pair of clothes.

The steam was coming off the grass as the first sunlight began to warm things up. The horses were already straining with the heavy load of the wagons. Besides the building supplies, the wagons also contained some food supplies for both of the ranches. The going was much slower than when they had come. By nightfall, they still weren't halfway to the Ortega ranch. It was nice to have a bigger group around the fire and listen to them talk.

Dutch thought of what a relief it would be to Victor Vargas to get the supplies he had ordered so that he could get his rebuilding underway. He also thought of his partner, Jacob. If he had known what women liked, he would have bought some of the material from the mercantile so Jacob could give it to Catrina. She would probably have liked that. He wondered how his partner was doing right about now. He sure would like to see him soon.

The third day found the wagons at the Ortega ranch. Luis planned for an early start the next morning. He wanted to send the six riders on ahead to help with the cattle at the Vargas ranch. If Dutch would go with the wagons and other men, it would be his job to be the front rider and watch out for any trouble. It was important to get the supplies safely to the ranch.

Some barrels of water were added now, and that made the load even heavier for the horses and wagons. Luis sent an extra horse along, just in case it was needed. The two builders rode on the wagons with the load. Every one had a rifle, so they could defend against any attackers. Any who dared try to take this load couldn't do it without losing some men.

When they crossed the water out in the meadow, Dutch could see the wagons' wheels sink deep in the sand. He was glad that they were going to have pretty solid ground to travel on for most of the trip. They stopped early that day, as the wagon masters said this was the last good feed for quite some time. They wanted the horses to have plenty before reaching the stretch where they would find neither water nor pasture.

Dutch worked around the area in a large circle, satisfied that there weren't any unwelcome visitors very close. It was getting near dark before he came back to the camp and the fire. It seems that they had lucked out pretty good, as one of the builders had worked as a cook on some cattle drives. The man set about fixing a tasty meal, and even made some biscuits.

The following day would be the hardest on the animals. The road became steeper as they moved into the rolling hills. The drivers had to stop and let them get a rest more often here. At noon they had to water and feed them and take about an hour rest.

Dutch changed mounts and continued to watch the trail ahead and the many places where trouble could hide. If the Indians knew they had food, they would try and get it. If the bandits thought they had something they wanted, they might try attacking, too. Dutch was the only one who could sound the warning if trouble came. Luis said that he hoped Dutch would be all right with this because it was dangerous. Dutch knew it was always dangerous, out here in this no-man's land. Any place he looked, a hundred Indians or bandits could be waiting.

*They continued on until nearly dark that day without many problems. Dutch kind of wished that some or all of the cowboys that had been sent on to the Vargas ranch to help out would have stayed with the wagons. He wouldn't need to worry so much then if he had more help. The one good thing about it, though, was that Jacob would know that he was all right. It would make things better.*

*After they had the horses ready to go the next morning, one of the drivers said, "We should reach the springs today."*

*Dutch knew the place he meant. He had stopped there before, on the way to the Vargas ranch. He could well remember standing watch there through part of the night, and it looked like that would be his assignment tonight, too. He rode on ahead to see if it was being used. Several Indian ponies had visited it, but it had been a while since they had been there. He could still see some of their old signs in the soft places. For sure they would need to be on careful watch tonight. By the time his wagon party dropped off the hill into the little meadow with the water in it, the sun had gone down. He told the men that they would need to be as quiet as possible, but they might have a small fire down in the meadow.*

*"Keep your guns close by," Dutch said. "We never know when they might come back through this way."*

*He selected one of the hands to climb up and stand watch the first three or four hours of the night. At last he could close his eyes for a short time before he took the balance of the watch.*

*When morning came without problem, Dutch was anxious to get the wagons on to the ranch. If all went well, they could expect to arrive before sundown on the fifth day. The next two days passed without incident, but the horses needed to stop and rest more often. It was a welcome sight when they pulled out of the last brushy draw onto the big meadow below the Vargas ranch.*

# Chapter 20

I had spent another long day with the rest of the hands in bringing cattle down from the high country. Since the new men had ridden in the night before with the news that my partner would be coming soon, I had been anxiously waiting for the ranch to come into view. It felt good when we topped the last rise and I could see all of the wagons around the area, loaded down with the building supplies. I started over to ask the foreman if I could go ahead of the rest to see my friend. He just smiled when he saw me coming and motioned me to go ahead. That's all I needed to be off and running down the pasture to the ranch.

Dutch was helping to unload the wagons. It was good to see him again as we exchanged a grip of both arms. He asked about Catrina. There wasn't much to tell, as we had all been so busy there was little time for anything but to eat, work, and sleep.

Dutch told me what had happened in the town. He said that he had seen his horse, but the bandits had run over the old brand. Luis had told him to leave things as they were for the time, as he couldn't afford trouble right then.

"I hope you hurt that Boracho plenty," I said. "He deserves it."

It was good to sit at the supper table with Dutch by my side. The table was getting pretty busy with the extra help, but we always had plenty of good food. Catrina was busy helping serve, but she stopped long enough to smile at Dutch and me.

I got to thinking; after she had my word to stay and help, maybe she didn't need to see me so often. I hoped that wasn't the case. Now, seeing that she still had that warm smile for me when I looked at her, I guessed things were still good between us two.

After supper, Victor called us over to come and sit by

the fire. We settled down in two of the empty chairs that were part of the circle in front of the big fireplace.

"I want you to tell me all that you can of what happened since you left the ranch, Dutch. Don't leave out anything that I might need to know."

Dutch gave an account of the past few days. Victor would stop him once in a while and ask some questions before he would continue on. It was getting late when Dutch finally finished. Victor asked us both to stay at the ranch the next morning. We were to help unload the wagons and start working on the bunkhouses.

This change of pace was welcome to me. I was starting to get tired of riding every day. Now that he had the extra hands, Victor felt that he should have a pretty good account of the cattle by the end of the week. There had been no sign of any thieves for a while now.

Work started as soon as it was light enough to see. The two builders had brought along some of the tools that would be needed. Before long, with their direction, we had a good start on the first building. The plan was to build the bunkhouses first, then the cook shack, and last the barns. When the wagons were all unloaded, Victor planned to send them back for the rest of the building supplies.

I was surprised when Dutch said that he would like to go back with the wagons and bring the next load. Victor knew that he would need to send someone to help out in case there was trouble, so maybe Dutch would be the one. He was familiar with the trail now. They would leave the next morning. I didn't want to see him go so soon, but he assured me that he would hurry back. I wished more riders were going with Dutch and the wagon masters. But he had been enough help the first time, so maybe he would be enough help the second time, too.

By the end of the fourth day, we had all four of the bunkhouse walls standing up and ready for the roof. It was fast going, since we built them all the same. Sometimes we got some extra help from vaqueros returning from their rides, and then the work would go much faster.

It was always nice to have Catrina bring something good to eat and drink throughout the days. Sometimes she would walk a little way off with me, and we would talk of how things were going. I could never get over her calling me Yacob. And every time I said her name, it was like some kind of music. "Catrina." It just kind of rolled off the tongue.

The work went well that week. We had the four bunkhouses up and the roof on each of them. We still had to put in the doors and one window in each, plus put the stoves in place. It would take some time to build the six bunks in each of them, too, but with them all being the same that should go fast. I thought often about Dutch, tracing his route first back to the Ortega ranch, then heading on to the Sonora Mercantile.

Victor Vargas seemed to have a load off him when he saw the shelters being built for the crew. We had put up the tents, so we didn't have to sleep outside any more; but this would be a lot warmer and better. The cast iron stoves had survived the fires and were put in place in the new buildings. New pipe was installed, and the first bunkhouse was completed. In a matter of two more days the other three were finished. We would put all of our effort into the cookhouse next. This would take a while, as it was much larger than the bunkhouses.

Victor Vargas said that he would have more help for us after the weekend. Since most of the cattle had been brought back near the pasture, he would be able to get by with fewer riders now. The others would be assigned to our building crew. Victor even said that some of the men could take a few days off if they wanted. They would need to take turns with this.

Four of the men decided to go to Moctezuma. Victor asked two of them to time their return with Dutch and the wagons from the Ortega ranch to his ranch. That would give some protection to the drivers. I was glad to hear this. It would help Dutch out a lot to have some extra help.

Tomorrow was Sunday, and it looked like we would have the day off. It had been a while. Maybe Catrina and I could go for a ride. That would sure be nice. When she came by in the late afternoon with the fresh water, I asked her what she thought of the idea. That seemed to bring a sparkle to her eyes, and she said, "Yes."

Sunday morning was kind of a get-up-late day if you wanted, but I was up early, feeding the horses and doing the chores. Catrina had said that we might take a ride in the valley and take a picnic lunch along. The sun was up and the gentle warmth of it felt good.

I had saddled her horse, and before long she came out of the house carrying a basket of food. A checkered blue and white cloth covered it, and she asked if I could carry it. She set it down while I helped her on her horse. She smiled down at me as I picked up the basket and got on my horse. It was good to be out and away. The air was still and crisp, and we could even see a few deer feeding in the distance.

"When do you think Dutch will be back?" she asked.

I tried to think how many days he had said it took the first time. "He should be showing up back at the Ortega ranch about today or tomorrow. That should put him here in about eight more days if everything has gone all right."

"Yacob, do you think we would have time to ride all the way down to the mountain today?"

"I don't think we should do that. I am sure your folks wouldn't want us to take such a chance."

"Yacob, we haven't seen any sign of rustlers or Indians for some time now. Don't you think we could do that again?"

It was awfully hard to tell her no when she looked at

me like that, and I could feel the redness creeping up in my face again. I thought of the time the large fish had jumped out of the water and how excited that made her, then of her showing me how to dance, and holding her close. How could I tell her no? She was riding close enough to hold my hand now, and I knew I was a goner.

I finally said, "Well maybe. But we must return home before it ever starts to get late."

"Thank you, Yacob! Thank you!"

We continued on down around the turn in the valley, where the view of the ranch would be lost. I felt a little bit of concern about this, but decided that we would be fine if we kept a sharp eye out and started home early. We could see the mountain now and imagine the clear, deep pool in our minds.

We crossed the place where more little streams were coming in from the east side of the hill and adding water to the main stream. It was just as I remembered from before. We stopped and got down to give our horses a drink in one of the streams. It seemed so peaceful here, but I remembered the Indians that came out of the willows a short ways from here, and decided that we didn't want to stay out in the open any longer than we needed to.

We would be at the rim of the deep water hole within the hour. It wasn't even noon yet, so we should be able to get back home early. When we got close to the place where we needed to get out on the bank and rim around to the water hole, Catrina wanted to go first, so I let her go ahead of me. We tied our horses in about the same place that we had done the last time and walked over to the edge of the bank and looked over.

It was just like we had left it. She took a little piece of bread out of the basket and pitched it out into the deep water. Two large fish came after the bread, and the water churned so much that we couldn't decide which fish got the bread. She did the same thing again, and another large fish came out of the water and caught the bread on the way down. She squealed with excitement. I told her we should have brought a hook and line. We could have taken some of them home to eat.

We sat on the grassy knoll a ways back from the edge and she began to put out the picnic for us. She had brought a larger cloth for the food and we started to eat.

"Yacob, what are you going to do when the cattle drive is done?" she asked.

I had thought about that some, and I really didn't have a good answer. Would Dutch and I continue on in our search for gold, or was it time to settle down and think about other things? I wished she wouldn't ask me things like this. Yet, I needed to give her some kind of answer. I finally decided that I would ask her the question, "What do you think I should do?"

She stopped eating and wiped her mouth with a cloth. Then looking me straight in the eye, and reaching out to touch my hand, she said, "Yacob, what does your heart tell you?"

That caught me completely off guard. My thoughts raced back for a moment to what my mother had told me when I was growing up. She had said, "Your heart will tell you." I thought about that for a minute and wondered just what my deep feelings were telling me. "What do you want me to do?"

"I want you to stay around for a while," she said.

We finished eating in silence. Eventually she asked if I wanted any more, and I told her I'd had enough.

"Do you still think you remember how to dance?" she asked.

We both stood up and moved away from the food basket. She began to hum the soft sweet song in my ear. It was so good to feel her soft and close again. I tried not to step on her toes too much. Now and then she would give a little laugh and tell me I was doing well.

It was as if everything seemed to stop, except for the two of us, and I found her soft warm lips on mine again.

I don't know how long we held each other and danced on the little grass knoll, but we finally sat down close together. She leaned her head against my shoulder and said, "Yacob, this is the most beautiful place that I have ever seen. If I were ever going to build a house here, It would be right up there," she said, pointing up the ridge to a small flat place on the hill. "From there, you could look out over this stream and pasture. Let's walk up there and take a look."

We started the gentle climb up to the place she pointed out. It was as she had said. We could almost see over the bend in the valley to the Vargas ranch.

"And look, Yacob, this flat extends right on around the hill. With some clearing, corrals and barns could be built. That little stream over there would supply all of the water anyone would need." She was carried away with excitement at the thought of one day having a home up here on the side of the big mountain she had named Montana Grande. "Of course there would be plenty of fish to eat. Have you ever been fishing, Yacob?"

"Oh, sure! That used to be one of the fun things to do out in California, as well as in the far away place from where I come."

"My parents are from a far away place, too, far across the water. They came from Spain, where they used to have a lot of money and property. But the government came and tried to take it all away. They said they wanted to divide it up with others. The Ortegas were neighbors there, too, and they decided to come along to settle in this land called Mexico. This is not an easy land, Yacob, but it won't always be this way. It will be easier someday."

It was peaceful sitting up here in the higher meadow with Catrina leaning back in my arms. I wanted this feeling to go on forever. Then I was brought back to reality by the shadows that were beginning to form across the pool on the other side.

"Catrina! It's getting later than I thought! We must get to our horses and head for home."

The sun wasn't quite down when we made it to the bend in the valley. When we could see the ranch house up ahead in the distance, we decided to run the horses a little bit. We wouldn't be out after dark this time.


*The wagons creaked along from the Ortega ranch toward Montezuma. They hadn't had any trouble coming from the Vargas ranch. Dutch was eager to get to town and see if he could find some time to see Rosa. He had thought of her many times in the past few days and wondered if she would see him at all. He would not have Luis along to get into the home or be invited to stay. What excuse could come along that would make it possible to get some time with her?*

*Dutch thought of Boracho and the rest of his bunch, too. Would he still be in town, or would he have recovered from the gunshot and be gone by now? What would Dutch do about his horse?*

*The town of Moctezuma was showing up in the distance now. He would soon know if Rosa was working at the store because he had decided to go straight there and try to buy some new clothes. He would check out the mercantile first, and leave the others to see about the second load.*

*It was about noon as they reached the town, and the drivers moved the wagons in back of the mercantile to be loaded. He went through the front door and looked quickly around to see if Rosa was inside. Armando gave a greeting and came over to him.*

*"It's good to see you again, Dutch. We have the supplies ready to load in the back."*

"We already pulled the wagons around there and we can start the loading as soon as you're ready," Dutch replied.

In a short while, Armando opened the loading doors, and they started to fill the wagons. They wouldn't be hauling much food this time, only a small amount to be used on the return trip. This made more room for the building supplies.

Dutch frequently went back inside the store to see if Rosa had come in. Each time, she wasn't there. He finally asked Armando if she was working today, and found out that it was her day to stay home.

By early afternoon, they had the wagons loaded. They had been able to fit in all of the supplies that had been ordered. Dutch had decided on some new clothes and even a new hat. He wanted to look a little better in case he was able to see Rosa again. Mr. Vargas had given him money for the expenses of the trip, so Dutch gave some of the money to the drivers so they could get something to eat. The horses had been taken over to the livery stable for the night. He would go pay the bill there now, so they could be on their way early in the morning.

When he walked passed the corrals, the first thing he looked for was Nighthawk. The corral was full of horses, but the black horse was gone from the rest. Would Boracho already be gone? He asked about the black horse and found it had been picked up yesterday.

With that bit of news, Dutch went over to the two-story cantina across the street. It seemed quieter now than it did the first time he came into it. Only five horses were tied to the hitching rail in front of the place. It looked like the outlaw bunch had gone.

It wasn't far to Rosa's house, and he thought he'd just walk by there and see if she might be where he could see her. He knew he wouldn't be able to go inside and ask for her, but maybe she would be out on the front porch or something.

When he got to the front yard, he felt better with his new clothes on. Someone was working in the flower garden when he came up to the house. It was one of the house servants that he had seen earlier. Dutch greeted him as he stood up from watering one of the plants. This man remembered Dutch from his last visit.

Dutch asked him if Rosa was home. He said that she had gone out to the riding stables, and pointed toward the back of the house. When Dutch walked around to the other side, he could see the stables and some of the men working with the horses, but Rosa was not in sight. When he asked if Rosa was there, one man said that she had gone for a ride and pointed in the direction of the military post.

Dutch thought about going after her and hurried back to get his horse. It might be dangerous for him to go too close to the many barracks and buildings of the soldiers, so he decided to skirt that area and go beyond. It was pretty open here and he could see a long distance.

He waited for some time, trying to decide if Rosa was at the military station or had ridden past the place and on out in the open. He would sure never go into the outpost looking for her, but if she was out here somewhere, he just might have a chance to talk to her.

It was a nice evening and the cool clear weather made for good riding. That was probably why she had decided to go for a ride. Perhaps she felt safe around the military post. It was about three miles to the other end of the clearing, which stopped at the base of some small rolling hills. Dutch decided he would ride on that way and watch for her. It was pleasant to think about her and her warm smile as he rode toward the end of the big mesa.

Just at that moment he caught sight of her riding fast from around the base of one of the small rolling hills. Four men were chasing her! He put his horse into a run, rifle in hand as he raced toward her. He could hear no shots, but it was evident that they intended to catch her without shooting her. She raced back toward the garrison and town. He could see that she had a good horse under her and she knew how to handle it. Her pursuers would not be able to close the gap. However, just as he began to think she was safe, he glimpsed two more riders coming out of the brush to the east, intending to cut off her escape.

Dutch pushed his horse as fast as it would run toward the two who had come out to stop her. They were so intent on getting her that they hadn't seen him closing the distance. It was about then that the four who had chased her out of the hills saw Dutch coming and opened fire toward him.

He didn't want to shoot for fear of hitting Rosa, but one of the riders pulled off a little and he shot him from his horse. The second one decided to give up the chase, too, and turned to the right. Dutch was close to him now and they exchanged fire. He felt something burn into his side at the same moment the man fell from his horse. Seeing this, the other four riders decided to retreat back the way they had come.

Rosa rode straight for Dutch. He could see the frightened look on her face. He waited for her to reach him.

"Oh Dutch!" she said as she rode up and grabbed his arm.

He wanted to tell her something, but suddenly the ground and the sky were whirling around. He hardly felt anything when he hit the ground.

The shooting in the valley caused a great stir in the barracks, and many soldiers came racing down to where Rosa knelt next to Dutch. One of the officers sent word for someone to go and get a wagon to take the injured man back to town. Rosa told the commander what had happened. He quickly sent a detachment in pursuit of the four that had ridden away.

Later on in the evening, Dutch came to himself enough to wonder what had happened. The last thing he remembered was holding Rosa's hand and knowing she was safe. When he opened his eyes, the doctor was working over him and he could see Rosa close by the bed. He could remember falling to the ground, but nothing about why he was waking up here. He could tell how nice the room was; this was not the doctor's office. Rosa must have brought him to her home. He could hear the doctor telling them that they must leave and give him some rest.

Dutch was awake when the doctor came again early in the morning to look at the wound in his side. He said that Dutch was one lucky hombre. The bullet had entered in at the small rib, which it broke, and continued on in, just missing the heart. He was able to get the bullet out, but Dutch would not be able to get up and move around for some time.

Dutch thought of the wagons and had them send for one of the drivers. He also had them find one of the ranch hands from the Vargas spread who was still in town. When they arrived, he gave them Victor's instructions and told them that they must be on their way. "Tell Jacob not to worry about me," was his only message. They were soon out the door.

When the doctor got through with the fresh dressing, he said Dutch would need to stay in bed about three days, if all went well. If he should get infection, then some other course of action might be necessary.

Dutch could tell when he tried to move that it was too painful. But he needed to be up and going as soon as possible. He sure couldn't help anyone lying there in bed. They brought a good breakfast to the bedside, but he didn't feel like eating anything. How did all of this happen anyway? And why were they trying to capture Rosa?

He hadn't seen her since last night. He must have looked an awful sight, judging from the blood-soaked dressing the doctor had removed. And he had been trying to make a good impression on her with his new outfit. Where were his clothes, anyway?

The house servants were coming around now to see if he needed anything. It was getting light outside, and he wished that he could be out on his horse, watching the sun rise. He'd never had to lie in bed for more than a day. This was going to be painful. On the other hand, if it meant getting to see Rosa once in a while, that would make things better. " Some way to get to see her, though!" he thought.

The door into the room opened and Armando came over to the bed to see how Dutch was doing. He said that he was thankful that Dutch had been able to get Rosa away from those who were after her. He might have saved her life. At the least, he had kept her from the bad ones chasing her.

Dutch asked him if she was all right, and Armando took him by the arm. "Yes, she will be fine. I have put the two outlaws' horses in the corral with mine. They will be yours, as well as the saddles and things."

"Was anyone able to catch the other four?" came Dutch's next question.

Armando shook his head and said, "They had too much of a head start and got away out in the hills."

Dutch tried to thank him for his hospitality and for bringing the doctor, but he brushed it aside. He said he was on his way to the store to make sure that everything was ready for the wagons to leave. He asked if there was anything he could do for Dutch. Since there wasn't, he left.

It was nearing noon when Dutch's door opened again. This time it was Rosa, asking if it was all right to come in. She came over to the right side of the bed. Reaching down and touching his hand, she said, "Thank you, Dutch." Her hand was soft and warm on his. She said, "The doctor thinks you will be up and around in a few days. You must get your rest now. We *will talk later."*

It was a good day at the Vargas ranch when the cook shack was completed. It made more room in the main ranch house when all of the tables could be moved back out. The only bad thing about it was that I didn't see as much of Catrina as I had when everyone was all crowded into the main house.

In a way this was better. I could be alone with my thoughts more. But I had difficult things to think about, things that Catrina had mentioned down on the Montana Grande. A home, corrals, actually another ranch and all that went with it. Now if Catrina came with it, then that would be something to think about. It had sounded that way to me.

It was while I was walking down to the corral that I saw the loaded wagons coming down the meadow. It would be good to see Dutch again. We would be starting on the barns soon. I hoped he would be working by my side.

As I watched the wagons enter the east end of the meadow, I could see that Dutch was not with them. It didn't take long for the story to spread about what had happened to him when he rescued Rosa from the bandits. Victor said they probably wanted to capture her and hold her for ransom. Even if the ransom had been paid, they most likely would have taken her life, too. One could only imagine what she would have to go through with a bunch like them.

It was good that Dutch was getting better from his bullet wound. I regretted that I hadn't been there to help him. Maybe he wouldn't be hurt again if I had been there, I thought. But, maybe my being there wouldn't have helped. In fact, he wouldn't have been out looking for this Rosa if he'd had me along. No, I guess I couldn't have done anything for him.

I would have to ask Catrina about Rosa. It was funny that Dutch hadn't ever even mentioned her. She must be something for him to risk his life for her.

The ranch was as busy as an ant hill the next morning. With all of the men back, we could start the barn construction. And, with the wagons and horses back, Victor had set about mowing some of the tall grass in the pasture. He said that we might have to move it twice; but if storms did come, we could still have the feed.

I asked Catrina that evening what she knew about Rosa over in Moctezuma. She had met the girl several times when her father had let her go along with him to make some purchases. They had spent time together and liked each other. She frowned a little when she told me that Rosa was the kind who would be given in marriage one day by her father. It was doubtful that Dutch would fit into the father's plans. They usually married other rich people. The father would decide.

This did seem like a lot of trouble to think about. Dutch no doubt had his eye on this Rosa, and she wouldn't be allowed to see him much, if at all.

"It just doesn't seem fair," I told Catrina. "Where are the feelings of the heart here?"

"I can only tell you how it is with the rich people," she said. "She may already be promised to someone."

This was a strange country and custom. The rich people did not want to have anything to do with the poor people. One thing was for sure: I was one of those poor people, but I could work hard and maybe have something again sometime. Maybe Dutch and I should go gold mining again.

*Rosa came each day to check on Dutch's progress. On the third day he was feeling good enough to stand up and walk around. He wanted to be on his way, but the doctor said he should stay where he could be watched closely for another three or four days.*

Dutch noticed that Rosa was friendly, but she would only get so close to him and she would only touch his arm. She would never allow him to hold her hand. He wondered what was the matter; maybe he was too plain for her or something. They had brought him new clothes again from the store. He thought he looked pretty good in the new outfit. He would just have to ask her why she didn't seem to like him a lot. "The very next time she comes in, I'll ask her!" he thought. At that moment, he heard her enter.

"Hello Dutch, good to see you up and around. Do you need anything?"

"Yes, there is something I need to know. You are pleasant and friendly, but you never let yourself go very far with me, and I am just wondering why."

He could see she didn't want to talk about this and she didn't want to hurt his feelings. She looked away, and there was a long silence before she spoke again.

"I am sorry, Dutch. My father said that he has promised me to someone, and I don't even know who it is. He doesn't allow me to see anyone when he does not make the arrangements."

"What about me? He lets you come in and see me every day!" Dutch said.

"Yes! But that is different; we are here in our home! And he told me to show you every kindness for all you have done."

So there it was! The answer must be that she was just being kind to him. Yet he thought he could sense the sadness in her voice as she told him these things.

"What about your feelings? What about what makes you happy?"

She turned to walk away, and said over her shoulder, "What I want makes little difference."

He decided that he couldn't stay in the house another night, or another hour. He didn't want them taking care of him because they felt sorry for him. And it looked like getting to know Rosa was going nowhere.

In a few minutes, over the objections of the servants, Dutch had made it outside. It was funny to see how weak he was from all of that rest. It kind of made him wonder if his body was working in the wrong direction. He should have been stronger with the rest instead of weaker. It would be good to get out on trail again and head for the Ortega ranch.

By the time he had taken the two horses from the stable in back of the house and picked up his own from the livery stable, it was almost sundown. Men were already crowding into the saloon and keeping the girls busy. Several horses were at the hitching post. As Dutch went past them, he was excited to see his black horse tied in with many of the others. He decided to go to one of the other places to eat and watch across the street to see if Boracho was riding the black.

He didn't feel too much like eating, but decided to sit it out until after dark. He knew he would never be any match with a handgun with any of those bandits. But with a rifle it might be another story. He decided he was going to take his horse back if there was any way.

He couldn't get Rosa out of his mind. She would know that he had gone by now, and her father, too. Dutch had told the hired help to thank them for him. Since he had some time to waste before it got real dark, maybe he had better do the right thing and go and thank them himself.

It was getting cool already, and there was a sharp pain when he pulled himself up into the saddle. He rode the short distance to their home. Tying the three horses up, he walked to the front door and knocked. He could hear the people inside and thought it was about time for them to be having supper. He hoped he was early enough that it would not interrupt them.

When the servant found who it was at the door, he invited Dutch in and made an announcement to the rest nearby.

Armando was the first one to greet him. "Señor Dutch, I was afraid you had planned on going without saying anything. Are you sure you are well enough to travel?"

Dutch assured him that he was. "I have just come by to say thanks for all you have done for me."

"It is my many thanks to you," he said. "How can I ever repay you? If you ever need anything, come and see me."

Dutch replied, "Thank you again, sir. Well, I must be on my way. Excuse me." He hadn't seen Rosa, but maybe that was best. Maybe this was the easiest for both her and him.

Getting off and on a horse was really painful for him, so Dutch decided to walk his horses closer to town and find some place where he could tie them for a while. When he returned to the saloon, it had gotten even noisier. He could see several of the soldiers' horses tied there, too. Maybe there was something going on between some of them and the cattle rustlers. That would explain why they hadn't responded to Ortega's request for help in arresting Boracho. He would just have to go inside, have a drink, and see for himself what was going on.

Dutch was confident that no one in the saloon would know him. Maybe he would see Boracho. He promised himself before entering that he wouldn't get into any trouble. He couldn't stand more of that right now.

It was as Dutch had pictured it. The crowd made for standing room only, and the smoke-filled saloon was doing a booming business. He found a place at the end of the bar. After ordering his drink, he turned to look into the dimly lit room. Several people were crammed together at the tables. Some were drinking, some playing cards, and some looking for trouble. A fight started over someone wanting one of the tables, and one of the locals was thrown outside.

306

Dutch decided to stand and watch for a few minutes. It was so crowded that he couldn't see across the room very easily. In the back and across from him, he finally saw Boracho and several of his men. They had a couple of the soldiers sitting with them. One of them looked like one of the commanders. Little wonder Luis couldn't get any help from the garrison, Dutch thought. They were all pretty good friends.

Boracho was still bandaged up. His arm was in a sling, and some of the linens were still wrapped around his side. He seemed in a pretty bad mood and was ordering people around. Dutch wondered if he were the mastermind behind the attempt to capture Rosa a few days before. From the look of what went on here, he could be involved with a lot of unsavory happenings, not the least of which could be selling stolen cattle to the army.

Dutch got pretty mad when he thought of Boracho. He and his partner had been through a lot of grief because of the man. However, this was one place where he couldn't just shoot him again. The piano player was banging out a tune, trying to drown out all the noise. That only increased the volume and added to the excitement of what was going on. When Dutch finished his drink, he decided it was about time to go and see if the black horse was still outside.

It felt good to be out in the fresh air, away from all of the commotion. His black horse was still tied up in the middle of all of the rest. Dutch wondered how many of the men coming in and out of the bar were part of Boracho's band. He decided to stumble up to the hitching rack. If no one stopped him, he would get on the black horse and ease out of sight. If anyone said anything, he would act like he had made a mistake.

He leaned on the hitching rail like he'd had too much to drink and had to have the support. No one seemed to be watching, so he made his way over to the black and climbed aboard. So far so good, he thought. He had moved halfway down the dark street before someone saw him on the horse and began to yell and point his way. It was no use to tarry now, so he gave the horse the reins. Shots rang out behind him as he pushed Nighthawk into a fast gallop until they were out of sight.

Dutch circled around the town and came back to the place where he'd tied the other three horses. He soon had all of them headed out from the town. The bandits would never know where he went in the dark, and that was lucky for him.

Back in the saloon, one of Boracho's men told him that someone had stolen his horse. He was furious. Throwing the table aside, he went out to see if it were true.

"Who was watching the horses?" he demanded.

No one volunteered anything, and they all hoped that he would soon cool down. He was as likely to shoot the one responsible as not, if he could find someone to blame. Everyone agreed that it was someone real smart who would come into this strong hold and steal the horse that belonged to Boracho.

# Chapter 21

Dutch continued his ride on into the night toward the Ortega ranch. It was a good road to follow, and even though the night was dark, the horses seemed to find their way. He would be miles from town by morning. He just wished he could have seen the expression on that big outlaw's face when someone told him his horse was gone.

His shoulder was painful from all this exercise, and he wished that he could just pull off the road and sleep the night. But is was necessary that he keep going. He stopped at one of the small streams that crossed the road and let the horses drink. He moved onto one of the other saddled horses and continued on.

The barking of the dog at the Ortega ranch announced his coming just a little before noon. One of the ranch hands helped tie his horses off. Even with help, he found it was hard to get off the horse. The long night's ride and much stress on his shoulder had caused blood to seep through the bandages.

The women gently took off the soiled linens. The bullet wound looked as though it had started to heal over. But these last few hours had pulled at the doctor's stitches, and they were now red and inflamed. They put what medicine they had on the wound and applied new bandages. Hopefully he would now be able to rest for a time and let his injury heal.

Luis came in with some of the riders. When he was told that Dutch had come back from Moctezuma, he was anxious to hear the whole story. Dutch was lying on one of the bunks when he came through the door.

"So, you are the one that saved Rosa from the bandits," he said. "That was a good thing to do. How bad are you hurt?"

"I was lucky. I was shot at close range with a pistol, and the doctor was able to get the bullet out. He left a nasty hole in my side where he tried to dig out some splinters from my broken rib. And then, having him dig for the bullet took a lot out of me. I think my left side is about all used up," Dutch said, "what with the knife fight, and now being shot there."

Luis smiled at what Dutch said. "What did Rosa think of you? You must be pretty high on her list about now."

"I don't know. She said she was promised to someone already. She didn't ever let me get to know her very much. She was kind and thanked me, but it seems that she is afraid of her father."

Luis listened in silence. "What do you think of her?" he asked when Dutch finished.

"I would like to get to know her better. I think she is some special young lady."

"She is a very special young lady, and someone needs to let her know that. I wouldn't be too put down by what she said.. Her father might be just saying that to keep every young man away from the door. If I were you, and I wanted to see her again, then that is what I would try to do."

Now this advice definitely made Dutch feel better. Luis Ortega was some kind of a guy. Of course, he might not have the same attitude when he heard the rest of Dutch's story. What would Luis think when he found out about taking the black horse back from Boracho? Maybe he hadn't ought to tell him about that right now . . . !

Of course Boracho was the very next topic they discussed. Dutch told how Boracho had his left arm in a sling, but it didn't seem to take any of the meanness out of him. Dutch also reported that Boracho seemed pretty chummy with some of the men from the garrison, even one of the commanders. This was of much interest to Luis. He didn't say anything more, but Dutch knew he was thinking about this information. Knowing that Boracho could ride again, Luis was on guard with the cattle, especially on the east end of the meadow. It continued to be busy around the Ortega ranch.

Dutch spent the next few days mending. His thoughts were on Rosa often, and he wondered how he would get around to seeing her again. Would she feel any differently toward him? He wondered how he could ever provide the kind of life style that she was used to living. He guessed he would never be able to give her all of the things that she now had, even if he and she ever wanted to get serious. Maybe this was the best way. Maybe he should just forget about her.

Dutch did have something to tell Jacob when he saw him again. Two of the horses had saddlebags on them. One had only some food, personal items, and ammunition. But the other, which must have belonged to Boracho himself, had enough Mexican money inside to equal about one thousand American dollars. Dutch guessed, with his bad shoulder, he just couldn't take them inside too easy. He smiled when he thought about this. Boracho was sure going to be in a bad mood for losing that money and that fancy saddle he had.

Dutch would give Jacob his half again. It was only part of the money Boracho had taken from them, but it was good to get some of it back. They would have a good laugh as they imagined Boracho wondering who would dare come in and take his horse right out from under his nose!


With the barn structures going up, Victor Vargas was using every available hand to help with the work. I never thought we could be busier that we had been, but the effort increased. I had little time to spend with Catrina, and Victor had asked all of us if we could work right on through Sundays until the barns were completed. Everyone agreed to do that as long as there would be some leave time before the roundup started.

I noticed that Chancey came by the corral or the barn each day for his rubbing and to get a handful of grain if I had time. Maybe he was looking for Dutch. "I sure wish he were here to rub your long ears," I told him. I hoped my friend was mending well and getting plenty of rest.

I knew that he had gone back after the second load of goods so that he might be able to see this Rosa again. With what Catrina had said about the father making all of the decisions for her, it sounded like Dutch wouldn't get much of a chance. I felt bad for him.

The mornings were getting colder now and it looked like we would just get everything undercover good before we got the rain and snow season. With the building pretty much done, Mr. Vargas told the men that they could take turns for a few days off before we began the roundup.

I asked the experienced men about what to expect with the roundup. I learned that it would take several days to move the cattle to the railroad at Batuc. There was a river crossing of the Yaqui River that would be one of the greatest challenges. Many cattle were sometimes lost in the crossing. On occasion some of the horsemen were lost, too, if the waters were too high. After that came the Rio Mayo, but it didn't offer such a challenge as the big river. Roundup was to start in about ten days.

Since men were now leaving for their turns to go into town first, I had less time to see Catrina. I guess everyone was getting ready for the big push. However, it was nice to sit with her sometimes in the evening hours and talk of the things that had happened the past few weeks. I knew that I didn't have much to offer someone like Catrina, so I tried not to let the talk get going about the two of us.

I had lost track of the time, but she assured me that it was fall and winter would be soon on its way. This news was both good and bad. One of the bad things was thinking about what Dutch would want to do and what I would be doing this winter. Mr. Vargas wouldn't need much help in the wintertime, and so he would have to let most of us go. Most of the hands would leave from the loading pens at the rail station and then return again in the spring.

In some of our travels I had talked with men who had seen the 'reales de minas,' or mining villages. They were much different that the ones over in California. The workers kept very little of the silver and gold that they dug out of the rivers and mud of the Sonora. The prospects for gold mining in Mexico didn't seem very encouraging.

The next few days passed quickly by and it was soon time for the roundup. Each day started early and ended late as all of the cattle were brought together in the big pasture. The large holding corrals soon filled up and a lot of feed had to be given to those being held, but the Vargas camp seemed equal to the task. In fact, as soon as the herd had been gathered, Mr. Vargas sent about half of the riders over to help with the Ortega gathering. In a few days we would all be headed toward the stockyards.

Catrina asked me one evening what I would be doing after the roundup. I didn't want to answer the question, but I knew she needed to know what was going to happen. I told her that her father wouldn't be needing me around after the cattle were delivered and I had found out that most of the hands went their way after the big pay day.

We sat there on the porch watching the sunset down the valley. She moved closer to me, and in her soft voice asked, "Yacob, what about us?"

What was she asking? I had so little to offer her right now; what could I tell her? I really didn't know too much about love, or what women wanted men to do. I had hoped that was the way she was feeling about me, and her question meant she was thinking about it not ending also. Was she talking about us going somewhere and making a home and a life, or did she want to settle somewhere near here? All I knew at this moment was that I never wanted this feeling for her to end.

It felt so right to turn around and hold her close. I finally whispered in her ear, "Catrina, what would you want me to do?"

"What does your heart tell you, Yacob?"

"I feel all funny inside and it's as if my heart is going to break when you are so close to me. Is this love?" I asked. I was afraid to look into her eyes right then, for sometimes it made me weak at the thought of her so near. I held her close and said, "Oh, Catrina, I never want to leave you, but I don't have much to get a start yet. I really have nothing that I can offer you except my feelings and hard work."

She whispered back in my ear, "Yacob, what else could anyone want?"

I held her close, unable to say anything more. We watched the sun disappear over the horizon. Relunctantly I whispered, "I must go and get a few things ready for tomorrow. We start the drive pretty early."

"Yes, I know," she said, as she held onto my hand for a moment longer.

As I worked to get my gear ready for the drive, thoughts raced through my mind at the hope of Catrina and I having a life together. Was I good enough for her? Would I be able to make my way and have something for the two of us? What would I tell my friend Dutch? Would he understand? Always Catrina's soft voice was there in my mind, repeating her questions: "What about us?" "What does your heart tell you?"

What did my heart say? What did I really want and need from life? I had come to know so many good people, and what more did I need than food and a place to stay? It was time to get this cattle drive over with. It wouldn't be a lot of money for me, but afterward I would make some kind of plan. Life was good.

All of the riders were back and assembled early to make our start toward the Ortega ranch. There we would join up with their crew and combine the herds. I quickly said my goodbye to Catrina and told her that I would return after we had delivered the cattle.

"Be careful, Yacob," she said. I thought I saw the slightest sign of a tear in her eyes as she held my hand tight for the last time for a while.

We moved the Vargas herd onto the Ortega range without too many problems. All of Ortega's cattle had been gathered, and one of his men kept an account as we put them through a chute and out onto the range. From the looks of the two bunches, they each had about equal amounts of cattle.

I was anxious to go and see my friend Dutch. He got up when I entered the main ranch house. He was much thinner than I last remembered. I could see by his movements that he was a long time from being well. It was so good to see him again.

I saw the twinkle in his eye as he said, "I guess the left side of my body is about all used up. Maybe next time I will ask for two right sides! Nothing bad ever seems to happen there." It was good to see a little smile from him.

Later that evening, we were able to spend some time together. It was easy for us both to drop into our native German talk. By now I had heard the story of his friend Rosa and the problems that had come to him because of her. It was better to hear it from him and get his feelings of those moments. We sat on two of the bunks in the bunkhouse and talked and talked. He told me of how he had gone to Rosa's aid and kept the outlaws from catching her. I could tell by the tone of his voice that he had some warm feelings for her. I waited for him to let me know about that.

He told me of getting his black horse back again. With that he reached under his bunk and came out with a saddlebag. As he opened it up, I could see that he had a small leather pouch inside. He reached in and began to pull out more money than I had ever hoped to see again in one pile. Then he began to divide it up and told me that it contained about one thousand American dollars, or five hundred apiece.

"Partners," he said, and pushed my half over to me. "I wish I could have found the rest of it, but I am happy to even get a part of our money back. You had better put it away before someone comes through the door," he warned.

I pushed it down deep into one of my pockets and asked him how he was able to keep it from being stolen.

"Mr. Ortega has let me keep it in his safe," he said. " I knew you were on your way, so I got it out so you would have it tonight."

I thanked him for being such a good friend. "Do you still have your three gold nuggets?" I asked him.

"Yes," he said. "They are in the safe, too. You have taught me to be careful of some things."

I smiled and asked, "Dutch, will you have Mr. Ortega put my money back into the safe until after the cattle drive? I'll pick it up later."

I thought of the little bundle of three gold nuggets that I had asked Catrina to put in a safe place for me. I didn't tell her what was in the wrappings, and until now, I had hardly even thought of them. With the money I now had and the gold nuggets, it seemed that there might be a way for Catrina and me to move ahead with our plans a lot faster. I worried, though, at how my friend would take the news. What were his plans and what would he do?

Dutch was well enough to ride, but needed to take it a little easy. His assignment was to ride the point and look out for any trouble that might be ahead of the drive. The days were dry and dusty for the most part, and I always seemed to be bringing up the drag. Mornings were the best. The dew on the grass and leaves seemed to help everything seem fresher.

I sometimes visited with Dutch, but each day was harder than the last. It was all we could do to keep the herd together and moving. After we had been traveling along for several days, the experienced riders told us that we would soon reach the Yaqui River. Dutch and I rode along with the advance group that went ahead to look at the crossing.

When we reached the banks of the river and looked at the crossing, the dismay on every face told us that the water was deeper and swifter than most normal years. Both Mr. Ortega and Mr. Vargas looked into the wide, deep waters and shook their heads. This was the only crossing for miles where cattle could get across and be able to climb out on the other side, and this year it wouldn't be easy. The river narrowed down just below the landing and became quick and deep. If any animals got that far down, they would probably be lost in the crossing.

The cattle were moved into a pasture about two miles away and held back where they could feed and rest. They would need to be well rested and get some extra grazing in order to give it a try. We waited two days for them to get stronger, but some dark clouds were building up the river toward the Sierra Madre Mountains. It was certain that we would need to make our move before those rains started.

Early the next morning the plans had been made and it was time for action. The herd would need to be put in as far up stream as they could, in order for them to have a chance to get across to the other side. The cow hands would be on the down side of the cattle to try to get them to move directly across to the opposite bank. The water was so deep that they would be swimming most of the way. The cattle weren't allowed to think much about their situation, but were pushed right out into the river. Some of the stronger ones were put in first. It appeared close for them making it onto the other side in time, but finally they reached the other side and staggered out on the bank.

By midday most of the cows had made it across, but the last ones began to panic about halfway across the river. I was right in the middle of them when some decided to go down the river instead of across. I could see the fear in their eyes as they came bawling and thrashing through the water. All of our yelling and shooting our pistols in the air didn't seem to change their minds, and they were soon upon us. I saw two come right at one of the riders and drag him and his horse under. Some of the cows were pressing down on me and I wondered if that might happen to me, too.

The water was cold and swift now and I saw the rider that had gone down come back up to the top of the water. I moved my horse in his direction and was able to get his hand just as he was going down again. I held on tight to the man, and slid off my horse so it might have a better chance to make it to the other side. Somehow I managed to hold onto the horse's tail and the fallen rider both.

Men were running up and down the bank with ropes in hand, waiting for us to get close enough to receive help from them. My horse finally found footing on the far bank and I held on. Several ropes came into the water and I grabbed one and put it around the shoulders of the vaquero I was trying to help. It was then that I realized who it was. It was my friend Pedro.

The men rushed into the water as far as they could and grabbed us both to safety. Pedro lay on the dry ground trying to get his breath. I was wet and soggy all over, but the first thing that I wanted to do was go over to my great horse Jake and pull the saddle off him and rub him down. "You did good, friend Jake," I said. He had saved our lives that day, and I wanted him to know that. I gathered one of the feed bags and put a generous helping of grain in it for him. Ortega and Vargas both nodded their heads in approval as I rubbed my horse down.

Twelve head of stock had gone down the river and were

probably lost in the fast water down below the landing. I asked if anyone would be going downstream to see if any of the animals might have made it across. Luis Ortega said that chances were that all of the twelve were swept away in the water. They would each take six off their count, since they had no way of knowing whom the cattle belonged to that were lost. Luis said that if that was our only loss, we would be doing pretty good.

I said, "Would you mind if I caught up another horse and went downstream to see while you are getting the wagons across?"

"Go ahead," Luis said. "But we will only be about two hours finishing up here and then we will need to move on."

In a few minutes I had caught and saddled another horse. I rode out around the landing to get a look at the river below. The brush was very thick as far as I could see. The sound of the water crashing down stream seemed to indicate the fate of those cows that had decided to go downstream. It took a few minutes before I reached a place where I could ride up to the bank of the river. There was no place upstream that any of them could have gotten out, and I still couldn't see very far down the river. Both sides of the fast water were choked with thick brush and high banks.

I moved back up the bank and rode down stream even farther. Could it be that all twelve drowned in the river? In moving farther downstream, I was able to find a small clearing that seemed to lead into the river's edge. It might be some place where cattle could climb out.

As I moved forward, I saw two of the animals standing on the bank trying to get their breath. I thought, if two could make it, maybe others would be found downstream, too. I moved back around and away from the two cows in search of the others. In a few minutes, I found six more cattle standing on a small sandbar that went out into the river. They, too, were trying to get their breath. From what I could see of the river down below, there would not be any more that could make it out, as the river went crashing into a deep gorge and then disappeared around a sharp bend.

It took about three hours to get the cows moving in the right direction and back up to the landing. They were much easier to herd now after all they had gone through. It made me feel good that I had come here to try and see if any had made it out of the river.

When I got to the landing, the ground was still wet where the wagons had been floated across the river. They had brought along some extra long ropes to tie off on both sides of the river to keep the wagons from turning over in their crossing. It looked like the rest of the bunch had made it across safely. They were out of sight, but I could hear the sounds of the cattle in the distance and knew I was not too far behind. My bunch were dried off now and wanted to get something to eat.

I considered trying to catch up with the others, but decided that these survivors needed some extra food right now. I moved them slowly along, allowing for some quick bites of grass. I had plenty of time to think about the big river we had just crossed. I had never seen one so big or strong as this one. No wonder that they had to pick and choose the way across.

It was nearing sundown when I finally caught up with the rest. It had been a long hard day, and I was glad to ride into camp with the eight from the river.

"All right, Jacob!" Luis called as he saw me coming in with the cattle. "You did good going after those lost ones!"

The word quickly spread around the gang about my saving Pedro and now saving eight of the cattle, too. I made my way to the camp cook, wondering if I had ever been so hungry and tired before. Of course, I knew the answer to that as soon as I remembered the trip Dutch and I had made across the Sonora high desert. Where was that partner of mine, anyway? As I looked around for him, hoping he hadn't had trouble with the river crossing, I spotted him heading toward the chuckwagon.

He poured himself some coffee from the pot and sat down beside me. "You know, partner," he said, "this life sure does have some hard places in it. It kind of makes me think of moving on, where things might get some better."

"Yeah," I answered him in German. "Sometimes it gets hard on the body and also hard on the heart."

He looked up at this and I knew it was something that had been on his mind for some time. He stirred the fire with a twig and asked what I was going to do about Catrina.

I answered and said, "I was wondering what you were going to do about Rosa."

We sat for some time in our thoughts. Neither of us brought up the idea of going gold mining, even though when we came into the country that was our purpose.

Finally he looked across the fire at me and said, "If I had someone like Catrina to plan a life with, I would give up on all of this foolishness of gold mining and figure that I had found my gold. She is one fine young lady, Jacob," he said. "And you are one lucky partner. I heard what you did for Pedro in the river today. You saved his life. Did you know it was him when you went in after him?"

"No," I said. "There was so much confusion and noise when those cattle panicked that I really didn't know who it was that went down."

"Just as I thought," he said.

We sat in silence for a few moments before I added, "I was just trying to save the horse. Pedro happened to be there."

That brought a smile on his face as he said, "Sure,

sure!"

"Tell me about Rosa," I asked.

"Not much to tell," he said. "Pretty as the wild flowers in spring, and I think she likes me. But her father keeps all of the young guys away. She said that she had been promised to someone when she is old enough, and that will probably be soon. I have never known or felt closer to anyone, yet it doesn't look like there is any chance for the two of us. I can see the sadness in her eyes about having a life with someone she doesn't even know. You know me, Jacob; I am no quitter. But with Rosa . . . " his voice trailed off in thought.

"I heard you saved her life. Doesn't that count for anything?" I asked.

"Well, you would just have to be there to understand. Of all my feelings, I wouldn't want to push myself in where I am not wanted. Helping her would be what anyone would probably do," he said.

"Not likely, with that many men all after her. It's no wonder you got shot up. Your heart can get you in a lot of trouble sometimes, huh?" I commented.

We sat for a long time nursing the fire and sipping from our coffee cups. Others would come by and have their fix of coffee, but most of the men were already on the ground sleeping with their heads against their saddles. Neither one of us had a call to watch the herd that night, so we got some extra rest.

# Chapter 22

In the morning we woke up to the sounds of the cook banging his pots together. We could hear the early stirring of the changing of the guard for the cattle. As we stretched and yawned to come fully awake, word came that we would push the cattle along for three more days and then stop for a day to give them a rest before we crossed the Rio Mayo. This would be our last crossing before we got them to the stockyards.

I had lost count of the days since we had been on the trail. Time wasn't measured in days any more, but in distance and trials. My thoughts were often of Catrina, and how I had promised her that I would return as soon as the cattle were delivered. Dutch hadn't said for sure what he was going to do, but I know he hadn't forgotten about Rosa.

We reached the last river to cross in a few days and there was relief that it wasn't running high like the Yaqui River had been. We should be at the railhead in about another week. Everyone was getting tired and a little bit short of temper with the many demands of the drive. The night before a small band of renegade Indians had tried to make off with a few of the cattle. No one was hurt, but it took us about three hours to get the cows all bunched up again.

I could see the tired faces of the men as they would come to the grub wagon. The ones who always had something to say were quiet now and only wanted to get this over with. Luckily the trail was now smooth and mostly flat, so we made good time getting the cattle to the holding pens at Batuc.

There were a couple of cantinas and not much else in the small town. The main thing that was different about this town were the steel rails on the flat that would take the cattle on to market. Vargas and Ortega were anxious to make the count with the buyers from the government.

We had arrived early in the morning and by early

afternoon the work for the cowhands was done. Every man was called forth to get his pay for the season. It seemed like most of them got the equivalent of about eight American dollars a month. When my name was called, I wouldn't let either Mr. Vargas or Mr. Ortega pay me anything. I told them that I was only happy to help them since they had done so much to help us. They each did insist on giving me a pick of the horse stock that they had. One thing about Mexican horses, they had some of the worst ones around and some of the best ones. Both of these ranches had some of the best, so thanking them I chose one from each ranch.

Most of the cowhands headed for one of the two cantinas, but others were anxious to be on their way back to their homes and friends. A few would be going back to the ranches to work through the winter.

I wondered what Dutch would do now. I had seen him head for one of the cantinas with some of his friends. Mr. Vargas came over to where I was standing and said that they would be leaving early in the morning for home. He said that he and Luis had talked it over and decided to give me the price of four of the eight cattle that I had brought in from the river crossing. He said if it weren't for me, they wouldn't have any of the eight cattle. He extended the money to me for the four cows, but I told him that I couldn't take any of that. He asked me what my plans were for the winter. I told him that I would need to get a job.

"Would you like to come back to the ranch to work and spend the winter? I can't pay much in the winter time," Vargas said.

One thing was for sure; a guy would never get rich in this country working for someone else. But it didn't cost much to live either, so I guess it kind of worked out. If I were ever going to have anything, I would need a new plan. These were all good people, but they could only afford so much for labor. I told Mr. Vargas thanks for the offer and said I would let him know in the morning.

With money in their pockets and something to spend it on, the boys were making a lot of noise in the cantinas. I decided to go to the only eating place in town and find something to eat. I wanted to be alone for awhile to try and plan what I should do next. When I entered the restaurant it was busy with the local people and some of the trail hands.

I found a place to share a table with a couple of the townspeople. They were surprised to hear me speak their language and began to open up to me more. They said that they were working for the government on the cattle shipment and they would be moving them to the big town of Hermosillo. I asked them what it was like there.

"There are always the poor and the rich. That is the way with Mexico," said one man.

We all laughed when a second man added, "Yes, and there are always more of us poor people than the rich!"

"Is it always that way?" I asked.

Nodding their heads yes, they answered, "Always."

I ate my meal in silence to think about what they had said. It was kind of the same way back home in Germany. Only a few owned the land and had the money. But there, a man could at least go to one of the cities and find a job. He could survive on his own. So Germans did have some choices that these Mexicans said they would never have. They told me they were lucky to have a job, even if it paid little more than enough for their food.

As I finished my meal, I knew I would have to go over to the cantina and see if I could find my partner and talk with him. We'd never really talked through all of our choices or made any decisions, and now was the time to do it. And besides, he was probably in trouble by now. Before I could get up to leave, Pedro came in and asked if he could sit down with me.

"Sure" I said, pushing a chair toward him.

"I want to thank you, Señor Jacob, for saving my life, for saving me from the river. What can I ever do to pay you back?"

I held up one hand for him to stop talking this way. "You don't owe me a thing," I told him in his native language.

"I will be your forever friend," he said. "I knew I was going to die in the river, until I felt your hand. Some have told me that you took a big chance with your life trying to save me. I will never forget."

He sat for a while, not saying anything more but looking steadily into my face. I said nothing more. Satisfied, he stood up and extended his hand in friendship to me. Yes! A lot of good people lived here in this land.

It was loud and noisy as I went into the cantina where I had seen Dutch go. Smoke filled the air, and it was hard to make out the figures around the room. There seemed to be some commotion in one of the corners with several men gathered around.

When I got closer, I could hear the yelling of a fight going on and could see two or three going at it. I could hardly get close enough to see what was going on, but there was sure enough a fight going on. Pretty soon some of those standing around were into it, too.

This cleared things out a little so I could see into the group. Sure enough, there was Dutch in there slugging it out with one big, big Mexican. He was about as big as both of us put together, but Dutch was managing to keep away from his big burly arms. I thought of the gunshot wound that he been nursing and that this just wasn't a good thing.

Suddenly Dutch held up his hands. Turning to the big fellow, he said in Spanish, "Hey! Why don't we call it off and I will buy you a drink?" The fight stopped right then and there, and with arms around each other they went to the bar to have their drink.

Some fought on, and some of the fighting went out into the street, but Dutch and his new big friend were leaning up against the bar talking and rubbing the sore spots they each had. He saw me close by and motioned me over.

"This is my good friend," he told the giant, who looked down at me.

I nodded and shared a drink at the bar with them.

"We need to talk," I told Dutch, but his left eye was just about swollen shut by now and the place he had been shot earlier was bleeding again. He was in no mood or condition to talk about anything. Tomorrow he would really be hurting.

"Do you want me to keep any of your money so it won't get lost tonight?"

He reached in his pocket and gave me a roll of money he had, and I gave him a few dollars back.

Knowing that I would not be able to start back with the bunch early the next morning as I had hoped, I went back into the eating hall and found Vargas and Ortega. They were sharing a table together and talking over the events of the past few weeks. I had heard them say that they had been paid a good price for their cattle, so that made me feel good. I told Mr. Vargas that I would like to stay on at the ranch this winter, but I might be a day or two behind them in my return.

With my three horses now, I moved my camp away from the others and out by myself. What would Catrina be doing right now? Would she be thinking of me? As I lay there looking up at the stars it was good to be out where it was quiet. Tomorrow, Dutch and I would have to do some talking and planning.

Morning came to the little town with the crowing of a couple of roosters. I hadn't even thought about there being chickens around the area when we came into town. I was sore from the long rides we had made, but not nearly as sore as if I had joined in the fighting. I wondered where Dutch could be found and where he had spent the night. One thing was for sure, I didn't leave him much to spend. So maybe he went out early.

The crowing of the roosters meant fresh eggs for breakfast and that was exactly where I would head first. When I passed by the corrals where the horses had been left, I noticed that most of them had now gone. Only a couple of riders were there now, making ready for their ride home. They nodded as I passed by them, and I held my hand up to them. I wondered if I would see them again next year.

The town looked quiet and only a few people were moving around the street. I noticed the two who had come to take charge of the cattle for the government. They said the train should be there in a couple of days. It was their job to see that nothing happened to the cattle, and they had been sleeping near the corrals when I came by.

Breakfast was really good with the fresh eggs and tortillas, along with some fresh meat. They never learned how to make coffee in one of these places, so I asked them if I could go in the kitchen and make my own coffee. They pointed the way, and in a short time I finally had a good dose going. When the coffee was ready I went back into the kitchen to get the fixings. They had some goat's milk along with sugar. I put some of the goat's milk into my coffee, but that was a mistake I sure didn't repeat on the next cup. The cooks were watching from the open door way into the kitchen and I guess I made some kind of bad face on my first drink of the stuff.

I asked a couple who were in eating if they knew what had happened to my friend, Dutch. I found out that he had spent the night in the cantina, I guess they didn't know he was out of money or they would have put him out.

With breakfast over, I thought I would feed my horses

some grain in case I was going to be leaving today. The sun was up now and the pesky flies were, too. I wondered how long it would be before there were any signs of life at the cantina. I didn't want to go over there and spoil my breakfast. There would be a foul smell coming from there at this time of day. I knew no one would be in a good mood, either.

As I sat on the water trough thinking about all of this, the bat wings on the door of the cantina opened. A big guy came through the door and started tossing those out who were inside, like sacks of grain. It seemed little effort for him to clear the guys out of his place. In a while, he had a pretty good pile of hats, boots and whatever didn't belong inside stacked outside in the street. Some just lay there, but the rough treatment as they were tossed onto the pile brought a few of them to their senses. They began rubbing their heads and looking for their hats and things.

Dutch was the third one that he tossed out. Before long he had pulled himself up and was leaning against one of the hitching posts. He looked a sight, and I could tell he felt just about like he looked. From where I sat, I could see his eye was nearly swollen shut. I just watched as he tried to figure out what had happened. I had seen him do this kind of thing before when he was trying to get over something. Maybe he was trying to get over his feelings for Rosa. I felt bad for him, but thought I would just let the sun get into his eyes and bring the world back to him.

He was rubbing his eyes already and pretty soon he yelled out at me, "Are you just going to leave me here to roast in the sun?"

With that I walked over to where he was. Reaching down, I pulled him to his uncertain legs and we made toward the horse trough. He seemed to know what was coming and started to hold back some when he saw the fresh cold water in the trough. By then it was too late. I pushed his head all of the way to the bottom. Half of his body went in, too. It was the only way I knew how to do things in a hurry. He came sputtering up using up some of his favorite German words on me. I was glad no one else could understand them.

I just left him sitting there on the horse trough. Soon the morning sun had his clothes steaming. It wasn't any use to come back for an hour or two, so I went into the only store and bought some hobbles and other gear that I would need for the horses. I visited with the store owner for some time. He had known of a fellow that had gone to the gold fields in California and come back again. I was interested to talk with the fellow, so he pointed to a house down the way where the man lived.

Kids were playing outside and I asked if they lived in this house. They said they did and I found out that their dad was inside having breakfast. With that I knocked on the door and heard "Come in!" from somewhere inside.

When I stepped through the door, I explained that I had just come in on the cattle drive and the man at the store had told me that the man who lived here had been to the California gold fields and back. He was anxious to talk when I told him that I too had stopped off there for a short time. He asked if I had been able to find a lot of gold. I told him I had found a little, but most of the claims were taken and it was hard to find a place to mine.

He said that he had gone way up there with two of his uncles to find this gold. He said the hills were full of people. Just trying to dig along any of the streams might cost a man his life. He was the only one to return, as his uncles had been killed while trying to find a place to dig for gold. They had just waited too long to go. He had only been back a few weeks.

I returned to the horse trough and Dutch. He was up moving about now and had tried to make himself look a little better, but his clothes were a sight.

"Do you think you could find out what I did with my

saddle and things and get me a change?" he asked.

I had seen the horse he had been riding still in the corral and several saddles were hanging on the top rail. In a short time I had found his stuff and brought it all back to him. He took everything into the barn and came back with his fresh clothes on.

"Now another dip in the trough and you will look good."

He held up his hand at me and said, "I can do it by myself this time."

"What happened last night?" I asked him.

"Well, you know everyone was feeling real good about having the drive over. It was crowded at the bar and hard to get a drink. After spilling a couple of times while reaching through the crowd, I noticed that this big guy was taking up a lot of the bar space. I guess I told him he was taking up more than his share. Well, you can just imagine what he said about that," he moaned, rubbing his eye that was still nearly shut.

"This was from his back hand," he said pointing to the eye. "Sure glad he never got close enough to really hit me. But I'm getting better, partner; I told him we would just call it a draw and I would buy him a drink. Besides, he made me remember where I had been shot. I think the darned thing has opened up again."

"Little wonder," I said. "When are you ever going to learn? I made some coffee over at the eating place. Let's go over and get you some."

"Jacob, I can't find any money. I guess someone made off with it while I was asleep. About every time I get into one of these things that happens."

"Come on, I think I have plenty for some food."

It was busier now than when I had been in to eat. It looked like the town was full awake and the sun had been up for some time. Dutch ordered his breakfast, and I told him the

331

eggs were fresh. He said he wasn't very hungry, but I told him a few cups of that coffee I had made would stir things up for him and he would be as good as new. Well, almost.

He told me that he wouldn't take any pay from the ranchers, but they insisted on giving him some horses and a job next season if he wanted one. He said he had brought some money down with him from the ranch, and now wished he had left it all back there. The thirty dollars was all gone that he had brought, but he would be able to pay me back when he returned to the ranch.

I pulled out his roll of money, which I had taken from him the night before. "Here! You can pay for your own food," I said. "It looks like you still have most of the thirty dollars left."

When he had finished eating, I asked him, "What are your plans?"

"I don't know. I would like to see Rosa one more time, and then I will make some kind of plan."

"Well, I've about concluded that gold mining in Mexico would not be good. Everything is pretty tough here. People work for nearly nothing. It looks like they pay the cowhands about eight dollars a month, probably half that in the wintertime. How long would it take anyone to get anywhere with that pay?"

He sat for a moment in thought. "I can't stay here, and I know that Rosa will not go away with me. I just can't give her the things she is used to."

"Maybe it's like the fight you had last night. Maybe you ought to leave the big ones alone."

That brought a smile to his face like I hadn't seen for a long while.

"Jacob, you sure have a way of getting a guy going."

We sat for some time in our thoughts and then he

332

asked me what I was going to do. I had thought a lot about my answer, and now I looked at him as I spoke.

"I want to return to the Vargas ranch and see Catrina again. She is waiting for me, and we need to decide more about our feelings. There is a lot to think about, and maybe she will change her mind about me. I don't know for sure." Doubt seemed to creep into my thoughts as I remembered Catrina's question, "What about us, Jacob?"

Dutch said nothing, and I kept on talking. "You know I don't know too much about women, Dutch, never was like you. I can see no way for anything to happen right away. I'd decided to ask her to wait for a year. But with you giving me back the five hundred dollars, added to the three gold nuggets that I have, I might be able to get things going much faster.

"Five hundred dollars in this country is a lot of money, when you think about your breakfast costing eight cents. I was thinking about a small spread to the east of the Vargas ranch. Mr. Vargas owns the land, and I would need to work something out with him."

I told him of the big mountain and Catrina's excitement about building a place there. It would be a ways from her folks, but with her by my side, I thought I could do about anything.

I went back to the store with Dutch so that he could buy a few things that he needed. We were soon headed back towards the ranch. With the extra horses we had been given, we were able to relay the riding and make good time. In some ways it was like old times, but something had happened this past few months. We were still good friends, but things had changed between us and would somehow never be the same. We both felt that as we talked on the way back.

One evening as we were getting close to the ranch, Dutch said we might be going different directions from here out. He said that there was still new country he wanted to see and many places he wanted to go.

I thought about this for some time and could see that he was probably right. Maybe it was because we were getting a little older, or that we had been separated for some time over the summer. Maybe it was the feelings I had for Catrina and his for Rosa. Whatever it was, the change in our relationship filled us with a bittersweet sadness.

I said, "Dutch, we will always be good friends. And if I am here or wherever, you come and see me."

He nodded his head in agreement. "It's too bad that we had to lose all of our money. Maybe we should go and find this Boracho and see if he has any of it left."

"I am sure that by this time he has used it all up and is probably trying to steal more from someone else to keep up his recent lifestyle," I said.

In a few days we were back at the Ortega ranch. Pedro was one of the first to see me and again show his friendship. I had given some thought to saving his life back at the crossing. As Dutch and I talked it over on our return, we decided that he had saved our lives that day when we were lost and without food or water. That made us even, but it was good to have a friend.

We were welcomed at the ranch and invited to stay as long as we needed. I wanted to get back to the Vargas ranch, but decided to stay a couple of days and see what my partner was going to do.

Signs of winter were on the high Sierra Madre range and it could be felt here even in the middle of the day. We helped with some of the chores around the ranch, but the need for the long rides for cattle was over. The only cattle that were left to be gathered were those that would have calves in the spring. They would be kept close to the ranch so they could be watched after.

One evening while we were in the bunkhouse, Dutch said that he had decided what he needed to do.

"I think I will go back up north over the border and see if I can find work. I might even make my way back over to California. At least I can find something to make a living there better than I can here. Who knows, maybe I can find another one like Rosa, without so much money. I know one thing, I don't want to have any more to do with those dance hall girls," he said.

I thought about this. I reminded Dutch that the gold fields were full of people and trouble now, and that the Mexican had said that the gold rush was pretty well over. This didn't seem to discourage him at all. I could tell that he had his mind made up. I also knew he was offering a plan for the two of us to go on together if I wanted to go.

"This time I can't go with you," I finally said. "I have decided to stick around for a while and see where things go from here."

Dutch left early the next morning. Luis Ortega had seen to the food he would need for the trip, and I insisted that he take Chancey along with him to keep him out of trouble. He, in turn, handed over the reins of the two horses he'd received after rescuing Rosa from their slain riders. "Here, take these two for your start, partner," he said.

Saying farewell was difficult, so we just both raised our arms as he left across the meadow. He was heading back the way we had come when we first entered the valley several months ago. He sat tall and straight on his big black horse, leading the one he had been given at the roundup. Chancey followed the two stride for stride.

I wondered if I would ever see either of those two friends again. I watched until they passed out of sight. A loneliness that I had never felt before swept over me as I stood there looking in the direction they had gone. It was like a part of me was missing. I thought of catching up my horses and following after them, but knew I needed to stay and make my own way now. If things didn't work out with Catrina, I too would head back to the North Country.

Luis Ortega came over to me after I had caught my horses for the trip to the Vargas ranch. "I guess you are staying, Jacob," he said. "I think you could do well in this country."

I thanked him for his help and friendship. I wondered whether he and Mr. Vargas had talked about my staying. He must have known that Mr. Vargas offered me a job for the winter. My horse Jake seemed to know that we were heading home, and broke out into a good fast pace down the valley toward the Vargas ranch.

It was nearly dark on the second day when I reached the ranch. Just as at the Ortega ranch, a watchdog announced my return. Some came out to see who would be coming in out of the dark. When I got close enough to the house I yelled out, "It's Jacob."

Catrina came out on the front porch. She looked just as beautiful as I had remembered. As I got down to tie my horses up, she came to me in the dim evening light and said, "Yacob, I was afraid something had happened to you."

She was soon in my arms holding and kissing me.

"I told you I would be back," I said, as we stood there for a moment just holding each other. I knew others would be looking our way and wondering what was going on, and I said, "Guess we had better go on in the house."

"Can we just have another minute alone?" she asked. And so we did.

When we entered the house Victor had already sent one of the servants to fetch something for me to eat. He wanted to know what the trip coming back was like. I told him that Dutch had come back with me as far as the Ortega ranch. I couldn't keep the sadness out of my voice as I told him how we had stayed only a couple of days before he decided to head out across the border to the North. I told them what he had said about even going back up to California if he couldn't find work soon.

"He told me to tell you thanks for everything you have done to help us. He said that getting to know good people like you and the rest made it worth the trip. I insisted that he take Chancey with his two horses. Chancey may help keep him out of trouble, since I won't be around."

Catrina came with the coffee, and a smile that showed her joy at my being here. When others looked at the two of us, I know I turned red and thought I had better excuse myself for the night and see about my horses.

It was good to be outside again. Sometimes a guy just needed to have some room to think things out. I still felt warm inside at the thought of holding Catrina tight. I must remember not to hold her too tight. I might break something.

I decided to throw my bedroll down outside the barn. I liked to look up in the sky when so many things were pressing on my mind. It sort of helped to get things unraveled. It had been a busy few weeks lately and it would be good to slow down and get a little more rest. The last thing I remembered were the horses feeding in the barn and wondering where Dutch might be right now.

An hour before light I could hear sounds coming from the house that told me the cooks and housekeepers would be up and getting the morning meal ready. I wondered if Catrina would be up helping them as I washed my face in the horse trough. I already knew the answer to that. She was a getting up and going type of girl.

One thing I had learned about ranch life was that everyone gets up and going unless they are hurt or sick. I worked with the others the next few days around the ranch. There was less to do, but the daylight was getting short, so it all evened out.

I had been able to spend more time with Catrina, and I looked forward to the evenings when we could walk and talk. She knew my feelings about my partner leaving, and said she wished it could have been different. She said maybe he should have gone back to Rosa to see if there was any chance for them to have some time together.

I told her that Dutch said it was because of his feeling for her that he thought it best not to try and change things. He'd said that he would not want to do anything to ever hurt her, so his leaving was probably for the best. He hoped she would be happy.

Catrina didn't say anything for a long while, but finally asked, "Yacob, what is it that would make you happy?"

"I was thinking more about you, and what would make you happy," I said.

The full moon was just coming over the hill and bathing the big meadow in its light. She came into my arms and we held each other close.

Then she said, "Yacob, will you build us a home on our mountain someday"?

I thought about what she had said. Who wouldn't want to do that? I wanted so much to say yes, but after a few silent moments, I heard myself saying, "We need to get through the winter and get your folks back on their feet. They need all of the help we can give them right now."

" Yes," she said, "you are right. We can talk of this later." I could feel the disappointment in her voice. She gave my right hand a squeeze and returned back around the barn and into the house.

Early the next morning, we were up in the east pasture looking for any cattle that might have strayed away when we noticed a rider moving swiftly in our direction. He was leading a saddled horse behind, and riding as fast as he could safely go. We stopped and waited for his rapid approach.

When he got a little closer, I could see that it was my friend, Pedro, from the Ortega ranch. Both horses were heavily lathered when he came up to us.   I asked him what was the matter, and he told us a story that made me boil inside.

Apparently one of Ortega's temporary hands had gone to town and had too much to drink. Boracho and some of his men happened to be in the cantina at the time and overheard his story about this German called "Dutch" who had come to town and stolen Boracho's big black horse, saddle and money bags.

Upon hearing this, Boracho became wild with anger. He told four of his men to catch up their horses and grub bags and go after his horse and money. They were to make sure they got his money and then kill this "Dutch" and bring him back into town tied over the saddle. In his fury, he turned on Lupe, the one who should have been watching his horse that night, and shot him dead right in the cantina.

This put the fear into the four he had directed to the job. They said they would ride early the next morning.

Pedro was still breathing hard from his ride. "I came as quickly as I could, because I thought you needed to know."

I thanked him for what he had done and excused myself from the others. "I must go back to the ranch right now!"

As I hurried along, I thought of what Pedro had said. I guess it was too much to hope for that Boracho wouldn't find out sometime what had happened to his horse and money. My temper reached the boiling point as I considered what Boracho had done in sending out four bushwhackers after Dutch. If they didn't get him, Boracho would get them. They would be dangerous men who rode with fear from both sides.

I told Victor Vargas the news that Pedro had brought. He had traveled day and night in his haste to get us the message.

"I must go and warn and help my friend if I can. He will only have about four days' head start on those outlaws. It won't take them long to determine that he is no longer at the Ortega ranch. It is likely they will send one rider by here just to check, and then be off on their search."

Catrina had come into the room when someone had told her I was in early from the pasture. "Can we go outside while I saddle up an extra horse?" I told her.

Catrina replied, " I will get food ready for you, Yacob. I know you must go."

I worked to get the grain and pack that I needed. I would take two horses saddled and ready and one pack horse. Catrina came quickly back with two large bags of food and some water containers. She stood and watched me in silence, though I could see the questions in her eyes.

When everything else was packed, I handed Catrina the money that I had, including the five hundred dollars Dutch had shared with me. "I may be gone a long time. If I don't get back before winter is over, use this money to help your folks."

I was quickly up on Jake with the two lead ropes in my hand. I felt Catrina's soft warm hand on mine and heard her say, "Oh, Yacob!" I dared not look down at her as I rode out across the meadow in search of Dutch.